Ice AND Embers

August Li

DSP PUBLICATIONS

Published by
DSP PUBLICATIONS

5032 Capital Circle SW, Suite 2, PMB# 279, Tallahassee, FL 32305-7886 USA
http://www.dsppublications.com/

Ice and Embers
© 2015 August Li.

Cover Art
© 2013 Anne Cain.
annecain.art@gmail.com
Cover content is for illustrative purposes only and any person depicted on the cover is a model.

ISBN: 978-1-63216-684-5
Digital ISBN: 978-1-63216-685-2
Library of Congress Control Number: 2014950609
Second Edition March 2015
First Edition published by Dreamspinner Press, March 2013.

Printed in the United States of America
∞
This paper meets the requirements of
ANSI/NISO Z39.48-1992 (Permanence of Paper).

This book would not have been possible without the support of my fantastic beta readers: Lena Grey, Autumn Schemery, and Eon de Beaumont. I can never express my gratitude for your honesty, insight, and willingness to help without much chance of recompense. This one is for the three of you. Thanks for telling me when I did well, but thanks even more for telling me when I didn't.

I also want to thank all the readers who took a chance on Yarrow, Sasha, and Duncan in *Ash and Echoes*. The reception my characters received was much warmer than I expected, and I appreciate everyone who stepped a little beyond the bounds of normalcy and sanity to become part of their world. The love and support I have received has meant the world to me and given me the courage to continue to take risks and be true to my characters.

Last but not least, this is again for Rosepetal. There would never have been a Yarrow without you. I hope I can give Yarrow everything I always wanted you to have. I miss you desperately.

—Gus, 2013

Glossary

Abode of Shades—The realm of the Cast-Down, the unworthy dead, and all those rejected by the goddesses.

Bairn—The second highest title of nobility in Selindria, after "valen."

Cast-Down—A term used to refer to those gods and goddesses disowned by The Thirteen because of their wickedness. Most pious Selindrians will not speak of them. In some rare cases, a person can be referred to as Cast-Down.

Emiri—An ethnic group, or possibly a completely different race of people, who arrived in Selindria about 150 years ago. Their name is derived from "*Emir*," the word for the sea in their language. Emiri have no formal homeland and are expert mariners. Their culture and values are quite different from that of Selindrians, and this leads to many misunderstandings.

Eru—The Emiri word for "wind."

Espero—A large and wealthy island nation to the southeast of Selindria, best known for the high population of mages and the arcane university there.

Estrella Lake—A huge freshwater lake in the northernmost corner of Selindria. Aside from providing most of the nation's water, it has a religious significance, is surrounded by shrines and temples, and is often visited by those on spiritual pilgrimages.

Everdale—A fertile valenny near the center of Selindria, which provides most of the kingdom's food, sister province to Merryvale.

Eyrle—The third highest title of nobility in Selindria, after "bairn."

Fane—A legendary mage-emperor who ruled over a period of unimaginable peace and prosperity eons ago. Eventually he demanded his people worship him instead of the goddesses, and the ensuing war destroyed the known world. No one knows if Fane ever actually existed, but his story is told as a cautionary tale and given as the reason mages are forbidden to rule.

Gaeltheon—A powerful nation to the east of Selindria, across the Kanda River, almost equal in size and wealth.

Kanda River—An enormous river separating Gaeltheon and Selindria. The Kanda is fed by Estrella Lake and considered holy by association.

Lapir Mountains—A huge, impassable mountain range marking the eastern border of Gaeltheon. No one has crossed them in centuries, and what lies on the other side is a subject of speculation.

Lockhaven—An ancient valenny, ruled by the L'Estrella family for as long as anyone can remember. Because it houses the sacred Estrella Lake, Lockhaven is highly respected throughout Selindria.

Meritage—The oldest and largest city in Selindria. Meritage is a port along the Kanda River, and while it is held by the Selindrian monarch, the territory around it is unstable and ruled by barbarians and warlords.

Merryvale—A fertile plain, sister province to Everdale.

Mir—An Emiri ship's captain.

Muri-ku—A very potent Emiri beverage made from fermented sea plants.

Narxium—A tree producing a fatally poisonous sap. It grows only in the Forest of Elwyd.

Order of the Crimson Scythe—A legendary and unstoppable cult of assassins. Thalil is their patron. While many people doubt the existence of the Crimson Scythe, their symbol, the red crescent, is still the most feared icon in the land. The Crimson Scythe are considered almost supernatural. When they have marked someone for death, that person has no chance of escape.

Selindria—The most powerful kingdom in the known world.

Starmont—The highest peak in Selindria, marking the northern edge of Estrella Lake. In the past, many Selindrians believed the goddesses resided atop Starmont, but that belief has been abandoned by all but the most superstitious.

Syrai—The Emiri word for "friend," used to express a wide variety of relationships from casual acquaintance to intimate partner.

Tam—The lowest title of nobility in Selindria as well as a common expression of respect, similar to "sir."

Thalil—A very powerful Cast-Down god associated with seduction, subterfuge, murder, and deceit. He is the patron god of assassins, particularly the Order of the Crimson Scythe. Thalil, usually portrayed as a beautiful youth, is also associated with male beauty and homoerotic love. The Thirteen Goddesses forbid his name from being spoken, and his worship is punishable by death. Thalil is known by many epithets, some of which are: He Who Stands Just Out of Sight, The One You See at the Last, The Whisper Heard Too Late, The Dark One, and The Invisible Blade.

The Thirteen, or The Thirteen Goddesses—The main and most important deities of Selindria and Gaeltheon. They have many sons and daughters, both benevolent and Cast-Down. They are sometimes referred to as the sisters. Each goddess presides over a month, or moon, of the year.

Valen—The highest title of nobility in Selindria, second only to the royal family. Valens rule large holds of land known as valennies.

THE GODDESSES AND MONTHS

Both Selindria and Gaeltheon observe a thirteen-month lunar calendar. Each month, or moon, is presided over by one of The Thirteen Goddesses.

Fayelle, ruler of the first month—A virgin goddess of purity. While compassionate, she is a very demanding goddess who expects perfection from her devotees.

Sarmine, ruler of the second month—The goddess of romantic love and marriage. Most weddings take place during Sarmine's Moon.

Mother Goddess, ruler of the third month—The only goddess without a name, she is the matron of all living things. Her month is a time of devotion and celebration. The Mother Goddess is said to love all her creations, even the Cast-Down.

Myint, ruler of the fourth month—The goddess of warfare, battle, weaponsmiths, armorers, and martial arts. She is the patron goddess of all knights.

Diarana, ruler of the fifth month—The goddess of travel and transition. She is the patron of children coming of age. Certain worshippers of Diarana maintain that the goddess loves and protects men and women who favor the clothing of the opposite gender. This belief is not widely accepted.

Vestrafori, ruler of the sixth month—The goddess of truth and justice, protector of the blind and mute. Vestrafori's priestesses conduct all legal proceedings in Selindria and Gaeltheon, and their verdicts are absolute.

Laud, ruler of the seventh month—A mysterious goddess associated with fate, the passage of time, and abstract concepts. Her devotees live hermitic lives of deprivation and contemplation.

Jelsyn, ruler of the eighth month—The goddess of artisans and merchants. She adores handmade items, particularly woven cloth. Jelsyn is also said to protect the poor.

Berris, ruler of the ninth month—The goddess of farming, plenty, and the harvest. Her festival is one of the most joyous occasions of the year.

Ix, ruler of the tenth month—The goddess of the wilds and protector of forests and animals. Ix is well-known to favor those who follow instinct over reason. Ix is also associated with the moon.

Strella, ruler of the eleventh month—The goddess of the sun, stars, and weather, Strella is also a liaison between humans and the goddesses. She carries prayers to the goddesses and guides the worthy dead to their rest.

Illira, ruler of the twelfth month—The goddess of music, poetry, history, and communication. She is the patron of all storytellers and scholars.

Pherara, ruler of the thirteenth month—The goddess of magic and arcane scholarship, and patron goddess of Espero. Most people feel Pherara values only her mages and turns her back on those without the gift. She is not widely worshipped outside Espero.

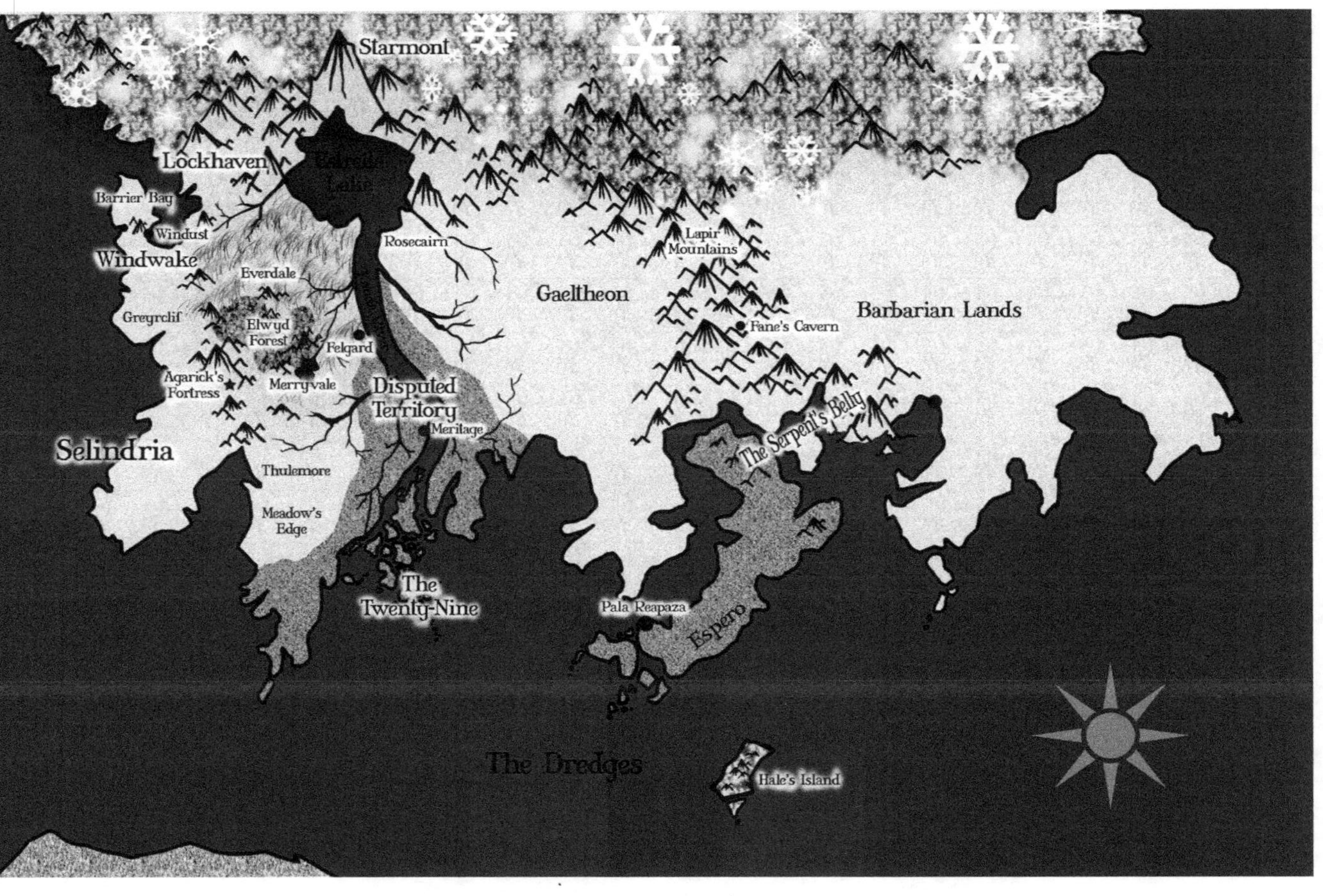

Starmont
Lockhaven
Calridan Lake
Barrier Bay
Windust
Windwake
Rosecairn
Everdale
Lapir Mountains
Gaeltheon
Barbarian Lands
Greyrclif
Elwyd Forest
Fane's Cavern
Felgard
Agarick's Fortress
Merryvale
Disputed Territory
The Serpent's Belly
Selindria
Meritage
Thulemore
Meadow's Edge
The Twenty-Nine
Pala Reapaza
Espero
The Dredges
Hale's Island

Chapter One

THE bairn of Windwake cast off his golden ceremonial cloak emblazoned with the crag eagle livery and let it fall heavily to the stone floor of his chambers. Duncan collapsed into an upholstered chair by the inglenook and rubbed his forehead. The fire had long ago diminished to embers, leaving the expansive suite dark and chill on this early spring night. Ruling Windwake had turned out nothing like he'd imagined, and the stresses of yet another day of listening to the demands of squabbling nobles wore on him. When Duncan had been granted his lands and title, he'd anticipated protecting and providing for his people, much as he'd done when he'd been a knight. The reality clashed hard against his expectations. He'd rather face an entire field of soldiers than those nattering, duplicitous aristocrats any day. At least men with swords were honest about wanting to destroy him, and he knew how to counter them.

Duncan had no sooner let his eyes fall shut and his head rest against the padded velvet of the chair when he heard a sound, even softer than the flutter of a night bird's wings, on the balcony opposite his hearth. He tensed, his exhaustion replaced by alertness. Many of his vassals couldn't be trusted; he found them avaricious, their only loyalty to their own treasuries. Some of them still owed fealty to Taran Edercrest, the traitor whose mantle Duncan had assumed after the man's death in a failed attempt to overthrow Selindria's true king. Duncan knew at least a few of the backstabbing nobles might stoop to murder if they could profit from it. He crept as quietly as he could to the weapons stand and picked up his greatsword. He held it in both hands as he approached the balcony, ready to defend himself.

With the sole of his boot, Duncan nudged the wooden double doors, and they swung open with a rasp and a groan. The red-tinged crescent moon provided little light as he glanced from one end of the parapet to the other. Nothing moved except a few leaves tumbling across the stone in the light breeze. Duncan blinked hard as sweat dripped into his eyes. He knew he'd heard something, but now he wondered if the combination of his weariness and the ever-present threat of treachery toyed with his mind. He'd never been a paranoid man, but as he stood looking out from the western side of Windust Castle, over the deep, round Barrier Bay, sheltered on three sides by high cliffs, he heard nothing but the gentle lap of the waves against the strong, gray ironstone that made up so much of Windwake. On a clear day, Duncan could see almost to the southern shore of Lockhaven from this balcony, but the gloom of the night and the chill mist rising from the water restricted his vision to the dozens of ships huddled close to the shore, bobbing gently on the calm tide.

"You should be more careful."

Duncan started and turned toward the low, velvety voice. He scanned the shadows but couldn't locate the speaker. Then, at the opposite end of the terrace, a sliver of shade separated from the wall, and a lithe silhouette tiptoed along the thin, stone railing before leaping down in front of Duncan without even disturbing the leaves. His boots met the stone silently, and the leather armor he wore didn't even creak or rustle.

Duncan blew out an extended breath and lowered his weapon. "Goddesses, Sasha. Why must you sneak around like that? I could have cut you in two before I recognized you."

Sasha answered with a sensuous laugh devoid of any genuine amusement. "I don't think you could have."

"Perhaps not," Duncan conceded, his happiness at his lover's return trumping his slight annoyance. Besides, he knew Sasha spoke not out of arrogance but simply stated the truth. Sasha had been trained by a cult of assassins so legendary and feared most doubted they even existed. The Order of the Crimson Scythe held mythical status throughout Selindria and Gaeltheon, and Duncan had witnessed Sasha's lethal skill on more than one occasion. If he'd been inclined, Sasha could have cut Duncan's throat while Duncan stood watching the boats like a dull-witted child.

Sasha's training was also responsible for what Duncan saw when he stepped closer to his partner: a face that, while exotically beautiful, betrayed no hint of emotion. Shrewd, black eyes offered no clue of the intentions behind them. Though they hadn't seen each other in weeks, Duncan looked into the cold face of a killer, not the warm smile of a lover. He tried, unsuccessfully, to staunch the hurt by reminding himself Sasha had been taught almost since birth not to feel love or attachment, let alone show evidence of what he'd been told was weakness.

Duncan reached up and stroked the soft, black hair that fell to Sasha's slender shoulders. Sasha batted his long, thick lashes and smiled mischievously. He had the most amazing, full, dark lips Duncan had ever seen, and the sight of them curling up and parting slightly sent a tremor of desire down Duncan's spine. He hoped Sasha showed sincere pleasure at his touch, as much pleasure as he experienced feeling the smooth skin of Sasha's cheek again after what seemed like forever. Sasha had no reason to perform with Duncan, but Duncan knew old habits held on tenaciously sometimes, like a cough that lingered after the fever had passed.

"I missed you," he said, pressing a kiss to Sasha's forehead. "But you could try using the front gate like a normal man. Or are you trying to impress me?"

Sasha curled his body against Duncan and brushed their bellies together. He rubbed his face against Duncan's whiskers and whispered close to his ear. "Did it work?"

Duncan glanced over the railing at the sheer, four-story drop to the sharp rocks surrounding the fortress. A wide gravel road wound out around those cliffs from the docks to the gate at the southern wall, on the opposite side of the fortress. Aside from that entrance, Windust was virtually impenetrable. "I suppose it did. Did your—" Duncan still felt uncomfortable discussing Sasha's work. "Were you successful?"

Sasha snorted as if insulted and crossed his arms over his slim chest. His devastating smile widened. "Pym Goodsal and his associates will cause no more trouble for your friend Garith."

"His Majesty will be pleased," Duncan said, taking Sasha's gloved hand, careful of the thin blades hidden at his wrists and the razor-like spikes over his knuckles, and leading him inside.

Sasha shrugged. "So long as he produces the agreed-upon gold."

Duncan almost asked what Sasha would do if Garith, High King of Selindria and Gaeltheon, the largest and most powerful kingdom in the known world, withheld the payment. He thought better of it, though, and went instead to add logs to the fire and stir up the coals. By now, Duncan knew Sasha regarded a prince and a beggar alike only as men who bled and died for his Cast-Down god.

Sasha removed his gloves, loosening the buckles and then tugging them off one finger at a time, while Duncan poked at the ashes in the hearth. Sasha unbuckled the belts over his hips that held daggers and pouches likely full of poisons, and then he unfastened the strap crossing his chest, along with the weapons it held, and let it drop onto a wooden bench. Sasha effortlessly disarmed himself in absolute silence. Duncan admired Sasha's grace and fluidity of movement from the corner of his eye as he tended the fire. The room soon glowed warm and bright as the flames flickered and grew. Orange light reflected off the snug, deep red leather wrapping Sasha's slender limbs and made shadows dance across his face. The fire couldn't melt the icy mask the assassin wore, but Duncan knew what might. He replaced the iron poker and crossed the room to Sasha, who stood only a few feet from the balcony door, as if waiting to be invited inside, seemingly unsure of his welcome.

Duncan curled his big hands around Sasha's waist, almost encircling it. He drew Sasha's chest against his, rubbed his palm up Sasha's back to his neck, and guided Sasha's head to his shoulder. Burying his face in the top of Sasha's hair, he inhaled the spicy fragrance that almost masked the scents of leather, steel, and blood. "Sasha, this is your home as much as mine. I wouldn't have any of it if it hadn't been for you. You don't have to enter it in secret."

Sasha laughed icily, but his lips and nose felt warm as he nuzzled against Duncan's neck. The tickle of his breath against Duncan's dampening skin when he spoke made Duncan shudder. "So, you'd parade me before your nobles and officials? Claim me as part of your household, as your friend?"

Holding Sasha's cheeks in both hands, Duncan tilted his face upward and made Sasha meet his eyes. He searched for some trace of emotion in those glittering, black orbs but saw only his own conflicted face reflected back at him in distorted miniature. "I would. Why do you make it sound so absurd? I'll tell them anything you like, anything that will make you happy. Sasha, you know I love you."

"I know." The assassin tried to look away as he furrowed his brow and turned down his lips, but Duncan held him, not letting him hide what he felt.

A fake smile replaced Sasha's concerned expression. "You'd lose your bairny if anyone discovered the nature of our association," he said with false cheer. "I understand better than most the need for secrecy. It's of little consequence how I enter the castle, anyway. I'm used to standing in the shadows."

Duncan hated it when his partner walled himself off, but he didn't know how to breach barriers that had been in place so long. Battering them down would not do, he'd learned. If he pushed too hard, Sasha would instinctively close him out, so he slid his hands down Sasha's lithe arms, clasped his hands, and led him to the massive bed canopied in gold and black velvet. They sat facing each other on the edge. Sasha pulled his heel to his crotch.

"Are you hungry?" Duncan asked, stroking up and down Sasha's thigh, savoring the feel of taut muscles beneath buttery leather. "Shall I have something sent up from the kitchens? My servants, at least, still respect my wishes."

Sasha edged closer and draped his hand over Duncan's knee. "Thank you, my friend. But not just now. Is there nothing on your mind besides food?" He moved his hand to Duncan's groin and cupped his balls as he leaned in and brushed his lips against Duncan's. When Duncan tried to return the kiss, Sasha pulled away with a grin. He wrapped Duncan's ponytail around his hand and tugged Duncan's head back so he could nibble up and down the side of Duncan's neck. As he dragged his magnificent lips over Duncan's rapidly heating skin, Sasha squeezed and fondled his balls through his cloth trousers. Duncan caught himself on his palms as Sasha pulled lightly on his hair, urging him to move farther onto the bed. Sasha swung his leg across Duncan and straddled him with his knees on the mattress and his thighs tensed and straight. When he looked down at Duncan with his lips even more swollen from Duncan's coarse whiskers and a beautiful, red flush across his high cheekbones and the straight, slender bridge of his nose, Duncan sensed a minute crack in the icy sheath Sasha wore like armor. Sasha never looked more desirable to Duncan than when he gave Duncan a glimpse at everything he hid from the rest of the world.

Duncan fell lightly on his back and grasped Sasha's hips just where the buckles of his armor crossed over the prominent curves of bone. He tried to pull Sasha into his lap so he could feel the contact between them he craved so much, feel Sasha's heat against him, but Sasha resisted, instead grabbing Duncan's wrist and bringing it to his mouth, where he ran his tongue over the sensitive skin and bit softly at the mound of flesh below Duncan's thumb. When Duncan reached for the tantalizing erection obvious beneath Sasha's skintight armor, Sasha again caught his hand, wove their fingers together, and let them fall next to his hip.

Sasha pressed Duncan's hand to his heart and just looked down at Duncan, his need and devotion radiating from him like a physical force. He smiled, and Duncan had no doubt he felt everything he showed in his expression, and it was Duncan's alone.

"I neglected to say I missed you too." Sasha released Duncan's wrist and scraped the back of his hand down Duncan's bearded cheek. "I'm not used to noticing the absence of another, and I was surprised how much it hurt to be without you. Truly, Duncan, I almost didn't enjoy my work."

"I'd hate to be the one who put you off murder." Duncan ran his free hand up Sasha's leg and over his chest until he could cup his shoulder. "Goddesses, you're beautiful." He worked the buckle over Sasha's throat free, then moved to the one across his collarbones, peeled the leather armor open, and bunched up the snug, hooded tunic beneath it. Duncan touched Sasha's warm, deep gold skin as he revealed it an inch at a time and watched Sasha's frozen blockade melt away with his arousal. Finally he pulled the armor open up the center and ran his hand over Sasha's lean, defined stomach, shaved, as always, and like silk beneath Duncan's palm. Duncan reached inside the leather to push it off Sasha's shoulder. "You could give it all up, you know. Never have to leave me."

Sasha shrugged out of his protective clothing and let it fall across Duncan's legs behind him. He pulled a small knife in a leather sheath from the waistband of his trousers and tossed it to the floor. "What, never leave your bed? Just be here naked and ready whenever you might want me?"

"All right." Duncan tugged at the buckle below Sasha's belly button, all his earlier worries forgotten. Nothing mattered to him but pleasing Sasha, feeling Sasha shiver with bliss and drop all the veneers he wore. Only in these intimate moments did Sasha completely bare himself for Duncan, and it drove Duncan crazy. He also knew Sasha liked to be in control, so when Sasha caught his hands, he allowed it. For the moment.

"So you'd turn me into a whore?" Sasha dropped a few inches, just grazing Duncan's swollen cock with his leather-encased bottom.

"No whore," Duncan panted, done with Sasha's teasing. He seized Sasha's waist and pulled him down, thrusting against the seam of his leather leggings, precome coating his cockhead and wetting the cloth of his trousers. "No sharing. You're mine, Sasha. Mine. Come here." He caught Sasha's shoulders and neck, bringing their faces and lips together. He nibbled Sasha's lips before thrusting his tongue between them, past Sasha's teeth and into the silken heat of his mouth. Sasha resisted, sparring with Duncan's tongue before submitting to it. Duncan growled and dug his fingers into Sasha's flesh. He wrapped his thick arms around Sasha's ribs and rolled so Sasha lay beneath him, and then he kissed him until his tongue ached and his lips felt ready to split, and he still wanted more.

"Tell me you're mine," Duncan panted. He stripped his linen tunic off and flung it beside the bed.

"You know I am." Sasha ruffled the hair on Duncan's chest and brushed his thumbs over Duncan's nipples, making them tighten to little pink beads. "I kill to protect you. I ask nothing in return."

"My love, you don't have to kill to show me you love me. I have guards—I—"

"I want to," Sasha said, yanking Duncan's fancy trousers to his thighs, making his erection smack him in the belly. "I want to show them what happens to anyone who threatens what's mine. In the order, I spilled blood for Thalil. Now I spill it for you, because I love you. Show me you love me even though I kill, Duncan. Take those silly clothes off."

Lifting one leg from the bed at a time, never taking his eyes off his beautiful partner, Duncan shed his trousers, boots, and stockings. Though a powerful, muscular man, he still felt a little self-conscious beneath Sasha's scrutiny. Where Sasha was lithe and graceful with uniform, bronzed skin, Duncan's body was pale from the neck down and covered in a dusting of dark brown hair and a network of battle scars. They had that in common now, he supposed, as he touched the pallid, raised, satiny strip on the side of Sasha's neck. He'd earned it when he'd chosen Duncan and their erstwhile companion Yarroway L'Estrella over his brothers in the order. A series of crisscrossing gashes, healed now, marked the inside of Sasha's forearm, and Duncan closed his eyes as he explored their texture. The scars felt like blades of grass scattered across Sasha's warm skin. Much about Sasha had horrified Duncan initially, and in those early days, he'd never thought he'd reconcile his code of honor with his love for this assassin and his beautiful, deadly, mad, broken Yarrow....

"You're thinking about him," Sasha said in a scratchy voice.

"No. I'm thinking about you, Sasha. About everything you've done for me. All you've given up. I'm thinking about how much I love it when I get you so aroused you'll submit to me, relinquish control to me. I love that the most." Duncan kept working on the buckles of Sasha's trousers, and Sasha lay contented beneath him, resting his arms on the pillow above his head. He even lifted his hips so Duncan could peel the leather away and remove the two hidden daggers crossed above his tailbone.

"Why?" Sasha asked as Duncan stood to pull his boots off, shaking his head and smiling when he found yet another knife at Sasha's left calf.

"Because I can see you," Duncan said, easing Sasha's legs open and sitting on his heels between them. "You don't hide from me. When you give yourself to me like that, I know you trust me. Goddesses, Sasha. You don't know how much that means. I know what your trust is worth."

Sasha spread his legs farther and arched his back off the bed. "You talk too much, Duncan. Show me."

"Don't order me, assassin," Duncan mumbled even as he found the vial of oil he kept under the bed and drizzled it over his hand and his cock. Funny how the title he'd once used to insult Sasha had evolved into an intimate endearment. Life could be strange, but Duncan didn't ponder it. Sasha lay looking up at him with trusting eyes, sprawled over the fancy, embroidered bedclothes in absolute complacency.

"Duncan, I'm yours."

Duncan bent to suckle Sasha's dark red nipple as he rubbed his slicked fingers over Sasha's cleft. His opening clenched every time Duncan caressed it, and Sasha pressed against Duncan's hand, practically begging to be entered. He tossed his head from side to side on Duncan's pillows as he opened and then closed his mouth without saying anything coherent. Duncan slipped his finger inside Sasha's open and very eager hole, easily sliding the entire length of it into his slick heat and feeling out the sweet spot within him. As soon as he grazed that clump of nerves, Sasha cried out in a language Duncan couldn't recognize.

"More," Sasha groaned.

"What is that language?" Duncan asked as he withdrew his finger and replaced it with his thumb, driving it home and watching Sasha twist his waist with pleasure. "I want to know what you're saying."

"I'm—Fuck." Sasha quivered as Duncan added another finger. "I'm calling out to Thalil. In… oh, that's good. In a dead language spoken by those who first worshipped him. Does it bother you?"

"No." It should have; Thalil was a disease: god of murder, seduction, and deceit. Even speaking his name was forbidden to the righteous. But as he pressed a third finger into Sasha's willing flesh and felt it squeeze him rhythmically, Duncan couldn't care. He loved this man, assassin or not, disciple of Thalil or not. This was his Sasha writhing beneath him, spreading his legs to accept Duncan's hand into him and flushing with delight at Duncan's touch. Duncan knew what it meant for Sasha to leave himself so vulnerable. It went against everything he'd ever been taught. "I love you for trusting me, for sharing your secrets."

"Duncan—"

"Tell me."

"Thalil, I need you. Need you now." Sasha rested one calf on Duncan's shoulder and wrapped his other leg around Duncan's waist, urging Duncan closer, clear in what he wanted.

Duncan slipped his fingers out of Sasha's body though Sasha's flesh clung to them as if unwilling to let them go. The desperation on his face as he looked up at Duncan spoke as loudly as his words, and it vanquished Duncan.

"I'll do anything for you, Sasha. I love you."

Sasha rolled his eyes. "Then stop talking."

Before entering Sasha, Duncan touched the small mark on the inside of Sasha's thigh: the crescent dripping blood, the sign of his order. That accursed symbol still unnerved Duncan, but it was a part of Sasha, and he'd accept it. "I love everything about you. Goddesses, tell me I can have you."

"Yes," Sasha breathed, spread his willowy limbs over the bed, and fluttered his eyelids. "Yes, yours."

Duncan gripped himself at the base of his erection and thrust into Sasha, burying himself to the hilt in Sasha's hot, clenching body. He looked down at Sasha's face, slack with ecstasy, and he couldn't hold back. Sasha curled his pelvis against Duncan, and Duncan thrust in, hard and deep, with no pretense of gentleness. Neither of them wanted that; they both wanted it hard, urgent, and raw, as if to reclaim each other after their time apart. Sasha dug his nails into Duncan's lower back to encourage him, and Duncan gave Sasha all he had.

"Bite," Sasha said, bowing his back and stretching his neck. "Duncan—"

Duncan knew of this peculiarity of Sasha's, and while he didn't share it, he enjoyed anything that brought his beautiful assassin pleasure.

He pushed deep into Sasha as he sunk his teeth into the muscle between Sasha's neck and shoulder, tearing the skin with his teeth because he knew Sasha liked it. The coppery tang of blood filled Duncan's mouth as he came into Sasha, his whole body convulsing and sprays of light erupting behind his eyes. His flesh melted after his release, and he fell across his partner's body as he rode wave after wave of pleasure.

Sasha made a small, dissatisfied sound that roused Duncan from his torpor. He lifted his forehead from Sasha's sweaty chest and kissed him before pulling out and flipping him to his belly. He lifted Sasha to his knees, guided his legs apart, and lapped at Sasha's open hole, tasting his own seed leaking out and mingling with the spicy flavor of Sasha's heated flesh. Duncan ran his finger along the rim of Sasha's distended opening before venturing deeper, his fluids easing the way. He gripped Sasha with his other hand and pushed his hood back to expose his moist cockhead. As he worked his hand into him, Duncan stroked Sasha in time with his thrusts.

Sasha's breath hitched and grew irregular; Duncan knew he was close. "Goddesses, I want to see you come. I want you to come for me." He curled forward and bit Sasha's ass cheek, sinking his teeth deep into the dense crescent of muscle until he tasted blood again.

Sasha loosed a raspy scream, dropped his head to the pillows, and came into Duncan's fist. His whole body seized, and his inner muscles clamped down on Duncan's hand. Duncan licked the blood from his lips and wrapped his arms around Sasha's chest, kissing gently across his shoulders as he whimpered and moaned. He'd given Sasha what he needed, so now Duncan could take his pleasure in the soft, slow kisses and caresses he relished.

When Sasha collapsed, Duncan pulled away, gently rolled Sasha to his side and lay down beside him, pressing their foreheads together. He held Sasha close, and Sasha wrapped his arms around Duncan's head. Neither of them said anything for probably a quarter of an hour as they drifted slowly down from the pinnacles of their bliss.

Finally, Sasha spoke in a low, contented tone tainted with melancholy. "You think of Yarrow too."

"There is no point in this," Duncan said, though his heart felt suddenly chilled, pierced by a cold, forgotten dagger.

"No. I'm tired of this unspoken agreement not to talk about him. I miss him. I long for him, and I know you do too. We should look for him. It's been over a year. He said he'd come back, and he hasn't. We should find him. Bring him back."

Duncan drew Sasha closer, enfolding him in his arms. It was true; their bed felt incomplete without their white-haired mage sharing it. "But I swore to him I'd let him go. He has much to work through, Sasha."

"It hurts," Sasha admitted in a small voice, like a boy who skinned his knee for the first time.

"I know. But right now, I have to try to bring some sort of order to Windwake."

Sasha rose to his elbow and propped his face on his hand, looking down at Duncan with those black eyes that cut to the core of him like the sharpest blades. "Windwake is yours. You are bairn. What more?"

Duncan rolled to his back and folded his arms beneath his head. "Bairn. High King Garith says so, but what are words worth?" He waved his hand at his finely furnished chamber, full of elaborate tapestries, posh benches, ornate weapons, statuary and paintings. "This is like a masquerade, Sasha. I wear the trappings of the bairn of Windwake, but it's a joke. The nobles are still loyal to Taran Edercrest, because he promised them money and lands. They care only about their own treasuries, not Windwake as a whole. Few of my vassals will even acknowledge me."

"I'll kill the disloyal ones," Sasha said, as if it were just that easy.

"No, love," Duncan said, burrowing his face into Sasha's neck, tired to his core of thinking about the greedy aristocrats. "It's not so simple."

"Why not?" Sasha asked and then yawned.

"Because it isn't. I'm too worn out to put it into words. I just want to hold you tonight. It's been too long."

"It has. Good night, my love." Sasha nestled against Duncan and fell asleep without another word.

Duncan drew Sasha so close their bones pressed together. He relished Sasha's slight weight against his chest, the way Sasha's breath moistened his skin, Sasha's come drying on his hand. In the world of deceit and illusion he found himself inhabiting, at least Duncan had one real thing, one thing he could trust amidst all the greed and deception. He touched the bite mark he'd left on Sasha's shoulder and kissed his forehead. Then Duncan let his head sink into the pillows. Tomorrow he'd have to face his vassals again, and he needed rest if he hoped to gain any ground. As he lay listening to his lover's slow breathing, the distant crash of saltwater against stone, and the evening breeze rattling the shutters of the ancient fortress he now called home, Duncan's mind conjured images of ice-blue eyes, hair like fresh snow, and a handsome face painted with blue ink. He wondered where Yarrow could be and if Yarrow thought of him and Sasha like this sometimes, just before falling asleep. The recollections ached like an old wound reopened, but Duncan didn't banish them, and his memories carried over into his dreams.

Chapter Two

SASHA ducked into an alcove as a pair of pages passed him in the hall. He pressed his back against the stone, and the boys in Windwake livery went on their way without ever noticing him. He watched them carefully for any sign that they might be other than they seemed. No one would suspect the grinning, rosy-cheeked boys, probably twelve years old, of treachery, and that made Sasha suspect them all the more. He'd used similar deceptions in the past, and could smile, blush, and gossip about the serving girls as convincingly as anyone. Sasha might have lost his innocence before he even knew he'd had any, but he could feign it as easily as any other emotion.

In the large room at the end of the hall, servants arranged platters of breads, meats, and cheeses on the long wooden tables that had been pushed against the walls. Others set out pitchers of water and ale, swept the stone floors, and stood on ladders to straighten the banners hanging from the rafters high above. Sasha attracted a few stares as he moved into the room where Duncan would once again face people intending him harm. The servants might have wondered what Sasha was up to as he moved around the perimeter of the room, dutifully scrutinizing the stone for any kind of trap, but they wouldn't know for sure. Sasha knew better than to come here in his distinctive order armor, and instead wore a simple pair of dark trousers, a rust-colored shirt, and a coarse brown cloak wrapped around his shoulders.

He still had half a dozen knives hidden in his simple garments, though, and he'd use them before he let anyone get to Duncan.

Windust Castle was an ancient structure, probably the oldest standing fortress in Selindria with the exception of Lockhaven, which meant dozens of twisting, hidden corridors, some of them boarded up, secret rooms, trapdoors, and plenty of other places that had been blocked off or obscured as the castle had been repaired and enhanced over the centuries. Sasha had made himself familiar with all of them before he'd allowed Duncan to take up residence here, and now he checked every place he might possibly hide if he'd been sent here to assassinate the bairn.

It took many hours before Sasha was satisfied. With the hall ready for Duncan's audience with his vassals, most of the servants scurried away to see to the midday meal. Sasha helped himself to bread and a few cold sausages, then made his way to a tiny balcony overlooking the room, another anomaly of the old building that served no practical purpose. Sasha had to climb over a section of fallen wall and pass piles of debris to reach the lookout. It was probably only large enough for three men to stand upon. Two long banners, one emblazoned with the Windwake crag eagle and the other bearing the royal ursine crest, hid it from the view of those below. From a tiny cleft between the two strips of cloth, Sasha had a good view of the dais where Duncan would sit. He readied his throwing knives in case he needed them.

Before long, Duncan entered and took his place on his heavy, wooden chair at the center of the round platform. Sasha didn't like the three tall windows surrounding the dais. Clearly the niche holding the bairn's throne had been designed for aesthetic value—to showcase the western light on the sea in the distance—rather than defensibility. An archer on a nearby tower could make deadly use of those silly windows. The two guards standing on either side of Duncan could do little to deter such an attack.

Nobles filed into the hall, followed by their servants, until the large space filled with people. Their chatter blended together into a din. Sasha waited, watching them all for any suspicious movement, even a chary facial expression. Finally Duncan's seneschal, Tam Allwynn Rathe, an older knight with gray-streaked hair and his long beard arranged into two plaits, banged his sword against his shield to call for order. He'd served the previous bairn, so Sasha didn't entirely trust him. The cacophony diminished and finally died.

"His Lordship, Duncan Purefroy, bairn of Windwake, will now hear your concerns. Who wishes to speak first?"

A woman in a dark blue gown elbowed her way to the front of the throng. A small boy of about six clutched her skirts. Sasha had made himself very familiar with the aristocrats of Windwake, and he recognized her: Friula Edercrest, the former bairn's widow. Watching Duncan's face, Sasha detected lethargy and a flicker of aggravation. Sasha couldn't blame his friend.

"Bairn Duncan," the woman said in a loud, shrill voice like a file on glass, "I have been before you now more times than I care to count. I have been ignored, my concerns have been dismissed, and no action has been taken on behalf of me or my household. Once again, I demand to know when my son's inheritance will be restored to him."

"My lady, with all due respect, the son of a traitor forfeits any right to inherit his father's title," Duncan said. "As I have told you many times before. I hold these lands at the behest of His Majesty Garith, High King of Selindria and Gaeltheon. I have no plans to relinquish them."

"And what of the gold my late husband set aside to sustain us, should anything happen to him? Can I assume it still fills your treasury, tam?"

"You can, and it will remain there," Duncan answered, his patience strained almost to breaking. "Taran Edercrest severely depleted this bairny's funds in his attempt at treason. Any gold he left will be used to help repair the damage he did, not only to the royal house, but to the people of this land, the subjects who depended upon him."

"And how are we supposed to survive?" she demanded. "We've been absolved of any wrongdoing by His Majesty, yet what's rightfully ours has been stolen—"

"Choose your words carefully, my lady," Allwynn warned.

"She's not alone." A man with dark, curly hair, well-built but with some fat around his middle, joined Friula Edercrest at the front of the assembly. "Many of us have had money we're entitled to withheld by this man!" He stabbed his finger at Duncan, and Allwynn stepped a little closer to his lord, his hand on the hilt of his blade.

Standing, Duncan pointed back and said, "Any funds used to finance Taran Edercrest's attempt to overthrow the rightful king will not be returned. They'll be used to repair the roads, wells, public buildings, temples, and ports the previous bairn neglected!"

"And how are we expected to pay the taxes you levied?" another man shouted from the center of the crowd.

"And what about the gold we paid Bairn Taran for lands and mining rights?" another man yelled. "How were we supposed to know what our money would be used for? Those bargains should be honored, or our money should be returned! We demand our money, or we demand our agreements be fulfilled!"

Many voices joined his in assent until Allwynn shouted above them all for order. The cursing and hollering died down to low grumbles and angry whispers. Sasha leaned in a little in a futile attempt to make out what the nobles said under their breath. It didn't matter; he already knew which of them were loyal, which conspired against Duncan and with whom, and even which of them were lovers. He knew all the alliances they'd forged and all the animosity some of them held against others. Therefore, he knew the matronly, gray-haired woman approaching the platform had three daughters she desperately wanted to marry to powerful men, and that she'd taken control of her lands and the lucrative mines on them because her husband was an invalid. Sasha had heard the other aristocrats describe her as a shrewd strategist and someone they wouldn't want to make into an enemy. Her name was Launa Ortean, and Sasha planned to eliminate her as soon as he could make it look like an accident.

Lady Ortean raised a frail hand, commanding the attention of everyone in the room with a gesture. Even Duncan stared intently at the stooped old woman in her ridiculously ornate purple gown. "Be careful what you say, my friends. A difference of opinion with Bairn Duncan is a dangerous thing to express."

"Just what do you mean by that?" Duncan, usually so slow to anger, widened his feet into a fighting stance and balled his large hands into fists.

"I think you know," Lady Ortean hissed, looking around at the assembled aristocrats, meeting some of their gazes. "I think we all know. You, tam, kill anyone who doesn't agree with you. You keep an assassin for just that purpose. Some of us have seen him, and we've all seen the evidence of his presence: our friends and neighbors, dead or vanished! You are a tyrant!"

Voices erupted in the hall, a few in support of Duncan but mostly in agreement with Lady Ortean. "Do you deny it?" she shouted over the others. "I bet he's here now. Tell us where you've hidden him, Bairn Duncan. And tell us how you're paying such a skilled murderer to terrorize us. Are you using the gold which should be returned to your nobles? Using our gold to pay an assassin to kill anyone who doesn't agree with you? Or are you securing his services in other ways? How is it a man your age is not yet married?"

Sasha put his foot on the edge of the railing, ready to leap down if he had to. The debate grew more heated by the moment, and Sasha planned to be at Duncan's back the second he saw the first glint of steel. As the nobles continued to yell and shove at each other, Lady Ortean stepped back and looked directly at the balcony where Sasha perched. She revealed a row of yellowed teeth in a cross between a smile and a snarl. Sasha ducked behind the Windwake banner just as the wooden doors to the hall flew open and a dozen of Duncan's knights entered the room with their swords drawn.

Allwynn pointed to the doors with his own blade. "All of you get out of here! Now! And be glad you're not on your way to the dungeons for treason."

Sasha waited to move until all the nobles had filed out and left Windust Castle and Duncan had slumped back into his chair, alone with his seneschal, Allwynn. Then he dropped lightly from his vantage point, making Allwynn flinch. "You're making a great deal of trouble for your friend, tam," the seneschal said. "Seems to me you'd leave if you truly cared about him."

"And leave you to protect him?"

Allwynn's eyes narrowed. "I don't agree with most of what those lacey fools spew, but they're right about one thing: your presence here is a disgrace. It's shameful and—"

"Enough, Tam Allwynn," Duncan said. "It's my decision and mine alone who I choose to keep in my presence. I'll ask you not to insult Sasha again. Besides, he isn't the problem. Gold is the problem. Edercrest depleted the Windwake treasury. I couldn't return those peoples' money if I wanted to. And the common people, miners and artisans, are suffering. Sasha is just a convenient excuse. These people want to replace me with a bairn who will cater to their greed and favor those who kiss his backside, at the expense of people who grow their food and make their clothing."

"Many of those people are traitors," Sasha added. "I've overheard them conspiring. They should be replaced with loyal men."

"That may be," Allwynn said cautiously. "But even so, they should stand trial, not be murdered in their beds."

Sasha studied the seneschal, satisfied by the way Allwynn's eyes darted to him every few seconds, watching him with trepidation. "So we should wait until the bairn is murdered while he sleeps?" Sasha asked. "I'm not willing to do that."

"We have laws in this land, tam. My lord, you cannot allow this to continue."

Duncan looked waxen and drawn when he patted his seneschal on the shoulder. "Thank you, Tam Allwynn, but I need to consider all of this. I'd like to be alone for the rest of the afternoon."

"Yes, Bairn Duncan." Allwynn bowed slightly. "Remember, my lord, tonight is the banquet you agreed to throw for your nobles. It should be quite an interesting celebration after what happened here today."

"I'm counting the minutes," Duncan grumbled.

"I suppose I should speak to the guards," Allwynn said. "We'll have to be ready in case of an… altercation of any kind."

"I'll see to protecting Duncan," Sasha said. Events like this made perfect opportunities for assassins, as he well knew. He'd taken advantage of them many times in his work.

"Do you really think that's wise?" Allwynn asked. "To antagonize them further, throw your presence in their faces? I assure you, *Sasha*, my men will keep the bairn safe."

"Oh? Could you keep him safe from me?"

"Enough!" Duncan finally lost his temper. "Tam Allwynn, see to your duties."

"Yes, my lord."

"Do you want me to go as well?" Sasha asked. As he waited for a response, he looked around for danger, because his skin chilled and his heart beat a little faster, just as it did when he sensed a threat. But he and Duncan were alone in the hall, so his anxiety made little sense.

Duncan shook his head. "I don't want you to go, but Seneschal Allwynn might have a point about the feast this evening. Perhaps you should avoid it. I'll only stay as long as I must to be polite."

"I don't want to be there because of some sense of vanity or a desire to be fawned over by you," Sasha said. "I'm trying to trust and feel affection, though it's strange and wrong sometimes, but I haven't become quite that needy, friend. Events such as this one, with all their chaos of people milling around and servants running back and forth, are perfect distractions for work such as mine. You need me there."

Duncan looked up and held Sasha's gaze with his muted green eyes. The conflict behind them said he didn't know what to make of Sasha's words, whether to be flattered or offended. Sasha knew Duncan loved him, valued him as no one ever had, but at times like this, Sasha saw Duncan wasn't completely comfortable with him. He didn't understand Sasha yet. It made Sasha's stomach churn. He didn't know how much more he could change.

"Sasha," Duncan said, choosing his words carefully, "I've been a knight over half my life. I can defend myself against almost any threat. I *do* need you, love, just not at the banquet tonight."

"Look me in the eye and tell me you truly believe that," Sasha said. "Before you do, think back to the night we fought those other members of my order." He canted his head so Duncan had a clear view of the deep scar the other assassins had left on him. It was perhaps a little cruel, but Sasha needed his friend to understand, and it worked.

Duncan shuddered and rubbed his forehead. He clasped Sasha's hand for just a second before letting go. With his hand still covering his eyes, Duncan said softly, "Very well. Perhaps we should return to my chambers. Rest. We're in for quite a night, my friend."

THE cloying scent of spring flowers overpowered the savory smell of the feast. Garlands woven from soft pink and lavender blossoms festooned the stone columns of the hall, and dozens of bouquets sat on every table. Sasha's nose itched as he moved among the guests. To the Shades' Abode with any accusations they might throw at him. Only Duncan's safety mattered.

In the Order of the Crimson Scythe, Sasha had been taught not to feel love or attachment, that valuing another person gave that person power, and power could always be exploited. Caring about someone meant others could use the person against you. Anything one held dear others could threaten to take. In some ways, life had been simpler when Sasha had felt certain he'd eliminated those weak feelings, made himself invulnerable to that sort of pain. He'd never had anything he'd feared losing, and he now couldn't help feeling like he'd handed an enemy one of his daggers and then left his back exposed.

As the fifty or so nobles sat down to the first course of their dinner, Sasha dipped behind a pillar and reminded himself for the thousandth time that he'd gained more than he'd lost, but exposing himself like this took a completely novel sort of courage. He hadn't quite mastered it, and found it a very subtle skill.

Duncan looked remarkably handsome in an emerald tunic embroidered with bronze thread and sprinkled with tiny orange gems. His rich dark hair spilled down his back, highlighted with deep red and gold by the firelight. His broad shoulders shook as he laughed at something one of the young women said. Sasha grinned and rolled his eyes at Duncan's pitiful attempt at guile. He hardly sounded convincing, but then, these aristocrats hadn't been trained to read a man's every expression. They didn't expect treachery in everything the way Sasha did.

The dull dinner dragged on and on, the nobles alternating between sniping at each other, offering hollow compliments, and just chattering on about nothing because they felt they should. Things left unsaid in even a few silent moments clearly made them uncomfortable. In contrast, Sasha adored the deep quiet that let him hear a target's every breath, heartbeat, and tiniest movement. Finally a quartet of musicians set up in a corner and began to play a lively tune. Servants cleared trenchers away and filled goblets with fine Lockhaven wine, from the chilled mountainsides where the vintners let the fruit freeze on the vines, trapping the sweetness in the ice crystals. Platters of pastries, fruit, and soft, pale cheeses were brought out to accompany it. Yarrow would have found it delightful. One by one, the nobles moved from their seats to the center of the hall to dance.

Duncan approached Lady Ortean and her three daughters. He scooped up the eldest girl's hand, kissed it, and said, "Would you do me the honor, my lady?"

"The honor is mine," the young woman said as she hooked her elbow with Duncan's and let him lead her to the center of the room. He twirled her around, making the layers of her blue and silver skirts billow around her, before passing her off to another young lord and taking a different partner for himself.

They performed a dance called Falling Blossoms. Sasha knew it well; he knew nearly every dance popular among the aristocracy, and better than most of the dancers he watched spinning across the floor. He found it bitterly funny that if he so chose, he could easily captivate and charm these frivolous nobles. He could have them lined up to receive his attention, have the maidens ignoring their partners to watch him, as many now watched Duncan.

The music paused, one of the performers smacked the skin head of his drum twice, and the dancers clapped twice in response. Duncan, along with the other men, lifted his partner by the waist. High-pitched female laughter filled the room as the reel reached its end and the dancers lined up facing each other, men on one side and women on the other, to perform the Loom and Shuttle dance to a slower, rhythmic melody.

Duncan looked genuinely happy as he stepped between two ladies in elaborate, conical headdresses and kicked up his feet. He danced gracefully in spite of his stature and brawn, and he commanded everyone's attention. The women, and even a few of the men, stared at him with undisguised longing, and Duncan cordially returned their smiles, though the brief grin he gave Sasha over his shoulder showed his other expressions for the pale imitations they were. Duncan's true passion burned only for Sasha. All the rest was an act, and Duncan was no skilled deceiver.

Sasha winked at Duncan, but he felt a tiny tug inside his chest, because he would never be able to dance with his partner at a celebration like this one. Such things had never bothered him before. Rather than try to analyze his tangled emotions, Sasha scanned the room to check for anything dubious. His gaze fell on the musicians, and he watched them perform for a few moments. A lovely young man, lank and supple, with thick waves of dark red hair, played a double flute. He wore snug leggings, one leg brown and the other yellow, and an oversized shirt with bell sleeves. He puckered his full lips around the tip of his instrument provocatively, but his taupe eyes looked icy and calculating as he cast his gaze around the hall. His handsome face lacked both the concentration and the joy in performing the other three artists displayed.

With the hair standing up on the back of his neck, Sasha followed the pretty piper's gaze. The musician made eye contact with another man for a heartbeat, this one dressed in unassuming but high-quality garments and as striking as the performer, who turned and disappeared down a darkened corridor. A few minutes later, the song ended and all the musicians bowed to enthusiastic applause. The lute player fiddled with the pegs on his instrument while the two drummers went to a table for refreshment. Predictably, the flutist wove far too elegantly through the merrymakers, avoiding all notice until he reached the same hallway and melted into the darkness.

Sasha gave the two men a few minutes' head start before following. He noticed right away that neither of them made a sound as they bounded between the scant patches of light the torches cast and the long stretches of shadow. As fast as he moved, Sasha could scarcely keep up with them, and his unease multiplied by the second. His quarry descended the stairs to the cellars. Ghastly possibilities played out in Sasha's imagination: thoughts of traps and poisoned ale casks. Whoever these men were and whatever they planned to do, Sasha intended to stop them before they could harm Duncan. He slipped a dagger from within his sleeve and felt the reassuring cold of hard steel.

Sasha crept down the crumbling stairs and into a large vault, where cured meats hung from the ceiling. Their smoky smell was strong, and he couldn't see in the pitch-blackness, but he'd explored these underground storerooms enough to navigate through to the wine cellar and down another flight of even narrower steps. They led Sasha deep below the fortress, to dank caverns filled with brackish water. Sometimes, during the high tides, the sea filled the caves completely, so most everyone avoided them. As he splashed through, wincing at the racket he made, Sasha still saw no hint of the other men and started to wonder if they'd somehow escaped him. He couldn't let that happen, couldn't risk what he knew were skilled assassins coming back when he didn't suspect them, or when he was away on a mission.

Finally he saw a flickering bluish light beyond a narrow cleft in the stone. Sasha reached beneath his left arm and drew a second blade from a sheath hidden within his shirt. As he pressed his back to the rock just outside the opening and listened, he watched the eerie luminescence reflecting off the serpentine blade. This dagger had been the first weapon given to him by his masters in the Order of the Crimson Scythe. He'd once thought of the other assassins as his family, and the order as the only place he belonged. Since they'd cast him out and branded him a traitor, he'd struggled to discern who exactly he was if not one of them. He gripped the hilt of the knife and remembered all the lives it had reaped for Thalil. His dark eyes reflected back at him from the polished steel. He was still an elite killer, the best of the best, and he'd protect what he cared about.

What he loved.

Sasha peered beyond the crack and into a natural room containing nothing but a glowing orb floating among the stalactites, casting severe shadows across the damp, shimmering wall. He'd known mages, one of them *very* well, and he recognized enchantment when he saw it. Cautiously, his every perception as sharp as his blades, he stepped into the space.

Sasha crouched just in time to avoid the swipe of a serrated knife. He sprang up and leapt back against the wall, raising one of his daggers above him and holding the other straight out. The two men he'd been following seemed to materialize from the scant shadows hugging the walls. Order assassins trained to conceal themselves, and while an ordinary man might have missed them, Sasha knew he would have detected their presence. More magic must have kept them hidden.

The man disguised as a noble stabbed down toward Sasha's chest with the speed only the Crimson Scythe could instill in its disciples. Sasha deflected the blow, and steel scraped against steel as they struggled. The other assassin concentrated on overpowering Sasha, and Sasha used his distraction to thrust the blade in his other hand at his enemy. The man dodged backward, but the tip of Sasha's dagger sunk into the flesh just above his hip, drawing a spurt of blood when Sasha yanked it free. When his adversary doubled over and pressed his hand to the wound, Sasha kicked him hard beneath his chin and sent him sprawling on his back in the fetid, foamy water. He barely managed to raise his arm and protect his face from the young assassin in the musician's costume. The jagged knife he held nicked Sasha's wrist, drawing blood but inflicting little damage. In one motion, Sasha stepped forward and brought his elbow down on the other man's nose, breaking it with a sickening crunch. The other assassin howled and cradled his face as blood poured down his chin.

Steel swished against leather, and Sasha spun as the man on his back threw a small knife. He dove to the side, desperate to avoid a blade almost certainly laced with deadly poison. A stone beneath the water caught Sasha's ankle, sending him down hard on his side and knocking the wind from his lungs. The assassin posing as the piper took advantage, diving on Sasha and tackling him.

"Filthy traitor," he hissed, blood from his mangled face splattering Sasha and getting into Sasha's eyes. "I hoped I'd have the honor of killing you." He raised his blade above Sasha's throat, but Sasha was quicker, throwing his weight to the left and knocking his enemy off balance. Before the other man could recover, Sasha plunged his serpentine dagger into his side, piercing his lung and releasing a rush of air. He drew the knife out and stabbed down again. The enemy assassin gurgled and spat up blood and white foam, his limbs convulsing before he fell still.

Sasha staggered to his feet, soaked in blood and frigid water and wiping gore from his face with his sleeve, just as the remaining order assassin slashed out at him with one of the slender, hidden blades they all kept hidden in their leather gloves, at the insides of their wrists. Razor sharp, it sliced through Sasha's simple clothing from the base of his rib almost to his spine. He'd dodged, and the cut wasn't deep, but it would need dressing, and soon. If the weapon had been treated with a toxin, he might never get the chance, but Sasha couldn't worry about that now. Blood poured in a sheet down Sasha's right side, staining the briny water around his knees. Ignoring the pain, he drove his knife into his opponent's thigh and twisted it, sending the other man down in the muck again. Sasha had raised his blade to finish it when he found his muscles suddenly weak and trembling. The dagger felt too heavy to hold, and it slipped from Sasha's fingers and disappeared beneath the fouled surf. At first he feared poison, but this… this felt like something else.

"I… recognize this spell," Sasha grunted with a great effort. "Why are you here? Who hired you to kill the bairn?"

"Kill the bairn?" asked a smooth but mocking voice. "How very far you have fallen, *brother*." The final word dripped with contempt.

Sasha's head felt like a boulder as he struggled to look up at the man who had appeared out of nowhere. He recognized the slim, sallow face with the pleasing features and slightly deranged eyes. When he saw the mage's single, wide sleeve, he also recalled the man had lost his arm just above the elbow. "I remember you. You came after me before. What are you doing here? What do you want with Duncan?"

The mage cackled as his wounded associate crawled to shelter behind him. "Poor fool. How utterly pathetic you've become. Killing you will be a mercy. To think, a former brother of Thalil could be so easily deceived. We're here for you, friend. Not your noble lover. If I doubted you were unworthy of serving the Dark and Beautiful One before, those doubts are gone now."

"What do you mean by that?" Sasha asked, trying to buy himself some time as he discreetly searched his pockets.

"Don't you see what's happened to you?" The mage-assassin waved his remaining hand around in front of his face. "You've become weak. You put that man's interests before your own. You value him, and we took advantage of your silliness. You ran after us without a second thought, right into our trap. Is that how a son of Thalil conducts himself? You barely gave us a challenge. And to think, the others once spoke of your talent and how far you'd go within the order. You handed us the very weapon we used against you. Have you forgotten everything you've been taught?"

"I remember it, but I'm no longer sure of the validity." Sasha closed his hand around a small cloth pouch, still dry, thank the Cast-Down. With one hand, he slowly worked the cord around it loose and dug his fingers into the powder it contained.

"And now I finally get to kill you," the mage said softly. "I've dreamed of this."

"Think twice," Sasha warned. "I have powerful friends."

"Yarroway L'Estrella," the mage said, and Sasha, so well-trained and adept at reading inflection, tone, and facial expressions, couldn't tell if the other assassin expressed awe, respect, hatred, or veneration. Maybe he felt them all at once. If anyone could inspire such disjointed and contradictory emotions, it would be Yarrow.

Sasha didn't ponder it. While the mage stood lost in thoughts of the man who took his arm, Sasha seized a fistful of sand combined with stinging herbs and hurled it into his face. The other assassin cried out and scrubbed at his watering eyes with his fist. Knowing he'd have only one chance, Sasha bounded up and prepared to strike, fighting through the magically induced torpor by sheer force of will.

The mage pointed his palm toward Sasha, fingers spread. A burst of sickly greenish light emanated from his hand, striking Sasha like a bulwark and knocking him down. Sasha's head pounded and spun; he could barely manage to push himself up on his elbows so the water wouldn't cover his face and drown him. Saltwater stung the wound across his waist. The walls of the small cavern rotated around him as he dragged himself toward the fissure in the rock without any real hope of saving himself. What a fool he'd been, blinded by his need for Duncan. He managed to hoist himself up on a small shelf of stone before the world went cold and black.

Chapter Three

THE red stain surrounding him told Sasha his blood had been dripping steadily into the water while he'd been unconscious. His body ached, and the saltwater made his wound feel like hot coals against his skin, burning into his bones and muscles, carried by his blood to every inch of his body. When he tried to stand the first time, his stomach lurched, and he spit up a mouthful of bile. He gripped the uneven stone and pulled himself to his feet, cursing himself for his failure, for his weakness.

The other assassins had gone, and their absence compelled Sasha to move in spite of the agony tearing him in every direction. He'd left Duncan unprotected. The other members of his former order might be on their way to him even now. Sasha had to reach him first. Dropping down in the foul, cold liquid, he searched frantically for his serpentine order dagger, irrationally upset over its loss. Finally he closed his hand around the familiar hilt and scrabbled back to his feet. He ignored his pain and the fuzz flooding his vision as he stumbled back through the caverns, to the cellars, and then back into the hall.

DUNCAN had never been so happy to see his hall empty out as he was after the so-called celebration. Faking smiles for his vassals, offering them insincere compliments, and pretending to enjoy the aggressive attention of their daughters had worn him down, like a piece of steel hammered too thin. He'd barely tasted his food as he felt their scrutiny on him as he ate, so he wrapped some rolls and a few slabs of salted meat in a napkin to take to his chambers. He just wanted to strip out of these ridiculously fancy clothes, stoke his fire, and relax in his bed next to Sasha. Goddesses, he craved the company of someone who'd offer no false flattery, who enjoyed his company not for what he might gain, but just because of who Duncan was.

Duncan rubbed his eyes and raked his fingers through his hair, pushing the leather loop out and letting his locks fall loose around his shoulders. At least the worst was over, or so he thought until Sasha stumbled into the empty hall, soaking wet, pale as a cadaver, and trailing blood behind him.

"Dear goddesses!" Duncan cried, hurrying toward his friend. "What happened?"

Sasha opened his mouth to reply, but his eyes rolled back and he crumpled on the floor. Duncan scooped his small body into his arms. Sasha's forehead felt ice cold when Duncan pressed his lips to it. Seneschal Allwynn burst through the door just as Duncan reached it. The older man, an honorable knight, looked from Sasha's limp body to Duncan's face. Duncan knew Tam Allwynn probably wanted to bombard him with questions, but the loyal soldier held his tongue.

"What can I do, my lord?" Allwynn asked.

Duncan felt grateful for Allwynn's dedicated service, and he trusted him as a fellow knight. "Please, tam, bring healing supplies, water, and mulled wine to my chambers. Tell no one what you've seen, I beg you."

Allwynn bowed. "Of course, tam. See to your friend."

Duncan hurried to his room, stripped away Sasha's sopping wet, filthy clothing and got him into bed. He wrapped Sasha's shivering, nude body in his blankets and held Sasha against his chest, offering a prayer to the Mother Goddess to ease Sasha's pain. He also prayed to Sarmine, the goddess of love, not to take another partner from him. The death of his first love still haunted Duncan, and the loss of Yarrow plagued his thoughts every day. Duncan didn't think he could bear to lose another man he loved. It took Allwynn forever to deliver the items Duncan had requested, but eventually he set them on a stand by the bed without a word of judgment. Duncan would be forever grateful to his seneschal for his discretion.

"Here, love," Duncan whispered as he tipped the decanter of heated wine toward Sasha's mouth. Sasha's eyes fluttered halfway open, and he parted his lips to accept what Duncan offered. His Adam's apple bobbed, and he winced as if it hurt to swallow. Duncan alternated between giving him water and heated wine until Sasha became alert enough to lift his head and look around the chamber.

"What am I doing here?" he asked.

Duncan smoothed Sasha's wet hair out of his face, grateful for the returning warmth of Sasha's skin, grateful for the clarity in Sasha's eyes and the lucidity in his question. "Thank the goddesses you're all right, Sasha. You… frightened me. What in the Shades' Abode happened to you?"

"Answer my question first." Sasha frowned and furrowed his brows. "How am I here?"

"You collapsed in the hall," Duncan said. "I carried you."

"You carried me." Sasha spat the words like tainted wine and looked away. "The others were right. I'm pitiful."

Duncan tried to cup Sasha's chin, but Sasha pushed his hand away.

"How have I come to this place?" Sasha moved to sit up, but then he winced and relaxed back against Duncan.

"As I said, I brought you here when—"

"No," Sasha snapped. "That isn't what I mean. *Baska.* You wouldn't understand."

"Why don't you give me the benefit of the doubt?" Duncan asked. "I'm not a simpleton."

Sasha sighed and closed his eyes, still pale beneath his deep tan. He opened his mouth to speak, shook his head, and nestled his face against Duncan's chest. After taking several moments to himself, he said, "I'm sorry, my love. I appreciate you protecting me, but I should not need it."

"Every man needs a bit of help sometimes. There's no shame in it. Please, tell me what happened."

"It was my former brethren," Sasha said. "The order. They… used my desire to protect you against me. I can't believe I fell for such an obvious ploy. I should have seen what they were doing, resisted it—Thalil, my time away from my colleagues has softened my mind as well as my body."

"You just made a mistake," Duncan said. "You are just a man."

"No! I am a disciple of Thalil! I shouldn't hand my enemy a weapon to use against me. I should be above this weakness. I should not make mistakes."

Duncan couldn't suppress the curl of his lip. Sasha had led an unusual life, but Duncan could dismiss only so much. "So you regard your love for me as a weakness? Goddesses, a mistake?"

"I never said that. I—I don't know." Sasha pressed his fist against his lips and scrunched his eyes shut.

Instead of pressing Sasha further, unsure if he wanted his questions answered, Duncan said, "Tell me why your former associates were here."

"They were here for me, of course. They meant it when they said they'd never let me go. No one leaves Thalil's service, except to go to his side. They aren't going to stop, Duncan. I'm putting you in danger by being here. Perhaps I should go. Lead them away from you instead of toward you."

"I don't want that."

"Why?" Sasha asked.

"I love you."

"Enough to put yourself in danger? To risk your life?"

Duncan pinched Sasha's chin between his thumb and finger and made Sasha meet his gaze. "Yes."

They looked at each other for a few minutes before Sasha finally smiled and wiggled closer to Duncan, insinuating his lithe thigh between Duncan's legs and draping his arm over Duncan's ribs. He extracted himself from the blanket Duncan had wrapped tightly around him and arranged it over both of them. Duncan felt the heat of Sasha's skin through his fancy clothes, and he wanted to feel it against his bare flesh, even if Sasha's wound prevented anything except cuddling close.

"The good news is the order isn't hunting you," Sasha said, moving his face close to Duncan's on the pillow they shared. "I'd initially feared one of your duplicitous nobles had managed to hire us… I mean to say, them. I'm relieved that's not the case."

Duncan grew drowsy as the anxiety he'd balled up inside his belly at the feast slowly fizzled from a flame to a coal. The warmth beneath the coverlet and the calming proximity of Sasha made him crave nothing more than a good night's sleep in his lover's arms. But he also noticed the sticky wet of Sasha's seeping wound. He disentangled himself from Sasha's limbs and sat up. "Your injury needs cleaning, or it could fester."

"Don't trouble yourself," Sasha said. "I'll see to it."

"Nonsense." The air in the drafty room chilled Duncan when he got out of bed, and he stoked the fire before taking a basin of water, some pricklefruit soap, and a soft cloth from the bedside table. He pushed the blanket to Sasha's knees. The mattress and rope supports groaned as he sat down next to his assassin. Duncan plunged the rag into the tepid water and twisted it to wring it out. The sight of Sasha's beautiful body, all those lean, defined muscles playing against each other as he shifted on the sheets, sent Duncan's blood straight to his root. Sasha looked like a bronze sculpture, but fluid, possessed of so much grace—Goddesses, he stole Duncan's reason without even trying.

Duncan shook his head. Sasha was hurt and needed tending. He dabbed the cloth along the deep cut, letting the pricklefruit essence seep into the wound. It would banish an infection, but Duncan knew from much experience it stung. Sasha took it with only a few muffled grunts, and soon the inflamed flesh around his gash looked less swollen. The redness faded away. Duncan opened a jar and smeared some greenish salve on Sasha's injury. He'd had the Emiri remedy shipped all the way to Windwake from Meritage, as he'd never seen a medicine so effective against septicity.

"Thank you," Sasha said, brushing Duncan's cheek with his fingers.

Duncan smiled, pleased Sasha had accepted his care, pleased to attend to the man he loved. Nothing gratified Duncan more than seeing Sasha's contentment, knowing Sasha felt safe at his hands. "I'm happy to do this for you. This and anything you need. I love you."

"I love you, Duncan. By Thalil, I feel it, but I don't know how to show you."

"You show me by just staying there, trusting me to see to you when you're hurt. Letting me take care of you. Drink some more wine; you've lost a lot of blood."

Sasha obeyed, and after Duncan cleaned his wound, he wound strips of clean, white linen around Sasha's waist, as Sasha refused to have his cut stitched. When he finished, he stretched out beside Sasha and pulled the covers over them. Though he wanted Sasha, wanted to satisfy himself within Sasha's flesh, Duncan felt content that Sasha had accepted his ministrations without argument. He knew how hard it was for Sasha to depend on another.

"Lady Ortean's eldest daughter, Aurauna, danced with me seven times," Duncan said, attempting to lighten the mood. "By the fourth dance, she was already hinting at marriage."

"Did you accept?" Sasha asked.

Duncan chuckled. "You're joking."

"I'm not." Sasha curled around Duncan, pressing his bare cock into Duncan's groin and his lips next to Duncan's throat. "It would be a strategic match. Will you pursue it?"

"No. You must be kidding." Duncan stroked Sasha's hip and thigh, relishing the softness of his skin, even though its warmth contrasted so harshly with the iciness of his words.

Sasha planted tender kisses up Duncan's neck and across his whiskered jaw before settling in next to Duncan's ear. As he spoke, he rubbed Duncan's lower back with the heel of his hand. "Your subjects will grow suspicious if you don't choose a wife eventually. Besides, you'll have to father a son to inherit your bairny. One of Lady Ortean's daughters would be a good choice. Their family is wealthy and respected. Also, you'd turn a powerful enemy into a friend."

"And that wouldn't bother you, Sasha?"

"Why should it?"

Duncan squinted to discern the details of Sasha's face in the dying firelight. Sasha looked tired and contented, his eyes half shut and his body languid beside Duncan.

"I want it to bother you," Duncan said, gathering Sasha closer and burrowing his nose into Sasha's hair. "I want you to be possessive. I want you to want me all for yourself."

Sasha wove his arms around Duncan. "I am. I do. Thalil, I do, but I'm also realistic. I must always stand outside your world. I know you can never acknowledge me as your partner. You can barely acknowledge me as an acquaintance. I understand. I'm accustomed to others avoiding me, turning away from me in disgust. Choosing a woman to bear your sons, one who can forge valuable alliances for you, is something completely different from what we share. I accept that it's inevitable."

"I don't," Duncan said, squeezing Sasha as hard as he dared, mindful of Sasha's wound. "This love we share should be sacred. It is sacred to me. It would hurt me deeply if you took another lover, Sasha."

"I have no desire to do that."

"Yet you suggest I should?"

"No, not exactly. A wife is a political pawn, an incubator for the future rulers of Windwake. Little more."

"You are cold," Duncan said.

"Yes. Life is cold and hard. Much more a battle than a soothing respite in a garden," Sasha responded. "We're not alive if we aren't fighting, are we? Every minute we must fight to survive. You should know I'll never let you be unhappy. I won't allow any wife you take to make you unhappy for long."

Duncan shuddered, still stunned at how naturally Sasha resorted to murder. It disturbed him, but he knew Sasha meant it as a gesture of devotion. "I… I appreciate it, the sentiment of it, but no. No poor wench deserves a husband who cannot love her. She certainly doesn't deserve death for failing to satisfy me when such a thing is impossible. I'd rather remain a bachelor."

"People will talk," Sasha said.

"Let them."

"My dear friend, you should reconsider," Sasha said. "As a knight, you had reasonable cause not to marry: the lack of a permanent residence, the danger of your calling. But now it will seem very suspicious. What will you do for an heir? You're always talking about your responsibility to the people of this land. Whose hands will they fall into if you don't have a successor? I'll never deny you my body. I'll be right here anytime you can sneak away from your wife's bed."

"I don't wish to discuss this any further," Duncan said, torn between hurt at Sasha's willingness to share him and gratitude at Sasha's concern for his reputation. He didn't know how to make Sasha understand that he wanted much more than Sasha's body. "Besides, we have more pressing problems at the moment. I don't appreciate anyone threatening you, and I won't stand for it. I won't sit here and wait for those serpents to come back. I say we go after them. With your knowledge of their customs and the army I can raise, we can rid the world of their pestilence once and for all."

"You despise the order, and not just because they attacked me," Sasha observed. "How can you love me when I am a part of something that disgusts you so deeply? Sometimes I worry you're merely distracted by the pleasure we take together. I offered from the beginning to be your lover with no strings attached."

"Stop it," Duncan said through gritted teeth. "I don't know what you're trying to do, Sasha. I don't understand most of what you do, the things you place value in and the others you dismiss, but don't tell me I don't know my own heart. Goddesses, I've had enough casual bed partners to see the difference between them and you, and—and yes, I hate that vile order of murderers. I hate that, because of them, I can never see you smile without wondering if you mean it or if it's manipulation, the means to an end. I hate that you have to calculate and ponder before you'll let me show you kindness. They stole away your goddess-given right to just feel happy in my arms with all that rubbish they told you about weakness. I would like to see them destroyed to their last member. But you would not. You still feel loyalty to them, don't you? Even now that they're hunting you."

"I—I don't know. They were the only family I ever had. It was all much simpler when I was with them. I would not see the Crimson Scythe ended, not that either of us, with or without this army of yours, could accomplish it."

"We certainly scared them off back in Felgard," Duncan said.

"Yarrow scared them off. I admit they're afraid of Yarrow. I'm sure word of what he did has reached most of the order by now. With him here, we might stand a chance at what you suggest. Without him, we have none. The order is scattered across the world and very well hidden. It's not the sort of battle you're used to, my friend. It wouldn't be a matter of facing an enemy on a field and fighting until the stronger force won. It would be like trying to defeat darkness in the middle of the night."

"I'm still willing to try," Duncan said.

"What would your nobles say about the expense of leading such a campaign? They'd see no benefit to themselves in it and accuse you of spending their gold on a personal crusade. What would happen to Windwake if you left and took all your loyal soldiers with you? You might as well hand it over to those who oppose you. You're always telling me you have a duty to the people of the bairny, and that it comes before anything else."

"I have always put my duty first and never considered doing otherwise," Duncan said, almost to himself. "I never had any problem until it meant putting you second. It's difficult for me to accept, and I honestly don't know what's right."

Sasha kissed Duncan softly and said, "Yes, it's much easier when everything is black and white, isn't it? There's just no set of rules one can apply to every situation he might wander into, not your knight's code of honor, not even the ways of Thalil. Most of the time, we have no guidance at all to rely on. Sometimes it seems to me that by choosing to protect one thing, something else must always be sacrificed. I couldn't have my place in the order and keep you and Yarrow. Duncan, what if you can't do your duty to your people and keep our friendship? What if you have to choose?"

Duncan felt like a diluted poison swam in his blood, making a dull ache spread from his chest to the tips of his fingers and toes. He tucked the blanket under Sasha's chin and his own and wriggled closer to Sasha, but he couldn't banish the shard of ice poking against his heart. Sasha needed reassurance, needed to believe he'd made the right choice by abandoning the cult of assassins, but Duncan couldn't find even a single word to say to him. He couldn't answer Sasha's question, because he honestly didn't know how to make a decision like that. Before, he'd have fallen back on his duty, but he now realized that was just taking the smoother path.

"It won't come to that," Duncan finally said in a scratchy whisper.

"Yarrow chose," Sasha said. "He chose our safety over his own happiness."

"It isn't the same," Duncan protested weakly. Goddesses, he missed Yarrow. The mention of Yarrow's name tugged a whole welter of memories, longing, and phantom sensations behind it. Duncan could almost smell the cool, crisp scent of Yarrow's hair. In the dark, with the fire perishing and the shadows thick, Duncan felt sure that if he reached behind him, he'd find a warm body with slender limbs and the softest skin he'd ever felt. If he looked over his shoulder, bright blue eyes glowing with their own luminescence would be looking back. Instead of glancing at the cold, unoccupied portion of the bed or grasping at a shade, Duncan let himself believe for a few seconds.

Sasha ran his fingertip along the globe of Duncan's shoulder, barely making contact. "Do you remember how little it took to please him? The smallest touch would make him moan with pleasure. I never met a man more responsive or more grateful for the slightest sliver of attention."

"I remember," Duncan said.

"Do you think he'll come back?"

"It's been a very long time, Sasha."

"I hope he isn't alone. Being alone made him miserable. Do you think he found someone else?"

"I can't know that, my love. Perhaps," Duncan said. "He'd be glad you and I are watching out for each other, though."

"Yes," Sasha said, wriggling his arm beneath Duncan's and clutching tight to Duncan's waist. "At least we have that, for now. I'm glad too. I do love you."

Duncan kissed Sasha's forehead and wrapped his arms around Sasha, holding onto him because Sasha seemed like the only solid, tangible thing in a nightmare world of twisting paths, fading hope, and frightening illusions. For the first time in his life, Duncan wanted to turn his back on all the people he'd sworn to protect, relinquish his title, and live the rest of his life by his sword with Sasha by his side. He didn't want to owe anyone anymore, but the idea of living without his duty to guide him felt hollow. As much as he might want it sometimes, Duncan couldn't lead such a selfish existence. He didn't know what to do, but he knew one thing with absolute, unwavering certainty: he loved Sasha. He didn't always understand him and sometimes he struggled to reconcile Sasha's skewed morals with the honorable and loyal man he knew hid behind the icy façade, but he loved him. He didn't know how he'd include Sasha in his world or make Sasha a full part of life, but he loved him, and he'd figure something out. He had to believe they'd find their way through the world together, because considering any alternative was unbearable.

Chapter Four

THE sprawling grounds of the ancient university of magic in Pala Reapaza almost reminded Yarrow of a nursery. The young mages and scholars sheltered behind its walls played with shiny baubles, read from fancy, leather-bound books, and sat on soft grass beneath grand old trees discussing metaphysics and the nature of enchantment, oblivious to any hardship the world might theoretically contain. Like sheltered children, the fledgling sorcerers never considered life beyond their secure and beautiful bubble. They didn't even think about their food or the people who prepared it; they simply went to the dining hall when they felt hungry and found it waiting. If Yarrow told them of people struggling to find enough to eat, wandering filthy alleyways and begging for scraps, the students would probably accuse him of making up frightening stories.

Oh, come now, beloved, said the voice of the ancient entity sharing Yarrow's body and consciousness. *They aren't such a bad lot, are they?*

They're just so innocent, Yarrow told it. *They're almost living in a different reality from the rest of the world. I don't blame them, but it's difficult to relate to them.*

They've been more welcoming to us than most, the creature said.

I bet that would change if they understood the situation. You would horrify them.

Its cruel laughter echoed inside Yarrow's skull and bounced down the knobs of his spine, making him shiver despite the heat of the afternoon. His muscles tensed and trembled as the tendrils of its perceptions wormed down his limbs. *You're so theatrical, my beloved. I miss the days when you did whatever you liked without considering the consequences. That damned fool knight and the pretty little assassin changed you. You waffle over everything now. I should make them pay for spoiling our fun.*

They are beyond your reach, creature, and I'll die before I let you near them.

Why are we still here, anyway? I can teach you more about magic in a day than you could learn over a lifetime at this place.

Yarrow knew it told the truth; the ancient, unfathomable being possessed more power than he could comprehend, but it asked a terrible price for its wisdom. For everything it helped Yarrow understand, it demanded the use of Yarrow's body. It couldn't experience sensation except through Yarrow's flesh, and it had excessive and monstrous appetites. Yarrow's purpose in coming to Espero had been to uncover information about the creature, to either banish it or learn to control it, so he could return to Sasha and Duncan without putting them in peril. While not a formal student of the university, he'd gained permission to use the libraries and attend any lectures he wished, but in almost a year, Yarrow had discovered nothing he could use against the entity. He was no closer to understanding it than he'd been on the frigid day it had fused itself to his consciousness and body.

How dull. When will you realize the futility of all of this and give it up, beloved?

When I'm rid of you.

You'd miss me, sweet Yarrow. Besides, you wanted me. I certainly didn't force you. I couldn't believe how quickly you accepted me into yourself. But that's nothing new for you, is it?

What do you mean by that?

Ah, beloved. Have you forgotten which of us burned thousands of men to ash without a second thought? I'd understood you left your lovers as much to protect them from yourself as from me. Yet you spend little time picking apart your own past, your own broken mind. Why is that, my little flower? Do you suppose it will all go away if you ignore it?

Ignore what? What do you see in my memories that I can't?

Do you really want an answer to that, beloved? I could provide it, but not for free.

I'll make no more deals with you, monster.

We'll see.

The ringing of dozens of bells roused Yarrow back to the physical world, and he sat up in the thick grass. Legends told that Pherara, the goddess of magic, had drawn the blood of the world up through the sea to form the island nation of Espero for her mages. The fountain tinkling softly behind Yarrow had been carved from the smooth, black rock she'd summoned, as had the buildings of the university. Centuries of enchantment had shaped them into impossibly beautiful formations: spindly columns and delicate buttresses covered in leaves and blossoms hewn from rock but so lifelike they appeared to grow and twist organically around the structures. The glass in the giant windows formed illustrations from Pherara's mythology in every conceivable color. Some of the garden walls were more delicate than the finest lace. Even the trees, hedges, and flowerbeds had been influenced by sorcery and grew more perfectly than nature would allow.

At the toll of the bells, dozens of doors burst open, and hundreds of students flooded the lawn. Yarrow stood and brushed the grass from his clothing as they split into groups to go in search of a midday meal or a quiet place to converse. In the heat of Espero, Yarrow had taken to wearing the native garb: loose, gauzy trousers, a long, sleeveless tunic dyed sea blue to match the permanent swirls of paint on his cheeks and throat, and a simple sash around his waist. He'd even traded his sturdy boots for a pair of light sandals with braided leather straps. His companion often teased Yarrow over the care he took over choosing his attire. Such things had never concerned Yarrow before, but then, he'd never imagined he could fit in anywhere.

A small group of students approached the mage, and Yarrow raised his hand in greeting. He ignored the taunting of his companion as he greeted his friends. A girl named D'Mesia hugged Yarrow, and a young man called Eucio slapped him on the back. Yarrow knew it was all just illusion, but the illusion of being a normal young man at the university pleased him, and he played along. At fourteen, Yarrow had been exiled while other boys his age studied poetry and learned to dance. He'd struggled to survive, alone in the world, while his peers contemplated what games to play to pass the afternoon or which doublet to wear to a feast.

You'll never be alone again, beloved. You have me now. It's no small wonder you accepted me so readily.

Can't you just let me pretend to be normal for a spell?

Sweet Yarrow. Where is the value in pretense?

I missed out on this part of my life, and I can't help playing along. Illusion has value sometimes, Yarrow told it.

Does denial? What about fear?

Enough. I have had enough. Let me imagine I'm a typical young man for a few hours. Is that so much to ask?

It acquiesced easily, which made Yarrow suspicious. He dismissed his doubts, though. He'd never had the opportunity to be a hopeful youth cavorting with friends and unworried over his future. Though he knew it was all as fake as the enchanted rainbow perpetually spread over the southern harbor, he enjoyed it, enjoyed playing out this part of his life that had been stolen.

"Hungry, Yarrow?" Eucio asked. "Had any lunch yet?"

"No," Yarrow said. "Where are you planning to eat?" He tried to imagine this was the extent of his worries, deciding where to go for lunch.

"Lessons are over till the day after the first of the Mother Goddess's moon," D'Mesia said. "I need a respite from studying. Let's go into town and find a place to eat that sells cheap drinks! I need a few, or more than a few. Maybe half a dozen!"

"I hope you'll join us, Yarrow," said a young man called Jorian. He was a classic Esperon beauty, with deep, olive skin, sparkling black eyes, and waves of dark hair that spilled over his shoulders and grazed his chest. Yarrow envisioned the ends of those lush curls teasing Jorian's dark nipples and tossing around in the throes of passion, and he knew Jorian entertained similar fantasies as he looked at Yarrow.

Yarrow returned Jorian's warm smile and stashed the books he'd been reading into a leather satchel. "I'd be happy to."

"Excellent!" Jorian looked delighted and waved another young man and two young women over to join them. He introduced his classmates to Yarrow: Lorris, Tianna, and Abelie. The group of students made their way slowly along the stone path leading to the gate at the end of the university grounds. As they discussed their lessons, their plans for the upcoming week of celebration, and how drunk they hoped to become, Yarrow fell in toward the back, next to Jorian. Soon they emerged into a section of the city full of shops catering to the students. They passed by establishments selling books, parchment, and ink, as well as cheery taverns boasting extensive varieties of wine and fresh, overpriced food. The tables and benches in front of them were filled to the brim with excited young mages. Carts offered cheaper fare, mostly an assortment of grilled seafood. Jorian stopped at one to purchase some skewered cubes of fish. Yarrow wandered to a stall and bought some biscuits filled with jam and glazed with honey. He licked the sweetness from his fingers as they passed more buildings hewn from the dark, volcanic rock and decorated with huge, bright flowers in every imaginable color. Here and there, musicians, acrobats, and puppeteers performed for spare coins.

"This is truly a remarkable place," Yarrow said.

The group of friends continued toward the quayside and the less reputable establishments frequented by the sailors and dockworkers. Seabirds cried out and feasted on discarded fish guts and refuse, but Yarrow found even this section of the city far cleaner and more orderly than ports like Meritage, where cutthroats, pickpockets, and whores waded through garbage up to their knees.

D'Mesia pointed to a lopsided little building next to a warehouse. The shingle above the door read "The Black Porpoise." The students went inside and sat around a long table in the far corner. A bar wench set a large jug of wine at the center and put a dented goblet in front of each of them. Glancing around, Yarrow noticed some rough-looking men, a dark-skinned woman of dubious morals in a low-cut chemise and snug bodice, and about a dozen other young people from the university. An old man at the hearth stirred the oily stew places like this always seemed to serve. The whole small room smelled of it, but Yarrow didn't mind. It surprised him how good it felt to be included in something like this. His unseen companion taunted him mercilessly, but even that didn't dampen his spirits.

"To the Mother Goddess," D'Mesia said, raising her glass. "Thanks to her, we have the next eight days free from musty old scrolls and practicing spells!"

They all toasted. Yarrow found the local red wine strong and slightly off-balance. The alcohol burn overpowered most of the other flavors, but he detected an earthy taste, like mushrooms or wet stone. Though he would have preferred something sweeter, he took another sip. He'd endured much worse.

"How are you planning to spend your time off, Yarrow?" Jorian asked with a hopeful glint in his eyes.

He's practically begging for it, beloved. We should give it to him.

Out of the question, Yarrow said, though he'd thought about it often, alone in his tiny room in the dormitories. *I'm going back to Sasha and Duncan one day, and I won't put Jorian in danger. He doesn't deserve it.*

To the other young man, Yarrow said, "Actually, I plan to continue studying."

"What?" Eucio asked. "Not taking any time off? Why? You're already better than the rest of us without even trying."

Yarrow bowed his head to hide his grin. They really had no idea. He'd been careful not to let the other students see the extent of his power, or they might start wondering about its source. As much as he enjoyed their company, he had to keep them at a safe distance. He couldn't let them see past the surface. "Oh, I have a project I'm working on, and I haven't made nearly as much progress as I'd hoped. I need to keep working."

D'Mesia refilled her goblet, sincere in her oath to enjoy more than a few drinks. "What are you working on, Yarrow? Maybe we can help you. After all, I never would have figured out that ice charm without your assistance. It just clicked in my head after you explained it, and I'd be happy to return the favor if I can."

"No," Yarrow said quickly.

"We wouldn't mind," Abelie said. "We can take a little time away from drinking and celebrating to help a friend."

Tianna nodded in agreement, and Jorian smiled. "Absolutely," Jorian said enthusiastically.

"I said I don't need any help," Yarrow snapped. "I'm more than capable of figuring this out on my own. If I wanted or needed assistance, I'd ask for it."

The other students frowned and looked at one another, clearly shocked at Yarrow's unexpected outburst. All of them lifted their wine to their lips to avoid speaking, and they wouldn't meet Yarrow's gaze.

Oh, well done, beloved. And you've been trying so hard not to be rude and push others away.

I have to push them away, Yarrow said. *I've let them too close already.* He raked his white hair, which he'd let grow past his collarbones in the Esperon fashion, out of his face and pinned it behind his ears. He downed his wine in a few large gulps, stood up, and pushed his chair against the table. "I'm sorry," he said. "I didn't mean to get angry. I'm just tired, and I have a great deal to do. I'm afraid I don't have time to waste in a tavern. I'll see you all again eventually, I'm sure."

He turned to leave, but Jorian caught his elbow. The handsome young man looked absolutely distraught. "You'll be at the parade and festival tomorrow night, though, won't you?"

"As I said, I'm very busy." Yarrow wrenched his arm free of Jorian's grasp much harder than necessary and hurried out of the Black Porpoise before Jorian or any of the others could say another word.

Out on the street, Yarrow walked a few steps toward the water and leaned his forearms on a thick wooden post draped in damp rope. Nearby, men loaded wooden crates full of bright, round koria fruit onto a ship. The gangplank bounced beneath their feet and the citrus smell was almost strong enough to negate the odors of moldy wood and old fish. One of the burly laborers raised an eyebrow at Yarrow as he passed, but Yarrow shook his head to decline the invitation.

He'd been indulging in a childish fantasy, pretending to be a student with no greater concern than finishing a scroll on time or locating the proper book in the library. Many young men and women from the university filled the streets now, walking in groups, drinking wine straight from the bottle and buying refreshments from vendors. Some laughed and some sang without a care in the world now that they'd been released from their lessons for a bit. Yarrow knew he wasn't one of them, and he'd never be one of them. He was, and would remain, an outsider. The time had come to stop kidding himself.

Does that mean we can leave this excruciatingly dull place, beloved?

No. I came here to try to understand you, what you are and how I can keep you from hurting others. I came to understand this awful power inside me, and I won't leave until I'm certain I've found all the answers this place has to offer. I won't leave until it's safe to return to Sasha and Duncan, or until I know what I must do next.

I'm growing very impatient, my little Yarrow. It's been months since you've allowed me to wear the flesh, to experience any sensation. You must let me have a little taste of something.

No.

Give it to me, beloved, or I'll take it.

I'll fight you. I'm getting better at resisting you, and you know it. And as I warned you, if I can't, I will kill myself and leave you trapped in my rotting shell. Then you'll have no experience. If you doubt I'll do it, go ahead and test me, creature.

A light touch to the small of his back snapped Yarrow's attention from the argument. He twirled on the ball of his foot and found Jorian watching him with concern, as if he expected Yarrow to hit him.

"I… didn't want to leave things like that," he said. "Don't be angry, Yarrow. I just want to talk."

"I told you I'm busy," Yarrow said irritably. Jorian flinched as if Yarrow had struck him. Yarrow shook his head, ashamed. "I really need to be on my own right now."

Jorian took Yarrow's hand and led Yarrow back across the street, into a narrow alley between the Porpoise and the warehouse. He stood in front of Yarrow and rested his hand lightly on Yarrow's waist. "Yarrow… I really hoped we might spend some time together over the holiday. You never talk about yourself. I want to get to know you better."

"No, you don't."

"I do. I really like you, Yarrow. I want us to be friends, and maybe…." Jorian trailed off, cupped Yarrow's cheek, and leaned in to kiss him. Yarrow turned away before their lips met, and Jorian colored and backed up, crossing his slender but muscular arms over his chest, clearly humiliated.

"I'm sorry," Jorian muttered, his gaze on his delicate sandals. "I… I should have asked if you felt the same way. I guess I imagined it all. I thought, sometimes… the way I'd catch you watching me… the way you'd look away when I noticed…. But you don't like me. Do you not like men? Or is it just me?"

"It's not you," Yarrow said gently, trying to patch up some of the wound he'd inflicted on a young man who wanted only to be his friend. "I'm glad we're friends, and I find you a very alluring man. And I like men very much. I just… I can't, Jori."

"Why?"

"I can't explain it."

"I know a little about you," Jorian said softly, stepping in front of Yarrow again but leaving a few feet of space between them. "I mean, we've all heard the rumors. I heard about that great battle in Selindria.

They say you defeated an entire army on your own. They say you've been all over the world, and that you've been a pirate alongside the Emiri." He reached out to touch the swirls of paint on Yarrow's cheek, the marks of the Emiri seafarers, but let his hand fall heavily against his thigh. "We… I must seem very common and boring to a person like you. I've never even been outside the city."

"I don't find you boring, Jori. I envy the comfortable life you've led. There's no shame in not having suffered. I have had to do terrible things…."

"Is that why you want to keep me from knowing you? Do you suppose I'll be put off?"

Yarrow shook his head. "I can't. I can't do this. Not again."

Jorian brushed the back of Yarrow's hand. "You don't have to be so lonely. I don't know what you want to punish yourself for, but I'm sure you don't deserve it."

Yarrow laughed, mocking himself, and the presence joined in. *Ah, my little flower! If he only knew!*

"Yarrow, stop that." Jorian sounded deeply disturbed, but to his credit, he didn't turn away. "Stop torturing yourself."

"I have to go." Yarrow hurried out of the alleyway and into the strong afternoon sun. The temptation to open up to the kind young man who, for whatever reason, cared about him, was becoming too great. "Find someone who deserves you, Jori."

"Will you at least come to the festival tomorrow?" Jorian called after Yarrow. "Just to have a drink and talk?"

"Very well. I'll find you there," Yarrow reluctantly agreed. Then he turned and jogged up the crowded street, toward the university, before he granted anything else he knew he should refuse.

Chapter
Five

ONLY magic could have produced the library of Pala Reapaza. It rose nine stories, a round tower twice as wide as the royal palace back in Selindria. Each level housed tens of thousands of books, scrolls, maps, diagrams, and drawings, more than one could hope to read in a lifetime. The tomes sat on stone shelves, as the whole structure had been carved out by enchantment instead of being built up block by block. The entire tower consisted of a single piece of shimmering dark gray rock. At the center, rising almost to the third balcony, stood a solid gold statue of Illira, goddess of communication, books and stories. In her hand she held a glass orb the size of a small carriage, perpetually lit by mystic energy. The domed ceiling was made entirely of glass.

Though he hated rising early, Yarrow had come just after dawn to sort through the writings for any mention of a creature like his companion. The people who tended the library, a mix of old scholars, young apprentices, and priestesses of both Illira and Pherara, had come up with a system of organizing the books according to subject matter. Yarrow had realized early in his studies here that the mages who penned the books did not necessarily keep to that system, though. A book on healing might contain a very enlightening passage about mystic ingredients that could be harvested from animals. The memoirs of great wizards were especially difficult to classify, but held some of the best information.

Yarrow yawned, thankful for the Esperon drink made from tarberries. He inhaled the fragrant steam and took a sip of the hot, bitter beverage so popular among the students, as it allowed them to stay awake and alert studying when they should feel exhausted. Even with three spoonfuls of honey, Yarrow hated the taste. He choked it down and closed the ancient travel journal he'd been reading. A growing stack of books that held no pertinent material sat on the floor by his left foot.

It's useless, beloved. You'll never find out about me from these moldy old tomes. And the only way you'll understand yourself is to face what you've been hiding from all these years. I can help you with both, and I ask so little in return.

Yarrow ignored it and opened another book, the diary of a priestess of Jelsyn who had traveled to lands south of Espero and observed the primitive magic of the natives. While interesting, Yarrow knew her account couldn't help him. He added it to the pile, rose from the padded bench where he'd sat all morning, and stretched his arms over his head.

Though he loved the library, it felt good to step into the sunlight and breathe the fresh, salt-tinged air. Few students reclined on the soft grass or studied on the benches, so Yarrow made his way without interruption to the hall where the senior mages lived. He ascended to the third floor and knocked on the door of the instructor who'd agreed to meet with him.

A tiny woman answered the door, her hair as white as Yarrow's and pulled into a tight knot at the top of her head. Though she reached only to Yarrow's shoulders, she radiated authority and knowledge. "Yarroway L'Estrella. Please come in."

"Thank you, Lady Brycia," Yarrow said as he entered the room. It had a fine view of the harbor, and wooden shelves lined with books and trinkets. He could feel the essence of the woman who called it home in every cushion and candleholder, and knew she'd lived here for a long time.

"You can drop the 'lady,' young man. I'm a student here, the same as you are. The study of magic is the endeavor of a lifetime." She indicated a pair of overstuffed mats in front of the inglenook, and Yarrow sat down and crossed his legs.

Brycia joined him, rubbing her hands together over the coals though the room felt balmy. "What can I do for you, my lord?"

"No lord," Yarrow said, sweating even in his scant, gauzy garments. "As you observed, we are all just students."

"We both know that's not true, Tam Yarroway, Hero of the Starlight Bridge. Now, what can I do for you?"

Yarrow took a deep breath and considered how to phrase his query. He decided to just be blunt. "Can I trust you with a very personal matter?"

Lady Brycia met Yarrow's gaze with her clear gray eyes. "As a servant of Pherara, I swear nothing you tell me will leave this room. Now, go on and speak. I'm not getting any younger, lad."

"Are you from Selindria?" Yarrow asked, recognizing the nuances of her accent. "Where from?"

"Meadow's Edge, as if it matters," she answered. "I've lived here for over forty-five years and consider myself Esperon. Do you have a question for me, or is this a social call?"

"I apologize," Yarrow said. "I know your time is valuable. I wish to tell you a story, something that happened to me, and it will be hard to believe, but I ask you to bear with me. I… I really need your help."

"Speak, then."

Go on, beloved. I'm eager to hear this.

Shut up. Let me concentrate!

"Tam Yarroway?"

"Yes. I'm sorry. You may know I left home at a young age to explore the world and seek knowledge."

"You left of your own accord, then?" she asked, her gaze on the embers in her hearth.

"No," Yarrow admitted. "The king of Selindria basically exiled me. He… abused me, but he blamed me for it and sent me away. This is not important, and I would rather not talk about it."

"Go on."

"I went into the Lapir Mountains. Everyone told me I couldn't make it across them, but I was so young and secure in my magic, I hired a guide and tried anyway. I suppose I just wanted to prove my worth. I was lost in a blizzard for days, I don't know how long. I almost died. I should have died, but I found a small crevice in the stone and took shelter there. It led to a series of tunnels. I had to crawl on my belly to get through them, and it felt like forever, but eventually I came to an underground room. You have to understand I was delirious at this point; I hadn't had food or water besides melted snow in a week or more.

"I sensed… *something* in the pool at the center of that cavern. It spoke to me. It promised to help me if I agreed to let it share my body. It had lost its own flesh to a terrible curse and was starved to experience any sensation: sight, sound, taste, even pain. I agreed. I really had no other option. It melded with my flesh, its awareness seeping into every drop of blood in my body, every hair and strip of sinew. It took days, and it almost killed me. That's what took the color from my hair and eyes. It saw my memories, and I saw the atrocities it had committed, but by then it was too late. This thing is a part of me now, and I would have it gone. It has killed with my hands and threatened people I care about. I came to Espero to learn a way to banish it, but I've found nothing."

The elderly mage closed her eyes and said nothing for so long Yarrow assumed she'd fallen asleep in front of her fire. He began to wonder if he should go when she looked at him, her gaze full of pity.

"You poor creature," she said in a raspy whisper. "You were so young. You'd never been taught to handle this gift you possess. It is strong in you, stronger than I have seen in many generations. Most mages I instruct struggle to conjure a sprig of flowers. Did you?"

"No. I could do it at six. Butterflies too."

She nodded. "I suspected as much. Child, I think you are mistaken about what you experienced in those frozen mountains."

"How so?" Yarrow asked, hopeful.

This ought to be rich indeed, the presence taunted.

"Mages have a wall built into them," the older woman explained. "It prevents them from accessing their power before they are ready to control it. Can you imagine what a child would do with the arcane ability to conjure rooms full of biscuits? Or what they might do to a nanny or tutor who angered or reprimanded them? Without this protection, many young mages would injure themselves or the people they care about. When they are older and ready to tap into their abilities, it is often difficult for them to bypass this safety net. They have to chip away at it, and their magic oozes out slowly from between the cracks. I have taught hundreds of young sorcerers, and getting them to lower this barrier is the most difficult lesson. Nature wants to protect them from their power. Usually, it takes them years of work to tear down the boundary between themselves and their arcane energies.

"You were dying. I believe the stress of your situation broke your wall down all at once. To ensure you survived, the magic flooded in to save you instead of trickling through the cracks in the usual way. When that safety measure shattered so quickly, I think it probably damaged your mind. As I have said, no mage is meant to come into his power so instantaneously. It isn't natural. I can only assume your mind created this other presence as a defense, to shield itself from forces it couldn't yet handle. Basically, you created for yourself someone who knew how to wield the forces you could not."

"You don't think it's real?" Yarrow asked. "But I've seen it, seen its memories and felt its desires. It is separate from me."

"I'm sure it feels that way," Lady Brycia said, laying a hand over Yarrow's knee. "But it is hard to say what so much esoteric energy unleashed all at once would do to a mortal mind. I think your magic rose up to save you, to preserve your life, but in doing so, it split your thinking in twain. This presence you speak of is merely the part of you that can handle the unfettered magic. It's the part of your consciousness that fights to survive, and maybe the part that is willing to do what is necessary to protect you."

"Assuming you're correct, what do I do?" Yarrow asked. It made his stomach twist into painful knots to consider all the atrocities he'd blamed on the presence had been perpetrated by him. He couldn't believe it. He'd always been arrogant, and he knew he could be abrasive, but he couldn't accept himself as a man who killed and tortured for sport.

"You must meditate, try to reconcile the part of your understanding that filters the magic with the part that understands the mundane world. You need to bring these two broken pieces together into the whole they are meant to be."

"What if I can't?" Yarrow asked, frustrated, unsure if he believed Lady Brycia's assessment of his situation.

She says I don't exist. Should I be offended, beloved?

What if you don't? What if you're me? Goddesses, what if all the disgusting things I've blamed on you have been me? What if... what if I killed Rini?

My sweet little Yarrow, I can assure you I am real. As for your little Emiri friend, I used your hands to crush his throat. I remember feeling all the life bleed out of him, his skin go cold as ice. If you'd like, I can show you what his face looked like before he died.

"No!" Yarrow clapped his hand over his mouth to hold in the sob desperate to escape.

"Yarroway?" Lady Brycia asked. "Are you all right?"

"It wasn't me! I never could have hurt Rini. I adored him. He trusted me, and I let it get to him. Please, I need to get rid of this thing."

She sighed and seemed to consider what to say next. "There is good and bad, fire and ice, within all of us, lad. The first step to understanding what is happening to you is to accept that. You may have to admit that you have certain desires you don't want to acknowledge. It is sometimes unfortunate that we mages have the power to indulge appetites others would not be able to cater to."

Yarrow got to his feet, his head spinning in the hot room. Bile stung the back of his throat as images of his companion's violence played behind his eyes. "You're wrong," Yarrow said. "It isn't me. I couldn't… I'd never…."

Yarrow's control over the other slipped with his distress and confusion. He felt it surfacing, rising out of the oily, dark water it inhabited. Sharp tines grazed his mind, causing a shudder of both pleasure and revulsion. The prongs sunk into his consciousness at the base of his skull. Yarrow clawed at his temples, but the presence of the other spread, filling his head and flowing down his spine and into his limbs. His skin began to numb, and his vision dulled. The other loosed a hungry growl, psychically salivating at the nearness of raw sensation. It turned its attention to Lady Brycia, and it envisioned shredding her flesh with its claws, feeling her hot blood spray against its face.

Its power flared with its appetite, and luminous, azure wings burst from Yarrow's back, the tips brushing the walls of the chamber and scorching the stone. Horns made of the same light and energy erupted from his forehead. A sheath of cerulean glow outlined Yarrow and spilled from the corners of his eyes.

Lady Brycia shrieked, backed into the corner, and lifted her hand to conjure a shimmering shield around herself.

Yarrow grabbed hold of the thing inside him, wrangling it down, sinking his nails into it to pull it back under. The light around him fizzled out as he subdued it and took back control of his body and perceptions. "Do you see?" He yelled at the elderly mage until his voice cracked. "Do you see how it takes control of me? That was not me!"

Wasn't it, beloved? Are you absolutely sure?

"Yes!"

"Yarroway, I think you should go." Lady Brycia pointed to the door with a trembling hand. "I'll do some research and contact you if I can help you. Until then, you should go to the library and read the work of Lavingierrio the Sixth. He pioneered many techniques for maintaining and controlling magical energy. Performing the rituals may help with your self-discipline. Learn them, and learn them well. Now please leave."

He staggered out into the hall and stumbled down the stairs, holding onto the wall to keep his balance. The few servants he passed eyed him warily, and he felt as if he wore his every dark secret like a placard around his neck. Certainly, the people he met in the ancient corridors saw him for what he was: a deviant, a murderer, a coward who'd sold himself to a monster in return for the power to protect himself.

"Leave me alone!" he shouted at a group of girls carrying baskets of laundry. "Don't look at me." They flinched and hurried away, whispering to each other.

Yarrow opened the first door he saw and retreated into the blessed darkness and isolation of a small cupboard. He slid down into the corner beside some pails and moldy-smelling mops, tucked his knees up under his chin, and rocked back and forth in an attempt to soothe himself. He wanted to cry, wanted the support of someone who loved him without judgment. The only two men who ever had were thousands of miles away, and Yarrow didn't dare return to them until he could keep them safe from the creature inside him and from himself. He didn't even dare send them correspondence, for fear they'd come looking for him if they knew where he'd gone. Right now, being so alone hurt more than freezing in the mountains had. He felt emptier and more miserable than he ever had while starving in exile. It made him feel like a pitiful child to want so desperately to be held.

Goddesses, I should be used to it by now.

You're not alone, my beloved. You're never alone.

Shut up. You've made a mess of things for me again. They won't let me stay here now. They'll think... they'll know I'm dangerous. They'll ask me to leave. Why did you have to choose that moment to take over?

I warned you, it said. *I told you if you didn't give it up I would take it. Besides, I don't want to stay here. This place is boring me to death. I'm tired of doing nothing but staring at old books. I want to drink, feast, fornicate, and fight.*

You're just afraid if I stay here. I'll find a way to get rid of you.

No, beloved, I'm not. I've never worried you'll get rid of me. You can't, and you know it as well as I do.

Where does that leave me? What will I do, forsake the company of others completely? Go and live in the mountains as a recluse?

Ridiculous, Yarrow. I promised to make you the most powerful sorcerer in the world, but you made promises to me. I want the flesh. I want to taste and touch. How about tonight at the festival? I'll certainly entertain your little friend Jorian.

It looks like I won't be attending the festival, then.

You'll hurt him if you don't show, beloved.

Not as much as I might if I do.

SINCE he knew his time at the university could end at any moment, Yarrow spent the afternoon and evening in the library, frantically searching for anything to point him in the right direction. He'd already picked up the Lavingierrio book Lady Brycia suggested. It waited in his satchel for after he found the answers he really needed. Beyond the small windows and above the glass dome, bright flashes of colored light exploded before taking the shapes of wyrms and unicorns. Yarrow shook his head. Back in Selindria, the advent of the Mother Goddess's Moon warranted a nice meal and a few words from a priestess, not a week of debauchery. As usual, he hadn't uncovered anything to help him. He'd been reading from a huge tome cataloging demigods and spiritual beings, the offspring of the goddesses and Cast-Down alike. Nothing among the hundreds of descriptions and illustrations resembled his companion.

I'm no child of your deities, beloved.

What are you? Where did you come from? With all the destruction you wrought, how can there be no mention of you anywhere?

Before it could answer, soft footsteps on the polished stone floor broke the silence, and a man's silhouette cast Yarrow in a beam of shadow. "I thought I'd find you here," Jorian said. "You could have just told me you weren't coming instead of leaving me to stand around waiting like a fool."

"I'm sorry."

"If you don't like me, just say so."

"Jori… it isn't that."

The other young man blew air out his nose and crossed his arms. "Right. You said that last time. What is it, then?"

Yarrow considered what to say. He couldn't tell Jorian the truth, couldn't explain how even being around Yarrow might put his life at risk, but he didn't want Jorian feeling insignificant or unworthy. He rubbed his tired eyes with the heels of his hands. "In another situation, I would be honored to spend time with you. I just can't right now, and I don't want to give you false hope. You deserve better than that. You should find someone who can focus all his attention on you. If things were different for me, I would love to be that man, but the truth is, I have someone waiting for me back home. I want very desperately to return."

"Why don't you? Why did you leave at all?"

"I had to," Yarrow said, his chest tight as he remembered the night he'd said good-bye to Sasha and Duncan in Meritage. He wondered if they still waited, or if they'd given up on him. He couldn't blame them if they had, but he couldn't let go of the possibility of seeing them again. It was really all he had. "I can't go back until I finish here. There's something I must figure out, but it isn't going well."

Jorian sat down on the bench next to Yarrow, seemingly satisfied with Yarrow's explanation. "Can I help?"

"Maybe. Do you know much about how the library is organized?"

Jorian chuckled. "It can be confusing, but I worked here as an assistant for my first three years at the university. What is it you're looking for?"

"Why are there no accounts of the world's history before Fane's fall?" Yarrow asked. "Why aren't there even any records of Fane's rule? I mean, we're told he reigned for, what, over a thousand years? Yet I can't find a single account from that time or before."

None of that is important, beloved. I can give you knowledge far more terrifying and beautiful. Oh, yes. We can certainly come to some sort of agreement. I'll make it easy for you. Just let me wear the flesh to bend your little classmate over the desk and I'll tell you anything you like.

Yarrow balled his fists until his nails pierced his palms as it tugged against the reins of his control. *Stop it. I won't let you hurt Jori or anyone else. Not ever again.*

You used to be so much more fun, Yarrow.

"Well," Jorian said, "I've always understood Fane ruled over a civilization even more advanced than our own, which means they would have kept some sort of records. We're also told he used his magic to provide for his people, so they didn't have to toil to make a living. That would have left plenty of time for them to pursue poetry and art. To keep accounts."

"Exactly," Yarrow said. "So how can there be nothing?"

"Fane's war with the thirteen sisters destroyed the world. Everything was lost. There's not a single brick left from the legendary palaces and temples Fane was believed to have constructed. After he and his mages fell, people basically had to start from scratch again, without even the knowledge of written language. I may know of something you can use, though most of the scholars here think it's a forgery."

"I'd like to see," Yarrow said, a faint, warm glow of hope penetrating the icy despair he'd been submerged in since leaving Lady Brycia's chambers.

"Down here," Jorian said, motioning toward a nondescript door Yarrow had never taken note of before. It led to a narrow stairway draped in cobwebs and reeking of neglect. Jorian conjured a small sphere of light that allowed them to pick their way down the crumbling steps to a series of vaulted rooms with ceilings so low even Yarrow had to duck to navigate them. Ancient relics lined the walls, most of them buried beneath years of dust. At the back of the space, a series of old books sat on a bowed wooden shelf that still looked old, but had probably been built long after the rest of the library—possibly for books the tutors wanted to keep from the students. Jorian grabbed one by the spine and opened it on a grimy table. It was a large volume, longer than the distance from Yarrow's elbow to his fingertips. Jorian flipped past dozens of pages covered in small, sloping letters before he found a map and traced the lines of rivers and roads with his finger.

"This is supposedly an account of a mage who studied with Fane," Jorian said. "According to it, he now resides on a hidden island to the south of here. It's unlikely he still exists, but he has documented some of the time he spent under Fane's tutelage."

"Astounding," Yarrow said, caressing the ancient sheets of vellum. He could almost feel the tug of fate against his fingers, urging him to follow the route of this forgotten sorcerer. If he had any chance of finding answers to his conundrum, he needed to possess the hand-drawn maps this book contained. They depicted territory far to the south of Espero, past any point people had ventured in recent centuries. His enthusiasm even undermined his surprise that such an ancient chronicle was written in the modern language.

"Jorian, is there any way I could keep these charts? They would mean a great deal to me."

"They're property of the university. There's an enchantment placed upon them that won't allow them to pass through the library doors."

"I took the manual about restraining magic, though," Yarrow said.

"The Lavingierrio? We have dozens of those. Help yourself. The new students always do. This one is very rare, though."

Yarrow placed his hand near Jorian's on the ancient pages. Their fingers brushed together as Yarrow looked into Jorian's warm brown eyes. "This is the first thing I've found since coming here that could help me."

"Yarrow, it's highly unlikely that this information is authentic. Do you realize how impossible it would be for a man who actually studied with Fane to survive long enough to write this? He'd be thousands of years old. Nearly every mage who's studied this believes it's a fake."

"Then why do they keep it down here, away from everyone?"

Jorian looked down at the pages, at the bluish light flickering across his hand, so close to Yarrow's. Then he met Yarrow's gaze, his expression sympathetic but confused. "It says some very controversial things about the thirteen goddesses. When this was found, hundreds of years ago, the Council of High Priestesses ordered it destroyed. The university fought very hard to keep it, but thought it unwise to anger the priestesses further by disseminating the opinions it held. Basically, if we leave it down here, the priestesses forget about it."

"I want to read it even more," Yarrow said. The presence in him watched him carefully, burrowing into the fibers of his thoughts and motivations, perhaps a little nervous.

"You can," Jorian said. "There aren't any rules that say you can't come down here to study."

Yarrow didn't want to tell his friend he'd likely be expelled from the university before long. He needed this book and felt sure he could defeat the library's enchantments if Jorian would agree to let him try. Since he could think of no other strategy, he just asked. "Will you let me take this? I think it can help me."

"Help you do what?" Jorian asked.

"Just help me… help me be all right, be safe. I can't tell you more than that. I wish I could. I'm sorry. I really need this book, though. I wouldn't ask you if I wasn't desperate. Please just trust me."

"It's hard when you won't be honest about anything," Jorian said. "But I want to. I… I'll leave you on your own, I suppose. I don't want to know what you do when I go." Without another glance at Yarrow, he turned and started back toward the steps.

As he watched Jorian go, Yarrow realized he might never see him again. "Thank you, Jori," he said softly. The other young man stopped walking but didn't turn to face Yarrow. "For everything you did and wanted to do."

"Good night, Yarrow," he said and disappeared into the shadows.

Yarrow stroked the spine of the large book with reverence and then closed it softly. He clutched it to his chest and crossed his arms around it, feeling like he'd finally made some progress.

It's clearly a fake, you fool. What good do you suppose it will do you?

I won't know that until I read it, Yarrow answered.

The Yarrow I knew would never have chosen a musty old tome over a tumble with such a good-looking man.

Yarrow looked longingly in the direction Jorian had gone. *I can't be a part of his world. I can't be with him or anyone else until I know I won't hurt them. I can't stand for anyone else to suffer because of me, or you.*

They are insects compared to us, beloved. Even the mages here. Their power is nothing compared to ours, so why should we not play with them and discard them when we're finished?

You're disgusting.

You agreed with me once. Part of you still does.

Enough. I must concentrate to break the enchantment on this book.

I could do it for you, beloved. Just let me wear the flesh—

No. Hush.

Yarrow let his mind go blank and slack as he picked apart the layers and layers of enchantment at work in the library and around the university. It was like trying to untangle a huge ball of knotted string, but he finally found the cord he needed and followed it as it looped around and jumbled among the others. By tugging at the right knots, he eventually separated it from the thousands of other interwoven threads and stretched it out, flat and straight in his mind so he could see how it worked. It didn't take him long to understand the simple but effective spell. The librarians had basically affixed a latent magical alarm to each book that would trigger when it crossed beyond the doors of the building. Yarrow wasn't sure what would happen when it activated—he doubted anything too severe, as the university probably didn't want to kill its students—but he didn't want to find out, either. He'd already done enough to arouse the suspicion of the tutors.

The spell was simple enough, but it took Yarrow some time to strip it away, as the magic had interwoven with every fiber of the old book, and he had to make sure he didn't leave any behind. It was like picking grains of sand out of a carpet with tweezers, and by the time he finished almost an hour later, Yarrow's head throbbed. He hurried from the cellar rooms in search of some fresh air.

Out on the normally quiet lanes of the university grounds, among the elaborate cut-out walls, statuary, shrines, and formal flower gardens, the festivities hadn't slowed down. Hordes of students in various states of inebriation sang, danced, or stumbled along, clinging to their friends. Flashes of magic in every color erupted around the lawn. Watching it all, Yarrow desperately wished he could take part in the revelry. He envied the students reclining on the grass, groping each other, kissing and sometimes more, without a care in the world, and he couldn't help feeling a little bitter that he'd never really been allowed to be a boy. The king had seen to that when he'd taken horrible advantage of Yarrow's sexual curiosity and then painted Yarrow as the deviant. At fourteen, he'd left home to avoid the scandal and wandered alone for more than five years.

Self-pity is hardly an admirable quality, beloved. Instead of feeling sorry for yourself, why not partake of the pleasure, find us some wine and a young man or two?

The men I long for are not here.

What will you do if you return and they have forgotten you?

I don't know. I'll worry about it if it happens. First I have to make it so I can return at all. If nothing else, I need to give them a proper farewell and wish them happy lives.

Yarrow pushed his way through the throng, in no mood to speak with anyone or even be in the presence of others. What had he been thinking, coming here and pretending to be one of the students? He had nothing in common with them. He'd deluded himself, and now it had to end. He hurried back to his room to ready his few possessions and end his time in Pala Reapaza, to disappear without explanation as he'd done so many times when others began to wonder at his peculiarities.

He had a single place he belonged—beside Sasha and Duncan. He had to get back to them, because he fit nowhere else in the world.

Chapter
Six

BY THE next morning, when Yarrow went to the dining hall for breakfast, the other students, most of them recovering from the previous night's cheer, gave him a wide berth. They cast wary glances at him over the rims of their cups and leaned in to whisper to one another as soon as they thought he wouldn't notice. He felt their suspicious gazes boring into him as he went to a table and filled a plate with a variety of sweet pastries and biscuits. No one waved him over to join them, so he found a secluded table in a corner and sat down to eat, though he found he had little appetite.

If Duncan had been there, he'd have told Yarrow to eat anyway, to keep up his strength, so Yarrow forced himself to finish at least a little bit of his food. Though it had often annoyed him at the time, Yarrow found he missed Duncan making sure he ate and drank. He missed having someone to look out for him and care what happened to him.

You're whining again, beloved.

I just miss them. Can you not understand at all?

Not really. I don't see what makes them so superior to the thousands of other men in the world.

Ignoring it, too broken down and weary to argue, Yarrow looked around the vast room. Only yesterday, he'd felt welcome here. Now the others quickly turned away if he attempted to make eye contact with them. *The rumors have started already,* Yarrow told his companion, not because he expected any sympathy, but because he'd just gotten used to speaking to it. For many years, it had been just the two of them, alone on the road, and before long, it would be again. *I didn't expect it so soon, I suppose.*

What do I care what these peons natter on about?

I never implied you should, creature. I was thinking to myself, except that I don't have that luxury anymore. This is awkward. I'm getting out of here. Yarrow left the rest of his food behind and hurried out of the hall with his cheeks and ears hot and stinging. He didn't even make it through the door before the gossip escalated. Out on the grounds, he encountered more of the same, and wished it wasn't too hot to put on his old, black cloak to hide inside. He'd hoped to have another week or so at the university to search for more books and speak with the older enchanters, but it seemed he'd have to leave. Fortunately, he had his clothing, armor, and books packed into his satchel.

It's very unlike you to place credence in the opinions of others, my beloved.

It was right; Yarrow prided himself on not weighing his own worth according to others. *All the more reason to get away from this place. I don't feel at all like myself. I'm far better at magic than anyone here. I won't let them intimidate me.*

Good boy, sweet Yarrow.

Yarrow practically jogged in the direction of the water, not slowing until he'd passed the fancy, black stone houses with the red-tiled roofs and elaborate grounds. When he reached the docks, he stopped to buy a bottle of wine from a stall despite the taunting of his creature about the early hour. Then he found a bench next to a fruit stand and sat sipping the strong local vintage, thinking and watching the men labor and the boats bob on the waves. The heat and sun beat down on him, the few, wispy clouds doing nothing to lessen the glare.

Several brawny, dark-skinned sailors gave Yarrow appreciative glances, but he ignored them despite the physical urges of his twenty-year-old body. To distract himself, he fetched his pilfered book from his pack, laid it across his thighs, and began reading. Before long he became so absorbed in the account of a young man working as a servant in Fane's court that he didn't even notice the din of the busy quayside. He found the writing itself overly detailed and a bit on the flowery side, but the glimpse into that long-forgotten world fascinated him. One day, the author, a man named Hale Trekellion, had been shoveling ashes from the hearth in the emperor's chambers when Fane had noticed the great amount of arcane energy he possessed. Fane had taken Hale as an apprentice.

"From that day forward," Yarrow read, *"the Emperor Fane, the greatest, most powerful, and most radiant of men who had ever graced this world, kept me at his side at almost every moment, from the time we*

woke in the morning to the rosy blush of dawn until we finally fell into bed long after night had draped the world in his dark and fuzzy cloak. Even through the long hours of darkness, my dear lord held me tight to him with his lips pressed against my cheek."

Yarrow smirked, thinking he'd found another reason why the priestesses wanted to suppress the information in this book. Turning the page, eager to continue, he'd just settled back into reading when a loud crash to the west snapped his attention away from the memoir. Ears ringing, Yarrow got to his feet.

All around him, men dropped the crates they carried and abandoned the nets they mended to sprint in the direction of the commotion. Unsure what else to do, Yarrow followed, gathering his magic in the pit of his belly as he shoved the book back into his satchel. Following the others, he ran about a quarter of a mile along the wooden walkway at the edge of the sea. The enchantment buzzing through the air and echoing like music made waves rise up and crash, frothing, against the piers. The mysterious energy vibrated up Yarrow's spine, making his bones wiggle and hum within his flesh. His companion also grew alert, the vast stores of power it held made ready, and its hunger and excitement contaminating Yarrow's reason. He wanted to fight, to spill blood and show his superiority over these masses of common people. It took all Yarrow's willpower not to let his glowing, azure wings sprout from his back and glide above their heads.

A group of sorcerers in dark blue robes stood in a crescent at the end of a pier, pointing toward a small ship. Espero had no militia; with so many mages, they didn't require warriors. The wards around the island kept hostile forces at bay. They did have an elite force of sorcerers who kept order on those rare occasions something threatened it: the men and women in the cobalt coats and silver sashes.

"Disembark and surrender yourself to our custody," one of the women called out. "If you do not, we will destroy your vessel." To punctuate her threat, she directed a gout of flame toward the small, brightly painted ship. Fire surrounded the blue-and-green-striped sail before consuming it and sending a spiral of sickly yellow smoke into the clear sky.

Yarrow elbowed his way through the gaping crowd, toward the mages on the edge of the pier. He didn't know what motivated him to loose a cloud of frigid air and ice crystals to douse the fire devouring the sail, but the spell left his hand before he reached the edge of the water.

"What do you think you're doing?" one of the sorcerers in blue shouted as he turned away from the boat to face Yarrow.

Yarrow didn't know, so he couldn't respond. The sight of an Emiri ship under attack ignited something instinctive within him. The Emiri had been far better to Yarrow than most, and he would defend them if he could.

"Stand down, young man," another wizard yelled.

"What are *you* doing?" Yarrow answered.

"Apprehending a thief," the man said. "Stay back." He shot a magical bolt toward the ship, shattering the mast and sending wood splinters flying into the choppy surf. "Show yourself, you swine!"

Yarrow followed the line of the man's outstretched arm to the deck of the ship. A small man with dark skin and blood-colored knots of hair emerged and came to the railing. Looking at his lithe, paint-covered, tan arms protruding from beneath his scant leather vest, Yarrow felt sure he regarded his long-dead Emiri lover, Rini. He shook his head to dispel the impossible vision.

I recognize him, the presence said.

Yarrow squinted at the Emiri shipmaster, and a spark of familiarity sprung alight from the embers of his memory. "Sai!" he called. "Sai, is that you?"

The red-haired Emiri's laughter rang out across the harbor. "*Syrai!* Imagine meeting you here after so long. The sweet sea is good to me, bringing you to me."

"Can I come aboard?" Yarrow asked in Emiri, knowing no one around him except the man he addressed would understand. While a simple language on the surface, it took many years to master the nuances of Emiri, as one word could have half a dozen meanings depending on context and tone.

"Most definitely, *syrai,* though aboard might be underwater before long. You can take your chances, though, Yarrow."

Yarrow, determined to save the man who'd done so much to help him in the past with little hope of recompense, pushed through the onlookers and toward the mages at the end of the pier. All of them abandoned attacking Sai's ship, turned, and focused their attention on impeding Yarrow. They ran toward him with spells ready. When they tried to grab his arms to restrain him, he let his energy pour out in sapphire flares. One of the mages, an older man with a deep scar running from his hairline to his chin, jumped back as Yarrow's power singed his hands. The other five mages surrounded him, but Yarrow's energy pulsed farther from the body hosting it and kept them a dozen feet away.

Saving this Sai won't bring back your Rini, beloved.

Oh, come on, creature! You said you wanted to have some fun. Well, here you are. Plenty of fun for everyone!

An excellent point, my sweet mage. Let's show them what we can do.

Yes, indeed. "Stay away from me," Yarrow warned. "I don't want to hurt any of you."

But I do.

"What in Pherara's sacred name are you doing, boy?" another of the mages asked. "Why do you seek to defend this criminal? Why would you impede us in our duty?"

"Because we can," Yarrow answered in a voice echoing the other.

The man made a complex gesture in front of him. To Yarrow, in his heightened state, the restraining spell the other mage cast appeared to drift slowly through the air, like a fallen leaf on the wind. Barely thinking about it, Yarrow swatted with his hand and volleyed the enchantment back at its conjurer. The spell intended for Yarrow wrapped around the enemy sorcerer, binding his arms to his sides and cementing his feet to the waterlogged wood of the pier.

Sai laughed out loud and slapped his thigh. "Take that, you deadweight dirt-striders."

"You shameless outlaw!" the female mage responded. "Surrender! You don't stand a chance."

"Can't say I agree, land-bound," Sai responded. "The tides seem to be rising in my favor."

Another spout of fire issued from her fingers, but Yarrow expected it this time. It took little effort to siphon the heat from her spell, to steal the air needed to feed the flame. Yarrow's companion always said Yarrow could take much easier than give, and Yarrow played to his strengths against the female guard. Her eyes widened, and she stumbled back as what she'd surely intended to be a devastating enchantment fizzled out like a pissed-upon campfire. Nothing remained but a few pitiful streaks of smoke.

The woman called for assistance, and one of the mage-guards hurried to her side while two others attempted to aid their immobilized comrade. Yarrow turned and sprinted toward the end of the pier, letting his ethereal wings trail behind him, spilling blue sparks as he rushed toward the water with five Esperon enchanters close on his heels. They flung all manner of spells at Yarrow, but his mystic appendages moved to deflect them without his conscious intent. When he needed them, the cerulean wings folded around Yarrow and protected him from anything aimed his way.

Sailors, laborers, and the residents of the area gathered around to watch the altercation. Some of them tried to help the mages pursuing Yarrow by casting feeble spells or trying to grab him from behind. Yarrow deflected them easily enough, but his companion, irritated, rose up and took control for a few moments. Against his will, Yarrow spun around to face the throng. His arms raised independent of his intention, and no matter how much he called out to the creature to stop, it wouldn't relent. It was enjoying itself far too much.

Yarrow grasped at the presence and fought to rein it in, but he couldn't get a firm hold on it. Its deprivation of sensation combined with its love of conflict to make it desperate, famished, and reckless. Yarrow could no more hold it back than he could restrain a starving harrow-wolf on the scent of a bloody carcass. It directed a bolt of arcane energy at the center of the crowd. Shards of wood shot into the air, and people screamed as they flew back from the impact. They struck those behind them and sent them sprawling with an effect like dominoes. They looked absurd, and Yarrow couldn't help chuckling.

Sai echoed his amusement. "Run, then, *syrai*. I long to have you near me, and in so many ways."

Yarrow finally managed to wrestle his companion down, though he allowed it a portion of his perception, hoping to keep it satisfied. Doing so forced him to walk a delicate line between his own goal of reaching Sai, saving him and escaping, and the creature's desire to rain death and havoc down on these simple people.

Up ahead, a group of sailors and laborers had gathered from nearby ships to block Yarrow's way, brandishing oars, clubs, and simple swords. He skidded to a halt just before colliding with them, raising a hand wreathed in blue flame as a warning. Unimpressed, the large men formed a crescent around Yarrow. He held his palms flat in front of him and released a strong gust of air. Some of the men closest to him stumbled and a few fell, but dozens more kept advancing.

What are you waiting for, beloved?

"Come on, *syrai!*" Sai called. From a gap between the seamen and work hands, Yarrow saw a small fleet of rowboats closing in around the Emiri ship. Sai hauled an enormous apparatus similar to a crossbow up and positioned it on the rail of ship. Though the weapon was as long as he was tall, Sai aimed it expertly, and a large harpoon pierced the hull of the nearest rowboat. The city guards inside it called out for aid as it filled with water. Sai's laughter rang above the cacophony of the harbor as he loaded another bolt.

A big man with a bald head and a gold ring through his nose swung a cudgel at Yarrow's head. Momentarily distracted, Yarrow barely managed to duck in time to avoid it. He lashed out with the edge of one of his ethereal wings, catching the big sailor at the midriff and knocking him down. The other men rained blows down on Yarrow, and it took all his concentration to shield himself with his magic. Exertion forced him to his knees. His pampered year at the university had left Yarrow unused to combat. Gathering the last of his strength, Yarrow fired a thick streak of lightning in front of him. The men it hit directly fell to the pier, twitching. Others scattered, some of them plummeting into the churning water. Yarrow stumbled to his feet and ran for the opening he'd created.

He managed to sprint a few dozen feet, shouldering through the gathered mages and sailors, before something caught him around the ankle and sent him sprawling on his chest, the wind knocked from his lungs. He looked over his shoulder. One of the mages held a glowing, red thread of energy. When he tugged it, Yarrow slid backward, scraping his stomach and chest against the rough wood. The rest of the guards soon caught up. One of them tethered Yarrow's wings with another arcane rope, and they blinked out of existence, leaving him vulnerable. The affronted sailors regrouped, scowling down at Yarrow and smacking their weapons against their palms. One of them kicked Yarrow in the side, bruising his ribs. With the mages' restraints sapping his energy, Yarrow couldn't retaliate.

I have suffered enough of this insult, beloved. Do something about these worms, or I will.

Before Yarrow could respond, something whooshed over his head, and Sai yelled out a stream of obscenities. Yarrow couldn't see Sai or his vessel over the men surrounding him, but he couldn't miss the small spheres of fire sailing over their heads or the thick sheet of black smoke wafting up from the water.

Beloved....

Wait. Just... just do nothing! Let me think!

The time for thinking is past, Yarrow.

"Restrain his hands," one of the mages said. "Use any necessary force. You men, get to the boats and haul that Emiri vermin to shore. He has nowhere left to go now. Both of these slugs are going to the dungeons. The rest of you, while we appreciate your assistance, we have this situation under control. Please return to your ships with our thanks."

Men hunched over Yarrow's supine body, and chains clinked behind him. The presence of their large bodies above him and the smell of their sweat raised an irrational panic in Yarrow as some phantom memory brushed the edges of his consciousness, and he lashed out with rage. It was better to be angry than weak, better to be cruel than let himself be hurt or violated.

"No!" Yarrow cried in a voice not entirely his own. "Not again! How dare you touch me?"

Something cracked and then shattered within him, and his power poured out from his deepest stores, rising up to keep him safe when he couldn't do it on his own. It disintegrated the bonds the other mages had placed on him. Though Yarrow saw nothing beyond the blinding blue enveloping him, he heard screams and smelled scorched wood and singed flesh. He'd never had a mastery of fire, but raw, arcane energy such as this had always come as naturally to him as walking. As it had only once before, Yarrow's body became nothing but a conduit for the magic. Magic couldn't be injured as flesh or a human mind could. He no longer felt made of skin, muscle, or bone, and power sang through his veins in place of blood. The ecstasy of it threatened to overwhelm him, and the temptation to let it just pour forth and wash away all those who intended him harm was almost impossible to resist. They deserved it. They all deserved it for hurting him.

Go on, my beloved. Show them all their place at our feet.

No! If he let go now, he'd level a section of the city. He'd probably destroy Sai along with it. This was why he'd had to leave Sasha and Duncan, even more than because of his companion's threat. He was dangerous. Sometimes this need to tear down the world, to make it pay for all it had taken from him, overtook him, and the power to accomplish it followed. He wanted nothing more than to reduce it all to ash. *No! I don't want to hurt Sai!*

Desperate to regain control, Yarrow recalled that silly book he'd taken from the library. Seeing little alternative, he performed one of the childish rituals it described, pressing his fist between his eyebrows, feeling the bones of his hand against his skull, feeling solidity return to his limbs as he concentrated his energy at that junction. He drifted down a foot or so, and his feet landed lightly on the pier. Following the book's instructions, he held his hands out to his sides, his palms toward the heavens. He shifted his focus from his forehead to his right hand, left foot, right foot, left hand, and back to his head. As he repeated the steps, Yarrow felt the magic compacting, every bit as powerful, just not allowed to flow unchecked like a spring flood down a mountainside. He let it bounce back and forth in the prescribed order, growing denser, more controlled. The bright, cerulean sheet before Yarrow dimmed. All around him, people cowered on their knees, shielding their heads with their arms. Only soft crying broke the eerie silence.

Forehead. Right hand. Left foot. Right foot. Left hand. Forehead... Ignoring the others, Yarrow repeated the ritual until he held all his chaotic power in a glowing ball in his right hand. Then, calm and focused, he walked to the end of the pier. No one dared to stand in his way. When he reached the water's edge, Yarrow spread his azure wings and glided to the deck of Sai's ship, touching down next to the Emiri captain.

Sai cocked his head and grinned. "Took your time, *syrai*." He embraced Yarrow and kissed him hard on the mouth. Their teeth pressed together through their lips. "Sweet Emir, it's good to see you, Yarrow."

Yarrow clamped his eyes shut, conflicted. Sai should be afraid of him, disgusted by what he'd just seen Yarrow do, but it comforted him that Sai accepted him without a trace of wariness or doubt. He was being selfish in a way he swore he'd never be again, putting his comfort ahead of Sai's safety.

"You've done a great deal for me already," Sai continued, "but if it wouldn't be too much trouble, could you see to my poor, lovely ship?" He waved his hand to indicate the burning sail and smoldering main mast.

With an errant thought, Yarrow sucked all the heat and vitality from the flame. It faltered and died. Not even embers remained, and a soft breeze whisked away any remnant of smoke.

"And now we should find a way out of this port." Sai pointed back at the pier, where dozens of mages in blue robes gathered in a circle, likely preparing a large and devastating enchantment. A wall of people lined the harbor, some just watching with morbid curiosity, but many more holding weapons, ready to defend their city. Others appeared along the parapets of nearby buildings.

A rowboat bumped against the hull of Sai's small vessel. It held four archers with their bows drawn and trained on Yarrow and Sai, civilian guards who stood as an absolute last resort should the mages fail. Just in time, Yarrow erected a pane of magical essence to shield them. The arrows bounced off his barrier, but the archers prepared to fire again, and other boats approached them from different angles. Yarrow didn't know if he had enough strength left to shelter the entire Emiri vessel.

Sai reached inside the tight, torn leather vest he wore and pulled out a small vial. He yanked the cork out with his teeth, stuffed a scrap of cloth inside, and lit it from one of the lanterns swaying from the rigging before tossing it at their enemies. Flames burst forth and washed over the rowboat. The archers and the man piloting the little vessel dove overboard and swam for shore.

"Can you get us away from here, Yarrow?"

Yarrow nodded. "What direction do you want to go?"

"West, and angle us slightly to the north," Sai answered. "Toward the southern shore of Selindria and the mouth of the river. We'll be safe among so many of my people."

Yarrow couldn't help smiling. Garith, his cousin and the king, had promised Yarrow those lands once the crown reclaimed them. Asking for them had been the only way Yarrow could conceive to keep the Emiri race safe, and now it would reciprocate and keep him sheltered as well.

Closing his eyes, Yarrow drew the seawater up and against the stern of Sai's ship, giving it a strong push out of the harbor. Sai stumbled and grabbed a rope to retain his balance as the vessel shot beyond the edges of the bay. Yarrow directed the water, and it pulled the ship in its wake, until they'd put a safe distance between themselves and their pursuers. When he knew they'd be unhindered for a while, Yarrow dropped to the deck and sat cross-legged on the smooth wood, so lovingly polished and swabbed, but damaged by the attack. At the moment, Yarrow couldn't ponder the scratches and scorch marks. The frantic rush to survive, fight and flee ebbed out of him, leaving him exhausted and apathetic.

Sai sat down in front of Yarrow, pressing his knees to Yarrow's as the ship continued to drift leisurely away from Espero. Yarrow took a moment to actually look at him, now that fear for his life didn't sway his attention. Ropes and braids of crimson hair, some twisted with bits of twine or ribbon and others tipped in clay beads or seashells, hung to Sai's waist. Beautiful, dark brown paint in intricate patterns edged his androgynous face and swirled down his limber, unmistakably masculine arms. Brilliant orange eyes looked Yarrow up and down. Sai wore a tight leather vest and trousers, ripped open in many places and held together with rawhide cords and patched with odds and ends of fabric and hide. Strips of tantalizing, sand-colored skin showed through at the gaps.

He's quite enticing, Yarrow's companion observed.

Don't even consider it, creature. He is off-limits to both of us.

What? Why? Do you see how he's looking at us, beloved?

He is not looking at you, and I have pledged myself to others. Besides, I won't let either of us put him in danger.

Sai clasped Yarrow's hand. "You seem so far away. Are you all right?"

"I'm just tired," Yarrow said. "How are we going to reach Selindria with no sails? I don't know if I can keep compelling the water to pull us along. We have a bit of a head start, but the others will catch up before long. I doubt we have more than half a day's lead. Maybe less. Just what do you have below deck that they're so intent on recovering?"

Sai stood and shielded his eyes with his hand. "Many fine things! But they'll do us little good if we can't get away. Not far from here is a swift current we can ride almost to the southern coast. But we will need the winds to pick it up."

"How?"

Sai opened a hatch and began pulling out rolls of canvas. Once he'd unfurled several feet of sturdy cloth across the deck, he opened a wooden box and handed Yarrow a long fish-bone needle and a spool of twine. He took out a pair of shears and cut into the fabric. "We should repair the sails, *syrai*, and in a timely manner. Then we'll rig a jury mast and hope blessed Emir shows us her favor."

Yarrow nodded at the simplicity of Sai's wisdom and prepared to sew.

Chapter
Seven

"LET him answer for himself," one of the nobles shouted at Duncan.

Duncan rubbed his eyes. His head ached, and tension reached down his neck and back. He felt like his muscles had been wound into knots for weeks now, and he couldn't spare a second to relax. He wondered how his life had become this repetitive nightmare of irrational aristocrats shouting at him and making unreasonable demands. Each time he endured it, he wanted more than ever to relinquish his title. No amount of wealth was worth this, but he feared what would happen to the common people under his protection if he left them at the mercy of these vultures. Before, he'd simply faced enemies with his sword drawn. The intricacies of court politics had proved much more insidious than an honest battle.

I'm a soldier, Duncan thought. *An uncomplicated man. I'm not meant for this life, and I don't want it. But only a coward retreats from a challenge and leaves others to fend for themselves. I have committed many sins before the goddesses, but I am no coward.*

When he'd left Windust fortress early that morning, he'd hoped to distract himself from the disorder and doubt with a long ride across his lands. Sasha, still healing from his wounds, had barely stirred when Duncan disengaged himself from his sweet assassin's limbs and left the bed. Sasha had only argued against Duncan going out alone and unprotected for a few moments before he'd acquiesced and gone back to sleep. As much as Duncan loved Sasha and valued his counsel, he'd departed anticipating a few hours on his own. He adored the early spring, with all the new life abundant around him, as if the whole world grew in hope. Everything smelled fresh and green, and a soft breeze ruffled his hair as it carried his worries away.

A mob had met him just outside the castle gates on his way to the stables for a mount. Aristocrats accompanied by their personal knights and guards filled the field between the inner and outer walls of the fortress, crowding around the small outer buildings where blacksmiths worked, weapons were stored, and animals kept. Duncan never traveled without his trusted greatsword strapped to his back, but it would do him little good against so many. Though he wore thick leather trousers and heavy, knee-high boots, he'd left his plate armor on its stand in his room.

"Bring out your assassin and let him face our questions, if you have a shred of honor, tam!" The dark-haired man, Tam Myrior Fennsour, demanded again. Lady Ortean stood just behind him with her arms crossed and a smug grin on her wrinkled face. Sasha had informed Duncan that the old woman and the younger man engaged in an intimate association.

"You may address any questions you have to me directly," Duncan replied, trying to maintain a calm and measured tone.

"Tam Elloransy was found dead this morning!" Fennsour bellowed.

"And? The man was eighty-nine years old and had been ill with a cough for quite some time," Duncan said.

"He also went to the goddesses without an heir. Very convenient for you, tam. As the bairn, his lands default to you. Your personal estate has just expanded considerably. Do you honestly expect us to believe this was a coincidence? When we know full well you keep a professional murderer in your employ?"

"A sick old man died," Duncan said, looking over his shoulder in the hopes that his knights had noticed the commotion. It was too early for the craftsmen to be in their shops, and no one would be in the stables but the boys attending the horses. "I'm sorry to hear of his passing, but I'm afraid a similar end waits for all of us."

"Do not continue to insult us, tam," Lady Ortean said, coming to the front of the group. "I want to know the whereabouts of your personal assassin! We have a right to know. Not even a bairn is entitled to such criminal activities as you've engaged in since assuming your title, which, I might add, you have no blood claim to hold."

The rest of the nobles and the armed men in their employ shouted vehement agreement. Some of them took out their weapons as they closed around Duncan, but Duncan refused to be intimidated by curs who would outnumber a man dozens to one. Cowards! He couldn't tell them Sasha had been in his bed all night, waking nearly every hour with a fever and muttering nonsense, but he wouldn't cower before them or sink to their disgusting depths. "I don't need to explain myself to any of you. I hold this title by the will of His Majesty, High King Garith of Selindria and Gaeltheon. Your tales of assassins and my schemes are pure delusion. I won't honor them with a response. All of you are in dangerous proximity to treason, and I demand you stand down!"

"We will not!" Lady Ortean cried in a shrill, scratchy voice. "If you will not provide the answers to which we are entitled freely, we will force them from you. We have suffered enough. Bring out your assassin!"

As the mercenaries around him drew their weapons, Duncan held his sword out in front of him. He couldn't believe his vassals would attempt such treachery in broad daylight, in full view of the goddesses, but he prepared to stand against it, even if it proved futile. At least he would die on his feet, fighting.

A man in mismatched bits of armor rushed toward Duncan from behind Lady Ortean with a battle-ax raised over his head. As he prepared to block the attack, Duncan saw half a dozen men ready crossbows in his peripheral vision. He retreated until he felt the rusted iron of his castle gate against his back. He cursed himself for instructing the servants to lock it behind him, but when he'd left, his concern had been for the safety of the people sleeping within the castle walls and not his own welfare. Now he only hoped one of those servants might notice the commotion and rouse his warriors. Until then, he would have to stand alone. The man with the ax dove toward Duncan, and Duncan parried. Before their steel connected, though, Duncan's enemy fell on his back, a tiny dagger protruding from his left eye.

"No, no, don't!" Duncan yelled, too late.

One by one, the soldiers with ranged weaponry crumpled to the ground with knives stuck in their necks or poisoned darts piercing their faces. The throng panicked. Screeching, the aristocrats scrambled to cower behind their armored hirelings. Duncan looked for Sasha along the walls, but he knew he wouldn't find him if Sasha didn't want to be found. As much as he wanted to stop his friend before he exacerbated an already volatile situation, Duncan had to turn his attention to defending himself as a man with a spiked mace ran toward him. He deflected the blow with his sword and succeeded in pushing his opponent back down the steep hill a few steps, but the enemy quickly recovered. He swiped at Duncan's head, and Duncan barely managed to raise his blade in time to repel the blow.

The force of the strike made him stagger, and the other warrior used his momentary interruption to swing at Duncan's legs. The heavy, studded metal ball struck him in the shins, tearing leather, clothing, and flesh and sending Duncan down to his knees. Duncan lifted his blade just seconds before the mace connected with his neck. Fighting through the pain in his shins, he got clumsily back to his feet. As Duncan stepped to the side, avoiding another swipe of the mace, he drove the pommel of his sword into his attacker's face, bloodying the man's nose.

Two other soldiers joined the first, one with a nasty-looking flail and the other wielding a sword and shield. They surrounded Duncan and raised their weapons to attack. Duncan tried to back away, but the castle gate stopped him, and he had nowhere else to go, so he prepared to fight. He refused to die on his knees at the hands of a cowardly pack of traitors. With a wide swing of his massive blade, he knocked two of his enemies off their feet and sent them tumbling down the hillside road toward the outer wall. The third man butted Duncan with his shield, catching him in the groin and making him double over at the sharp pain.

Duncan dropped to his knees again as he raised his sword to shield his head. The bruised base of his body throbbed, and blood poured from his shredded legs. The men who gathered around him began to grow blurry through the pain Duncan suffered, and he knew he wouldn't last long against such superior numbers without his knights. Then a dark streak fell from the sky and stood in front of him. Sasha easily deflected the other knight's sword thrust and cut his throat before he could raise his shield. The assassin kicked the defeated man in the side, sending his lifeless body rolling down the path with a trail of blood following him. He flicked his wrist, and the dagger he held flew from his hand and imbedded in the forehead of a man with a crossbow. Blood seemed to flow in slow motion down the man's face, the crimson stream splitting around his nose and converging again at his chin before he fell facedown in a bright red pool.

As Duncan had known it would, Sasha's interference enflamed the nobles' outrage. Their guards rushed forth, and Duncan grasped the iron bars, staggered to his feet, pressed his shoulder to Sasha's and prepared to fight alongside his friend, maybe for the last time. Then a cumulative cry sounded from behind him, answered by cursing and shouts from the traitors. Duncan spared a second to glace over his shoulder. Tam Allwynn led a regiment of three dozen knights out of the castle barracks and toward the gate. Enemy archers tried to prevent the seneschal from unlocking the heavy barricade by firing on him, but Allwynn's men shielded him, and before long the gate swung open. The loyal men of Windwake burst through and defended their bairn against the soldiers opposing him. Sasha grasped Duncan's arm and pulled him aside as the soldiers ran past them. Steel met steel, and arrows sang through the air. From the edge of the fray, Sasha used the remainder of his throwing knives wisely, eliminating or immobilizing the archers. Before long, Duncan's knights pushed the traitorous warriors past the outer wall and almost to the cliff overlooking the sea.

"Take them all into custody," Sasha shouted, cradling his side.

"Wait—" Duncan called. His men already moved to obey the assassin, but Duncan wasn't sure throwing a group of citizens and wealthy landholders into the dungeons would help his popularity. "Let's consider this first."

"Duncan, they are traitors," Sasha said in his infuriatingly calm and cold tone. "This is necessary."

Tam Allwynn and his knights seemed to agree, and they quickly apprehended the enemy soldiers, binding their hands and then gathering them in front of the gates. To Duncan, such a move only added timber to an already out of control fire. But as he saw a few of his knights lying on the ground and realized they'd died defending him, any sympathy he'd felt for these filthy cowards bled out of him. Lady Ortean and Tam Fennsour protested vehemently as Duncan's men rounded them up and restrained them with no hint of gentleness.

"You will not get away with humiliating us like this," she spat at Duncan, her face purpling with rage.

Before Duncan could respond, Sasha stepped in front of him, yet another knife pointed at the traitorous woman. "You would be wise to hold your tongue," he said with no more emotion than if he'd commented on the fair temperature of the morning.

"I know what you are," she snarled at Sasha. "I'll personally see that your execution lasts for weeks, Cast-Down piece of filth."

"Enough!" Duncan yelled out. "Get them out of my sight."

Suddenly dizzy, Duncan gripped the iron bar of his gate. His aching, torn, and bloody legs could no longer hold him, and he sank down in the gravel. Sasha hurried to his side but refrained from touching him in front of others. "You need a healer," the assassin said. "Can you make it to the barracks if I help you, or should I have him sent here?"

"I can make it," Duncan grunted. He'd been injured worse, but he was getting too old for this nonsense. Goddesses, he grew weary of it. "Give me your hand."

Though much smaller, Sasha planted his feet in a wide stance and stood steadily as Duncan grasped his forearm to pull himself to his feet. He staggered and almost landed back in the dirt, but Sasha caught him beneath his armpits and draped Duncan's arm across his back like a shawl. Duncan hated to put so much of his weight on the slighter man, but he really had no choice, and Sasha bore the burden without complaint as they made their way slowly through the inner courtyard to the part of the castle where the soldiers and guards lived. Not far ahead of them, a queue of aristocrats and their knights and hired soldiers in manacles trudged toward the stairs that led to the dungeons.

Sasha helped Duncan limp down the uneven stone steps and past the rows of neatly made cots where the common soldiers slept. They entered a large room at the end of the long, narrow corridor. A few men lay in the beds lining the walls, and an elderly man with a long white beard and functional beige clothing sat at a table. He hurried over when Sasha lowered Duncan onto the nearest cot and grabbed the heels of Duncan's boots to gently stretch his legs out. Duncan winced and screwed his eyes shut as his blood soaked the coarse brown blanket. When he opened them, he saw Sasha holding his waist, a wide strip of crimson painted across his shirt.

"Sasha, you're hurt," Duncan said through gritted teeth. He addressed the Windust healer: "Never mind me, Tam Fulgrig. See to my friend."

The healer Fulgrig was a man of few words but very knowledgeable when it came to patching up wounded soldiers, as he'd been doing in Windwake for half a century. He turned slowly toward Sasha, but Sasha held up his hand and took a step backward. "I'm fine. The bairn needs your services. Do your job."

Fulgrig merely nodded, pulled a wooden stool beside Duncan's bed, tugged his heavy boots off, and began to cut his trousers away with a sharp pair of shears. Duncan gasped as the healer used tweezers to pick something, probably bits of cloth and leather, and maybe gravel from when Duncan had fallen, out of his wounds. The old man hunched over him and worked in silence while Sasha slumped against the wall. Finally Duncan's assassin abandoned his pride and collapsed onto a nearby stool.

"How did you get to me so quickly?" Duncan asked, making conversation mostly to distract himself from the burning as Fulgrig scrubbed his cuts with pricklefruit astringent. "You were fast asleep when I left you."

Sasha arched a slender black brow, clearly surprised Duncan spoke so freely in front of others. Duncan shook his head. Old Fulgrig didn't concern himself with such things, nothing in the world could shock him, and the healer certainly wasn't one to gossip. He never even lifted his head, Duncan's injuries his only concern. "How did you dress, arm yourself, and get to me as soon as you did? You were asleep," Duncan persisted.

"Was I?" Sasha said. "You think I would loaf about in bed while you went off riding alone? Into the forests, where you could be ambushed and no one would ever hear you cry out?"

Duncan bolted up, earning a stern look from old Fulgrig. "So… what? You intended to follow me?"

Sasha shrugged. "Yes."

"But, Sasha, you told me, you swore to me, you'd stay in bed. You—" Duncan hesitated to call Sasha a liar after Sasha had just saved his life, but he couldn't help feeling slightly betrayed. "You did not do what you told me you would. I need to be able to believe you when you promise me something."

"Then next time, don't be so stubborn and just agree when I want to protect you."

"You miss the point completely," Duncan said, watching as Sasha's features glazed over with the layer of ice he so often hid behind, even from Duncan. Sasha had simply seen deception as more efficient than debate, Duncan realized. Lying to Duncan had been a strategic move.

"We should continue this conversation at a later time," Sasha said. "You must decide what you'll do with the traitors. There may be others. I should look into that, and soon."

"Out of the question! No. Do nothing until I've had a chance to think and consult with Tam Allwynn. I absolutely forbid you to target anyone else without speaking to me first."

Sasha widened his black eyes and flared his nostrils. "You… *forbid me?*"

Duncan sucked in air as Fulgrig stitched the deepest of his cuts with a curved needle, applied another salve to the gashes on his legs, and began wrapping them tightly in clean bandages. "Sasha, I didn't mean it like that…."

"I think you did." Sasha's chill armor melted with his anger and affront. He gripped the wall and stood, though it obviously aggravated his wound. "I want you to remember who I am. What I am. I'm your friend, but I won't be ordered, Duncan. Only one can command me. Besides, you'd be wise to let me roust out the rest of the turncoats while you execute those you captured."

"Execute?" Duncan almost choked on the word, felt it scratch his throat raw, like a bone hidden in a piece of meat.

Sasha crossed his arms and tilted his head. "They tried to murder you in front of your own gate. What else would you do with them?"

"They must stand trial," Duncan protested weakly. "You cannot just kill anyone who inconveniences you."

"They made an attempt, albeit a feeble one, on your life," Sasha said.

"They will pay for it, but according to the rules of civilized society. I will summon the priestesses of Vestrafori, and they will be judged by those holy women and their noble peers. Only then will I hand down punishment. To do otherwise would be tyranny."

"You must kill them and any others conspiring against you," Sasha continued in an emotionless speech that chilled Duncan's blood and made him shiver against the hard bed. "To do otherwise is foolishness. While they live, they may try again. They may succeed. Dead, they stand no chance against you."

"It isn't that simple." Duncan grew frustrated; he just couldn't make Sasha understand.

"It's the simplest thing in the world," Sasha said. "Most things in this life are tepid, but a few are still frozen or boiling, perfectly clear. This is one of them. Killing them keeps you safe. I see no conflict."

"Please, Sasha. I'm asking you as a friend not to do anything without speaking to me first. If you care for me, promise me you won't."

"Fine."

"And do you mean it this time?" Duncan asked. "Tell me you're not just agreeing because it's quicker and still planning to do whatever you like as soon as I look away."

"If that's what you think of me, Duncan, I doubt anything I can say will change your mind. You either trust me or you don't."

To Duncan, trusting Sasha felt like another of those lukewarm areas. He loved Sasha and placed absolute faith in Sasha's desire to protect him. It was the assassin's methods of protection Duncan couldn't quite reconcile with what he understood of justice. Though he couldn't comprehend what passed as morality for Sasha and didn't know if he ever would, Duncan had no doubt as to Sasha's loyalty and the purity of his motives, so he said, "Of course I trust you. Do the same for me, and let me handle this situation as I feel I must."

The healer Fulgrig finished bandaging Duncan's legs. He stood and said, "You were very lucky to avoid any broken bones, but you'll probably see some severe bruising before long. Your boots took the worst of it. Keep weight off your legs as much as possible for at least a week. Wash the wounds once a day, and be sure to eat meat and drink wine to keep your blood strong. As long as you can avoid the wounds festering, you should be fine before long." Without another word, he left them to wash his bloody hands in a basin on the other side of the room.

"How do you plan to handle these traitors?" Sasha asked, finally calming enough to sit and rest his elbows on his knees.

"I plan to send a messenger to His Majesty and ask for reinforcements," Duncan said. "Perhaps the presence of a hundred royal guards will dissuade another attempt. As I said, the nobles who attacked me will be put on trial, and I will carry out whatever the priestesses say, as well as considering any advice His Majesty can provide. You must understand that I have always lived by a certain code, and I can't abandon it for my own safety."

"I abandoned my calling and code for you and Yarrow," Sasha said under his breath. "I would do it again."

"I know."

"Well, don't expect me to leave your side until this silly trial is finished," Sasha said. "I'll hear no arguments. I'm not venturing more than a few feet away."

"The only good thing to come from this wretched situation," Duncan said, smiling, elated when Sasha returned his grin without pretense.

"Come to think of it, I'd be far more comfortable in my own bed. Do you suppose you can help me to it?"

Sasha leaned so close his breath tickled Duncan's whiskers. "Make it worth it to me?"

Duncan's eyes fluttered shut, heat spread across his face, and his skin tingled from the place Sasha's lips brushed all the way to his chilly bare toes. "I promise," he managed to whisper. "Goddesses, Sasha, help me get out of here before I embarrass myself. My feelings for you are becoming… obvious."

Sasha grasped Duncan's armpits to hoist him off the rickety cot. The old healer only shook his head and rolled his eyes as the two of them staggered out of the sickroom, holding each other, smiling and laughing.

Whatever would happen with the treacherous nobles could wait a few hours, Duncan thought. Sasha mattered to him right now, and Duncan couldn't wait to show him how much.

Chapter
Eight

WITH the damage to Sai's ship, it took Sai and Yarrow almost two weeks to reach the southernmost point of the Selindrian coast. Doing magic almost nonstop over the course of their voyage had stretched Yarrow thinner than a worn cloth full of holes where the fibers had simply disintegrated. He'd had little choice. They'd needed the winds, so he'd summoned them. They'd needed drinking water, so he'd made it rain, and when ships from Espero pursued them, he'd conjured a thick fog to hide them while they absconded. For the last half of their journey, he'd eaten nothing but whatever sea creatures Sai could catch and roast at the little brazier at the center of the quarterdeck, and hunger and the craving for fruit had added to his weakness.

Yarrow slept on a pile of mismatched cushions and blankets, the strong sun beating down on his almost naked body. He'd stripped to nothing but his gauzy trousers only hours into their excursion, tucking the ends into his old, leather boots so they wouldn't tangle on the riggings. Though he'd never minded the intense, southern heat, Yarrow found himself dreaming of chilly Lockhaven and the first night he'd spent with Sasha and Duncan in the fortress where he'd grown up. He could almost taste their skin as he writhed and tossed on the deck of the ship, sweating even as he recalled the cold, the ice crystals catching the prismatic light of the moon they'd viewed together.

He stirred when he felt a hand grasp his bare shoulder and looked up at Sai smiling down on him. "I hate to disturb you when you look so luscious in repose, but I could use some assistance guiding us into the harbor."

"Of course," Yarrow said, shaking the dreams from his head and letting the coastal breeze carry them away. He stood and stretched, trying to dwell on all the good things around him instead of pining for those lost. He loved ships and the sea, the way the gentle tide lapped at the hull of the brightly painted little boat, the smell of the pitch sizzling in the powerful sun, the little white birds circling across the crystalline sky. He went to adjust the aft sails while Sai stood at the helm. In the short time he'd been aboard the ship, tugging the coarse ropes had calloused Yarrow's hands, and the sun had baked him almost as brown as Sai.

Yarrow breathed in the aromas of saltwater and heated wood as he climbed the rigging to adjust the topsail. It caught the wind with a satisfying crack, pushing the little vessel toward the sprawling settlement of sand-colored buildings in the distance. After the immaculate order of Espero, Yarrow had forgotten the overcrowding common to Selindria's port towns. Buildings stood practically on top of each other, covering the series of small islands they approached, and piers jutted out into the harbor anywhere they'd fit. Shoddy bridges connected some of the islands. Hundreds of ships choked the narrow passages between landmasses of various sizes. Yarrow smiled at the sails in stripes of every color.

"What's the name of this port?" Yarrow called down to Sai.

The seafarer's vibrant cords of hair whipped around him as he looked over his shoulder and smiled. To Yarrow, Sai's every gesture oozed innuendo. The way he tossed his hair sent Yarrow's imagination alight, and he wondered if Sai did it on purpose.

"We call it *Kimula Artai O-Fortan*, Twenty-Nine Pieces of Paradise," Sai said. "There are so many places to hide amongst these islands that it's almost impossible to be found. Sweet Emir carries everything we need to us, and it practically washes up at our feet. Don't worry, *syrai*. I'll show you all the pleasures of the Twenty-Nine." He finished with a wink and turned his attention back to steering the fleet little boat between two of the larger islands.

From his perch, Yarrow took in the vista to the limits of his vision and found it aptly named. The warm air filling his lungs made him feel buoyant, as if some of the weight of the past fettering him fell away for a moment. As Sai skillfully guided his vessel and they skirted islands of various sizes, Yarrow smiled and waved at the beautiful people wandering the shores or lounging on the docks with their feet in the water. The deeply tanned, lithe, androgynous Emiri raised their painted hands in greeting with none of the suspicion Yarrow's countrymen displayed.

Though it said nothing, Yarrow felt the presence watching, trying to dissect his happiness. In an instant, Yarrow's burden returned, heavy on his heart. If the creature discovered something he loved or enjoyed, it would try to control him by threatening it. Yarrow struggled to bury his excitement at the brilliant sapphire water speeding by beneath him and the sea breeze in his hair. He couldn't leave himself so bare; he had to be more careful.

Sai steered the boat into a deep, narrow bay on the eastern side of a midsized island. He called for Yarrow to help him drop anchor, and they moored the ship a few hundred yards from the sandy shore.

With just the tip of his finger, Sai traced the deep blue ink twining down Yarrow's neck, across his collarbone, and over his arm. "You wear the paint of the Emiri, Yarrow. I wonder, can you swim like one of us?"

"Oh, I'm not so bad." Yarrow returned Sai's smile, his gaze locked on Sai's enormous orange eyes.

Sai leaned in, and Yarrow felt his breath on his cheek. "I bet you're not bad at all." The Emiri gave Yarrow a quick peck on the cheek, climbed up to stand on the railing, and then dove into the water, cutting the surface with barely a splash.

Yarrow followed, arching his body with only slightly less grace. Blood-warm water engulfed him, and he kicked wide, curving toward the surface amidst a flurry of silvery bubbles. He broke into the sultry air and mopped his fringe off his forehead. Sai had a good head start, and Yarrow, while a strong swimmer, wasn't Emiri. Emiri were practically amphibious, and often bragged seawater ran through their veins. Even the name of their race translated to "People of the Sea," or simply "seafarer."

Sai dipped beneath the water and then resurfaced, moving as naturally through the tides as Yarrow would cross a field of soft grass, and reached the beach well before Yarrow. He rose from the ocean and threw his head back in another devastating motion. Light played across the planes of his face, magnifying his androgynous appeal. The droplets flying from his hair looked like molten gold in the late-afternoon sun, treasure raining down on the sand. Though he didn't need assistance, Yarrow clasped Sai's hand when he offered it and didn't let go as Sai led him along the glittering coastline. He still honored his pledge, unspoken or not, to Sasha and Duncan, but Yarrow didn't see much harm in walking hand in hand. Emiri were a much more tactile people than his own—friends frequently greeted one another by kissing—though the way Sai stroked the length of Yarrow's finger pushed the boundary.

Looking down, Yarrow thanked the goddesses only Emiri seemed to inhabit this particular spit of land. The water had left his thin, Esperon trousers almost translucent. He untangled his fingers from Sai's, as he had no hope whatsoever of hiding what Sai's suggestive fondling did to his body.

"This is my land home," Sai said, pointing to a little stone building the same color as the sand. "I live here with my *syrai*. You are most welcome here, Yarrow. I'm honored to call you a friend."

"Thank you, Sai." After Emiri custom, the simple, two-story cottage had been painted with colorful, abstract designs in teal, purple, ochre, and rust. The designs resembled the swirling patterns the Emiri inscribed in their skin. Similar decoration adorned the exteriors of the nearby dwellings, and like Sai's home, the Emiri residents had removed the doors and window shutters, preferring to drape gaily dyed cloth over the entrances to encourage airflow. Yarrow had always found Emiri more clever than his own kind in many ways, but he also found them a bit eccentric. Instead of gardens, patches of gravel packed full of shiny baubles lined their walls: metal vases, opalescent shells, bits of elaborate architecture, and shards of precious metal sat in heaps that nearly reached the windows. The uniquely Emiri art of cobbling together colorful bits of broken glass into round lanterns made a fine showing on the island. Dozens of the mosaic orbs dangled from cords strung between the house roofs and swayed from the eaves of the porches.

Emiri could also be a bit slovenly. The idea of putting items in order rang foreign to them. As long as they could find what they needed, they didn't see the point. When Yarrow entered Sai's home, discarded garments and bedclothes were strewn all over the floor. Empty clay cups covered a table carved from driftwood, and chests of valuables overflowed along the walls. Yarrow didn't mind. He saw order as an illusion, a pitiful attempt by powerless people to pretend they could control their lives. Emiri harbored no such illusions, and Yarrow loved them for it.

"The sweet sea takes us where she will," Sai said, as if on cue. "Today, she has brought me home to my *syrai*."

"Sai! *Hai mira, syrai-tama*," said a slight woman with ropes of bright yellow hair. She held a plump infant on her hip as she embraced Sai with her other arm.

"Yarrow, do you remember Lala?" Sai asked.

"Of course," he said. *"Hai mira,* Lala."

"And Toumo." Sai tilted his head toward an Emiri man in nothing but a floral-printed loincloth who leaned against the wall with a sensuous tilt to his waist. Yarrow raised his hand in greeting, and Toumo winked his bright, golden eye and blew Yarrow a kiss.

"Good to see you well, *syrai,*" Toumo said. "And you too, Sai, you crafty sea-worm. How was your time in Espero?"

"Profitable," Sai said with a smirk.

"So, a celebration tonight?" Lala asked, beaming. "I can make *mubo.* I have plenty of fresh shellfish."

Sai kissed her. "Is there ever a bad day to celebrate being alive? We never know if today might be our last." He took the infant as she hurried off to make preparations, sitting the rosy-cheeked boy on his shoulder and heading back toward the beach.

Yarrow, Sai, and the rest of the household spent the afternoon preparing for the evening festivities. Sai spent so much time playing with the baby boy called Yei-Ri that Yarrow wondered if he'd sired the lad. He knew better than to ask; it would be impolite to the Emiri, who traced their lineage only through their maternal line because they placed no restrictions on coupling. They formed families based on friendship and trust rather than blood; they supported their *syrai,* their trusted chosen. As he watched Sai chasing the small boy into the foamy tide, Yarrow understood completely. Sasha and Duncan had been more like kin to him than anyone related by birth. They were his family, and he still felt connected to them across the time and the distance between them. As he lay on the beach beneath a broad-leafed tree, he recalled every moment they'd spent together.

Yarrow sat lost in his memories as the sun slid lazily into the sea, leaving the sky streaked with fuchsia and mauve and the water sparkling like gold dust. At dusk, the Emiri lit fires on the beach and candles inside their lanterns. Shards of colored light danced across the shore, but Yarrow couldn't be cheerful. Watching the Emiri made him miss his dead lover, Rini, and his living partners, who stood almost as far out of his reach.

Come now, beloved. Why try so hard to be miserable when they are so many pleasures here to enjoy?

I deserve to be miserable. Look what I did to Rini. He should be living on a beautiful island like this, but he had the misfortune of meeting me. I won't let the same thing happen to Sai. I should leave. He stood to gather his things and hopefully sneak away unnoticed, but Sai approached him with a bowl of the spicy shellfish stew called *mu-bo* in one hand and a jug of strong Emiri liquor in the other.

"You don't seem in a festive mood," Sai said. "You should be happy. I plan to share the goods I acquired from Espero with you. After all, I wouldn't have escaped with them without your help. We did well together. Let's celebrate."

"I have to be on my way," Yarrow said. "I appreciate your hospitality, but I… I just can't stay."

"What? Not even for a meal? Not for a single night? I have *muri-ku*. I've never seen a land-bound drink it like you did back on my old ship. I hoped we might share some. Yarrow, I hoped we might share many things finally. I haven't forgotten you. I've thought about you often and cursed myself for the opportunity I missed. I don't want you to leave again without us truly enjoying our time together. What if the sea never carries us to each other again?"

"I can't do that, Sai."

"I don't understand."

This supple little Emiri and I agree on one thing, beloved. What possible reason can you have for turning him away? You and I both know Emiri boys know what they're doing with other men. How long has it been since we've had one beneath us? Why not take a tumble with this one, feel his pliant little legs gripping us, his tight—

Because of Sasha and Duncan!

They're probably over a thousand miles away. How will they ever know?

Damn it, creature! I'll know.

You are very different from when I first found you, beloved. You used to take your pleasure where you found it, not deny yourself everything as punishment.

"I can't," Yarrow said through gritted teeth, balling his fists, energy crackling over his skin. "Sai, please just leave me on my own."

"I know you find me beautiful, Yarrow. I've seen it in your eyes. Tell me you don't desire me, and I'll never bother you again."

"It isn't that," Yarrow said, defeated. Trying to explain sexual exclusivity to an Emiri would be like trying to tell Sai he couldn't eat proffered food even while starving. Emiri regarded sexual play almost like a handshake. He couldn't try to impart to Sai the danger the creature, or maybe even Yarrow himself, could pose. He didn't want Sai to remember him as an abomination.

"I have my reasons," Yarrow finally told him, remembering he'd given Jorian the same watered-down excuse. "That's all I can say."

Sai shrugged. "You don't know what you're missing, *syrai*. But do as you will. If you don't want to lay with me, at least have some of Lala's fine *mu-bo*, and have a drink with me. You need shelter for the night; you can't deny that. Tomorrow I'll give you a share of the loot. Don't argue. It's the Emiri way to share treasure amongst everyone who helped acquire it. Then I suppose I'll tell you good-bye again."

It wasn't an easy task to inspire melancholy in an Emiri, since it took little more to please them than a strong drink, a sunny scrap of beach, and the free time to enjoy them. As much as they loved wealth, they didn't hoard it, ever optimistic they could find more. Sai would squander the fortune he'd come by in Espero until he depleted it on any fleeting fancy, then he would go in search of more. It hurt Yarrow that he'd brought such a miserable expression to Sai's blithe face. Yarrow patted his forearm, but his words of apology and explanation stuck in his throat like fish bones. His companion roared with laughter and mocked Yarrow's weakness.

"But no matter," Sai said, most of his cheer returning though a hint of regret remained, like a dark cloud on the distant horizon. "There's no point in concerning ourselves tonight. Anything could wash up at our feet with the sunrise. Tonight is for enjoying." He handed Yarrow the bowl, and they sat together in the sand with their legs folded under them and their knees pressed together.

When Yarrow finished picking the sweet and spicy meat from inside the shiny black shells, Sai passed him the clay jug adorned with bits of sea glass. Emiri always drank *muri-ku* from the jug and never poured it into a cup. It was like a kiss, pressing one's lips to the mouth of the vessel still warm and flavored by the last drinker's lips. Yarrow worked the cork loose and took a conservative pull since he hadn't enjoyed *muri-ku* in more than a year. Even though his throat burned, his eyes watered, and his lungs froze for a few seconds, Yarrow grinned as he passed the jug back to Sai. Sai drank, sputtered, clapped Yarrow on the back, and then returned it.

The strong brew, made from a secret concoction of ocean plants and creatures, had Yarrow's head reeling after his third drink. The fires farther down the beach blurred, splitting into separate images but rejoining if Yarrow concentrated. Dozens of Emiri had wandered from the nearby homes to join in the merrymaking, and their dark silhouettes twisted and whirled across the sand. Sai pressed the jug against Yarrow's belly, splashing his bare skin. It trickled down into his trousers, and both of them laughed until they had to hold each other's shoulders to keep from collapsing. With his sides aching, Yarrow lay back and looked up at the silver smears against the deep blue sky. Sai lay so close to him Yarrow felt Sai's ribs expand and contract with his breath.

"Ya know, Sai," Yarrow said, "all this will be my lands someday."

"How's that?" Sai took Yarrow's hand, kissed the back, and guided it to rest over his heart.

"My cousin's prince, er, king now. He gave it to me. I'm officially valen of this place, or will be when Garith reclaims it."

"What will happen then?" Sai asked, taking a drink and spilling some down his cheek. "We'll have to obey all those strange land-bound rules? Sweet Emir, I can't even remember most of them. And the thought of doing work, the same day after day, well, that sounds crueler than death. Is that what will become of the Twenty-Nine?"

"No, not at all. I wanted this place so I can leave it the same. I love everything the way it is. I asked for it so I can stop them from changing anything. I want this place for the Emiri. I don't want to rule anything, just want a place where I can lay on the beach like this without anybody bothering me. I feel safe here with you. I mean, with all of you. Your people."

Sai laughed. "Most of your kind consider us a pack of lazy thieves."

"You *are* thieves."

"You have me there, Yarrow. The thing I can't imagine is only making love to one person. Can you understand that?"

"A little," Yarrow said. "Maybe two."

"But there's so much beauty, so many interesting people. It's all beyond me, and thinking of it makes my head hurt."

Their conversation lulled into companionable silence. The high tide moved in, and the waves lapped loudly against the shore. The other Emiri laughed and shouted to each other. The smoke from their fires spiraled into the sky before a gust of wind off the sea whisked them away.

This is dull, beloved.

"I love it. I wish life could truly be this simple."

"Why can't it?" Sai turned toward Yarrow and gave Yarrow's hand a gentle tug until Yarrow faced him. He stroked Yarrow's cheek with his free hand and raked his fingers through Yarrow's hair. The tips of their noses brushed together, their lips barely touching. Sai slid his hand to the back of Yarrow's neck and angled his head to kiss him. Yarrow kissed him back, responding to Sai's warm, slick, and skillful lips before his inebriated mind could catch up. He wound his arm around Sai's waist, and Sai arched into him with a ravenous groan.

Much, much better, little Yarrow. Bite him. I want to taste his blood. Tear his soft flesh with our nails. Want to... want to hear him scream... feel his bones shatter....

"No!" Yarrow pushed Sai away, stumbled to his feet, and backed up. He looked down at Sai's bright red hair and confused orange eyes, and it horrified him to realize he, Yarrow, wanted to hurt him, wound him, make him bleed and cry out. "No! Stop it! Stop it, damn you! I don't want that!"

"Yarrow, don't get angry. Lie back down beside me. I don't expect you to do anything you don't desire. We'll just have another drink and look at the stars."

Sai looked so much like Rini Yarrow had to turn away. His hands trembled, and violence coursed through him. He didn't know if it came from him or the hideous thing inside him.

Tell yourself I'm to blame, if it makes you feel better, beloved. I don't care. I just want to toss your little fish-boy on his belly and fuck him until he can't walk.

"No," Yarrow protested, but he felt the creature flooding his senses. Its control wormed down his spine and into his limbs, making Yarrow's skin and muscle feel insubstantial as it stole his perceptions. The world grew cold and flat, the stars dull and the darkness of the sky faded, until everything smudged together in a uniform gray. The sea sounded miles away, and then Yarrow couldn't hear it at all. Yarrow felt dissolved, like he'd disintegrated and his ashes had dispersed on the breeze. He tried to get hold of the thing, but it slipped through his hands like a fish coated in oil. He clawed at it desperately, but it proved much harder to control when Yarrow was drunk.

I won't let you.

I'll make you a deal, little flower. Stop fighting me, and I won't kill him.

Not good enough. Yarrow pawed around for his magic, blind and incapacitated in every possible way. Something icy and sharp grazed the edges of Yarrow's consciousness. He clasped it and held on to that shard of power for all he was worth, using it to slash at the other and drive it back a few precious inches. Sensation rushed back into Yarrow's fingers so fast he screamed. He swallowed great gulps of air, relieved to be able to feel his lungs filling again. Light and shadow returned to the world with such vibrancy it scorched Yarrow's eyes.

"Are you all right, Yarrow?" Sai, less than a foot away, reached for Yarrow's face. "Feeling sick from the *muri-ku?*"

You won't defeat me, Yarrow. Not on your best day, and certainly not drunk on that Emiri swill. You should have let me have the body when I asked. Now I'll have to punish you.

Yarrow's arms and hands throbbed as if his blood wanted to escape his veins, and then they went numb, more than numb; they felt gone as if severed. As Yarrow watched in horror, they reached for Sai's throat, and Yarrow couldn't stop them. He fought, delving into his darkest places for the power that had defeated the Esperon guards, the power that had burned an army to cinders. When he felt the chaotic pulse of that energy, he didn't hesitate. It crashed through whatever dam normally held it back, making Yarrow's long white hair stand straight up in the rush of power. The creature howled with psychic pain and retreated, but only a few steps.

"Sai," Yarrow panted, unwilling to waste his moment of lucidity. "I do feel very sick… I… I need to go."

"Let me help you to bed." Again, Sai reached for Yarrow, as if to take Yarrow's elbow and guide him.

Yarrow swatted Sai's hand away, turned, and ran. He ran until his thighs trembled, his lungs burned, and the stitch in his side made it almost impossible to breathe. When he couldn't run any longer, he staggered along the beach, thanking the goddesses he'd reached a desolate patch where heaps of brown stone tumbled into the foaming surf. Yarrow picked his way gingerly over the uneven and sometimes treacherous terrain. The other stalked around the perimeters of his consciousness, waiting for the tiniest gap in Yarrow's defenses, so Yarrow feared slowing down or stopping. He wanted to put as much distance between the creature and Sai as he could, so if it overtook him it would have a long way to go before reaching the Emiri. Yarrow wished he could cage himself, restrain himself somehow, but nothing physical would hold his companion.

About a dozen feet ahead, a group of shoal pups emerged from the water. Yarrow had never seen one so close up before, and he stopped to watch them, transfixed. They had long snouts similar to a dog's, and they were about the same size, but the resemblance ended there. The creatures dragged their gray, gelatinous bodies ashore with squat front legs, leaving oozing trails behind them. They had no mouths because they consumed their pray by draping over them, absorbing them into their acidic jelly, and dissolving them, much like their land-bound cousins, the sangorms. Some of them had fed recently and held partially decomposed fish within their mucinous forms. Yarrow wasn't afraid. Smaller and much less intelligent than sangorms, the shoal pups posed him little threat. Still, he raised his hand and pointed it at the nearest one, striking it dead with a bolt of cerulean power.

In a repetitive sequence, he aimed at and slew the next creature, and the next. *Locate, aim, fire. Locate, aim, fire.* He found it calming to let the simple exercise command all his attention, and it helped him regain his focus in much the same way as the Lavingierrio ritual. He repeated it until he ran out of shoal pups, and then he wandered inland.

By the time Yarrow found a patch of sea oats, smoothed them down, and erected a simple ward to protect himself, he practically collapsed. He curled on his side, listening to the plants' little pods popping softly as he crushed them and breathing the clean, almost citrus fragrance they released. The Emiri gathered the hollow husks and brewed a tea they claimed eased the effects of too much drink. Yarrow would need it in the morning. He'd have to find fresh water and make it himself. He'd put Sai and the others in danger if he returned to them. He could never see Sai again.

Oh really, beloved? Have you forgotten your precious book is inside his house? I have you now, little mage. I win either way. Go back for the book and hand me your little playmate, or leave it behind and never find out—

It stopped abruptly, a tremor of anxiety flowing through it, and Yarrow recognized its mistake: it had admitted the Esperon book, Hale's journal, held something useful, something Yarrow could use against it.

YARROW didn't know what reception he could expect when he arrived at Sai's home late the next morning. He almost hoped Sai would toss Yarrow's possessions out the door and order him away. But Emiri rarely held grudges except against serious slights. Sai sat on the sun-bleached boards of his simple porch, naked except for an orange floral-printed scrap around his waist. The infant Yei-Ri sat on his lap, gnawing the pulp from a melon rind. Sai looked a little rough after his night of revelry, but he smiled at Yarrow and raised his hand in greeting. Farther down the beach, many of the other Emiri still slept in the sand, Lala and Toumo among them.

"Feeling better this morning, *syrai*?" Sai asked. "There's breakfast."

"Is it fish?"

Sai laughed. "We're Emiri. Of course it's fish." Yarrow groaned and shook his head, and it was as if nothing awkward had ever passed between them. Sai handed Yei to Yarrow and went inside, then returned with a long platter covered in different sea life grilled to a char and resting on a bed of the sweet, crunchy grain the Emiri called *bori-bori* after the sound it made when one chewed it. Sai took his child back, unfurled the boy's fingers from one of the plaits Sai had made in Yarrow's hair, and handed Yarrow a small steaming cup. Yarrow smelled the distinct aroma of sea oats.

Making himself as comfortable as possible atop an overturned barrel, Yarrow sipped his tea and began to eat, hungrier than he'd realized.

"If you don't mind me asking," Sai said, "how do you know so much of Emiri ways? Why do you wear our paint? Did you live amongst us?"

Yarrow nodded, his mouth full of food. He swallowed and said, "I had a *syrai*, a *syrai-tama*. He was more precious to me than I can ever express."

"What happened to him?"

The presence within Yarrow roared with mocking laughter. *Say it, beloved. I killed him.*

Yarrow's response silenced it in an instant. "I killed him. It was… an accident."

The infant Yei wrapped his chubby hand around Sai's finger, and Sai kissed it. Then he met Yarrow's gaze, a rare, serious expression on his face. "Is that why you push me away? Because you think the same will happen to me? Do you think I'll be scared off so easily? Yarrow, I desire you desperately."

"I don't know what to say."

"Say you'll stay here. You said you like this place. Stay, and have nothing to trouble you. Fish, swim, and nap on the beach. Kin and Izu will be back soon. You'll like them too. Be our *syrai*. Yarrow, be mine."

Toumo walked groggily up the porch steps, sparing Yarrow from answering. Goddesses help him, it was tempting to agree. If everything was as simple as Sai had described, he would have. But then, without his current complications, he'd still be with Rini.

Oh, now. If not for me, little Yarrow, you never would have found your way into the arms of that big, strong knight. And that assassin of yours is like a pliant twig that you can practically bend in half and—

Shut up. Goddesses, I'm so weary of you. You make it all sound so base. You could never understand what Sasha and Duncan mean to me.

"Planning to retrieve the things you took from Espero?" Toumo asked Sai. "I'm dying to have a look at them."

"I'd love to," Sai said. "I'll go now if you'll watch our boy."

"Happy to." Toumo grinned at little Yei and picked him up when the boy reached for him. Yei giggled when Toumo tossed him into the air. Then the two of them pressed their faces together and kissed each other's cheeks. The little child wrapped his arms around Toumo's neck and tugged at his marigold clumps of hair. Toumo made a dramatic show of yelping in pain. "Our lad is a terror, my sweet Sai."

Sai chuckled, turned, and looked down at Yarrow. "Mind helping me?"

"Not at all."

Sai caught Yarrow's hand and led him to a square raft lying upside down on the beach. He bent to brush some sand and brittle, dried rushes off it. Together, they flipped it into the water and waded out to get aboard. Sai handed Yarrow an oar, and standing back to back, they rowed out to Sai's anchored ship. When they reached it, Sai said, "Wait here. I'll pass the items down to you."

Yarrow couldn't help his surge of excitement at discovering what Sai had pilfered from Espero, so he nodded. Sai ascended the rope ladder dangling from the side of his ship quicker than an erkit shimmied up a tree. Yarrow couldn't help enjoying the stretching and bunching of the lithe muscle beneath his wet brown skin. Looking harmed no one, after all. Before long, Sai lowered a large wooden crate with a rope, and Yarrow steadied it when it reached the raft and then untied the knots. The raft dropped a few feet lower in the water. One by one, Sai lowered down three more full chests before he joined Yarrow again and they rowed back to shore.

Toumo and Lala helped Yarrow and Sai drag the crates back to Sai's home. Once they got them inside, Sai pried them open with a metal bar, and the others marveled at the riches within, mostly gold coins and elaborate jewelry. Despite the early hour, the Emiri opened another jug of *muri-ku* to toast Sai's success. Yei gummed an emerald the size of his palm while Toumo draped strings of pearls around Lala's neck. Sai placed a delicate silver tiara on Yarrow's head and slid a ring with an enormous blue stone onto his finger.

"It's the color of Emir," Sai said, looking at Yarrow with unveiled longing. "It matches your paint, *syrai*, and your beautiful eyes."

"Thank you, Sai. Truly."

Sai shrugged. "Help yourself. Without you, all of this would be laying on the ocean floor, along with my bones."

Yarrow kissed Sai on the forehead and waited a few more minutes, smiling as the Emiri enjoyed their good fortune. All he really wanted was to inspect Hale's journal, especially after his companion's reaction the night before. As soon as he thought he could slip away without being rude, Yarrow made his way to the second floor. His possessions waited within a room that stood empty but for a pair of thick, comfortable sleeping mats. He quickly found Hale's account, flipped to the central map and unfolded it across the smooth wooden floor. Though he sat studying it for at least half an hour, Yarrow could make little sense of the swirling lines and arrows around the Selindrian coast and Espero. Beyond them, to the south, lay areas he'd never seen or even heard mentioned.

The soft slap of bare feet drew Yarrow's attention from the confusing maps. Sai stood at the threshold, cradling more wealth in his arms. "I chose a few more things I'd like you to have, *syrai*. There's more waiting for you downstairs, as well. I thought you might like a look at some of the books and scrolls—Are those charts?"

Sai dumped the riches unceremoniously in a corner and sat on his heels in front of Hale's journal, widening his eyes in fascination. "Sweet Emir! I've never seen anything like this. These maps show currents around the Dredges."

"Dredges?" Yarrow asked.

Nodding, Sai pointed to a large, blank area far south of Espero. "We don't ever sail this far south, because the sea in this region is completely still, and there's no wind. Any *mir* who ventures very far into the Dredges finds himself trapped there. But according to this, there's a western current one could ride around that whole cursed patch." He used his finger to trace along a wavy line. "Imagine sailing beyond the Dredges! I wonder what waits on the other side. We have always thought the world ended beyond that bit of ocean. But look! There's land waiting on the other side, at least according to this."

Yarrow stared down at Sai's tanned finger, girdled in gaudy rings from his newest stash. Sai pointed straight to the island Hale had supposedly retreated to after his split from Fane.

Don't be an imbecile, Yarrow. Fane fell over ten thousand years ago. There is no way this man still lives, if he ever did. More than likely this is just a ridiculous fiction, someone's silly fantasy written to entertain simpletons.

You didn't think so last night. I felt your fear when you realized you'd told me this book had value. I can use this against you, and you know it. There is a power in these words, these charts and diagrams. Besides, Fane ruled for over a thousand years. He'd obviously discovered immortality, and maybe he passed it along to his apprentice. Even if Hale is gone, he might have left something behind, something that could help me.

You're a fool. You cannot get rid of me, and you'd be wise to keep me happy, beloved.

Ignoring it, Yarrow looked up and met Sai's gaze. "*Syrai*, do you think it is possible to reach that island?"

After studying the map a few minutes more with his head cocked to the side, tracing his fingers over the markings illustrating the ocean currents and winds, Sai smiled wide and said, "It would be great fun to try."

"Really? You think it could be done?" A tiny flicker of hope burst alight in Yarrow from coals long ago gone cold. Not even his companion's belittling laughter could completely squelch it.

"Sure," Sai said, "provided you find yourself a very capable mariner. I happen to know a *very* capable mariner."

It took a moment before Yarrow realized what Sai was suggesting. "No. No, Sai, I can't allow that under any circumstances."

Sai arched his crimson brows and blinked once, slowly. "You stand much less chance without me than with me. You may stand no chance without me. I know you still feel pain about your lost *syrai*, Rini. I have lost people I cared about, and I understand, but it doesn't mean the same will happen to me. The winds are always changing, Yarrow, and all we can do is adjust our sails. I'll leave you to decide. The rest of us are going to walk down the beach to a little cove and try to catch some *tiburi* fish. You should join us."

Without saying anything more, Sai stood and left the room, leaving Yarrow alone to wonder what under the heavens to do. He needed Sai's help, but could he dare subject Sai to a threat he couldn't even completely comprehend? He wanted to be rid of the creature, but he no longer knew if it even existed beyond a fractured part of his own mind. If he agreed to this, the danger Sai faced might come from Yarrow himself, from something he could never excise. He didn't think he could survive the loss of another person he cared about.

Chapter Nine

GARITH, High King of Selindria and Gaeltheon, thought the sight of his daughter asleep in her cradle beside the window was the most miraculous thing he'd ever seen. Her wisps of black hair looked even softer in the hazy sunlight filtering though the leaded glass. She had such small ears, barely larger than the tip of Garith's thumb. As he stroked her chubby cheek, he almost envied women, whose sole concerns were looking after children, holding them close and watching them learn and grow. He missed so much of the little Princess Denna Borea's progress because the things considered important to men called him away: war, conquest, gold and power. They called him away even now, when all he wanted to do was sit beside his precious daughter, less than half a year old, and enjoy a book.

"Rest well, princess. Grow strong. You're so beautiful." Garith tucked the pale yellow coverlet edged in the finest lace around the baby's tiny shoulders. On his way out of the nursery, he passed his wife, Queen Cothryn, and kissed the back of her hand.

The royal estate in Meritage was even more expansive than Garith's palace back in Selindria, and it took him nearly half an hour to reach the room where he met with his advisors, a separate room from the one he used to hear the concerns of his vassals. At least he preferred this cozy, book-lined space to the formal hall, where he had to sit enthroned on a dais. A cheery little fire burned in the hearth when he entered, and four of his generals and two advisors sat around the table. A page stood ready with a scroll and quill. Tam Lysander, Garith's personal and most trusted guard, stood in the corner near the door. Garith met Sander's gaze and smiled before taking his place at the head of the table.

"How is our campaign progressing?" Garith asked, trying to suppress the boredom in his tone. It seemed he asked the same questions and received the same answers every afternoon.

One of the knights cleared his throat. "The news is promising, Your Majesty. My men have had excellent success reclaiming the lands around the northernmost borders of the Kanda River, with one exception."

"Go on," Garith said.

"The territory claimed by the mercenary band known as the Thorns of Rosecairn has been especially difficult to assimilate into the kingdom. The Roses, as they're known to the local people, share much of the money they earn with the residents. They do not terrorize the people as so many other warlords do, and I'm sorry to report the farmers and merchants in the area support them. They don't want to see them gone, and they're making our job quite a challenge."

Garith considered. "I have thought a great deal about this matter. Approach the leader of these mercenaries. I know of them, and they are mostly an honorable lot. Tell their leader to swear fealty to me, and I will make him a bairn and give him the very same territory he now holds. I will name him bairn of Rosecairn, and so long as he does nothing opposing the crown, I'll allow him to continue on as he has done."

"A brash move, Your Majesty."

"Is it?" Garith asked. "Compromise costs far less than conflict. If we can appease these men, we'll have not only saved the lives of many of our own by avoiding senseless combat, but procured the service of skilled warriors, should the need arise. I ask you to find the leader of the Roses and treat him with respect. Tell him I very much want him at my side, as his men stood beside mine at the Battle of the Starlight Bridge. Bring me word of his response as soon as possible. If he wishes it, invite him here to meet with me in person and discuss terms. Assure him he will be shown all the hospitality any of my other nobles would receive."

"It will be done, my king."

"Good," Garith said. "What other news?"

Another knight spoke. "Our progress in the lands to the south is not so encouraging, Your Majesty. The Emiri are stubborn, to say the least. Driving them out will take more men."

"I have no more men to spare," Garith said for what felt like the hundredth time. "My forces are stretched thin as it is."

"Then I don't know if we'll ever succeed in ridding our good kingdom of the Emiri vermin. They outnumber us at the mouth of the river, and we don't stand a chance against their fast ships and knowledge of the islands. What will you have us do?"

"We'd find it less of a challenge if your mad cousin would return and help us reclaim his own valenny," another knight grumbled.

"Yarroway disappeared even before my wedding," Garith said. "No one has seen him since then, and even if they had, I don't know that he would aid us against the Emiri. He's very fond of them."

"So we're expected to die to secure his lands while he does goddesses know what? Preposterous—"

Garith raised his hand to silence the man before he ventured into inflammatory territory. "One of the main goals of the union between Selindria and Gaeltheon was to bring order to the disputed lands between our nations along the Kanda. We're hardly doing this merely as a favor to my cousin. Continue our efforts, but conservatively. Do not risk our men or resources. Do what you can to claim this territory, but know we may need to wait until we have a greater force to dedicate to the effort. For now, let us work our way down from Estrella Lake. I want to regain this land, but I don't want good men losing their lives for no reason. I want to be kept up to date on the casualties as well as our progress."

"Very good, my king."

"If there's nothing further, I'm very busy today," Garith lied, looking over his shoulder to have a quick glimpse of Sander. If he could get rid of his generals and advisors, the two of them might have a few moments alone to speak. Garith didn't know what had happened between the two of them or when it began, but at some point he'd started to see Sander differently, to appreciate the sunlight on Sander's disorderly, copper curls, to delight in the way he smiled and the sound of his voice. He caught himself enjoying just watching Sander cross a room; he moved so beautifully. When Sander wasn't around, and especially when Garith didn't see him for a few days, he felt a dull ache in the pit of his stomach. Then, when they could be together, just be in the same room, Garith felt warm and giddy in a way he'd never experienced. When Sander stood behind Garith as he sat on his throne, just stood there, stoic in his duty, Garith couldn't stop smiling. He wanted to laugh aloud and dance across his hall.

Garith couldn't pinpoint the moment when he'd gone from seeing Sander as a brave and loyal knight, a trusted friend, to... to whatever he now considered his guard. Not that it mattered; the king could never act on his feelings. He didn't even know what actions he wanted to take beyond touching Sander's hand, his rosy cheek, running his fingers through his hair….

A smile tugged at Garith's lips as he daydreamed. It all made little sense. He loved his queen, a kind, beautiful, and intelligent young woman who'd already given him a child. What more could a man want in a wife? Still, his innocent fantasies about his friend made Garith feel an odd mixture of toasty heat and chilly numb in his chest.

A scrawny, freckled messenger boy burst into the room, tripping over his feet and panting. The commotion made Garith snap his head up from the lacy cuff he'd been staring at.

"Urgent… urgent message… for the king," the poor lad choked out between heaving breaths.

"Give it here, child," Garith's oldest advisor, Tam Vartanan of Gaeltheon, snapped with his customary irritability. The messenger handed him a thick scroll tied with black and gold ribbons and looked very pleased to escape the room. The elderly man unfurled the parchment and took a large glass from within his sumptuous, purple robes to inspect the document. Everyone else, Garith included, almost held their breath as they waited for him to report.

The slouched man finally cleared this throat. "This is an urgent missive from the bairn of Windwake, Your Majesty. He claims several of his nobles have committed treason and even attempted his assassination. According to this, he barely survived. He writes that most of his aristocrats are demanding things promised to them by the former bairn, Taran Edercrest, and that when denied them, the aforementioned aristocrats responded with violence. Bairn Duncan and his men captured the offenders, and he now holds them in his dungeon awaiting trial. He wishes for Your Majesty's counsel on how to proceed."

Garith pinched the bridge of his nose and rubbed his eyes with his thumb and finger. "Goddesses, what next?"

"Your Majesty?"

"Good Tam Vartanan, make a note. Tell Bairn Duncan to do nothing until I can assess the situation. I know him to be a good, honest, and loyal servant to the crown, but his actions may have implications he hasn't considered."

"Quite right," Vartanan barked. "The lady Ortean, one of this man's prisoners, is the sister of Maury Damasca, a respected and wealthy lord of Gaeltheon, and, I might add, one who has provided us with many knights."

"Damasca is also a nasty piece of work," one of the knights said. "Likes to cause conflict. He's the kind of man who will even hurt his allies, just because he likes to watch people suffer. Makes him feel powerful, I suppose."

"That is a harsh statement, tam," Vartanan wheezed out.

"But not an inaccurate one," another of the generals said. "That bastard Damasca is a petty son of a whore, and everyone knows it."

The third knight agreed. "Tam Maury thrives off arguments. He likes to turn people against each other, and he's the kind of man who'll pull your trousers down to kiss your ass while he stabs you in the back with his other hand. Be wary of him, Your Majesty."

"Even so," Vartanan said, "the man commands a large portion of our kingdom's resources, and many follow his lead. You must tread very cautiously, my king. In my opinion, you should instruct this bairn to release Lady Ortean."

"And let outright treason go unpunished?" another knight said. "A dangerous precedent to set, don't you think?"

"A strategic move," Vartanan continued. "We show ourselves to be a friend of a man who can aid our cause immensely. Ask restitutions from the sister, but by the goddesses, let her live! Damasca will make her into a martyr if you do not, Your Majesty. Mark my words."

Garith heard the clink of Sander's greaves as he took a step nearer. Goddesses, Garith just wanted to feel Sander's supportive hand upon his shoulder, but he knew Sander didn't dare.

"These traitors deserve exile at the very least," a knight said, and the others muttered agreement. "Allow this to pass unpunished, and you invite more of it in the future. The bairn of Windwake was lucky to survive this treachery."

"He survived it because he keeps a Cast-Down assassin, a disciple of a foul being I will not name within these walls, as a personal bodyguard. The good people of Windwake claim their bairn sends this… *creature* to put an end to anyone who disagrees with him. That, my friends, is the foulest of tyranny! It is no wonder the nobles are outraged. They should not have to fear death for speaking their minds," Vartanan said, disgust thick in his tone.

"They also should not attack their leader because he doesn't line their pockets," one of the generals said, beating his gauntleted hand against the wooden table and making the trays and goblets tremble at his outrage.

"The fact remains," Vartanan said more calmly, "that Tam Maury Damasca is valuable to us. He should not be made an enemy, under any circumstances. If I may be frank, Your Majesty, your rule over this so-called Blessed Epoch is not completely secure. It is difficult for seasoned men to place their faith in one so young, and it doesn't help to have an heir to the throne, its only heir, with an Esperon name. And a little girl at that! You need every possible noble household behind you. You need to secure their trust and loyalty at any cost. Goddesses help you if Damasca convinces others you condone Bairn Duncan's use of a—of that man."

Garith shook his head. As much as he wanted to rub his eyes and temples, he didn't want to demonstrate weakness before his vassals. "I will have to consider this matter. While what you say is true, Bairn Duncan is also my vassal, and a very valued one."

"You must find a way to appease both parties, Your Majesty."

"I need to think about this," Garith said. "It is complex, and I must weigh all the implications carefully. Please leave me."

When the knights hesitated, Sander banged his sword against his shield. "You heard His Majesty. Be off."

When all but Sander had left, Garith rested his elbows on the table. "I'm thankful to the goddesses for you and your strength, Sander. I—"

Sander curled his hands over Garith's tense shoulders. He kneaded the stiffness from Garith's overwrought muscles and helped Garith relax. He leaned in, his face only a few inches from the top of Garith's head. Garith felt Sander's warm breath in his hair. He closed his eyes and breathed Sander's scent: leather, steel, and warm skin underneath. Then he patted Sander's hand, and Sander sat down in the chair next to Garith, the look of regret in his sea-blue eyes mirroring the hollowness in Garith's chest. They had already indulged more than they should, and both of them knew it.

"What am I going to do?"

"It seems simple enough to me," Sander said. "We both know Duncan is a good and honest man. If his nobles committed treason, they should be put on trial and punished. Is it really wise to grant them a royal pardon? What kind of message does that send? That wealthy and important people can ignore the law? That they're above it?"

"I have ignored the law when it suited me," Garith said, knitting his fingers together and staring down at his knuckles. "The Windwake nobles make a fair point about Sasha. Imagine if they knew I had employed him on occasion."

"You are the king!"

"So I'm above the law?"

"Yes," Sander said.

"And that doesn't bother you?" Garith asked. "It sits well with you?"

"It's necessary," Sander replied. "You cannot rule this great kingdom under constant threat of treason. Those people who stood against your father, who would stand against you, had to be eliminated."

"But shouldn't they have been taken into custody and given the opportunity to stand trial?"

"That would have taken forever," Sander said, forcing a laugh.

"So convenience excuses it? Goddesses, I paid a man to slaughter others while they slept."

"Others would have done the same to you, Garith, given the opportunity. Why is this troubling you so deeply? As king, you have a goddess-given right to do as you must, as you see fit."

"All the more reason to consider what I do carefully," Garith said, standing and smoothing down his red velvet tunic.

Chainmail rattled softly as Sander also got to his feet. He put his hand on Garith's shoulder and said, "You are a good man, my friend. Never doubt that."

Looking at Sander's sincere, blue-green eyes, smooth, rosy skin, and lush pink lips, Garith wanted nothing in the world but to kiss him. In that moment, he'd have traded his crown for five minutes of freedom to show Sander what he meant to him. Instead, Garith embraced him, though he couldn't feel the planes of his body beneath Sander's armor, and goddesses, he wanted to. He pressed his forehead to Sander's temple and whispered, "Thank you for listening to me rant."

Sander stroked Garith's hair. "I would do nearly anything for you, my king."

Garith pulled away. "Will you come riding with me later? Just for a few hours before dinner?"

Sander chuckled. "Garith, you are High King of Selindria and Gaeltheon. You hardly need to ask one of your guards to accompany you on a ride."

"But I am asking."

"Then I am honored." Sander crossed his arm over his chest and bowed, his wild, burnished locks tumbling into his face.

WHEN Garith returned to the nursery, it pleased him to see not only Queen Cothryn reading from a book of devotions, but his mother embroidering by the window. The wet nurse fed his daughter on a chair in the corner.

The queen looked up and frowned. "You look very tired, Your Majesty. What's on your mind?"

Garith sat down on the padded bench beside his wife. While he knew other kings and nobles kept military and political matters separate from their domestic lives, Garith had always found his queen clever and insightful, and even though he'd known her less than a year, he valued her opinions, as well as those of his mother, so he recounted to them what had transpired during the meeting. Sensible advice was sensible advice, no matter who it came from.

"To my mind, the solution is simple," Cothryn said. "Send Lady Ortean, her husband, and her daughters to her brother, and strip her of her lands. Damasca will have no choice but to see her life as a gift from Your Majesty. Do the same to Tam Fennsour: take his estate and demand he leave Windwake and never return. You will be seen as merciful while removing the threats to Bairn Duncan and increasing his estate significantly."

"Lady Ortean will be absolutely humiliated to be sent to beg scraps from her brother," Garith's mother said. "She'd probably rather be executed. She's a very proud woman, and a shrewd one. She'll not just let such a slight go."

"If I kill her, I make an enemy of Damasca. And what of the knights and hired soldiers? I won't spare aristocrats and send common men to the noose. The opinion of the knights and soldiers carries almost as much weight as that of the nobility. If I just leave them to rot in the Windust dungeons, Duncan has to feed them."

"Send them to fight the Emiri, or one of the other barbarian factions along the Kanda," Garith's mother said. "Let them earn their pardon through two years of service."

"A good plan," Garith admitted. "Even with the combined forces of Selindria and Gaeltheon, I can always use more men. Provided they don't desert at the first opportunity."

"It's too bad my nephew couldn't be with his friend in Windwake," Garith's mother said, wistfully looking out the window. "These traitors would not dare be so bold against Yarrow. He would put them in their place."

Garith snorted. "Or he would go mad again and burn the entire bairny to the ground." Even after all these years, the fondness and near awe his mother used when speaking about Yarrow stung Garith. He could hardly help that he'd disappointed her by not being born a mage. "Besides, Yarrow doesn't care about this kingdom. He'll tell you so himself. I care about it. I'm the one who's here, protecting it instead of off doing goddesses know what. I'm afraid I'll have to do in my legendary cousin's absence."

"I never meant to imply you wouldn't, Garith," his mother said gently. "I'm proud of all you've accomplished. You are a fine king."

Garith nodded, unwilling to start an argument. "I think I'll do as you advise; it seems the only reasonable option. I must go and draft a message to Duncan. He's going to be disappointed in the reinforcements I'm able to provide. Then I'm going riding with Sander. I'll see you both at dinner tonight. Good afternoon, my queen. Mother."

Garith left quickly. It would do his reputation no good to be seen spending his days in a nursery and seeking the counsel of two women.

Chapter Ten

SASHA felt like Duncan had chained him to the wall by making him swear not to eliminate their enemies. For the past several weeks, he had been restless in a way he'd never experienced. He spent each day watching his partner, almost hoping something would happen. He would welcome anything that required action. Sasha was tired of waiting; he'd been trained to anticipate an enemy's attack and act first. He knew this conflict couldn't end without loss of life. Such conflicts never did. The world contained many blurred areas and questionable courses of action, but Sasha knew one thing with absolute certainty: there were two kinds of men, the victorious and the dead, and no subtle distinctions stood between them.

Crouched on the wooden shingles of the highest tower of Windust fortress, clinging to an iron spire built in to channel lightning, Sasha looked out over the bairny of Windwake. Agitation and a sense of helplessness had stolen his rest for several nights now. The wind whipped his hair around his face as the first feeble rays of dawn fought through the darkness to illuminate the rocky terrain. He detected movement on the trail to the castle gates, a significant force, enough to raise a faint cloud of dust. That meant at least a few horses. Sasha dropped lightly from the roof to the parapet below. He ran quietly along the rocky ledge before lowering himself to Duncan's balcony and dipping in the door.

Sasha's entry didn't disturb Duncan. Of course it didn't; the man slept like a corpse. Sasha envied his ability to shut out the troubles of life for a few hours, as such comfort eluded the assassin. Now, though, he needed Duncan alert and ready to face whatever approached the castle. When saying Duncan's name a few times didn't rouse him, Sasha shook the knight's shoulder.

Duncan snorted, rolled on his side, and tucked his blanket under his chin like a boy who didn't want to get up for his lessons. While Sasha found it endearing, he needed Duncan ready to use his sword and defend his bairny.

"Duncan, you must wake up."

"Sasha? Yarrow? Is the prince safe from the ice wyrm?"

Sasha grinned. Duncan's sense of duty permeated even his nighttime fantasies. "Shake off your dreams, my love. A party approaches Windust fortress."

Finally, Duncan sat up in bed and rubbed his eyes. "Sasha? What are you doing out of bed?"

Since he saw no advantage in telling his partner he hadn't spent more than an hour in his bed for days, Sasha said, "I observed a fair-sized force heading toward the castle. A dozen horses, if I have to guess."

Before Sasha finished speaking, Duncan was out of bed and dressing. Within minutes, he donned his dented old plate, secured his ceremonial cloak across his shoulders, and strapped his greatsword to his back. "I know better than to hesitate when I hear concern in your tone, Sasha. You're not a man who is easily spooked."

"No," Sasha responded. "Hurry. You should have your knights ready to meet the approaching force."

"I know it, assassin," Duncan said with a playful smirk. "I've been commanding men since you were still learning to use a knife and fork."

"I learned to use a knife before you had the strength to lift that huge blade of yours," Sasha teased back.

Duncan laughed brightly, with his mouth open and his head thrown back. "I could use this sword at twelve. That would mean you held your daggers in the womb."

"Practically," Sasha said.

"Well, I can show you how well I wield my big sword, if you need convincing."

"Oh, I do," Sasha responded as his body reacted to Duncan's words. He thought he might manage a few hours of rest if Duncan satisfied him. By Thalil, he needed both. "Hopefully we can make this quick and return to our bed while we still have a scrap of the morning left to enjoy. You have servants to deliver our breakfast, do you not?"

Duncan nodded his agreement. "Let's go."

They stood side by side and kissed brusquely. Both of them checked their weapons before they proceeded out of Duncan's chamber together, ready to face whatever threat might arise.

DUNCAN'S heart plummeted at the twenty royal guards approaching his outer gate, their bright blue cloaks flapping in the breeze and their polished armor reflecting the sunlight. He'd requested five times as many, and had hoped Garith might grant at least half his entreaty. Still, Duncan intended no disrespect to these loyal men or their service. They did as he had done when he'd been a knight: they went where they were ordered. As he approached them, Duncan crossed his right arm over his chest and bowed as a knight would to another knight, seeking no superiority over these honorable men. Despite his title, he felt much more comfortable with them than with his nobles.

"Bairn Duncan of Windwake," their commander said, "We bring a message from His Majesty Garith, High King of Selindria and Gaeltheon."

"Speak, tam," Duncan said. "Though you need not use such formality. King Garith and I are old friends. At the very least, dismount your horses and take a bit of refreshment. As your host, I shall be offended if you refuse."

The knights on horseback looked at their leader. When he nodded, all of them dismounted and stretched, clearly glad to be out of the saddle. If Duncan knew one thing about young knights, it was that they were always hungry. Servants emerged from the stables to take the men's chargers and lead them into the barns. The knights followed Duncan across the courtyard, through the inner gate, and into the hall, where he invited them to take seats at the long, central table. Sasha didn't join them, but stood leaning against the wall in a shadowy corner, his arms crossed over his chest.

"The journey from Meritage is a long one," Duncan said. "I'll have some refreshment brought up from the kitchen."

"That would be most welcome," said the knight-commander, a man about Duncan's age but whose hair had started to gray above his temples and along the top of his head. "We appreciate your hospitality. My name is Tobin Muire of Launceton, a small village tucked in the southwestern corner of Thulemore. I'm sure you have not heard of it."

Duncan chuckled. "I grew up in Birtsweth, only a day's ride away. I'd be surprised if we don't have kin in common. Are your people cattle farmers?"

The other knight smiled warmly back at Duncan, both of them seeming to agree business could wait until after a hot meal. "I was raised on a dairy," Tobin said.

"I don't suppose you brought butter or cheese from home," Duncan jested. "It doesn't seem as sweet when made anywhere but Thulemore."

"No, tam, it certainly doesn't."

The kitchen servants brought loaves of fresh bread, wine and ale to dip it in, platters piled high with ham and sausage, salt fish, cheese, beans, and plenty of boiled eggs for the hungry knights. In rocky Windwake, swine who could survive on acorns and scraps were more plentiful than cattle, so beef was only served on feast days.

While they ate, Sasha continued to stand in the corner, making no more sound than a statue. The knights who'd eyed Sasha's unusual armor, barely concealed by a light cloak, seemed to dismiss his presence in favor of their food. They conversed easily over their breakfast, and Duncan enjoyed the meal immensely, feeling like he was back in the barracks for a time. Everyone lingered over his food, and more than an hour passed before the clink of crockery and the sounds of chewing ceased.

"How is His Majesty faring?" Duncan asked Tobin, easing into the conversation. "It's been too long since I have seen him."

"He fares well, as does the queen and their daughter. The king has a great deal of respect and affection for you, Bairn Duncan. That much is plain."

"I'm honored to hear you say so. What is it King Garith sent you all this way to tell me?"

Tam Tobin's smile dropped, and he knitted his brows together. "His Majesty has considered your concerns in regards to the charges of treason against Tam Fennsour and Lady Ortean, as well as the knights and soldiers supporting them."

"What does the king say?" Duncan wiped his sweaty palms on the sides of his trousers. Tam Tobin's hesitation didn't encourage him.

Finally, the other knight spoke, though with strain, as if his words scraped his throat on their way out. "His Majesty has issued a pardon to Tam Fennsour and Lady Ortean. Tam Fennsour will be exiled from Windwake, and Lady Ortean will be sent to her brother in Gaeltheon. You will take possession of their estates. Those men who abetted them will be given the option to join His Majesty's army and earn their lives and freedom through service."

Though Duncan prayed to all the goddesses at once Sasha might hold his tongue, Sasha spoke from just behind his shoulder, though Duncan hadn't heard him cross the few feet of space, not even in the silence following Tam Tobin's announcement.

"This is unacceptable," the assassin said in his flat tone. "Do you honestly propose to simply set the bairn's enemies free to try again? To avenge the loss of their lands and the blow to their inflated pride? Is Garith a fool, or does he completely disregard Windwake and one of the men to whom he owes his crown?"

Chairs scraped the floor as the knights got to their feet, gasping as one. Duncan clamped his eyes shut and swiped his hand over his face. As much as he loved Sasha, right now he wanted to throttle him, to finally teach him a scrap of respect.

"Who is this man and where in the names of the thirteen sisters does he get the nerve to speak that way of his king?" Tam Tobin pointed at Sasha with a hand trembling with rage.

Duncan didn't know what to say; he couldn't defend Sasha this time. Sasha had no reason to be so disrespectful.

Sasha threw more kindling on the flames. "These people attempted to murder the bairn of Windwake. If Garith doesn't want them executed, he must find them more valuable than Duncan. I have seen many men sacrificed to politics. I won't stand by and let this king of yours put a price on my friend's life."

"What a preposterous thing for *you* to say." Duncan couldn't help raising his voice. "Just stay out of this. It's none of your affair."

Sasha's eyes widened, and Duncan expected him to yell. His infuriating calm ratcheted Duncan's anger even higher.

"Your life is none of my affair now?" Sasha asked.

Duncan couldn't do this; he couldn't have a lover's quarrel with Sasha in front of twenty royal guards. He put a stop to it the quickest way he could. "Sasha, please just leave."

Sasha took a step back, and the icy mask fell from his face to reveal his shock and hurt. It took all Duncan's force of will not to reach for him, but he knew he couldn't. In seconds, Sasha had replaced his armor, protecting himself from the pain Duncan had caused. He nodded once in faux-acquiescence and nonchalance, turned on the ball of his foot, and stalked out of the hall.

"We will speak later," Duncan called after him, but Sasha didn't turn back.

"I have more news from His Majesty," Tam Tobin said, breaking the awkward silence that followed Sasha's exit.

Duncan nodded, and all the knights sat back down. For the next few hours, they continued to discuss Garith's wishes and the reasoning behind them. Every few minutes, Duncan looked to the door, thinking—hoping—Sasha might return. Duncan's lover had been so concerned with his safety he hadn't even eaten. He wondered why Sasha hadn't partaken of the huge and elaborate breakfast. Then, feeling like a dull dagger pierced his heart, Duncan realized he'd never invited Sasha to join them.

UNBEKNOWNST to Duncan, he'd done Sasha a favor by asking him to leave the hall. By sending him away, he'd spared Sasha from making some excuse to leave—spared Sasha from lying after he'd sworn he wouldn't.

Hidden behind a weathered buttress, Sasha watched the company of knights escort the nobles and their traitorous soldiers through the Windwake gates. Lady Ortean stumbled behind them with her head in her hands. Her three sobbing daughters waited just down the path to join her in exile. Plump Tam Fennsour had to be compelled from the castle by a knight with his sword drawn. The disgraced aristocrat turned and glared back at the ancient fortress. Sasha, so well trained in reading facial expressions and body language, easily discerned everything the man felt. He'd seen it all before. Fennsour had lost his title, his land, his hope for the future, and even his well-connected lover. Sasha could tell from the look in his eyes he'd never let it go. Fennsour had nothing left but vengeance. Experience had taught Sasha nothing was more dangerous than a man with nothing to lose. For that exact reason, his former order made sure its assassins held nothing close.

The royal knights split into three groups: two each to escort Lady Ortean and Tam Fennsour and six to accompany the soldiers conscripted into Garith's army. At the thought of the prince, the king now—it hardly mattered to the assassin—Sasha's blood burned. Garith only lived because Sasha had let him, and he only held his throne because of Duncan's leadership and Yarrow's magic. By Thalil, Sasha missed Yarrow. Yarrow would have hated this farce; he would have agreed with Sasha and done what needed doing without philosophy or empty talk of justice. In Sasha's experience, and in what he knew of Yarrow's life, justice was a delusion. But Yarrow wasn't here, so it fell to Sasha alone. The desire to spill blood sang in his veins. The Crimson Scythe taught anger and hatred could hamper their work as much as weaknesses like love or compassion.

The assassin should be cold, he'd been taught. Emotion had no place in any decision he might make.

But as Sasha watched the procession, staying hidden on the rooftop above them and letting them get far enough ahead for him to follow unseen, passion, love, and hatred all boiled in his belly. How dare anyone threaten what was his? If Garith wouldn't protect Duncan from the forces menacing him, Sasha would. Contrary to what he'd learned from his masters' whips, Sasha retained his clarity and purpose in spite of his powerful feelings as he dropped lightly to the ground and darted behind a jutting rock.

One pair of knights led Lady Ortean west toward the harbor. She and her household would likely travel to Gaeltheon by sea. Her infirm husband probably already waited on a ship. Sasha dismissed her; her brother would likely keep her on a short leash to avoid any further embarrassment to the family. Sasha decided Fennsour posed a more immediate threat, so he followed the paunchy aristocrat down a trail to the east, grateful for the many rock formations offering him cover.

Careful to keep concealed, Sasha stalked Fennsour and his guards until well past evening. The small party reached a trade outpost somewhere between the northern border of Everdale and the southwestern edge of Lockhaven in the dead of night. The knights shoved Fennsour to his knees at the edge of the small settlement, ignoring his curses as they turned to leave. Sasha ducked behind a low shed housing half a dozen goats until they passed, then he returned his attention to the exiled noble. Fennsour, predictably, made his way to the nearest tavern. Sasha pulled the hood of his cloak over his hair and followed Fennsour inside, staying as close behind him as he dared. Taking Fennsour's coin had apparently been too cruel a punishment for Garith's knights, and the former noble went to the bar to purchase a drink and a room for the night. Sasha took note of the location of his chamber.

For the next several hours, Sasha stood in a corner near the hearth, nursing a clay cup of tepid, bitter ale so his presence wouldn't rouse suspicion. No one questioned a patron buying drinks and not causing trouble. Sasha wasn't alone in maintaining a degree of anonymity. Here on the road, removed from any established village, one encountered mostly traveling merchants, their hired guards, and men roaming the edges of society for more disreputable reasons. Not a single woman stood at the bar or sat at one of the inn's rickety tables, not even a whore. Tam Fennsour didn't surprise Sasha when he bought a round for every armed man in the tavern, asking obscure questions about hiring mercenaries. The man wasted no time planning his revenge against Duncan, just as Sasha had predicted.

When Fennsour started to grow groggy and drunk, Sasha slipped up the stairs, picked the lock on his rented room, and waited among the shadows within. Three-quarters of assassination was waiting.

Eventually, Fennsour stumbled through the door and lit the lantern beside his narrow cot. He never noticed Sasha crouched in the corner as he stripped off his tunic, scratched his balls, farted, and collapsed on the bed. He never even noticed when Sasha crossed the room and locked the door from the inside.

"This isn't over, Launa, my love," Fennsour muttered.

"Actually, for you, it *is* over." Sasha stepped from the darkness at the edge of the room and into the light, a dagger in his hand. Legend said the brethren of the Crimson Scythe could materialize from shadow, and the order's agents perpetuated the myth to inspire fear in their prey.

"You? No—Goddesses!" Fennsour sat up in his bed and tried to scream, but Sasha pressed his free hand over the man's mouth and twisted him around so the back of his head pressed against Sasha's chest. Tears poured down Fennsour's fat cheeks and over Sasha's fingers as Sasha leaned in close to whisper next to his ear.

"Duncan of Windwake is important to me. Threatening him will be your last act in this world. Go to Thalil, and may he accept my offering even though you are filth and completely unworthy."

Fennsour shouted into Sasha's palm and thrashed on the bed. In a smooth arc, Sasha drew his dagger across the man's throat, severing his most vital blood vessels and slicing into his windpipe. The aristocrat died within minutes, gagging into Sasha's hand, blood pouring down his chest. Sasha let the corpse fall against the mattress. It twitched a few final times before falling still.

Sasha wiped his dagger on the moth-eaten sheets and cleaned away the few drops of blood spattering his leather glove. Then he slipped off the gold and ruby ring Fennsour wore on his pinky, tucked it into a hidden pouch near his waist, opened the window, and dropped lightly to the dewy grass below.

In spite of his exhaustion, Sasha jogged around the side of the building and back to the steep, rocky trail. Without the burden of staying hidden, he hoped to make it back to Windwake by morning, ideally before Duncan rose. With Fennsour dead and Lady Ortean on her way across the world, Sasha felt the fetters that had weighed him down for the past few weeks fall away. Other conspirators might remain to threaten them, but they'd be safe enough for a time that Sasha could relax. He could finally get some sleep.

When Sasha reached the castle just as the starlight began to surrender to the sun, he expected to find Duncan asleep, curled on his side as he did on chilly evenings. Instead, Sasha opened the door from the balcony and saw Duncan sitting on a stool next to a fire that had burned to coals long ago. The cinders barely even glowed to drive back the shadows, but they allowed Sasha to see Duncan's strained face and swollen eyes. He stopped just inside the room, unsure if he should have returned.

The two of them just looked at each other for long, agonizing moments. For maybe the first time, Sasha couldn't intuit Duncan's thoughts or intentions by his countenance. He noted nothing on Duncan's face but pain.

"Sasha, I—" Duncan sniffled and cleared his throat. "I didn't know if you were coming back."

"Did I make a mistake in returning?" A cold and unfamiliar pressure settled onto Sasha's chest, and he realized it was fear.

Duncan shook his head. "Goddesses, I—Please just come here."

Sasha went quickly into Duncan's open arms and let out a breath of relief as they closed around him. Duncan rested his head over Sasha's heart, and Sasha combed his fingers through his knight's soft, thick hair.

"Where did you go?"

"Just away, like you wanted." Sasha decided his words didn't truly constitute a lie.

"I didn't mean it," Duncan said. "It was a very tense situation."

"You're not angry with me?"

"I suppose I should be, but I just can't. I'm probably a fool."

They just stood holding each other until the last coals in the fire burned to ash and the room went dark. Duncan reached up and slowly picked apart the buckles of Sasha's armor, peeling it from his damp skin an inch at a time and then tracing Sasha's exposed form with reverence. The way Duncan touched him sometimes, slowly, and with so much devotion, made Sasha feel like the most beautiful man in the world. Other men had wanted his mouth, his ass or his cock, but Duncan lavished praise and affection on every inch of Sasha's skin, down to his eyelashes and ankles. Sasha wondered if Duncan knew how his caresses melted Sasha's heart.

After they'd both undressed, Duncan turned down the bed. They lay down, and Duncan wrapped his large, strong, but gentle body around Sasha protectively and nestled his face into the nape of Sasha's neck. In minutes, he snored softly after having been awake an entire day and night.

Sasha, content in the arms of the man he loved—one of them—and with fresh blood on his hands, slept more peacefully than he had since his days of absolute certainty within the order.

Chapter Eleven

THE heat coming off the smooth wood of the ship's deck felt good against Yarrow's bare feet as he walked from the stern to the helm, where Sai stood leaning against the railing. He loved the smell of the ocean and the wind in his hair. After several weeks at sea, without fresh water to wash it, his hair had formed ropelike clumps similar to Sai's. Sai had encouraged the knotting of Yarrow's hair by braiding some strands and adorning them with small shells and rubbing others with the fat from a porpoise he'd harpooned, encouraging Yarrow's hair to clump tightly together. The dense locks hung past Yarrow's collarbones, and their decorations rattled as he walked.

"The *eru* favors us today, *syrai*," Sai said. "We'll soon catch the current shown on your charts, and sail around the Dredges. I can't wait to see where Emir will take us. I don't suppose I can convince you to celebrate our good fortune."

Sai wet his lips with his tongue and traced the swirls of blue paint down Yarrow's side, raising gooseflesh over Yarrow's skin in the wake of his fingers. He trailed his hand lightly along the line curving over Yarrow's hipbone and traced down the V of muscles, stopping just a hair's width above the waistband of Yarrow's faded trousers. "Are you ever going to let me see the rest of your paint?" Sai asked in a rough whisper.

Oh, go on, beloved!

Goddesses help me, I want to! It's getting harder to say no to him by the day.

Then say yes, little Yarrow.

No. I shouldn't even be here with him. I put my goals before his safety. I was selfish again. What's wrong with me? I should have found another way.

"Yarrow? What is it? What are you thinking about when you look so distant? Sometimes your eyes cloud over, and I don't think you even see me anymore."

"Nothing. It's not important."

Sai's warm, rough hand still rested just above Yarrow's hip, and though only a few inches separated their bare chests, Sai made no move to get closer. "Are you thinking about your *syrai*, Duncan and Sasha? How come you aren't with them? Are they the reason you don't want to lay with me?"

Talking about this made Yarrow feel like he'd burrowed his fingers deep into a fresh wound, but after all Sai had done for him, he owed Sai some explanation. "Duncan has an obligation to Selindria and her king. He is serving as the bairn of Windwake. Sasha… I don't know. I hope they're together. I know this will be hard for you to understand, but it would hurt Duncan to know I laid with you. His ways are different from ours, and he is my *syrai*. I don't want to cause him pain."

"That part I can understand," Sai said, letting his hand fall away from Yarrow's side. "I may not understand the rest, but I know you wouldn't cause my *syrai* harm, so I won't cause harm to yours. I'll stop trying to tempt you."

You'll miss it, beloved.

I know. "Thank you. You'd almost broken my resolve. You're an extraordinary man, beautiful and brilliant. Your *syrai* are very lucky."

Sai's full, expressive mouth turned down at Yarrow's praise, and he looked sadly out at the horizon. Yarrow didn't know what to say, and for a long time, nothing broke the silence but the waves swishing against the hull and the wind stretching the sails. They'd come so far from land not even birds circled the ship. It felt to Yarrow like he and Sai were the only living beings for hundreds of miles.

To change the subject, Yarrow asked, "Where are we exactly?"

As he turned, Sai shrugged off whatever melancholy or regret he'd felt a moment ago. "Espero is about two days behind us, off to the east. Four days behind us, really, but the *eru* have been especially kind. Normally, I would sail no farther in this direction for fear of being pulled into the Dredges, but by evening, we should reach the current shown in your charts. If you can man the sails."

"Of course," Yarrow said, understanding tasks would remove the opportunity for both of them to say things that might hurt the other. He went to the main mast and easily ascended the rigging while Sai returned to the helm.

For the rest of the afternoon and into the evening, they sailed in relative silence. After the sun set, they stopped working to enjoy a meal. Selindrian sailors had only recently realized what the Emiri had known for centuries: eating dried fruit on a long voyage kept them from getting sick. Yarrow relished the sweetness; he craved sweet things almost daily, and the wrinkled, red slices of *pomatora* and chewy *ata* berries provided a welcome change from fish. Both Sai and Yarrow refrained from *muri-ku*, though they had it in plentiful supply. Yarrow couldn't allow the drink to loosen his control over the other, and Sai would have to do some skillful sailing to pick up the elusive current illustrated in Hale's memoirs.

Yarrow had often thought Emiri possessed an innate and intuitive magic in regards to the sea. They seemed to sense Emir's whims and accommodate, and their sense of direction when surrounded by nothing but water was uncanny. Sai reinforced Yarrow's theory when he rose from the deck, abandoned his meal, and went to the helm.

"We're nearly there," he said, gripping the well-worn wooden pegs. He canted his head to the side and let the red ropes of his hair fall over his face. "Sometimes, I can see the stars best from the corners of my eyes. They don't seem as bright if I look at them straight on."

Yarrow trusted Sai and said nothing to break his concentration. Sai moved the helm as if in a trance, navigating carefully between the constellations Hale indicated in his journal: the Firebird and the Three Priestesses. The Emiri knew them as the Angelfish and the Pieces of Gold. Rini had explained it all to Yarrow over the many nights they'd spent lying on the beach and looking into the sky.

The little boat pitched from side to side as it cut through a patch of choppy surf. Yarrow clutched the rigging to keep his balance as Sai steered carefully. A gust of wind caught the sails and turned the vessel almost about, but Sai compensated and kept them on course. Yarrow waited to be directed, but Sai focused all his attention on guiding his precious ship into the obscure stream.

What if he can't do it, beloved? What if he's not as talented as he led you to believe?

He can do it. Faith and adoration flooded Yarrow's heart as he watched Sai manipulate the helm. He didn't doubt his friend for a second, and he knew the creature didn't either, and that made it nervous.

Sai rewarded Yarrow's confidence in him when he hopped and punched the air. "We did it, Yarrow. We caught the current! Do you feel it?"

Yarrow shrugged. He couldn't tell the difference.

Sai embraced him and kissed him hard on the mouth. "Can't you feel it tugging us along? *Syrai, Za-kamei!*"

"*Za-kamei.*" Yarrow repeated the Emiri word that translated loosely to victory or success but also sometimes meant treasure. He pressed his mouth to Sai's sweet lips. Goddesses, Sai felt and tasted good. Yarrow lingered, closing his eyes, enjoying the contact, the delightful heat. It was only a kiss. He'd go no further, but he couldn't help delighting in it. Sai ignited his desire, and if his love for Duncan and Sasha hadn't been so strong, he would have given Sai such pleasure....

Loving him doesn't mean you love them less, Yarrow-flower. Love does not exist in finite quantities to be divided up.

What do you know of love, monster?

More than you might imagine.

Really? Are you speaking of your first beloved?

Horrid, rotten little insect! How dare you taunt me? I'll raze everything you've ever cared about to dust! It circled Yarrow's mind, drawing closer, tightening around Yarrow's perceptions like a noose.

Peace! Peace! Yarrow held up his hands in surrender, shuddering at the creature's murderous rage. *I'm not trying to taunt you. I honestly wondered. I've seen your memories, seen him beneath you. As much as you crave causing pain, with him you were gentle.*

If I'd known of his treachery, I'd have torn him in half. He taught me not to waste my energy caring about the pleasure of others. My own pleasure is all that matters now. None of you insignificant creatures are worth my consideration.

Not even me? Yarrow asked, surprised at the sting he felt. *Sometimes it almost seems like you care about me.*

It laughed, mocking him. *My poor, clinging babe. Do you need me to find you a teat and sing you a lullaby?*

Curse you. I'll show you and everyone else I'm not some soft babe to take advantage of.

Reassure yourself, my final beloved. I have no doubt you'll accept my wisdom in time. And then we'll be radiant, perfect and unstoppable—

If you don't shut up, I'll drown myself.

The presence said nothing more, though it continued to chuckle to itself. Every echo of its laughter felt to Yarrow like the jab of knuckles against bruised ribs. He couldn't believe he'd actually fished for approval from the very monster he despised, the thing that had ruined his life and removed any chance of happiness. He had changed; before, no one's opinion mattered to him but his own. He'd known he was clever and strong, and if others saw him as a vagrant or a deviant, so what? Goddesses, he'd really convinced himself he could survive utterly alone, but now everything had changed, and maybe not for the better....

To distract himself, Yarrow turned his attention back to Sai, who leaned with his elbows on the ship's railing and his hip tilted up in such a devastating pose Yarrow thought it must have been some sort of a spell. With the aid of the elusive current and a beneficial wind, the little boat bounced and glided over the surface of Emir like a leaf in a gale. It left a trail of thick, white foam in its wake.

Sai dropped to the deck and folded his legs beneath him. "Far away again, Yarrow. Like a faint glimmer of light where the horizon dips over the edge of the world. Maybe it's just a trick on my eyes. Come sit by me. Talk or not, as pleases you."

"Sai...." As if his bones and muscles had suddenly liquefied, Yarrow flowed down the wall of the ship until he rested in a heap beside his friend. Without considering the implications, he caught Sai's hand, kissed it, and pressed the back of it against his forehead. Goddesses help him, he loved Sai, even if could never express it. "You have been so good to me. Better than I deserve. I doubt I'll ever be able to repay you."

Sai's laughter was like sunlight banishing the darkness and gloom. "Well, we can talk when you're tam or lord or whatever your people call it of the Twenty-Nine!"

"I'll give you a palace if you want one," Yarrow said, crushing his lips against Sai's painted hand again.

"I don't want a palace. I already have everything I want: my *syrai*, my ship, the sun, sky, wind and sea. I have a son! I have more *muri-ku* than I could ever drink, and Emir won't run out of fish for my supper. The world is beautiful, and I have everything I could ever wish for, with one exception."

"I'm sorry," Yarrow whispered, his words almost stolen by the rush of the water they passed through at such speed.

"I named our boy after you, you know. Yei-Ri means—"

"White fire. Or snow and fire. I don't deserve an honor like this."

"It's also the name of a small flower that grows at the very southern tip of Espero. We Emiri may not care about much, but we name our children very carefully. All five of us agreed to call our child after these wonderful things. Two strong things and one delicate, beautiful thing."

Yarrow couldn't help wondering if he contained the same. Were he and his presence the two strong things? Was anything about him beautiful?

"A fine name," Yarrow said. "And thank you, *syrai*."

"If we're *syrai*, the boy is yours too," Sai said. "That's the way children are raised among the Emiri."

Yarrow gasped and dropped Sai's hand into his lap. The enormity of such honor and responsibility frightened him. "If I can ever do anything for that child, I will."

"I know," Sai said, unlacing his fingers from Yarrow's. "I've never known a land-bound who cared about the Emiri as you do. The others despise us."

"Fools." Yarrow let his head rest against the solid wood of the ship, very tired all of a sudden. Sai dropped his head to Yarrow's shoulder. "But should we sleep? Don't we need to steer the ship to the island? Man the sails?" Yarrow yawned. "The rudder?"

A warm, thick mist engulfed Sai's boat. It wrapped around Yarrow like a blanket, making him feel as secure and drowsy as a child tucked in for the night by his mother. It smelled good—like Sasha's leather and spice and Duncan's steel plate and honest sweat, with a note of Sai's sea breeze, hair grease, fruity breath, and salt-encrusted skin. Yarrow slid lower down the walls of the boat until his back lay flush with the deck. The fog grew so thick he could barely see Sai, who curled on his side and wrapped his arms and legs around Yarrow, his magnificent, orange eyes already closed and his lips mumbling words from his dreams.

YARROW'S dappled gray mare munched red clover while Sasha's black horse, Duncan's bay charger with the four white feet, and Sai's even-tempered roan stallion drank from the clear blue stream. The four of them rode from Windwake to Yarrow's valenny of South Coast, for no other reason than a change of scenery. They were basically on holiday, and so they stopped to spread a cloth over the soft grass and eat a lunch of raisin-studded muffins, cinnamon rolls drizzled in white glaze, preserved fruit, biscuits filled with nuts and figs, bread and jam, and the sweetest ice wines of Lockhaven.

Yarrow regarded his flute of syrupy, golden nectar and said, "All my favorite things."

"Of course," Duncan answered. "We love you and want you to be happy."

"It's your birthday," Sasha said. "We wanted it to be special."

For a fleeting second, Yarrow thought he didn't deserve such contentment, but his doubts quickly passed. Why not? He'd never harmed anyone, with the exception of the mages he'd encouraged to drink too much at the university in Espero. Even so, he'd graduated with honors, and his mother had been so proud. He felt a small twinge of guilt at knowing he was her favorite son. Yarrow pushed his dirty-blond fringe out of his eyes as he sat up. "Thank you, my friends."

"After all your studying, you deserve a good time," Sai said, cuddling into Yarrow's embrace and nibbling along his jaw. "I'll show you one. Or twenty."

"Me too." Duncan sidled up to Yarrow's opposite side and nipped the edge of Yarrow's ear. Yarrow found that odd, Duncan's acceptance of Sai, but he couldn't puzzle it out with both of their mouths teasing his skin until the gooseflesh almost hurt.

Sasha insinuated himself between Yarrow's legs, resting his hands on either side of Yarrow's waist, and kissed Yarrow deeply. As they twisted their tongues together, Yarrow relaxed back into the soft grass and fragrant wildflowers. All the men he loved surrounded him. Sasha's erection pressed against his own.

"As much as I regret saying so, we should restrain ourselves until we reach an inn," Duncan said. "We don't want the local shepherds pleasuring themselves while watching our lovemaking."

Another strange declaration from Duncan, Yarrow thought, but he supposed he agreed. "Let's find an inn soon, then, my friends."

"Very soon." Sasha sucked Yarrow's lip between his teeth and bit lightly. "I need you, sweet *syrai*."

"Sasha, you are not Emiri. Why call me *syrai*?" Yarrow asked.

"Our beautiful Sai has rubbed off on me, I suppose," Sasha responded.

Sai laughed, bright and pure. "I have, and would like to do so again, lovely Scythe." Sai and Sasha kissed passionately above Yarrow's chest. The sun danced across their intermingling crimson and ebony hair. Yarrow smiled and Duncan clucked his tongue.

"Come on, let's get back on the road," the knight said as if to a group of willful but cherished children.

A smile graced Sasha's miraculous lips. He rolled his eyes and said, "Yes, Tam Knight."

"It's bairn now, assassin." Duncan gripped his saddle and swung his leg across his mount's broad back. Looking over his strong, wide shoulders, he urged the rest of them to mount up with a grin bursting with promise.

Yarrow couldn't have wished for a more perfect day to ride. The light decanted softly through the few puffy clouds, painting the ground with warm, golden patches broken only by the occasional soft shadow. The gossamer breeze tempered the afternoon heat. It had to be halfway into Diarana's moon; wildflowers in shades of blue, lilac, and magenta bloomed along the gravel path they took. For a second it surprised Yarrow that he didn't even know what moon it was, but he dismissed his doubts in favor of enjoying the lush emerald canopy of grass rushing past beneath his cantering horse. It added its scent to the warm air as he rocked in his saddle next to all the people he loved most.

Yet Yarrow felt like something watched him, ran along beside their cheery procession just beyond the limits of his vision. Though the pursuer seemed to want Yarrow's attention, it faded away when he tried to look at it directly. He felt something missing on this ideal, summer day. As absurd as it might sound to another, he found himself ready to converse with someone who wasn't there, and it left him feeling hollow.

Sasha rode up alongside Yarrow on the black horse complementing his dark attire and pointed a little way up the road to the loveliest inn Yarrow had ever seen, an inn straight out of a young girl's storybook. The little stone building, surrounded by expansive porches and wooden balconies, stood a bit off the road. An elaborate garden, vegetables and flowers, almost obscured the gravel path to the front door. Their horses would be comfortable in the clean stables and large paddock behind the tavern. Yarrow smiled and slowed his mount, thinking of a leisurely meal and a night with the men he loved. But something whispered at the periphery of his senses; maybe it was just the wind in the fruit trees, but Yarrow felt it wanted to impart something to him. It was like he heard a mouse scratching, but he couldn't locate the wall it moved behind.

Beloved....

Yarrow turned in the saddle toward Duncan, who rode just behind him. "Did you say something just now?"

The big, gentle knight laughed. "Yes, my love. I said we should stop here for supper and to spend the night. What a beautiful place."

"This looks nice, for a land-bound inn," Sai agreed. "It will do."

Their horses kicked up gravel as they reined them in, and men hurried from the barn to attend to the animals. Duncan offered them a few coins, and they led the horses down the curving lane.

No insects. Midsummer, and not a single nipfly....

The observation came from outside Yarrow, but he acknowledged the validity as he ascended the stone steps with his precious friends. Someone was missing. Yarrow felt another presence skirting the bounds of his perception, but Sasha caught his hand and led him inside. Vases of summer blooms, Ix's necklaces and windblossoms, adorned every orderly little table. The yeasty scent of fresh bread filled the small room. They seemed to be the only patrons, and almost as soon as they sat down, a plump wench with rosy cheeks brought a basket of steaming rolls, a crock of butter, and another bottle of Lockhaven dessert wine.

Beloved....

"Did one of you speak?" Yarrow asked his three lovers. They looked back at him in confusion. He relaxed his neck and let his head droop parallel to the tabletop. "You say it's my birthday. How old am I? How old am I, and why don't I know?"

Sai reached across the checkered tablecloth and squeezed Yarrow's hand. "You're twenty, *syrai*. Are you testing us?"

Duncan and Sasha joined Sai in a laugh. The innkeeper brought burleberry pie, fresh from the oven, and set it down between them. As one, they leaned in to inhale the sweet fragrance wafting from the pastry.

"I'm so happy," Yarrow said to himself.

Duncan squeezed his shoulder, and Sasha and Sai beamed at him. "Glad to hear it, sweet Yarrow-flower," the knight said.

"What did you call me?" Yarrow shrugged out of Duncan's grasp. "Something isn't right."

"Everything is wonderful," Sai said.

"That's it exactly," Yarrow continued, staring at his healthy, pink fingernails. "I'm happy. Content and unafraid. How can this be real?"

"Oh, my love," Sasha admonished. "What a horrible thing to say."

"It's not. Sasha, you know. Happiness is an illusion, and security is fleeting at best. What's going on here? This isn't natural. I may not know much, but I know it isn't my fate to be satisfied and lead an easy life."

Good... good boy, beloved.

"Who are you? I know you...."

Yes! See me, beloved Yarrow. Think about what you really *want.*

What? "What do I really want?"

"A piece of pie?" Sasha asked, a thin veneer of faux-innocence over pure mischief. He rubbed Yarrow's knee beneath the table.

"No," Yarrow said, a little irritated. Not knowing what was going on didn't sit well with him, not at all. "What I really want... is power. Power to punish my enemies and protect myself."

"You have no enemies and nothing to threaten you," Duncan said.

If you believe that, beloved, there is no hope for you.

Yarrow stood from his bench and ran out of the inn into the warm, floral air. When he cast around for the source of the voice, he noticed a silhouette near the patch of woods beyond the stables and ran in its direction. Though he crossed a half a mile or more, he never ran short of breath or felt the slightest ache in his muscles. Soon, he stood face to face with a bizarre but oddly familiar creature. Its stature made Duncan look like a child; the top of Yarrow's head reached barely past its broad chest. Brilliant, azure wings, wider than three carriages standing end to end, extended from shoulders rippling with muscle. The nude, male being possessed a savage, angular beauty, and Yarrow felt a tingle of desire. Majestic, curving horns jutted from its forehead, and it regarded him with eyes of solid black. But it also wavered as Yarrow watched, fighting down the urge to touch it. He could see the shapes of the forest through its body.

"I know you…."

"I should hope so, beloved. You and I have been one for half a decade. You must snap out of this foolish fantasy, little Yarrow."

"But I'm happy here."

"That alone should prove none of this is real."

"Yes…." He had no right to contentment; there was something he had to do….

"Be quick, beloved. I don't want to be stuck in this honeyed farce even a minute longer. If I had a true stomach, I'd have emptied it at all your foolishness."

Gradually, like a painted temple window shattering in slow motion, the ideal world broke apart and fell away. Yarrow wanted to grab hold of the spiraling shards and clutch them to his heart, but he let them drift off on the arcane breeze whisking them away, allowing Yarrow to see the reality behind the elaborate illusion. He pushed his chest up from the deck of Sai's ship, his arms wobbling as they struggled to support him. Nothing surrounded him but that warm, placating mist.

Well, that was tiresome, the familiar presence said to Yarrow.

Why did you save me? I thought you didn't care.

I didn't want to trap myself in that disgusting, honey-choked world your mind conjured, beloved. How tedious. You are a simpler creature than I ever imagined.

The desire for safety and happiness makes me simple? Yarrow raked his damp, matted hair out of his eyes. He couldn't dam the surge of disappointment he felt at Sasha and Duncan's absence.

Like all your kind, the creature responded.

A few feet away, Sai lay with his knees against his chest and his willowy arms wrapped around his calves. The fog had condensed over his still form, leaving his skin and hair sparkling beneath the lantern dangling from a rope. Beyond him, Yarrow saw nothing but shifting sheets of gray.

How do I free Sai from the enchantment that gripped us? Yarrow asked his companion.

Why should I care?

Fool. The ship is moving in a tight circle. We need him to get us back on course.

I don't want to follow the course you've set, Yarrow. It benefits me to leave him to his fancies. Unless you'd like to trade....

No. Do you truly want to circle this little section of sea forever? How will that satisfy your craving for new sensation? Not to mention I'll perish here when the food and water runs out. Where will you be then?

I'll let your body grow weak, and then I'll take control of it. I may keep control and shut you out for good, beloved.

Yarrow looked down at the sleeping Emiri blanketed in a net of sparkling droplets. He knelt beside Sai and plowed the heavy, damp ropes of hair off his peaceful face. "I won't abandon you, *syrai.*"

Tilting Sai's head to face him, Yarrow stared hard at his closed eyes. He shook him, but the Emiri didn't respond. Yarrow knew Sai was suspended in a dream similar to the one he'd just escaped.

How do I free him?

Why would I care? the creature asked. *Don't depend upon my assistance, Yarrow. I have no desire to reach this likely nonexistent isle. I certainly don't care about this creature. Plenty of Emiri are willing to spread their legs for us.*

I'll do it myself. Yarrow moved Sai's head into his lap. Extracting him from his dream would be a delicate operation, because he'd have to project a sliver of his essence into Sai's mind. That would leave less of him to keep his creature at bay. He'd have to be very careful not to sink too far into Sai's fantasy, or the beast would seize the opportunity to take over Yarrow's body. For all Yarrow knew, it might leave him suspended in Sai's vision forever. But he had no choice. He couldn't forsake Sai and leave him to waste to nothing.

Their connection gave Yarrow a glimpse of the creature's thoughts, and he saw it biding its time, ready to barrel through any gap in his defenses. He'd have to guard it closely. This would be the most difficult bit of magic he'd ever performed. He'd essentially have to guide a ship through rock-spattered waters with his right hand while fending off a skilled attacker with the sword in his left. If he faltered at either, he'd fall.

For the first time since he was six years old, Yarrow's confidence in his magic quavered. He couldn't let on; the presence would scent his doubt like a harrow-wolf smelled blood and attack. With a last deep breath, he summoned his gift and let a fraction of his attention drift free of his mind and body. When the wisp of his essence shaved off, he had to concentrate to direct it in search of Sai.

The presence lunged, pulling the leash tethering it to Yarrow's control taut, but not snapping it yet. He spared a little of his perception and arcane energy to keep it restrained. Yarrow lost all awareness of his physical body as his attention stretched thin between his two tasks, dangerously close to ripping down the center. If that happened, Yarrow might never be able to mend his mind. He had no idea what would become of him if his awareness cleaved permanently asunder. He had to do this quickly.

Sai's spirit was like a slow, playful wind, warm and redolent of tropical fruit and the sea. Yarrow perceived it as a pure, amber light unblemished by anything dark. With one eye still on his companion, Yarrow latched onto it and let it tow him into Sai's dream.

The Emiri captain's fantasy was as vibrant and unsullied as a child's drawing of a beach done all in primary colors. Sai lay naked in the sand beneath a bright yellow sun. Water so blue it almost hurt Yarrow's eyes rolled gently up the sand to lick at his feet and ankles. Kin and Toumo dozed at Sai's right side, while a nude imitation of himself with long, white ropes of hair and a few interesting additions to his paint lay perpendicular to Sai, the other Yarrow's sleeping face pressed against Sai's warm, flat belly. Farther up the shore, Izu, Lala, and Yei hunted for shells. A basket overflowing with fruit sat nearby along with a jug of *muri-ku* and a huge chest of gold coins.

Yarrow spared a fraction of a second to wonder what it might be like for one's life to mirror one's fondest dream so closely. Other than the addition of Yarrow, Sai's days passed very similar to his fantasy. Yarrow said his name, hoping to rouse him from the illusion.

Sai petted the false Yarrow's cheek and spoke without opening his eyes. "What did you say, *syrai*?"

"Nothing." The dream-Yarrow grazed Sai's ribs with his fingertips, making Sai giggle.

As he looked down at the languid, brown bodies with their limbs tangled like old fishing line, Yarrow felt the presence testing its bonds, finding them weaker....

"Damn it, Sai! Listen to me! You have to wake up and snap out of this!"

Sai lifted his head and looked around. His gaze settled on Yarrow, and he squinted and furrowed his brow, but in a few seconds, he lay down to return to his nap. He couldn't see Yarrow.

Performing a delicate balancing act, Yarrow stole a few droplets of concentration from the part of him guarding the presence and let them fall, a drop at a time, into the phantom form standing on the beach. He looked down at his hands as they solidified and grew denser in color. Yarrow still saw the waves breaking on the beach through his ghostlike fingers, but he couldn't divert any more of his attention from the creature or it would break through and take his body. Its first act would probably be to violate and kill Sai while he slumbered. Hoping he had enough energy to insinuate himself into this reality, Yarrow yelled, "Sai!"

Thunder tumbled in the distance, and dark clouds spilled across the sky. Frightened, Sai sat up and brushed sand from his back, looking up and down the beach with wide eyes. Yarrow knelt and tried to grasp his shoulders, to shake him out of his fugue, but his hands moved through Sai's flesh. "Look at me, Sai! You have to see me. Damn it. Look from the corner of your eye."

Yarrow didn't know if Sai heard him, but the Emiri canted his head and let his hair fall into his face. With a yelp, he scuttled backward and stumbled to his feet, knees shaking as he looked from the Yarrow drowsing on the shore to the Yarrow standing in front of him.

"What in the name of Emir's swollen tits?"

"Calm down, Sai. You're dreaming. We sailed into a spell." Yarrow swept his hand along the horizon and over the reclining, naked bodies. "None of this is real. You must realize that."

Taking a few steps back, Sai jabbed his finger at Yarrow. For the first time, Yarrow saw him angry and afraid. "I think you're the one who isn't real. You're some foul enchantment sent by a sea witch to deceive me. Get out of here!"

"Sai, you must believe me." At the other end of his consciousness, Yarrow felt the creature butting hard against the barrier keeping it in check, almost able to shoulder through. He spared a sprinkle of energy on stopping it, but it cost him.

"Believe you? You're already fading away. Nothing but an evil trick."

"This isn't real!" Yarrow screamed until his voice split.

"Nothing here seems especially miraculous," Sai said, looking at the beach and the friends he'd known for so many years. His ship was festooned about a quarter mile to the east, the bright sails billowing in the wind.

Yarrow couldn't keep this up. Within seconds, his creature would break free if he didn't focus on subduing it. But that would mean leaving Sai here, never to awaken in the real world. He had to make a choice: let Sai die here in his delusion, or awaken him to be ripped to tatters by a monster. Yarrow just couldn't focus on both points anymore. Then something occurred to him, and he tilted his head toward the version of himself stretched out on the sparkling sand.

"This isn't real because I'm here with you," Yarrow said, ashamed at the pain growing in Sai's orange eyes. "I would never leave Sasha and Duncan for you, and in your heart you know it."

Sai's heart shattered like delicate glass struck by a thrown rock; Yarrow saw it on his face. Only seconds after the cold, cruel words left Yarrow's mouth, Sai's paradise crumpled in on itself and faded like the stars at dawn.

Yarrow lifted his aching face from the fog-bloated boards of the deck. His head throbbed, and blood poured from his nose and dripped off his chin. All his bones felt broken, ground to powder, his muscles torn as if he'd spent hours on the rack. He didn't try to stand; he knew he couldn't do it for at least a few more minutes, but he struggled to focus his blurred vision and locate Sai. The young Emiri sat a few feet away, hugging his knees to his chest, a haunted expression on his face. Yarrow wanted to say something to comfort him, but he didn't have the strength. He let his head drop and rolled to his back. A fair wind swept away the thin shroud of fog still spread across the sky. Warm sunlight kissed Yarrow's face, and he managed a wan smile.

Still think me so simple and pathetic, creature? Yarrow couldn't resist a bit of boasting.

That... was an impressive bit of magic. It didn't tease him. It was impressed—and afraid. *I don't know if my first beloved could have managed that. And you did it without my assistance.*

Ha! I did it with you working against me.

It was risky, though, little flower. You could have severed your spirit permanently.

Don't call me that. Besides, I didn't. I'm too competent a mage to let that happen. I'm a great mage, the greatest born in generations. Everyone says so.

Is there a point behind this shameless bragging, beloved? Are you still trying to convince yourself of your worth? It's a sad thing to witness.

I just want you to know I'm going to beat you.

Chapter Twelve

On the last day of Myint's Moon, every fortress, keep, and military outpost held a feast in honor of its knights and soldiers to thank them for their service and honor the goddess who protected them. Duncan had spent the past few days preparing for the festivities: directing the kitchen staff, scheduling the parades, and speaking with the priestesses who would perform the blessings. Incense was scheduled to arrive later that afternoon. His mood had inflated greatly after the treasonous aristocrats had been dealt with and he and Sasha had reached an understanding, and Duncan actually enjoyed the frivolous tasks he performed. He whistled a battle hymn as he knelt to unfurl one of the musty Windwake banners brought out just for this celebration.

The clamor of armored boots against stone made Duncan lift his head from the bundles of faded black and gold cloth. He smiled when Tam Allwynn entered the courtyard, and he raised a hand still holding dusty fabric in greeting. "Good man, Allwynn. Help me sort these out."

"I've actually come to deliver news, Bairn Duncan."

"No need for titles, Allwynn. As far as I'm concerned, we're both just simple, fighting men."

"Yes, tam. I must inform you of a rather grievous incident."

"Yes?" Duncan got to his feet, his skin tingling with the premonition of bad news.

Allwynn ran his fingers down one of the plaits in his beard and wouldn't meet Duncan's gaze. "Three nights ago, tam, on the outskirts of your bairny, Tam Fennsour was found murdered in his room at a small inn."

Duncan's blood turned to ice, cementing him where he stood. "How?"

"His throat was cut. I was told it was very clean, very... *professional.*"

"A robbery?" Duncan choked out.

Allwynn deflated with his sigh. "We're soldiers, just like you said, tam, and I'm not going to insult you by giving you some candied version of the truth. Not when we both know what likely happened. Fennsour might have deserved it, but even so—"

Duncan had never suffered from a quick temper. Even on the battlefield, he took no pleasure in bringing pain and death to his enemies. He'd always seen his role as knight as a protector of the farmers, bakers, and seamstresses who couldn't bear arms themselves. A rare rage now coursed through Duncan's veins, making his balled fists vibrate. "Where is he?"

Goddesses bless him, Allwynn didn't pretend not to know who Duncan wanted to find. "I last saw him practicing in the field beyond the stables."

Duncan clasped his seneschal's hand as he stomped past. "Thank you, my friend. Go back to your duties. I'll see to this."

"Tam, I think it might be wise for me and a few of the boys to come with you."

"No," Duncan growled. "It's time I claimed responsibility for all of this."

"But your safety—"

"Do as I say, Tam Allwynn."

"Yes, my lord." The seneschal bowed, turned on his heel, and departed.

Duncan wanted to turn his face toward the sky and scream. He couldn't remember the last time he'd been so angry. Instead, he ground his teeth as he took a few deep breaths through his nose to calm himself enough to walk to the practice ring.

Every step he took across the rocky terrain of Windwake fueled Duncan's ire. By the time he reached the small field lined with a simple, wooden fence, he felt as ready to explode as a pool of pitch touched by a spark. The bastard had looked in his eyes and promised him....

Sasha stood in the middle of a circle of trampled, yellow grass, wearing snug black trousers and a too-large white shirt he'd probably taken from Duncan's armoire. The leather straps crisscrossing his chest barely kept it from falling off. Even enveloped by his cloud of outrage, Duncan marveled at the assassin's fluidity of movement as he launched his throwing daggers at the three bales of straw surrounding him. Each of the knives imbedded at the center of a bale. Goddesses, the slight little Cast-Down was fast.

"Good morning, Duncan," Sasha said as he went to pull his daggers free from the targets.

"How did you know it was me?"

Sasha finally faced him, holding his right hand up, a razor-sharp knife glinting from between each of his fingers. "I recognize the sound of your steps. You have always had the tiniest limp in your left leg, especially when the weather's on the change. Don't worry. No one else can tell."

An icy trickle of fear combined with the heat of Duncan's smoldering anger; goddesses, Sasha identified the rhythm of him walking, and across a field. The two of them stood regarding each other across a few dozen feet of wind-beaten sward, neither speaking, neither moving except for their hair fluttering in the breeze. Sasha offered Duncan a meaningless smile and put on a pretty mask, just as he had when he'd made his promise to Duncan while he murdered Tam Fennsour in his mind. What kind of fool did he think Duncan was, the arrogant, duplicitous little bastard, to think his false-friendly expression would dupe Duncan a second time?

Duncan grew angry beyond articulation, balled his fists, and closed the distance between them at a jog. He just wanted to swat away the lie Sasha wore on his face with the back of his hand. Instead, he restrained himself and seized Sasha by the front of his baggy shirt, lifting the smaller man off his feet for a second before shoving him so hard even Sasha's grace faltered, and he staggered back a few steps. When he regained his balance, Sasha stayed slightly crouched, his legs spread wide and his knives still in his hand. His face expressed the antithesis of Duncan's burning rage; Sasha's features went blank and as cold as one of the ice fields beyond Starmont that hadn't thawed in a thousand years. Only the slight arch of a slender dark brow in challenge betrayed any emotion at all.

While part of Duncan's mind told him to be afraid, his anger shouted over the small voice and obliterated it. He held his arms out to his sides and puffed his chest out, exposing his heart. "Go on," he yelled. "Are you going to kill me too?"

"If I'd wanted you dead, I'd have simply turned my back and let someone else do the heavy lifting."

Sasha's tone, devoid of anything but mockery, incensed Duncan more than his words. "You think too highly of yourself, assassin. As if you alone can protect me! Do you think I'm helpless?"

"Just blind and deluded."

Before he knew what he was doing, Duncan drove the heel of his hand into Sasha's shoulder, shoving him back several feet. He stopped himself just before swinging his fist at Sasha's defiantly raised chin. His entire body trembled with rage, and he spoke through tightly clenched teeth. "You promised me, and you lied. You looked me right in the eye and lied to me."

Sasha shrugged without uncoiling muscles wound tight and ready to strike. "It was necessary. Fennsour was too much of a threat."

Duncan shoved him again, satisfied when he saw Sasha's frozen façade splinter and a hot vein of anger bubble to the surface. "That is not for you to decide. *I* am bairn of Windwake. We have laws here, and you will abide by them the same as anyone else."

"I am not the same as anyone else! I'm Crimson Scythe, and I am outside your ridiculous rules."

"Damn you, and damn that foul order of yours to the Shades' Abode! You are not a part of that any longer!" Duncan grabbed Sasha's wrist and dug his nails into the flesh, feeling the delicate bones grind together in his large fist.

"I'll tell you one time to let go of me, Duncan."

"And then what?" Squeezing harder, Duncan dragged Sasha closer and twisted his arm, wanting to hurt him as he'd hurt Duncan with his betrayal, wanting to make him show some trace of humanity.

Sasha set his features in a stony expression as he spun out of Duncan's grip and kicked at Duncan's shin's in a single smooth motion. Duncan, his legs swept out from under him, landed hard on his ass, his teeth knocking together. Sasha flicked his wrist, and his daggers sailed toward Duncan, one embedding in the ground on either side of him and the third sticking between his legs, only inches from his groin. Sasha straightened and sneered down at Duncan, as if they'd settled the matter.

Duncan didn't agree. "You need to learn some decency. Some damned respect!" He swung at Sasha's waist with all his considerable might, but Sasha stepped nimbly to the side and avoided the worst of it. Still, Duncan felt his knuckles brush across the rungs of Sasha's ribs, and the assassin winced and clutched his side, giving Duncan enough time to get back on his feet.

"What exactly am I expected to respect?" Sasha asked, circling around Duncan with wide steps, placing one foot behind the other and lowering his shoulders.

"Me!" Duncan roared, punching his fist against his chest. "You claim to care for me. Do you feel nothing when you tell a bold-faced lie right to my face?"

"I don't feel," Sasha said with maddening calm. "I think. You should try it. And if you *think* you can teach me to be other than what I am, Duncan, I invite you to try. It's been a long time coming."

"Very true words. For once. Time for you to learn that those serpents of your order aren't the only ones who can fight. A man who wields his sword with honor always has the upper hand."

"You have no sword, friend," Sasha hissed. "And you talk too much."

Neither of them said much after that. Duncan realized he was unarmed, and Sasha almost certainly wasn't. He could only be sure Sasha concealed no weapons when the assassin was completely naked. The risk that Sasha might produce a poisoned dagger from somewhere didn't quell Duncan's righteous anger. He drew back and aimed a roundhouse at Sasha's sneering face. The assassin raised his forearm to shield himself, but the force of Duncan's blow drove Sasha's arm into his lips and knocked him back. He snarled at Duncan, revealing teeth coated in blood. A crimson rivulet dripped from the corner of his mouth and stained his white shirt.

Part of Duncan hoped maybe Sasha had had enough, but another part still had anger to take out on the assassin. To be honest, a pool of resentment had been building up in Duncan for a long time, and now that he'd let it surface, he couldn't dam the torrent. "I have gone out of my way to trust you and accept you when any sane man would have turned away! Look how you repay me!"

"I have saved your life many times over!" Sasha swatted Duncan's hand away when Duncan tried to land another punch. He smashed his fist into Duncan's jaw, making Duncan bite his tongue.

Duncan spat frothy blood on the ground. "And I have saved yours! I don't use it as an excuse to lie to you or hold it dangling over your head!" He tried to catch Sasha's hand, but the assassin was faster than any warrior Duncan had ever seen or faced, and he aimed a series of quick jabs at Duncan, connecting at Duncan's diaphragm, ribs, and lower belly. When Duncan doubled over, Sasha moved behind him in a blur, grabbed Duncan's ponytail, and wrenched his head back. He dragged his nails down Duncan's stretched neck.

Blood spattered Duncan's face as Sasha spoke an inch from his cheek. "I could cut your throat right now if I wanted to."

Duncan slammed his elbow into Sasha's ribs and knocked him into the air. Miraculously, Sasha managed to land on his feet and skid backward, tearing up the grass with his boots. "You're overconfident," Duncan said as he turned on his heels and raised his fists.

With an agile leap, Sasha closed the distance between them and brought the side of his hand down toward Duncan's collarbone. When Duncan raised his arm to protect himself, Sasha drove his knee into Duncan's side. Duncan grunted and gasped for breath.

Sasha, also panting and holding his ribs, backed a few steps away from Duncan. "How… how can you just wander contentedly through life when you're surrounded by threats? How have you remained so hopeful after everything that's happened?"

"Because… because I thought I could trust *you*."

His words gave Sasha pause, and a shadow of regret flitted across his face, but it passed over as quickly as it had appeared, and Duncan couldn't be sure he'd seen it at all. Seconds later, they were trading blows again, each of them landing a hit now and then but mostly blocking and dodging each other. Despite Duncan's years of experience, superior strength, and size, Sasha's speed and the intensive training he'd received from childhood made them almost evenly matched. Duncan couldn't remember the last time he'd faced an opponent who presented him with such a challenge. They fought on and on, Sasha employing his misleading, acrobatic style and Duncan countering with the solid techniques he'd perfected over twenty years on the battlefield.

With a painful stitch in his side, Duncan panted and held his bruised ribs, scraped, swollen, bloody, and aching all over. He wasn't as young as he used to be, and his muscles quavered with exertion. It took every scrap of discipline he owned to lift his arm and deflect the kick Sasha aimed at the center of his chest. Swiping the side of his fist against Sasha's knee, Duncan managed to send the assassin sprawling on his side. He lunged for Sasha, but the quicker man tucked into a roll and avoided his grasp.

Sasha was slowing with fatigue and heaving for breath, but he arched his back off the ground and landed on his feet in a graceful arc. Almost instantly, his foot stretched out behind him and his front knee bent in a fighting stance. Duncan understood; their brawl wouldn't conclude until one of them proved superior. Most of Duncan's anger had drained away with his exhaustion, but he still had his pride to defend. He didn't intend to lose to a whelp of an assassin, not even one he desperately loved.

Duncan watched Sasha's black eyes. He'd seen his partner fight enough to know at this stage, hurt, drained, and in danger of failure, Sasha would resort to some sort of ruse. Though he hated to admit it, Duncan didn't have much left, and he needed to bring this skirmish to a hasty end.

"What… what's wrong? Tired out?" The words left Sasha's throat as if he'd coughed up broken glass. A dark bruise painted his high cheekbone, and strands of dried blood flaked from his sweaty skin at a variety of intersecting angles. Even so, the assassin's stance was solid, and his shrewd gaze trailed Duncan's every twitch.

"Wishes won't win this for you, assassin." Duncan forced his voice to remain steady and strong as he lifted his fists. Sasha sprinted toward him with long, bouncy strides, pushing off with his back foot just before he reached Duncan. He twisted in the air and aimed both of his heels at Duncan's chest. Duncan waited until the last possible second, then dropped into a crouch, and Sasha sailed over his head.

With a soft rustle of grass, Sasha landed lightly behind Duncan. Duncan knew Sasha wouldn't be able to resist flanking him, so instead of turning, he clasped his knee and pretended to gasp for air, all the while listening to Sasha's approaching footsteps and watching the shadow he cast draw closer. As soon as Sasha grabbed for Duncan's throat, Duncan reached behind himself, clasped the back of Sasha's neck, tucked his head, and flipped Sasha over his shoulder. Sasha's back hit the ground hard, the wind slapped from his chest. Before he could recover, Duncan straddled him and pressed his wrists against the shredded lawn. While extraordinarily skilled, Sasha couldn't compete with Duncan's strength, no matter how much he struggled and writhed.

"Do you yield, Sasha?" Duncan asked, looking down at his partner's flushed, sweaty face, dilated eyes, and parted, crimson-stained lips, swollen even fuller than usual. Gripped by a sudden and irresistible urge, Duncan leaned down and kissed him hard, tasting fresh blood as their tongues sparred and their teeth bumped together. When he pulled away, both of them panted harder than when they'd been fighting. "Sasha... do you yield? Admit you're fairly bested."

Sasha circled his hips beneath Duncan, his excitement obvious through the simple trousers they both wore. "What will you do if I won't?"

Duncan kissed him again, the taste of their mingled blood more intoxicating than the strongest spirits. "I'll have to find some other way to subdue you, you little nightmare."

Sasha chuckled, and the vibration of his lust-laden laughter moved across the root of Duncan's body and up his spine, making him growl with need. He pressed his injured mouth against Sasha's, and Sasha held his lower lip between his teeth. As senselessly aroused as he was with the mélange of battle lust, desire for Sasha, and the heightened sensitivity he always felt during and after fighting, Duncan hardly noticed the pain. He did notice when Sasha's laughter faded abruptly, and he sat up to look down at his assassin's serious face.

"Duncan, I do respect you. I always have, but even more after today. I knew you were a talented warrior, but—"

"So you'll yield?" Duncan released one of Sasha's hands to run his rough and battered fingers along the contours of Sasha's beautiful face, a face left split and swollen by Duncan's fists.

"I didn't say that, Tam Knight. Maybe you'll yield this time. Let's go back to the castle, and I'll show you what I mean, if you fail to grasp it."

"I'm no fool, assassin." The possibilities in Sasha's suggestion crystallized in Duncan's imagination, and his already hard cock felt ready to split in two. "And I'm also too tired to carry you all the way back to the castle."

"Carry me—?"

Duncan stood and scooped Sasha into his arms, cutting him off. As he held Sasha's head against his shoulder and supported Sasha's knees with his other arm, he stopped his assassin's wiggling and protesting by kissing him as they crossed the practice field. When they reached a small shed that held spare swords, bows, arrows, targets, and scraps of leather armor for the most novice fighters, Duncan kicked the wooden door open without lifting his face from Sasha's.

THE little room smelled strongly of leather, horses, steel, and sweet summer straw. Sasha had relaxed in Duncan's strong arms by the time they entered, his affront at being carried like a woman ebbing with the growth of his lust. Duncan lowered him gently onto a heap of fleece saddle blankets before barring the door from the inside with a board. Then he knelt down, spread Sasha's legs wide, and slid between them.

"Since you've already spoiled my shirt, assassin…." By the Cast-Down, the way Duncan said "assassin," drawing out the S's into an expectant sigh….

Duncan grasped the loose linen shift Sasha had taken from his room and tore it open. Buttons carved from twirl horn bone flew in every direction and got lost among the heaps of straw. Then he quickly unbuckled the leather straps holding Sasha's knives and pushed them off Sasha's shoulders and chest.

Sasha sunk into the horsehair-coated blankets and curled his body up against Duncan's warm lips as he explored Sasha's neck, chest, waist and belly. The scent of their sweat, blood, and arousal drowned the other fragrances, and it acted as an inebriating perfume to Sasha. He burrowed his fingers into Duncan's damp, disheveled hair and guided his knight's head down past his belly button. By Thalil, Duncan's rough whiskers felt exquisite against Sasha's smooth-shorn stomach.

Duncan grasped the waistband of Sasha's trousers with his teeth and tugged it past Sasha's engorged, leaking cock. Cast-Down help him, Sasha almost came when Duncan dragged his battle-worn lips up his length and around his crown. He grasped Duncan's shoulder and pushed him away.

"No."

"Sasha, I want to touch you, taste you…."

Sasha wrapped his legs, hampered by his halfway-down trousers, around Duncan's hips and held Duncan firmly as he rolled so Duncan lay beneath him. He looked down at Duncan's blood-spattered, grass-stained shift and said, "This shirt is ruined too. Take it off."

Duncan stretched his arms over his head to help Sasha peel the soiled garment away. Sasha flung it aside, eager to bury his fingers in the soft hair decorating Duncan's chest. He ran his thumbs over Duncan's tiny, firm nipples and earned a pleased shudder from the man beneath him. And what a man—he'd bested a Crimson Scythe assassin whether Sasha would admit it aloud or not. He was a man worthy of Sasha's body, his submission, but Sasha didn't want to be the passive party today. He wriggled his thumbs beneath the waistband of Duncan's trousers and whisked them down until his own legs stopped him.

"Stay there," Sasha said as he stood to disrobe. "And don't tell me not to order you. I'm ordering you, Duncan, and I want you to do as I say."

Duncan looked up at him, his bloody, swollen face absolutely trusting. Bruises edged his waist and spread across his chest, inflicted by Sasha as they'd scuffled. The memory of their battle ignited Sasha's blood; it had been like an erotic dance to him, power exchanged back and forth, surrendered and won. He'd been aroused from the first meeting of their fists, and now he wanted to complete what they'd instigated.

After he stripped his filthy clothing away, Sasha knelt to pull Duncan's boots off and slide his trousers down his thick, muscular legs. Duncan lay still and allowed Sasha to slowly undress him. Afterward, he remained complacent as Sasha ran his fingertips and nails along Duncan's ribs and then up the beautiful, taut muscles of his arms. Gooseflesh followed the path of his nails, and Sasha bent down to feel that dimpled flesh against his lips, loving the way his lightest touch could subdue his powerful partner. As he ran his tongue along Duncan's bicep and over the globe of his shoulder to nip at the side of his neck, Sasha hooked his hands under Duncan's knees to bend and spread his legs. He thrust a few times against Duncan's belly, and Duncan pushed back against him with a groan.

Duncan ran his rough hands down Sasha's back, cupped his ass, and pulled Sasha hard against him. Delightful heat wafted off him, especially from his proffered ass. "Get on with it, Sasha."

"I'll give the orders," Sasha said. He wanted to drag it out, to show Duncan he was in control and would set his own pace, but he just couldn't wait. Strains of battle lust still echoed in his blood and beat out a steady tattoo in his head. With a low growl, he sunk his teeth into Duncan's dense muscle and stretched his legs even wider.

Duncan made a sound between a shout and a squeal, arching his back off the blankets and almost throwing Sasha aside. Sasha tightened his grip on Duncan's legs to hold him down. "Stay still."

"I can't." Duncan circled his hips, jabbing his erection into Sasha's belly and leaving a slick trail. He already started to shudder, and his breath hitched as his eyes rolled back.

"Oh no you don't," Sasha said, pulling away and breaking the contact between them. "You're not coming till I'm inside you." He gripped his cock at the base, thumbed his foreskin back, and rubbed his moist crown in circles around Duncan's opening. He, too, felt extra sensitive and acute, his mind and body still in fighting mode, and he closed his eyes as he enjoyed the contact. Sasha couldn't help pressing forward against the resistance of those tight muscles.

Duncan gasped, and Sasha looked down at his wide eyes and trembling lips. He was worried, and Sasha felt a shimmer of shame. Duncan thought Sasha was going to harm him in a selfish pursuit of his own satisfaction. "I'm not going to hurt you." He leaned down to kiss Duncan, but the gentle reassurance he'd intended soon turned to nibbling, slurping passion. In moments, they were grinding against each other again, both of them ready to tumble into release.

Sasha broke away, his lips aching and his cock throbbing with his pulse. On a shelf near a weapon rack sat a little ceramic pot of leather polish made from arn-nut oil, beeswax, and windblossom nectar. Sasha reached for it and dug his fingers into the thick paste. It softened as he rubbed it between Duncan's cheeks. He circled Duncan's opening, and it twitched at his touch.

"Relax," Sasha whispered. He thrust in to the hilt; he couldn't stop himself. Duncan cried out, and Sasha threw his head back and matched his shout of pleasure as Duncan's heat and pressure enveloped him. Sasha curled his fingers around Duncan's shoulders as his body moved independently of his will, his hips snapping back and forth with increasing need.

"Goddesses," Duncan panted, splaying one leg out beside him and hooking the other over Sasha's shoulder. A shadow of pain drifted behind his eyes even as he pushed back against Sasha and rolled Sasha's nipple between his thumb and finger.

Sasha didn't want to hurt Duncan, but he didn't want to—he couldn't—stop. "Duncan," he grunted, all rational thought abandoning him, "Duncan, good?"

"Don't stop, love. Oh, Sasha. More."

Free from worry, Sasha kissed Duncan hard and gave into everything his body demanded, thrusting hard and deep into the man he loved. Both of them groaned, groped each other, and cried out as their skin smacked together. Duncan seized Sasha's waist, pressing into freshly bruised ribs and making Sasha whimper.

"Goddesses, I'm sorry," Duncan said, going still.

"Thalil, I wouldn't care if you broke one of my bones right now," Sasha said, resting his forehead against his partner's and raking his fingers through Duncan's whiskers. "I—"

"Tell me." Duncan covered Sasha's hips with his big hands, encouraging Sasha to keep moving.

"I—Cast-Down, Duncan, I'm going to come! Come with me." He grasped Duncan's cock and jerked it with short, quick strokes, twisting his fist over the head. Their mouths met, opened, and they swallowed each other's cries as they fell apart against each other until Sasha's body felt like a pool of warm liquid spread atop Duncan, held together only by Duncan's strong arms around him.

They separated, and Sasha flopped on his back, coated in sweat and still trembling. As he drifted down from the heights of ecstasy, he turned to Duncan and propped his head up on his hand. "I didn't hurt you, did I?"

Duncan chuckled. Sasha would never get tired of that warm, honest sound. "Insecure, assassin?"

Sasha grinned and arched a brow.

"All right. I admit it; I'll be tender at the ceremony tonight. I don't care. It was wonderful; you were wonderful. I love you. I might add that that was hardly the performance of a man who values intellect over emotion. Tell me again how you don't feel anything."

Sasha balled his fist around the equine-scented blankets, a ripple of his earlier annoyance shattering his contentment. "I killed Fennsour because I love you!" he blurted before he considered his words.

"Peace, friend. I know. That's why I can't stay angry. But I need a partner, Sasha. A man I can trust, one who shares his plans with me, finds me worthy of his secrets. Tell me we're in this together. I… can only forgive the deception this last time. There will be repercussions from what you've done, but I'll deal with them somehow. But I need to know where we stand."

"You cannot ask me not to protect you when you're threatened!"

"I ask only that we face threats together. I love you, Sasha. Tell me you'll try."

Duncan looked up at him with his heart completely exposed, more vulnerable than he'd been standing unarmed before Sasha's knives. Sasha didn't think he'd ever find that particular form of courage in himself, and he couldn't shatter it in Duncan. If he wished it, Sasha knew he could destroy Duncan with a word. He spoke very carefully. "I'll do everything I can not to deceive you again, but I am what I am, and I'd rather have you drive me away than stand by while something happens to you. Standing idle while you face danger is not something I'll ever be able to do. I hope you can try to understand."

Gathering Sasha into his arms and resting his chin on top of Sasha's head, Duncan said, "Drive you away. I'd rather die than lose you, too. But enough of this. I have to clean up your mess, after all. We should get back to the castle. And Sasha, perhaps you shouldn't attend the festival tonight. Do you agree?"

Sasha nestled against Duncan's neck and closed his eyes. "It will be a prime opportunity for an attack, with all the knights and soldiers drunk and carousing. The chaos could tempt a traitor, or it could coax my brethren. Now, I'll tell you anything you like about what I plan to do, but I'll still do it. I won't be seen. Does that explanation satisfy you?"

Though he said nothing, Duncan hugged Sasha tighter and held him until he absolutely had to let him go.

Chapter
Thirteen

THE strong breeze coming from the south finally whisked away the thin mantle of mist hovering over the surface of the water. Sai steered his vessel clear of the last of the haze and left the helm after many hours. He crossed the deck and stood next to Yarrow in the shade of the aft sails. They hadn't said a word to each other since waking from their trance.

Sai met Yarrow's gaze. Emiri eyes were so different from those of Yarrow's people: large, luminous, and sparkling like jewels in shades of crimson, orange, and gold. Yarrow could have lost himself for hours in the flecks of pigment in Sai's brilliant irises, had he not seen an uncharacteristic darkness behind them.

"You're troubled," Yarrow observed.

"Not as troubled, I think, as you, *syrai*. You left a little of yourself behind in my head, just a ripple from the wake of a ship long passed, but it is a foreboding current. I had no idea the depths of your pain."

"I'm sorry."

Sai shook his head, making the small shells and clay beads in his hair rattle softly. "I'm not looking for an apology. You're hurting, and you're my *syrai*. I want to help you even more."

Yarrow blinked his stinging eyes and wondered how he always found his way to wonderful people he didn't deserve. The presence within him howled with laughter and tormented him for sentimentality. For some reason, the creature hated Sai even more than it hated Sasha and Duncan. It wished him harm with every ethereal spark of its being. Yarrow decided that as soon as they reached Hale's island, he'd send Sai away, even if it meant finding his own way home.

I know you won't let me starve.

Perhaps, perhaps not. I will let you suffer, beloved. Pain is just another level of sensation to me. It might be entertaining to watch you grow so hungry you chew the meat from your own fingers.

"Look there!" Sai touched Yarrow lightly on the bare shoulder and pointed at the horizon.

Yarrow squinted in an attempt to see what excited Sai so much, but he found nothing but blue sky and water for as far as he could see. "What is it?"

"You can't see that vast expanse of land?" Sai asked. He took a distance glass from a pouch tied to his belt and handed it to Yarrow.

Looking through the leather tube and the lens at the end, Yarrow discerned a blurry brown line far in the distance. "Goddesses, the island? We actually made it?"

"You doubted it? I'm actually a rather passable sailor, *syrai*."

"You're brilliant." Yarrow hugged Sai and lifted him off his feet, twirling him around before setting him back down on the deck. "When will we reach it?"

Sai, still encircling Yarrow's waist with his arms, shrugged and smiled. "By nightfall or not long after. Which leaves us with several hours to spend at our leisure."

"Sai—"

The Emiri captain released Yarrow and stepped away. "I'm sorry. I'm just used to the companionship of my *syrai*. I'm not used to being without it, and it's no secret I find you alluring. I said I wouldn't tempt you, though."

Yarrow, already hard, his neglected needs crying out for fulfillment, had to turn away. "You tempt me just by existing, but I… I cannot."

"I know, Yarrow. Come on. At least have a drink of *muri-ku*. We've done the impossible. We deserve at least a small reward."

"All right," Yarrow conceded. "One, and no more."

True to Sai's prediction, the small vessel reached the shore of the island at twilight. Sai maneuvered his boat within a half mile of the beach and moored it in the calm water. "Should we expect opposition?" he asked, sliding into his tiny vest and then strapping one of the curved swords his people favored to his hip.

"I don't know," Yarrow answered honestly. "I suppose we should be ready for anything. Who knows how long it's been since anyone has set foot on these shores."

"That entices me," Sai said. "Come on. You're a strong enough swimmer that we shouldn't need the dinghy."

Both of them dove into the water and swam, Sai reaching the coast well before Yarrow. He helped Yarrow over the smooth stones, and Yarrow pushed his heavy ropes of hair out of his eyes.

The island looked bleak and desolate beneath the silvery light of the moon and stars. Reaching out with his senses, Yarrow sensed no threat. In truth, he sensed nothing, not even the faint life pulse of a small animal. Though the rock jutted up into impressive mountains, he felt no energy from the twisted trees and gnarled brush growing along the slopes.

"Sai, stop. Something is wrong."

"*Syrai?*"

Yarrow shushed him and stepped in front of him as he wandered a little way inland, up a path that wound between the rocks. As his eyes adjusted to the light, he kept expecting to see or hear something: a bird call, a crab scuttling over the gravel, even an insect, but there was nothing. He'd been in many wild and desolate places, but never one absent of even vegetation. It wasn't natural.

"What was it you hoped to find here, Yarrow?" Sai asked. "It's strange to see such a large island so completely abandoned."

"There must be something," Yarrow said, trying to ignore the dread settling heavily in his belly. "Let's keep going."

You've made a mistake, beloved. There's nothing here. You should have listened to me.

Yarrow ignored it as he and Sai ascended the winding little trails. If it was right, he'd be back where he started, with no compass to point him to a way to get rid of the creature. He couldn't return to Espero after the chaos he'd caused. Where would he begin if this one glimmer of hope he'd found turned out to be an illusion?

Give it up, Yarrow. I'm not going anywhere.

The farther they walked, past gnarled, leafless trees that looked scorched, the blacker Yarrow's mood became. After traveling for hours, they came to a precipice from which they could see for miles, and they saw more of the same. Sai sat down on a large rock and rubbed his thighs.

"It isn't possible," Yarrow said. "There would be something, a mushroom, at least. I wonder if magic could do this."

"We should go," Sai said. "There's nothing here, and this place makes me feel very uncomfortable."

What terrible power could do this to an entire island? Have you ever seen anything like this?

Why would I tell you if I had? I'm not helping you, the creature said.

"Yarrow, I'd like to leave," Sai said again.

"Give me just a few more minutes." Anything that had been touched by magic, especially magic this tremendous, would bear a mark, much like the grooves stonecutters left on building blocks for castle walls. Yarrow closed his eyes and mentally ran his fingers over the essence of the island, feeling for the furrows and ridges. The caster had been very adept, though, and left his creation polished almost to perfection. Almost.

Yarrow sensed the tiniest resonance of an old, old spell. It was subtle, complex, and beautiful. He'd never witnessed anything so delicate or precise. As he studied the enchantment, turning it over to see it from every angle, he realized it hadn't been created to syphon life or prevent growth.

"This is an illusion," he said in a voice soft with awe. "A cloth thrown over the whole island to hide something underneath."

"No, *syrai,*" Sai said as he reached over and snapped off a blackened branch. "This isn't just something we're seeing. We can hold it in our hands."

Yarrow considered, making connections and getting excited. "Yes, and weren't you sure, while you were dreaming, that you could feel the sand beneath you? Couldn't you reach down and squeeze someone's shoulder?"

"Yours," Sai said wistfully.

"I think whoever cast that fog did this as well," Yarrow told him. "Every spell a mage casts bears a little hint of him, a signature, almost. What would he go to such lengths to hide? Do you want to find out, Sai? If you'd rather go, I understand, but I'm going to try to break this."

"Maroon you here to starve to death?" Sai asked incredulously.

"This might be hard to believe, but I won't die. I just can't go until I at least try. This is the only chance I have."

Sai squeezed Yarrow's hand. "You weren't doing so well after you broke that last spell. It worries me."

"I promise I'll be fine." Yarrow stroked Sai's cheek with the back of his hand before finding a patch free of sharp gravel and desiccated bracken where he could rest his back against a stone. He was in for a long night. This enchantment had been in place for a long, long time, and it had taken root in the bones of the island. Yanking it up would be no small feat, and Yarrow hadn't completely recovered from his previous exertion. But giving up now would mean giving up any chance of a future with Sasha and Duncan and any chance of a life free from the thing's influence. It would mean a life alone.

Yarrow took a deep breath and tried to release some of the tension in his neck and shoulders. The shroud covering the island was vast, and Yarrow had no choice but to pick it apart thread by thread. Worse yet, he soon discovered that when he pulled a string loose, the mystic fabric compensated and wove back together. He had to burn it off at the seams behind him every step of the way.

After experimenting with several different techniques, Yarrow found the magical blue flame that had always come so easily to him effectively stopped the illusion from weaving itself back together. A filament at a time, Yarrow drew the threads of the spell toward him and incinerated them. The more he unraveled, the more elaborate he found the tapestry. He had no choice but to be patient and diligent and pick it apart meticulously. Now and then fortune favored him and his mystic flames managed to travel along the cords of the enchantment and dissolve an entire patch, but mostly he worked thread by thread. The few times Yarrow opened his eyes, he saw a shimmering, cerulean web extending from his fingertips, draped over the black island stone, sizzling slightly as the two enchantments battled for supremacy.

As deep as they ran, Yarrow had almost depleted his wells of arcane energy by the time he finished. Slowly, he remembered he had limbs and felt solidity returning to them. He felt the ground beneath his numb, tingling backside and legs, the heat of the sun on his face and shoulders. He flexed his fingers just to make sure he had control of them, and the small gesture exhausted him. He opened his eyes and squinted at the intense, late-morning light.

Sai lay a few feet to Yarrow's left, curled on his side in a patch of high, wind-strewn grass, sleeping peacefully with his hair fanned out around him. The sight of lush, green vegetation where there had been only parched soil before should have surprised Yarrow, but he was so tired he couldn't really consider the implications. In fact, Yarrow knew if he didn't lie down soon, he'd fall over. He could barely spare the energy to focus his vision. Sai was safe; everything else could wait until Yarrow had refreshed himself. For a few minutes, Yarrow just watched Sai and wondered what he could be dreaming about as his eyes moved behind his lids and a smile pulled at the corners of his slightly parted lips. Yarrow decided he looked too content to disturb him, so he stretched out in the grass beside him, and within seconds fell unconscious.

They didn't wake until late in the afternoon, judging by the sun's position. Yarrow sat up and rubbed his eyes, his throat dry. For fresh water, they'd have to backtrack several hours and swim to their stores aboard the ship. What he saw as he looked around made him forget his thirst. He'd been too tired after unraveling the spell to notice what it had been concealing. High, yellow-green grass swished in the light breeze between tan rocks worn smooth by the ocean winds. The trees, while stunted, drooped beneath clusters of fruit or healthy foliage. Here and there, clumps of flowers Yarrow didn't recognize scented the air.

"*Syrai*, are you sure we haven't fallen under the influence of another spell?" Sai asked. "This place is beautiful. All of this was really hidden beneath that dark, dead world?"

Yarrow nodded and stretched his arms over his head. His muscles ached and trembled. He'd likely flexed them tight without realizing it as he'd worked to negate the illusion. Now the question of why anyone would smother this pristine paradise beneath such an ugly nightmare gnawed at his thoughts even as it encouraged him. No one went to this much trouble except to hide something valuable.

Sai echoed his reasoning as he got to his feet and shielded his eyes to look out across the startling vistas. "We should look around. I bet there's treasure here. Why else would someone make the island look so dismal? Someone clearly doesn't want anyone to stay. Do you think the mage who cast that spell is still here?"

I hope so. He's powerful; he can help me.

If he's willing, the presence said. *You don't have much to offer him in return, beloved. Unless he enjoys pretty young men who like to whine and wallow in self-pity.*

Say whatever you want, monster. You're worried, and I can feel it.

"Yarrow?"

"I'm sorry. I was just thinking. This mage has already erected two obstacles to keep people away from here: the dream fog and now this artifice. He may have more in place, so we'll have to be very careful. Goddesses, this place is huge, and we'll need water soon. Where do we even begin to search for him?"

"Look there." Sai pointed to a tiny tendril of smoke winding up from the trees. "A fire means at least a man, if not a mage. I think we can reach it by morning if we travel all night."

"That might be too long without water," Yarrow said, concerned for Sai. Part of him wanted to send Sai away, but a larger fraction felt glad not to be alone. Selfishness again. Besides, Emiri were about as easy to order around as alley cats.

"Why don't you just make it rain?" Sai asked.

"I shouldn't use magic unless it's absolutely necessary," Yarrow said. "If there is another sorcerer here, he'll probably be expecting us after I unraveled his concealing spell. Casting could alert him to our exact location. I think it's better to stay somewhat hidden for as long as we can. Sai, tell me you won't risk your safety. If something happens to you—"

"I've been in tighter situations than this. Don't worry. This much vegetation couldn't possibly thrive without a water source. Trees usually mean fruit, and fruit means liquid. If we don't happen upon a spring, a stream, or at least a patch of berries, we'll dig down and find water beneath the soil, or we'll take from inside one of the plants."

"Are you sure?"

Sai laughed and clapped Yarrow on the shoulder. "Trust me, *syrai.* I'm Emiri. We have an extra sense when it comes to water. And treasure. Right now, it's telling me we'll uncover something precious here. So, shall we set off and find out what it is?"

"All right, but remember to be cautious."

Sai clasped Yarrow's hand, smiled wide, and tugged him toward the suggestion of a path leading into the forest. Yarrow couldn't name any of the trees surrounding them. Most were slender, with pale beige or nearly white trunks that curved at odd angles to reach for the sun. Some of them had heart-shaped leaves of a deep olive green that recalled to Yarrow Duncan's eyes, while others had long, slender leaves of bright emerald. Here and there, something between large bushes and small trees, with bright yellow, star-shaped leaves, broke the curtain of green. Clumps of dry, pale grass grew between them, but the abundance of large rocks kept the bracken to a minimum. Though it felt sparse compared to a Selindrian forest, the variety of foreign flora fascinated Yarrow as they passed through.

Sai's guess proved true once again, and they found a bubbling little pool feeding a rapidly running brook. Both of them hurried to slake their thirst, disturbing a flock of indigo birds picking at the berry bushes along the banks. Yarrow and Sai also ate their fill of the big, golden berries striped with green. Though tart enough to make Yarrow's lips pucker, the fruit at least filled his empty stomach. They rested for probably an hour before setting off toward the elusive column of smoke in the distance.

After walking all night, Yarrow could think of little beyond forcing one foot in front of the other. Sai trudged along beside him, swatting bugs out of his face. Ready to collapse, Yarrow was just about to suggest they stop to rest when the blush of dawn illuminated a much wider path than those they'd been following. Large stones lined the trail in a very deliberate pattern. Yarrow held up his hand, and an exhausted Sai bumped against him when he paused.

The Emiri pressed the heels of his hands against his eyes. "What do you think?"

"I don't know. Somebody put these stones here, and not long ago. There's no moss or vines growing on them." Looking ahead in the increased light, Yarrow saw rocky soil terraced almost into a staircase. "There's someone living here."

"And he might not take kindly to our presence." A profound yawn punctuated Sai's observation.

"Exactly. Maybe you should wait here while I go on ahead."

Sai only rolled his eyes in response before he and Yarrow stepped cautiously onto the steps cut into the packed dirt of a curving road that wound around a large hillock. Yarrow expected to find a citadel at the summit, something worthy of the mage who'd cast the two amazing spells they'd encountered. Any sorcerer who could construct those masterpieces of magic could drag a castle up from the bedrock of the world. Yarrow held his breath as they rounded the final corner, awaiting the sight of the majestic fortress.

Instead, he saw a small stone cottage with a thatched roof, neat and tidy but little more than a peasant's hovel. Expansive vegetable gardens surrounded it; squash and beans grew fat in the southern clime while the plants would barely be pushing through the soil back home. Beyond the back fence, trees heavy with round, red fruit Yarrow had never seen grew in orderly rows down the opposite side of the knoll. Yarrow relaxed, his hunger trumping any anxiety as he looked at the yield of the well-tended garden. "This must be the home of some servant of the great mage," he told Sai.

"So much work to grow food you could just take," Sai said. "Or take the gold to buy."

"Let's be off."

"What?" Sai said, shocked. "Without eating some of this? I'm starving." He plucked a fat tomato from a vine and bit into it with a groan of delight.

"Maybe a little." Yarrow knelt, picked a cucumber, and dusted it off on his trousers. It was the most delicious cucumber he'd ever tasted, juicy and almost sweet, without any bitterness in the thin skin. Next he split a long pod open and ate the tender beans within. He was just about to take a round orange squash from the vine when he heard boots on the gravel trail behind him. He summoned his magic but held it in check as he slowly turned around, his mouth still full of fresh beans.

"You're stealing from my garden," said an unassuming young man, his tangled brown hair held out of his face by a strip of cloth. Dirt stains covered his simple russet tunic and matching trousers. Soil caked his hands and worn boots. His brown eyes, while warm, cut straight to Yarrow's core.

"I'm sorry," Yarrow said, swallowing half-chewed beans. "We were lost at sea, and frantically hungry. We can offer you compensation for the vegetables. We're not thieves, just a pair of men needing food."

"No, not thieves." The young man shifted his weight and rested the basket he held against his upthrust hip. He narrowed his eyes. "You're the one who broke the illusion I placed on the island. And you made it through the mist. Tell me how, and quickly, before I decide I don't care and just kill you."

"Hale?" Yarrow asked.

The other man flinched. "Who in Fane's name are you? How are you here, how do you know of me, and why should I let you live?"

"I am Yarroway L'Estrella of Lockhaven. I have been searching for you, Hale. I need your knowledge, your help. We mean you no ill will. I just want to speak with you. Will you allow me that?"

"No. Leave this place."

Yarrow shook his head. "I can't. I desperately need to talk to you. I can't depart until I do."

Hale looked tired and annoyed as he raised the hand not holding his basket and shot a gout of white-hot fire at Yarrow. Before he even had a chance to think about it, Yarrow summoned his azure wings and closed them in front of himself, deflecting the missile. It ricocheted back at Hale, who had to jump aside to avoid it. A tripod of beans caught fire. Yarrow choked the flame, denying it the air it needed to thrive, and it flickered and died. "Please. I don't wish to fight. I'm only asking for a few hours of your time. Hear what I have to say, and when I'm finished, if you can't or won't offer me advice, we'll leave."

The white fire wreathing Hale's fist dissipated. "It's so strange to hear a human voice after all this time. The spoken word has undergone much less evolution than I'd have predicted. But tell me, what manner of creature is your companion?"

"Sai's Emiri," Yarrow said. "How long have you been here alone, Hale?"

"I've had no way nor any desire to measure the time since Fane fell."

Yarrow gasped. "It's been thousands of years. So long, many don't believe Fane ever existed. No evidence remains of him or his kingdom."

"I'm sorry to hear that," Hale said, "but it isn't unexpected. Now, say what you feel so compelled to say. I have fruit to harvest and my solitude to return to."

Yarrow had so many questions he felt like they'd burst from him in a torrent. Why would one of the world's most powerful mages tend his gardens by hand? How did Hale maintain his youth after such an unimaginable length of time? Why did he choose to live in total isolation?

Yarrow forced his curiosity aside so he wouldn't offend his reluctant host and make Hale change his mind. Instead, he said, "My friend and I have been walking all night, and my story isn't a brief one. Is there somewhere we might sit down?"

Hale set his basket down. "Of course. I forgot the most basic rules of human interaction long ago. You do look very tired, Yarroway L'Estrella."

"Yarrow. And yes, breaking your spells wore me thin. I've never encountered such complex and powerful enchantment. It was… marvelous. Beautiful."

If Hale appreciated the compliment, he gave no hint of it through words or expressions. "I thought them impenetrable. You must possess a rare combination of arcane energy and the ability to comprehend the structure of a spell. I did not think this tired, old world capable of producing another such skilled mage. Please, come inside and sit down."

Yarrow and Sai followed Hale into his rustic one-room dwelling. It contained little beyond a hearth, table, narrow bed, and some cupboards for storage. Some crates and baskets holding fruits and vegetables sat on the stone floor. Beyond the window, Yarrow noticed a few utilitarian garments drying on a line. The tub and washboard sat nearby. Most of the furnishings had been carved from wood, probably with the crude knife hanging from Hale's belt, and Yarrow wondered how they'd endured for thousands of years. But he wasn't here to talk about woodworking and gardening.

"Sit down." Hale indicated two long benches on either side of the table. He took his place across from Yarrow and Sai, putting his back to the pot of stew bubbling over the fire. "Tell me your tale, and then I'll invite you to stay for a meal. That's how it was done, if I recall."

"That would be most welcome, *syrai*, and thank you," Sai told him.

It fell to Yarrow. He hadn't considered, before this moment, that Sai might be witness to the information he needed to share with Hale. Though he worried Sai would fear and despise him after he heard Yarrow's account, after all he had done, Sai deserved the truth. If he turned away from Yarrow in disgust, he was entitled to his feelings. As Yarrow prepared himself to tell the story for only the third time in his life, he felt his creature watching, pondering, and planning.

"I hail from Lockhaven," Yarrow said.

"I have never heard of such a place," Hale replied, "but go on."

Yarrow hesitated. Everyone knew of Lockhaven, the oldest and most respected valenny in Selindria. The L'Estrella family had ruled it since before recorded time. "Yes, anyway. When I was fourteen, I was sent away. Exiled."

"Why?" Hale asked.

"I have never spoken of this," Yarrow said softly, "but I'll tell you if you wish to know." He resisted the urge to clasp Sai's hand beneath the table. "My uncle, the king, took certain liberties. I… admit I was becoming curious about men and their bodies at that age, but I didn't want…. No matter. This part is not important. When people started to talk of what had happened, the king blamed me, stopping just short of saying I bewitched him. My family was humiliated. They wanted me gone to lessen the gossip. Out of sight, out of mind."

He proceeded to tell the story of his time in the Lapir Mountains, where he'd encountered the presence, sparing none of the gory detail. He needed Hale to understand why he had to be rid of it. As he spoke, Yarrow expected the creature to taunt him, maybe to correct his account, but it stayed eerily silent. As the morning wore on and it grew hotter inside the little cottage, Yarrow spoke of his adventures with Sasha and Duncan, and how the presence had threatened them. He told Hale of the Battle of the Starlight Bridge and the advent of the Blessed Epoch and all that had happened after he'd left his partners, stopping at the point he and Sai had fled Espero.

"And so, I don't even know if this thing inside of me exists. One of the mages at the university suspected my mind had split in two, and what I perceive as the presence is just the part of me that's willing to do what needs done. My survival instinct given voice, I suppose. She suggested I unconsciously created it because I couldn't deal with certain appetites I possessed. Could it be the aspect of me that can access my most powerful magic?"

Hale drummed his fingers on the tabletop and ruminated on Yarrow's tale for a few moments. "No," he finally said.

Relief washed over Yarrow, and he closed his eyes to hold back the tears. *Thank the Goddesses! It wasn't me. I didn't hurt Sasha and Duncan. I didn't kill Rini.*

If you're willing to go on nothing but a single word from this fool, beloved.

What? I thought you wanted me to acknowledge you! If you've changed your mind, it's only to try out a fresh way to torment me. This is Hale! Fane's apprentice!

So he says. He looks more like a dirt farmer than a powerful sorcerer to me. Why would a mage of such legendary skill choose to live like this?

"Yarrow? Are you all right?" Sai rubbed his back and moved closer on the bench.

"Yes, and thank you, *syrai*." Yarrow sniffled and scrubbed at his eyes, but he refused to let his tears fall. He looked up at Hale, and saw sympathy in eyes that, unlike the rest of him, betrayed his great age and the toll the years had taken on his spirit.

"You must understand, both of you, that I would have died if I'd refused it. I just wanted to hone my magic, so I could protect myself. I never wanted anyone to take advantage of me again. A paltry excuse, I know. But you're sure this thing exists independently of me? Do you have some idea what the creature could be, where it could have come from? Is it possible for me to unravel this bond I share with it?"

Hale held up his hand to stem Yarrow's frantic inquiries. "To make you understand, I have to tell you a tale of my own, and I'm afraid it's even longer than yours. But now is the time for the midday refreshment. Let's have some stew, and I'll speak to you of things I've never shared with another living soul."

Chapter Fourteen

HALE smiled sardonically as he flipped through the book Yarrow had stolen from the library in Espero. "While some of this information is accurate, none of it came from my hand. I can only assume the story was passed down through gossip for many years, maybe even centuries, before some entrepreneurial soul thought to make a bit of gold selling it. I'm surprised, though. I didn't expect written language to survive the schism, and the preserving charm on these pages is quite competent. But I suppose I should start at the beginning."

He collected the wooden bowls they'd eaten from and dropped them into a tub of water before sitting back down. "Where to start…."

"Is it true you were Fane's apprentice?" Yarrow asked. He couldn't help himself. "Fane really existed?"

"Oh yes, child. I was his pupil and much more. I shared his bed, but I was one of many. I don't know if he ever reciprocated the devotion I felt for him, though he was good to me. I at least have the honor of knowing I was one of his favorites, though that fact made me enemies. Fane was already ancient by the time I began studying under him, though he never looked a day older than you are now."

"It seems he passed that skill to you," Sai observed.

"Yes, but I'll get to that part later. I haven't spoken to another person in a hundred lifetimes, so I don't think I'll be able to really describe to you what the world was like under Fane's rule. I admit I don't know what it's like now, but I saw a little of what became of it after he fell. Before that, it was truly a paradise. I don't exaggerate when I say Fane had stamped out misery and suffering. Through magic, we'd learned to cure almost every illness and heal every injury a person could suffer. Our crops grew almost without the need of labor. We produced more food than we could ever eat.

No one had to toil. People devoted their time to composing music, writing stories, creating art, and designing buildings of such complex beauty they would take your breath away. Has human society even come close to recreating what was lost?"

Yarrow shook his head and took a sip of Hale's homemade wine. It was wonderfully sweet, but not much stronger than fresh juice. "A few people can pursue such things, but they do it on the backs of hundreds of others who suffer endless drudgery to meet their basic needs. Survival, even for the wealthy, is a constant battle. One out of a hundred people are comfortable, but only because they exploit those beneath them."

"Sad," Hale said.

"It isn't so among my people," Sai said. "We have no rulers or masters. The idea of gaining, or even wanting control over others is incomprehensible to us."

"Where did your people come from?" Hale asked him. "Beings such as you were unknown before the schism."

Sai shrugged. "I was born on a boat near the eastern shore of Espero. My mother's kin came from the south of the mage's island. I don't know anything else. We don't put much stock in the past."

"That is both foolish and incredibly wise," Hale said. "The past can teach important lessons, but dwelling there can hold one down like the heaviest chain."

Impatient to know how Hale might help him and aware of Fane's mythology, Yarrow said, "What happened to that perfect world?"

"A complex question," Hale answered. "It wasn't anything singular or decisive. Fane… Fane was a distant man, quiet and often aloof, but he was a good man, a good emperor who cared about the welfare of his people. He enjoyed luxury and pleasure, but he made sure his subjects lived almost as well as he did. I think his age allowed him to keep many things in perspective, to see the difference between the profound and the petty. He harbored one irrational fear: a fear of creatures like the one you describe."

Yarrow's companion snapped to alertness after it had spent most of the conversation complaining of boredom.

"Though he had hundreds of lovers, Fane chose his wives from among the most gifted female mages. Just before he fell, he had thirteen of them, and he trained them well and taught them his every secret. Then he sent them to scour his kingdom and eradicate any of the creatures they could find."

"What were they?" Yarrow asked, his companion's anger roiling through his veins like poison, making him tremble, sweat, and feel like he'd be sick.

"I asked the emperor that same question," Hale said. "He believed they were a race that held dominion over this world before we even appeared here. He considered them vile and bloodthirsty, and told me they were the greatest threat to his subjects. He believed if these creatures were so inclined, a single one of them could massacre an entire city without feeling a shred of remorse."

"So… these creatures were created by the goddesses, the same as everything else?" Yarrow asked.

"What are you talking about?" Hale asked. "What goddesses?"

Yarrow couldn't believe what he was hearing. *What goddesses?* Everyone in the known world lived by the rules of the sisters. All life revolved around them, and even the moons bore their names. He'd never been especially devout, but even Yarrow rankled at hearing the goddesses dismissed. So far, he hadn't heard much he didn't already know, but he wanted Hale to continue. "Nothing. What happened?"

"Since these creatures Fane feared couldn't be killed, the emperor taught his huntresses a spell to dissolve them, negate their physical forms. It's not something I ever wanted to learn or even properly understood," Hale said with a shiver.

"It sounds like what happened to my companion," Yarrow said, ice in his blood. "But… it told me it had been trapped and deceived by a young man. I've seen this in its memories."

Hale rubbed his chin. "That makes little sense. As far as I was aware, Fane only ever sent his wives after the creatures. I once asked him why he didn't send me, because I felt my magic was as strong as theirs. He told me he prized me too highly."

"Did they get them all?" Yarrow asked in a whisper, sliding closer to Sai and clutching Sai's leg.

"They believed they did," Hale said. "But teaching that spell to those treacherous harridans was the worst thing the emperor could have done. Ultimately, they used it against him."

"His wives?" Yarrow asked. He'd been taught the thirteen goddesses had vanquished Fane as a punishment for his pride, for demanding he be worshipped in their place. "Wait… his *thirteen* wives—"

"Each of them became as powerful as the emperor under his tutelage," Hale said. "They grew to resent the love the people showed for Fane. They felt themselves just as worthy of public praise. They began to gather support, and when they had enough, they attacked the emperor and his army of mages. I was there. I watched the world burn to an ember, to ash, to nothing. In the end, those women couldn't completely destroy Fane, but they did to him what they'd done to all those creatures. A shred of Fane's consciousness still exists, but they erased the rest of him. I died that day. This immortal body just hasn't realized it yet."

Yarrow sat clutching the edge of the table, staring down at his white knuckles, replaying Hale's words over and over in his head, trying to reconcile what he'd just heard with everything he'd ever been taught, everything he thought he knew about the world. If he could no longer believe the goddesses, the thirteen sacred sisters, had made him and everything around him, what could he believe? He choked down bile and fought to keep his vegetable soup in his stomach where it belonged.

As if in answer to Yarrow's unspoken questions, Hale said, "You must believe nothing that you haven't seen for yourself to be true."

"Hale," Yarrow managed to say, though the single word felt like it cut his throat to ribbons on the way out. "I was taught, we are all taught, that there are thirteen goddesses who created the world and everything in it. They are revered by everyone, and temples and statues are built in their honor. We measure the passage of time by their thirteen moons. The story of Fane…. Well, it's told that Fane was an arrogant man who drew worship away from the goddesses. A blasphemer. The goddesses threw him down as punishment for his conceit. He's blamed for destroying the golden age of the world."

"What?"

The little room spun around Yarrow, and his hands felt too weak to keep hold of the table. Even sitting down, he felt like he'd lose his balance and fall over. "What—goddesses. Do you remember the names of any of Fane's wives?"

"I didn't know them well. I didn't care to. Ix, I remember, and Myint. Pherara."

"The goddesses of the wilds, warfare, and magic," Yarrow said.

"Goddesses?" Hale bellowed, knocking his bench over as he got to his feet. "People *worship* those vipers? Why? For how long?"

Yarrow's hands and feet tingled as he swayed on the bench, feeling like the very ground had disintegrated beneath his boots. "The oldest temple to the Mother Goddess has stood on the shore of Estrella Lake for more than two thousand years."

"Mother Goddess?" Hale swung his arm, and crates and baskets of produce cartwheeled across the room, sending peppers, corn, and berries flying into the air. "Only that manipulative harlot Amandira would have the arrogance to claim such a title! And all because she could drop spawn from her womb like an untended tree drops rotten fruit! Her spawn Thalil was a monster! Worshipped—as a *goddess*?"

"Thalil," Yarrow whispered, thinking of Sasha and his cult. All of it was based on a lie. The whole world operated according to falsehoods and deceit. *There are no goddesses.*

At least you know I'm real, my beloved. I never lied to you.

"I—This just can't—Sai? Sai, I need—" Yarrow tried to reach for his friend, but he didn't have the strength to lift his arms. He tried to fight the sparkling, gray fuzz pouring in at the corners of his vision, but he couldn't banish it or even drive it back. His eyes closed of their own accord, and he felt himself falling backward. He didn't even try to fight it because he knew he'd lose. He just let himself tumble down into oblivion. Hale's modest cottage disappeared, and Yarrow knew no more.

SURROUNDED as he was by soft warmth, Yarrow almost expected to wake up between Sasha and Duncan in a tent somewhere along the road, with the pure, winter cold waiting just beyond the edges of their bedroll. He tried to remember what he'd been doing before he went to sleep. Visions of an Emiri ship, a quaint, country inn, and mist over the sea flickered across his memory, disjointed and out of order. As he watched the images, Yarrow could assign no meaning to any of them.

Snap out of it, beloved.

Yarrow held tight to the voice. It was concrete. Real. Ever present. *Where are we? What's happened?*

"Onion soup," said a different voice. Hale. Fane's apprentice. Fane was real, and the goddesses weren't—The young man in the coarse, homespun clothes handed a wooden bowl to Sai.

Sai knelt down next to the bed where Yarrow lay—Hale's bed—and lifted the steaming bowl to Yarrow's lips. Yarrow drank down the rich broth his friend—his *syrai*—gently offered. Gradually, the details of the conversation solidified in Yarrow's mind, and he found the strength to sit up. A fire burned in the hearth, and lamps glowed from the table. Yarrow had felt faint not long after lunch, and now he awoke in the dead of night with no idea what had happened. He tried to ask, but his voice wouldn't cooperate.

"Please rest, *syrai*," Sai said. "This venerable wizard says you've worn yourself ragged pulling his spells apart, and I'm worried for you. You've had quite a shock."

Hale, standing behind Sai, said, "I am beginning to understand what happened after Fane fell, but I wish to hear more about what has become of his world. I would invite you and your unusual companion to stay here with me. I'll do what I can to help you with your problem, and all I ask in exchange is information."

"Thank you," Yarrow managed.

"Rest as long as you need to," Hale said. "I appreciate your surprise. I feel the same way. You are safe here, safer than any creature in this world, even from those you know as goddesses. They cannot find this place. Nothing can touch you here."

"The thing inside me," Yarrow started to argue.

Hale shook his head. "It's an unusual situation. I have never heard of any of the creatures defeated by the huntresses returning. I didn't know it was possible for them to anchor their essence to another form. I'll have to think on this. There are so many implications, but I will try to help you. You're welcome to remain as my guest as long as that might take."

"Thank you," Yarrow said again, too exhausted to feel any hope or happiness, too exhausted to feel anything at all.

"Rest," Hale suggested. "We have nothing if we don't have time."

Yarrow found it difficult to keep the room in focus, to keep his eyes open at all. "I don't want to be alone. Sai… *syrai-tama*, will you lay with me? Not like that. Will you hold me and stay close to me while I sleep? Just as a friend—"

"I'm happy to." Sai peeled away his leather vest and leggings, stripped naked, oblivious to Hale, and climbed into the narrow bed beside Yarrow. Yarrow rolled on his side, facing the wall, and Sai cuddled up behind him, his warm, smooth skin divine against Yarrow's back, wrapping his willowy limbs around Yarrow like vines, making Yarrow feel safe, feel valued, feel rooted to the physical world.

"We'll get through this, Yarrow." Sai crossed his bare arms over Yarrow's chest, nuzzled his face against the back of Yarrow's neck, and kissed Yarrow beneath his ear. "I love you."

"Sai—"

"Please, just sleep. Let me enjoy being close to you."

Yarrow nodded against Hale's pillows, his heart and mind pulled in every direction. He felt like he'd fall apart if not for Sai holding him together. He couldn't think anymore, couldn't ponder the astronomical conflicts he found himself enmeshed in. Knowing he'd have to face them when he awoke, Yarrow closed his eyes, hoping to sleep for many hours next to his sweet Sai and put it off as long as possible.

Chapter Fifteen

"Sai?" After two weeks in Hale's cottage, Yarrow wasn't used to waking up without his *syrai* curled close to him in the narrow bed. He knew he'd sorely tested the Emiri by asking Sai to sleep chastely beside him night after night. Goddesses knew the feel of Sai next to him had stretched Yarrow's resolve to the breaking point as well. He spent nearly every evening dreaming of things he could experience for real if he only asked. He stirred from slumber every morning to a fading vision of Sai straddling him and riding his cock until Yarrow couldn't move. At this point, Yarrow couldn't deny the love he felt for Sai, love that made them *syrai* and transcended physical longing. But, goddesses, the physical longing was ripping him apart.

Yarrow knew he should be concentrating on his lessons with Hale, but Sai's scent clung to the pillows and blankets, and just the ghost of his essence made Yarrow hard. He groaned as he sat up in the bed and his erection stabbed him in the belly.

Beloved, it's been forever.

And it feels like even longer.

Your fish-boy is so, so willing. Follow his lead and let go of the past.

I can't.

"Breakfast," Hale announced, his stern voice wiping away Yarrow's fantasies.

Yarrow stumbled to the table and ate fresh fruit and bread. Then he pulled his boots on and followed Hale to the garden. As per their routine, they tended the vegetable patch until lunchtime, pulling weeds, raking soil, and pruning away withered leaves and blossoms. Yarrow's back ached from bending over, and he thanked whatever manifestation of divinity he still acknowledged when Hale said they should break for the midday meal.

"Why do you subject yourself to such miserable work when you have magic?" Yarrow asked as he collapsed on the bench by the table. Blisters covered his palms, his legs ached, and his neck was knotted into a ball of painful tension.

"I don't find the work miserable," Hale answered as he placed vegetables fresh from his garden on the table beside a loaf of bread still warm from the oven. "I like working with plants and helping things grow."

"But all this—your fine home and orchards—they don't appear thousands of years old."

"They're not," Hale responded, dipping a corner of his bread in the herbed oil he'd drizzled over his vegetables. "Every few hundred years, I raze everything I've built to the ground and start again."

"Why?" Yarrow gasped. Performing mundane labor alongside Hale, hearing him speak of little beyond the health of his plants, Yarrow had found it easy to forget his tremendous age.

Penance, beloved.

But for what? What could he have possibly done to deserve all of this, over and over again?

"Why not?" Hale said with a shrug. "What else do I have to do? Though instructing you has proved an interesting distraction."

"Tell me, then, do these thirteen women still exist in the world? Are those my people worship as goddesses still here?"

"Probably," Hale said. "I'm sure Fane made them immortal. He offered it to anyone who pleased him. I made sure to hide myself just in case they still sought vengeance against me."

"Why would they do that?" Yarrow asked.

"Because Fane loved me more than he could ever love any of them. Because he preferred to spend his nights in my bed, even though he knew I'd never produce offspring."

"Could that be why we're taught love between men is a sin against the goddesses?" Yarrow asked. "Some vestige of their envy?"

"It wouldn't surprise me," Hale said. "All of them were jealous of the affection Fane showed his male lovers, me in particular. He needed his wives to ensure his progeny, but he *wanted* me. I miss him so much. You'd think these thousands of years would lessen my desire to be near him, to just hear one word uttered by his lips, but they have not. That's why I work so hard, to try to distract myself from the memories. Some wounds never heal, I suppose."

Yarrow squeezed Hale's hand. "I wish I could offer some relevant expression of sympathy. I'm afraid anything I say will be insignificant. I know how you feel on some level. My desire to return to those I love is the entire reason I risked seeking you out. I don't feel whole without them. It hurts like having part of my body hacked off with a rusty sword. After thousands of years… I can't even imagine your pain. I wish there was something I could do."

"Your intentions are admirable," Hale said. "I can feel the veracity of your sentiment. Having you here has been a welcome diversion, Yarroway L'Estrella. You are a great mage. I'd worried Fane's wives had hoarded all the world's magical energy for themselves."

"Many scholars say there are fewer mages born every generation," Yarrow said.

Hale nodded. "I am not surprised. Those witches are sucking up every shred of esoteric energy, leaving nothing but table scraps. Few are as powerful as you, as capable of taking the main course from under their noses."

"The goddesses are really just mortal women?" Yarrow still couldn't comprehend it.

"Not mortal, not anymore. But nothing divine," Hale responded. "Certainly not in the way you've been led to believe."

"I'd be publicly executed if I even suggested any of this," Yarrow said. "Yet I feel like people should know."

"People want something to follow, Yarroway. They *want* to be told what to do. Being told removes the burden of deciding what is right and what isn't. That's not a load most of these simple creatures are willing to take upon themselves, to hoist onto their shoulders."

"I used to feel that way, superior to those around me, but the past few years have made me wonder," Yarrow responded. "Hale, why don't you leave here with us? Start again? Maybe even find someone again?"

"No. I am finished with the world. I have no desire to watch it cycle through its endless phases of building up and tearing down."

"But you could help it. You have so much knowledge and power to share."

"Yarrow, you can't even begin to comprehend the years I've lived, the things I've seen. Why would I want to invest myself in human society again, aid in making it great, maybe even fair, only to watch it all torn down to nothing and forced to start again from the beginning?"

"Is it so inevitable?"

"In my experience."

All the more reason to live only for ourselves, my beloved, to pursue nothing but our own pleasure.

Yarrow was about to argue with it when the small door to the hut creaked open and Sai entered, his shoulders sloped down, hair dripping, and a miserable expression on his face. He flopped down on the bench beside Yarrow, and Hale slid a plate of food in front of him, but Sai didn't even glance at it.

"*Syrai?*" Yarrow asked, rubbing Sai's shoulder. His skin was warm from the sun, and his hair smelled of the ocean. "What's the matter?"

"I feel like I'm trapped in some version of your peoples' Abode of Shades. I can't imagine anything worse than waking up day after day and performing the same dull toil. Why go on living at all? Besides, I miss the companionship of my *syrai*. Sweet Emir, I miss making love! It's just not natural to deny one's body something it needs! Have you learned what you came here to learn, Yarrow? Can we be off soon?"

Yarrow looked at Hale. Over the past couple of weeks, Hale had examined the connection between Yarrow and the other. He admitted he'd never encountered such a spell and would have to think about how the bond might be severed. In the meantime, he'd taught Yarrow some very useful techniques for keeping control over the creature. Yarrow was now able to isolate and sequester it until he couldn't even hear it speaking, if he chose. But he still didn't feel safe to return to his partners, because he knew the creature would wait. It would bide its time until it caught Yarrow just tired enough to slip up, feeling ill, hurt, or distracted. Like Yarrow, it too could learn and create magical formulae. It might very well discover ways to negate everything Yarrow had learned from Hale.

"Have you figured out a way to get rid of it?" Yarrow asked the other mage.

Hale set his wooden fork on the table and rubbed his eyes, keeping them covered with his hand as he answered. "What has been done to you is unlike anything I've ever encountered. The essence of this creature has permeated every aspect of your being: your flesh, your mind, your magic, and even that piece of your identity some would call your spirit. I can't even begin to understand how it accomplished this, let alone how to undo it. I don't even know if this bond is the result of a spell, or something else entirely, something beyond the realm of even my experience. If I thought I might discover the solution in time, I would invite you to stay, but I honestly see no possibility of ever unraveling it. There is simply nothing more I can do for you."

The creature roared with laughter so hard it almost shook Yarrow's physical body. *I have been telling you from the beginning, beloved! Now, can we leave this boring hovel and find a man, a woman, a fine feast and some blood to spill?*

I cannot accept this. Icy sweat broke from Yarrow's pores as he staggered to his feet, stumbled through the door and out into the garden. The plants and vegetables looked garish and unreal with their bright colors. He grasped one of the branches supporting the tomato plants as he threw up. Then he fell to his knees in the dirt and hung his head, too broken even to cry. *If Hale cannot help me, if there was nothing in the vast libraries of Espero….* "What am I going to do?"

Live. Revel in sensation. Grow into your power. Take your place as the master of this world.

"I don't want that!" Yarrow yelled at the top of his voice. With a ragged cry of desperation, he lifted his hand and shot an eldritch-blue fount of energy from his fingers, disintegrating everything in its path and leaving a wide swath of the garden decimated. "I don't want to spend my life alone!"

There is no need for you to spend it alone. With what I can teach you, you can have anyone you want, thousands singing your praises, just like they did for this Fane. You can be even greater than he was. When I first met you, your only desires were knowledge and power. I have told you before you can make others love you.

I am not the same as I was then. I don't want to live as a pariah. I certainly don't want love that isn't freely given. That isn't even love. You know nothing about love. Dry sobs shook Yarrow as he dragged himself a few feet away from the puddle of sick and curled on his side in the dark soil. "It's all over. There's nothing left to hope for."

A patch of shade broke the sun beating down on Yarrow, and he looked up to see Sai, with Hale standing cautiously a few feet behind. The Emiri knelt down, and his clumps of hair blanketed Yarrow's shoulder as he squeezed Yarrow's hand. "It will be all right, *syrai*."

Sai's simple words threw fuel on the cinders of anger glowing inside Yarrow, igniting an inferno of rage and despair. Azure wings flashed as Yarrow stood and backed away from his friend. He pointed at him, light crackling from his hand, and shouted, "It will not be all right! Are you stupid? You heard what he said! He cannot help me, and that means no one can. You'll get on your ship, leave this place, and forget you ever saw my face if you have any sense!"

Astounding Yarrow with his bravery and devotion, Sai dared a step nearer to him. Yarrow couldn't allow it; he had to drive him away as he'd always done before Sasha and Duncan taught him to trust. But it had all been an illusion, as fleeting and delicate as ash on the wind.

The same as everything, beloved.

Yes.

Hale came to stand protectively in front of Sai. Goaded by his companion, Yarrow sneered at the other mage. He'd broken Hale's spells before, and he could do it again. He could probably relieve Hale of the burden of his tedious existence….

The presence barked out a victorious laugh: This *is the true you, beloved! This is not coming from me, you know. Are you sure I'm the dangerous one? The one that needs to be excised? Maybe it's been you all along.*

"What does it matter?" Yarrow screamed, his voice cracking and sparks of azure energy spiraling into the darkening sky. Thunder shook the heavens, and black clouds congealed across the dome of blue.

"Your friend has stood beside you when few others would have," Hale said. "You owe him gratitude, not insults and threats!"

"Leave me alone. You're useless," Yarrow told Hale.

"Am I? If you'll get a hold of yourself and at least pretend to be a civilized human being, I can suggest one last course of action, though you must look inside yourself, Yarrow. There's something festering in you beyond the presence of this creature. Now, control your magic and come back inside." Hale turned on his heel and went back inside the house.

Yarrow took a deep breath and let his power drain away, back into the deep pool inside him where, according to both Hale and his creature, something rotted far beneath the surface. He smoothed down the Esperon garments he still wore and went to join the others, his cheeks sizzling with shame. He couldn't meet their eyes as he sat down at the table. "Sai, I apologize."

"You're hurting, *syrai*. I understand."

Fresh anger bubbled up in Yarrow. He wanted to rail at Sai for always being so forgiving. Why would he do that? He should be furious with Yarrow. Yarrow *wanted* him to be furious, to not be the only one experiencing such rage. He dismissed it for the moment and forced himself to look up at Hale. "I owe you an apology as well. You've done far more for me than you had to. Please, tell me what to do."

"The plan I propose has a slim chance of success at best," Hale said. "It's far more likely you'll destroy yourself attempting it."

"I can't go on like this," Yarrow said.

Hale nodded. "I can do no more to help you, but there may be a sorcerer who can."

"Who?"

"Fane," Hale said softly, the name a reverent prayer on his lips.

"But, I don't understand. He was destroyed!"

"I thought so too, until I met you and learned of your situation. If some remnant of this creature remained, strong enough to communicate with you, then maybe the emperor survived the same spell. If it was the same spell. You may be able to find him and communicate with him, as well. I warned you it was a dubious idea, but I can think of no other. I can give no other advice than for you to seek Fane. I don't know that you'll ever find him, and if you do, the spells I placed around my island to protect it will seem like children's puzzles in comparison to what those bitches likely left behind."

So, we're to scour the world in search of a shred of a memory of a man vanquished ten thousand years ago, turning over every rock and scrap of wood in existence? Honestly, beloved. Your knight and assassin will be dust long before we canvas a tenth of the world.

"Where will I even begin?" Yarrow asked in a quivering voice.

Hale went to a chest, opened the lid, and spread a massive scroll over the entire surface of the table. Yarrow gasped; the map showed parts of the world no one living had ever imagined. Selindria, the great kingdom most considered the very center of the world, was only a tiny patch, scarcely larger than Yarrow's palm. Sai hooted and spread his hands over the map, as eager to get ahold of it as if it were made of solid gold.

"I'm reluctant to send you to your death, Yarrow," Hale said. "I'm afraid it will be on my conscience along with all the others."

"I can have no life as I am," Yarrow pleaded. "You're condemning me if you don't help me."

"Very well." Hale pointed to a spot east of Gaeltheon, on the far side of the Lapir Mountains. "They dragged Fane to a remote cave near here and performed the spell to destroy him."

Yarrow groaned. "No one has crossed the Lapir Mountains in generations. I nearly died trying, and would have if not for my creature. There is no known pass through them. They cannot be traversed."

"No," Sai said in an excited whisper, "but they could be sailed around! Look!" He pointed to a narrow, serpentine strip of sea between Espero and the land to the north. "Sailing through this part of Emir is not possible because of shallows, sharp rocks, whirlpools, and erratic, changeable currents. But here"—he pointed to a broken line curling along the southwestern edge of the mage's island and caressing the shore of the uncharted land beyond the impassable range—"is a current that might take us very close to where you want to go. Then again, it might not. No one has ever attempted it, as far as I know. But it will be fun to try!"

Ah, another few months on a ship with sweet Sai. Just the two of you—and me.

"No," Yarrow said firmly. "I cannot do that. Sai, I appreciate everything you've done for me, and I don't want to hurt you, but you won't be coming with me. I have let you face too much danger on my behalf already. I refuse to lead you into… into goddesses know what else."

"But, *syrai*, we've made quite a team—"

"No." Yarrow pulled his hand away when Sai reached for it. "You need to go home to your son and family. I'm going on alone. When we get back to the mainland, we'll part ways. I will not permit you to accompany me under any circumstances."

A mixture of hurt and anger twisted Sai's beautiful face into a scowl, and he hurried from the table and out into the garden.

"Though you've cut him deeply, I think you did the right thing," Hale said. "You've probably spared his life. You may stand a better chance with a companion. I don't know. I have no idea what that part of the world is like now, or what obstacles you'll face. If you can even find Fane."

"Why don't you come with me, Hale? You're exceptionally powerful, and you might get to see something of the man you love again."

"No."

"But why? Why stay here and continue to punish yourself like this when you have a chance of speaking with Fane?"

"I have let him go," Hale said. "I have no right to face him after failing him as I did. I will not discuss this further, but I will ask you to do one thing in exchange for the aid I've given you."

Yarrow clasped Hale's hand. "Name it."

"If you do find Fane, and he's suffering somehow, put an end to it."

"I swear it, Hale."

"Good. Go see to your friend's bruised feelings. I'll pack up these charts, and you can take them with you. I never want to see them again."

Chapter Sixteen

"MY BAIRN, you have a… a most uncommon visitor."

The uncharacteristically hesitant tone in Tam Allwynn's gruff voice made Duncan sit up straight from the financial records he'd been hunched over all evening. He blinked his tired eyes in the torchlight. What in the sisters' names could have perplexed the seasoned soldier? A visitor? His heart stuttering with the faintest hope, Duncan got to his feet. Sitting for so many hours with his treasurer and then on his own had left his legs cramped. "Is it a young man?" he dared to ask. Could Yarrow have really returned to them? "What color is his hair?"

Tam Allwynn's furry brows arched up at what he certainly found an odd question, but like any good knight, he answered it. "The most ungodly red, tam."

Duncan collapsed back into his chair. It had been a foolish expectation at best, but it had taken root and bloomed in his chest with only the slightest coaxing, just like a windblossom growing from a crack in the unforgiving stone. "I can't imagine what fresh torment this will prove, and after the day I've had, I can hardly wait for what will surely be a delightful surprise. Show him in, tam, and thank you."

The grizzled seneschal bowed and disappeared into the shadows of the hall, returning with a slight figure, the top of the stranger's head barely reaching the knight's shoulder. Though small, the lad walked with grace and confidence into the ring of brighter light where Duncan worked. Duncan squinted at his ropes of shell-adorned hair and tremendous orange eyes. "Mother Goddess," he gasped. "Sai?"

"I'm happy you remember me, Duncan." The Emiri looked much as Duncan recalled with his full lips always moving suggestively and his beautiful androgynous features, but strips of puffy black wreathed his bright eyes.

Tam Allwynn stepped between Duncan and Sai. "You will address the bairn of Windwake in the proper manner, Emiri."

Duncan lifted his hand with some effort. "Thank you for your concern, Allwynn, but Sai and I are old friends."

"You certainly pick yourself some… *unusual* friends," Allwynn grumbled as he turned to leave and stomped away. "Call if you need me."

Sai watched the seneschal depart with a smirk tugging at his lips. Without waiting to be invited, he sat down in the chair Duncan's treasurer had occupied hours before and leaned his elbows on the table.

"Please tell me you're not here to ask for money like everyone else, *Mir-Sai*," Duncan teased, hoping he remembered the proper honorific for an Emiri ship's captain.

Sai threw his head back, laughed, and clapped his hands. "Ah, very good, Tam Duncan! Though it is *Sai-Mir*, but still, well done! And no, I haven't come for gold, unless you're offering, in which case I'd tell you it would only be fair for me to earn it *somehow*."

He stretched his lithe brown body, barely covered in strips of worn leather, across the table toward Duncan. The beads in his hair rattled softly as they brushed the parchment-strewn surface. Duncan couldn't help chuckling as he rolled his eyes. "You've changed little. Why have you come all this way, then? I thought your people hated the colder climes."

"I bring news of Yarrow. Urgent and unhappy news, I'm afraid."

Duncan's blood froze in his veins until his body felt numb and as immobile as rock. He concentrated on dragging in a breath so he could ask the dreaded question. "Is he—?"

"No, not yet," Sai said. "But what he plans to do…. I don't think he'll survive it alone."

"Goddesses, what happened? Start at the beginning."

"Could I trouble you for some water first?" Sai asked. "I've been sailing hard for weeks with barely a couple hours of sleep each night. I didn't stop for supplies or even to maintain my ship."

Duncan hurried to fill a goblet from the clay pitcher at the center of the table. Sai drank deeply and then began. "I'll do my best to explain it to you, but I have little understanding of magery. Some of this was hard for me to believe even as I watched it happen, and I'm not easy to shock."

"Just take your time," Duncan encouraged.

"Where is your *syrai*, Sasha?" Sai asked. "I'd hoped he might be able to help Yarrow too. He is an able fighter, if I recall, as well as a beautiful man."

"That is a long tale in itself," Duncan said. "Much has happened since we left your ship. Sasha is… trying to uncover information about certain threats he faces. He's also making himself scarce for political reasons. He isn't in the castle at the moment and may not return for several days."

Sai groaned. "Land-bound power struggles confuse me even more than magery. I'm afraid there's no time for your story. You must hear mine, and the time is short."

Duncan's mind reeled with the bizarre yarn Sai spun, beginning with him and Yarrow sacking an Esperon port and absconding with a hold full of treasure. The story grew more surreal with every word Sai said, until Duncan finally interrupted him.

"Wait. Is this some horrific attempt at jest? Yarrow studied with Fane's apprentice, and now he's gone in search of Fane himself? That… that cannot be. Fane likely never existed. If he did, it must have been thousands of years ago."

"Ten, according to Yarrow and Hale. They talked about him at length, but most of it was beyond me. I have to confess I didn't pay much attention. I don't know much about your people's religion, and I didn't recognize the names of most of the people they mentioned. Besides, it doesn't matter if Fane, or whatever's left of him, is real or not. Hale thinks it's dangerous where Yarrow is going, and he doubts Yarrow will survive. That was the part I paid attention to, not so much the old tales and legends. What happened all that time ago isn't important. Yarrow traveling unaided to dangerous lands is. This part of the world is well beyond the place where we'd always imagined it ended. Until I saw Hale's charts, I had no idea of the scope of Emir."

"If you're so worried about Yarrow, why did you leave his side?"

When Sai frowned, he looked like a devastated child, eyes impossibly wide and lips trembling. "He does not want my company any longer."

"What makes you think he'll want ours?" Duncan asked, his memories fanned from cinders to decimating flames that threatened to devour his heart. "He left us too, and made us promise not to seek him out.

He thinks… he thinks some sort of ancient presence inhabits him, and he's afraid it will harm us."

Sai nodded. "He told me of this."

Surprised, Duncan asked, "He did?"

"Me and Hale," Sai responded. "I wasn't quite sure what to make of it all. I suppose he thought he was being noble by sending me away."

"I believe he thought the same when he left us behind," Duncan said, an ache in his chest. "And as I said, he did not wish for us to follow him."

"Yet you and Sasha have some claim over him I admit I can't understand. He needs you now, whether he knows it or not." Sai took Duncan's hand and held it in his clammy palm, not out of flirtatiousness, but clearly out of fear. "I can take you to him. I have Hale's maps, and I *think* I can make it."

"But you just said he doesn't want you there." Duncan felt like he'd stumbled into some ghastly nightmare.

"I don't plan to stay." Sai looked so small and broken Duncan fought the urge to comfort him. "I'll get you and Sasha to that nameless shore, and then I'll return to my *syrai*. I miss them very much. We have a little boy, you know."

"Congratulations," Duncan mumbled, still certain none of this could be real.

"You should make yourself ready to leave as soon as possible," Sai said, a deep yawn punctuating his words. "It took me almost an entire moon to make it here, and that was sailing twenty hours a day through mostly waters I know well."

"So, Yarrow could make his destination well ahead of us, and the entire journey would be for nothing? Sai, this will be hard for you to understand, but as bairn, I have a duty to the people of Windwake. I must protect their interests and stand as an advocate for them, now more than ever. I have dire troubles of my own here. Believe me, I'd give up these lands and this castle for a single day with Yarrow. But if we'll never reach him in time, what's the point?"

"I slowed him down for that very reason," Sai said. "So you'd have a chance of making it to him before he encountered danger."

"You slowed *Yarrow* down? This just gets better and better," Duncan said. "How did you manage that?"

"I put a powdered root my people use for easing pain into his drink when we made port and left him tucked in his bed at an inn. I knew he'd sleep for days. Then I stole his maps and all his money. He'll have a very difficult time reaching a destination no sailor has ever heard of with no coin to pay one."

"Maybe he'll just give up," Duncan said, his voice as rough as if he'd spent the past hour screaming. Goddesses help him, he wanted to scream, to go out on his parapets and just rail at the sky and the sea until he had no breath left in his lungs.

"If you can even suggest that, you don't know your *syrai* at all," Sai said. "Yarrow is a desperate man, and one in a great deal of pain. He would do anything for a respite from it. Sweet Emir, I hope he finds one. He left a little of himself in my thoughts when he rescued me from the sorcerer's dream. I never knew a man could suffer like that. I don't dare think about it, or it steals my sleep and makes me want to cry. It's like a cloud hiding the sun that no wind can drive away. How can anyone guide his ship without being able to see the sun?"

"You were a friend to Yarrow when he needed one," Duncan said. "I appreciate that."

Sai nodded, looking haunted. "And now he needs you. Can you be ready within the hour?"

"Goddesses, my friend, you look ready to fall over. You'll spend the night here, in a comfortable bed, and have a proper meal in the morning. It's the least I can offer after you took such good care of my *syrai*."

Sai smiled and nodded, his eyes already closing.

"Besides," Duncan continued, "the decision isn't mine alone. I'll have to see if Sasha agrees." Though he said the words, Duncan knew what his assassin would choose—Sasha wouldn't even consider it a decision. Sasha would want to leave that very moment. Duncan had only to return to his chambers and hope Sasha would appear from the thickening shadows draping the balcony, hope that his search for information about the activities of his former brethren would not keep his assassin for days this time. Sai, a member of one of the most indolent races ever known, had felt the danger so critical as to sail until he'd nearly killed himself. That, combined with a dread and solemnity Duncan had never thought Emiri capable of expressing, made him believe, if not everything Sai said, enough to feel the need to be at Yarrow's back, where he belonged.

The next time Duncan looked over, Sai was slumbering on his crossed forearms, breathing deeply enough to make the candles flicker. Duncan helped him to his feet and practically dragged him up the stairs to a guest room he usually reserved for King Garith's visits. After tucking the snoring Emiri into the gold brocade blankets of the lavish bed and stoking the fire, getting the grand chamber warmer than he'd enjoy himself, Duncan returned to his own room.

He could do nothing but wait, and every moment he spent looking out over the harbor felt a year. He felt closer to losing Yarrow forever than he had the night the mage had walked away from him, and just as helpless to stop it.

HAD he not been trained almost from infancy to hide his every emotion, Sasha might have rolled his eyes as Duncan's stout, gray seneschal repeated himself for the fourth time.

"Bairn Duncan, I must protest this course of action! This bairny is far from secure. We may have"—he coughed theatrically and glared at Sasha—"*eliminated* the most immediate threat, but with the loyalty of so many of your nobles still in doubt, do you think it wise to leave your lands unprotected? Your absence might be just the opportunity the traitors need to strike."

"Tam Allwynn, I trust in your ability to oversee this bairny while I'm away. You will have full authority to act in my stead. Now, I can delay no longer. I have something I must see to, and it cannot wait."

"Can you at least tell me where you're going with these… *men*?" Allwynn barked.

"No," Duncan said.

"And when will you return?" the older knight continued.

"I don't know that either," Duncan told him.

"You're leaving not only me but your entire bairny in a very vulnerable position!"

"Tam Allwynn, if you do not want the responsibility of ruling while I'm away, I'll choose another knight, but you're my most trusted general and advisor. I'd feel better about leaving my lands and people in your hands than any other's."

Tam Allwynn crossed his arm over his chest and bowed. "I am honored, and I will do everything in my power to protect this land."

"Good," Duncan said, clasping his seneschal's hand. "Do this for me, and I'll grant you the estate that belonged to Tam Fennsour, if you want it."

"I fear it may be home to vengeful spirits," Allwynn said. "Besides, I'll do my duty without the promise of a bribe."

"We should sail before we lose the tide," Sai called, already heading across the courtyard toward the opening in the outer wall that led to the curving road and the harbor at its end.

"Agreed," Sasha said, eager for the road and eager for Yarrow. Though he wore his Crimson Scythe armor and gear, his skills would do little to help Yarrow until he could use them against an enemy. If he needed to, Sasha would spill an ocean of blood to bring them all together again. Their strange little family was the only thing he'd ever valued in his life. Precious things were a liability, as they could hurt one if taken. Sasha would just have to make sure nothing took what he loved, and to do that, he'd have to be better than anyone or anything that tried.

Boarding Sai's small ship summoned a strange mix of pleasant and painful memories for Sasha. As he climbed into the rigging to watch Windust Castle receding, he recalled betraying his order when he'd let Garith live against their wishes. He'd been so conflicted during that voyage, torn apart by his loyalty to his brethren and his strange, new feelings for Yarrow and Duncan. At least this time, his purpose was clear. Recollections, sweet or bitter, would not serve him, so he pushed them away. He felt a restless need to practice with his daggers, become faster, stronger, and even deadlier. He wanted to be ready.

When he noticed Duncan looking up at him with concern, Sasha dropped lightly to the deck to join his friend. Talk would not aid their mission, but it would soothe Duncan's nerves, so Sasha would talk with his friend as long as Duncan wished. Sai stood at the helm, his hair looking even redder against the overcast, ash-gray sky.

The first month of their journey passed excruciatingly without event as Sai sailed south from Windwake, staying to the gentle, predictable waters along the coast of Selindria. It grew hotter by the day as they entered into Vestrafori's Moon and full summer. Since he could travel faster with a crew, Sai taught Sasha and Duncan to man the sails and rudders and to tie up the riggings. When they weren't needed, Sasha and Duncan sparred for practice, and Sasha made it harder and harder for Duncan to match him as he picked up on the nuances of Duncan's fighting. Though Sai played with and propositioned both of them, he spent most of his time alone at the helm. Something profound had changed about the Emiri, Sasha noted.

They stopped among an array of islands Sai called the Twenty-Nine to careen the ship, remove the barnacles from the bottom, do some repairs Sai had neglected, and apply a fresh coat of paint. After filling the hull with supplies, they set off again, east toward Espero. It surprised Sasha that Sai didn't want to visit his family while he was so close to them, but when he inquired about it, Sai just shook his head sadly and stared off toward the sunset. Later, he explained that if he went home, he wouldn't be able to force himself away from his family and child again. Sasha respected the ship's captain enough to let him keep the distance he needed, literally and emotionally.

A few days later, Sai allowed them a rare respite for a meal. Until then, they'd all eaten while at their posts. Sasha and Duncan spread a cloth on the blistering-hot deck and sat down while Sai went below for provisions.

"Have you wondered why he's doing all this?" Duncan asked softly. "Sai, I mean. It's very out of character for an Emiri. If he's not making a profit or finding some sort of amusement, why is he going to all this trouble?"

Sasha shielded his eyes as he watched Sai emerge onto the deck with his arms full of baskets and jugs. The Emiri moved beautifully, never faltering despite the rocking of the ship. With a bit of training, Sai could become a fabulous assassin, though Sasha knew he didn't have the dedication or attention span to pursue it. Only one thing could hold the Emiri's resolve for this long. "He loves him. Yarrow. Watch his face and gestures whenever he speaks of Yarrow. It's obvious, and… tragic."

Duncan harrumphed. "Obvious to you, maybe. I find it eerie you can tell such things by the speed someone blinks. But why tragic?"

"Because it was never reciprocated." Sasha didn't tell Duncan, but he found that very odd. The Yarrow he'd known had been free with his body and unashamed of pursuing pleasure. Sasha had seduced him just by asking, and Yarrow had made no secret of his fascination with Emiri men, and Sai in particular. The Yarrow he'd known would have worn Sai out. His needs had practically exhausted Sasha when they'd been together. The recollection of his slender, tanned limbs twined in blue ink, his lips parting in ecstasy at the slightest touch, and the enthusiastic sounds he made dragged Sasha back toward that strange place between chill bitterness and warm, glowing contentment. *Useless.* He banished the memories and the confusion they towed in their wake. They would only distract him.

Sai set out not only fruit, dried fish, hardtack bread, and water, but a scroll twice as long as the scrap of yellow cloth they picnicked upon. "I plan to sail through here." He pointed to a twisting, narrow passage between the island of Espero and whatever lands lay beyond the Lapir Mountains east of Gaeltheon. "My people call it the Serpent's Belly, because once you find yourself in it, you're not getting back out."

"Then why in the name of the goddesses would you sail into it?" Duncan asked, a forkful of fish paused halfway to his mouth.

"It's been two months already since I left Yarrow. Two months, and he was closer than we were. Sailing all the way around Espero will add weeks to our journey, and those weeks might mean everything. I think, if I'm at my best, I *might* make it out of the Serpent's Belly."

Sasha expected Duncan to argue in favor of reason, but neither of them saw reason when it came to Yarrow. They hadn't from the beginning. "It seems we have little choice."

"I just wanted you both to be prepared," Sai said. "If we sail hard through the night, we'll reach the Serpent's Belly by first light. I won't lie to you. This has never been done, as far as I know. I'm a capable mariner, but…. The two of you should spend the evening doing anything you might want to do once more in this world. You can use my cabin. I'll be at the helm, anyway."

Without saying another word or eating more than a few bites of fruit, Sai stood and went to the starboard rail and looked out over the sea.

"I feel awful for him," Duncan whispered.

"Well, we could ask him to join us," Sasha suggested. "I'm sure that would cheer him up. Besides, he's lovely. Don't you think? It could be quite enjoyable."

"I need more from coupling than just enjoyment," Duncan said, holding Sasha's gaze with his gray-green eyes, letting Sasha see all the way into his soul. "It hurts me that you'd seriously suggest such a thing."

"That wasn't my intention," Sasha said. "The two can be separated, you know, pleasure and…." He sat in silence, poking the tip of his knife into slices of *koria* fruit and making the ample juice spurt out.

"Love?" Duncan offered. "Why is it so hard for you to even say the word? I know you feel it, sometimes, at least. For me, love means commitment. Fidelity and devotion. Sasha, I don't *want* anyone else. You and Yarrow are it for me. I want to be enough for you too."

Sasha tipped his head slightly so he could look up at Duncan through his lashes and smiled with his lips slightly parted. The devastating gestures he'd practiced over the years worked even better when he meant them, he'd found. He also found it far easier to show Duncan how he felt than to try to force it into words. "Let's finish up our tasks around the ship, and then we can go to the cabin, and I'll give you a chance to prove you're enough. I suspect you'll rise to the challenge, as always."

"Goddesses." Duncan colored, and the black centers of his eyes dilated until they almost eclipsed the green.

THE creak of the boards outside the cabin woke Sasha even before the soft tap on the wall. The small chamber had no door, just a brightly printed curtain over the entrance, but it had afforded enough privacy for him and Duncan to enjoy a wonderful evening. Sasha had slept well, if lightly. He pulled on his undergarment, snug leather trousers, and buckled boots and then stepped out into a fuzzy, gray world tinged with the pink of dawn. Sasha expected some suggestive comment from Sai at his exposed chest, but none came.

Sai looked pensive and drawn; he'd clearly been up most of the night. Fat beads of moisture condensed on his tangled hair and smooth skin. "We'll sail into the Serpent's Mouth in a few hours," he told Sasha just as Duncan emerged, blinking, from the cabin. "We must prepare the ship. Tie everything down, and then we should eat something. We may not have time for another meal for days."

After they'd secured everything on deck and shared a solemn meal of a sort of stew made of fish, watery grain, and seaweed, Sai tied a rope around his waist and fastened it to the helm.

"Sasha, Duncan, tie yourselves to the main mast. Leave enough slack in the rope that you can move around the deck, but not so much you'll be more than a few feet away if you get washed overboard. This little boat will take good care of us as long as we can stay with her. If we don't make it, may you sleep peacefully forever in the arms of Emir. I'm glad she's carried us to each other for a time."

"I'm glad too," Duncan said, extending his hand toward Sai. Sai ignored it and stood on his tiptoes to throw his arms around Duncan's neck.

"None of us are going to die," Sasha said. He had no use for poetic sentiment. "Let's get this done and get to Yarrow."

Not long after, Sasha got his first glimpse of the Serpent's Belly. Based on the map, he'd expected a narrow passage, thought he might be able to see the land on either side. But then he remembered sailing on the broad Kanda and not being able to see from one bank to the other. The water grew choppier and the wind picked up, pitching them forward into overlapping sheets of mist. Sasha couldn't tell if the fog rose from the water or dropped from the sky, but he couldn't see more than a few hundred yards ahead. Now and then the boat crested a high wave, the bow angling up before sliding smoothly down the other side of the swell and cutting through the foam with a spray of spume, but so far, the journey didn't seem so bad. Even as the waves increased in height and frequency, Sai's ship bounced and surfed along them like a child's toy in a washtub. Sasha was no expert on seafaring, but he knew that, while his people constructed sturdy vessels meant to withstand storms, rough seas, and attacks, the Emiri preferred light, fleet ships that could outrun them. Emiri ships were both quick and exceptionally maneuverable.

The wind carried them so fast along the channel the little boat seemed to skim the ocean's surface. Only a few hours into their voyage, their ship began to pitch from side to side, tossing Sasha and Duncan almost from the starboard rail to the port.

Sai didn't look away from the helm as he yelled above the increasing volume of the waves crashing against the hull. "The waves will be coming in from both Espero and Gaeltheon, and they sometimes crash against each other when they meet. Hold on! We're in for quite a ride, and I have to keep her within a few miles of dead center or we'll hit the shoals."

"Goddesses guide us," Duncan yelled at the roiling gray sky as they caught an enormous wave that lifted the ship probably twenty feet into the air.

The bowsprit was almost vertical as Sasha skidded aft across the deck, barely staying on his feet. When the rope around his waist stopped him, he felt like it snapped his spine. He no sooner regained his balance than the boat dove bow-first toward the frothy sea. It hit hard, dousing Sai with a wall of water. He held tight to the helm with both hands but barely withstood the onslaught. More water surged onto the deck, covering Sasha's feet past his ankles.

They had no time to recover before a wave struck the portside like a stone wall, almost knocking the vessel over. Sai steered deftly into the swell, and though it drenched them and knocked Duncan down hard on his side, it didn't capsize them. The assault continued all day and through the night. The ship climbed waves like jagged mountains and sledded down the other sides while breakers struck the boat from every angle, sometimes laying the vessel almost flat on its side. Through it all, Sai guided his beloved ship masterfully, though they had a few close calls and all of them swallowed half their weight in seawater. A few times, Sai steered too close to the shoals, and they scraped along the boat's bottom, threatening to splinter the wood.

By the time the moon rose, nothing but a brighter blur in the thick gloom, Sasha's entire body ached and trembled from clinging to the mast or hauling himself back to it with the rope attached to his waist. He'd been battered from every direction, had never been so thirsty and would have given anything to wash the saline taste from his mouth and throat. Duncan looked half drowned and exhausted, and Sasha had no idea how Sai managed to stay on his feet clinging to his helm, let alone continue guiding them with such incredible precision.

When morning finally came, Sasha barely held on to consciousness as he dangled from the scrap of severed rigging he'd wrapped around his hand to stay upright. Though the sea still tossed the ship up and down and back and forth like a cat batting at a moth, his knees gave out and his eyes closed. More water dumped down on them, and he sputtered awake, disgusted by his weakness. Shoals caught the hull, and the wood groaned in protest before Sai steered them sharply away. The Emiri hung from the helm like a wet shirt on a line, his arms stretched up above his head and his knees almost touching the saturated deck. They pitched sideways again, and Sai compensated, avoiding the center of another huge swell only moments later and guiding them over the gentler curve at its edge. Sasha knew only his love of Yarrow kept the seafarer standing, love that would never be realized. Such motivation was difficult for Sasha to understand, but he felt sure Duncan would appreciate it.

By late afternoon, they reached what must have been the verge of the Lapir Mountains spilling into the sea. Sharp peaks, taller than Windust Castle, rose from the whitecaps churning around them. Everywhere Sasha looked, they jutted from the surf, some on their own like huge, jagged tombstones, and others lined up like a primordial fence. When the rough waves struck them, they shot spume dozens of feet into the darkening sky. In the distance, the cliffs formed walls Sasha had no idea how they'd cross.

"I need water," Sai croaked. "Sasha—"

Sasha staggered across the shifting deck to one of the crates they'd secured with a heavy net, falling twice before he reached it. Using his twisting dagger, he sawed through the wet rope, flung open the lid, and found a clay container stoppered with a cork. Clutching it tight to his chest, he hauled himself along the rail while the sea pelted him relentlessly. When he reached the helm, he opened the canteen and held it to Sai's lips. Sai closed his eyes and drank deeply, opening them just in time to jerk the spokes of the helm and whip them away from one of the smaller rock formations. A gust of air snapped the aft topsail taut, making the ship buck and the stern lift out of the water. Sai's chest hit the helm hard, and he cried out.

"Are you all right?" Sasha asked, worried. The Emiri looked just this side of the Shades' Abode with his dry, cracked lips, sunken eyes, and pale, waxy skin. If he fell, neither Sasha nor Duncan would be able to guide the ship through such difficult waters. Sasha needed him healthy to keep Duncan safe and to reach Yarrow. "Maybe you should rest."

Sai managed a parched chuckle. "I rest, and we die dashed against these rocks. Emir's tits, this passage is like a wind tunnel. I have to concentrate. Have trust in me. I can get us through this."

"Sai, it's very rare for someone to impress me with his skills—" Sasha found it difficult to compose a sincere compliment, though he could flatter and manipulate a cloistered sister out of her knickers or a miser out of his last coin.

The Emiri only nodded, looking weary to his spirit but determined, determined in a way Sasha had only ever seen in the eyes of his brothers on their missions for Thalil. "Thank you, Sasha. Have water. Take some to Duncan. If you don't, you'll die as surely as if you traveled with a land-bound sailor instead of a son of Emir."

Sasha pressed the large flask into Sai's hand, remembering how annoyed Yarrow used to get when Duncan reminded him to eat or drink. It had been endearing, the way their mage railed against concern and coddling when he so clearly craved it. Duncan had been better able to provide it than Sasha, though maybe when they reached Yarrow, Sasha could rectify that. *If* they reached him.

After retrieving more fresh water, Sasha made his way back to Duncan. Both of them wet their lips, and Sasha swore he'd never tasted anything as sweet. He reached up and buried his fingers in Duncan's tangled tresses and dropped his head to Duncan's broad chest. Duncan wound him in his arms, and it felt good to feel sheltered and stable, felt good to know someone would mourn if he sank to the bottom of the sea. A small, deeply ingrained voice told Sasha it was weakness to depend on another for comfort, but he ignored it more effectively than he ever had before.

"Are you all right, my love?" Duncan asked, holding Sasha tight, enveloping Sasha in his thick arms as a fresh fount of ocean bombarded them.

Sasha nodded. It would do neither of them any good to complain of his aching body, more abused than it had felt after any battle. "Are you?"

"Goddesses, I feel like I've been trampled by a hundred war horses. I should put Yarrow over my knee and spank him within an inch of his life for making us go through this."

"He might like that," Sasha said, smiling at the enticing vision, even though he knew Duncan would never really do it. Duncan would rather hold Yarrow on his lap, feed him sweets, and say silly things that would make a maiden roll her eyes. "I… I really love you, Duncan."

"Sasha…." The knight burrowed his face into Sasha's hair and squeezed him until Sasha felt like his bones would crack. Even as Sai steered a corkscrew pattern around the rocks that jostled them against the main mast, Sasha wouldn't have wanted to be anywhere else... except with Yarrow, where the three of them could be together at last.

The wind picked up behind them, hurtling them forward at such a great speed that Sai barely managed to dodge the oncoming rocks. When he sailed too far from the craggy coast and away from the middle of the Serpent's Belly, they wandered into the cursed shoals. Even with his skill, Sai couldn't keep steering them away from every obstacle at their current speed.

"We have to spill wind! Reduce sail!" he yelled, his voice hardly discernible over the howl of the gale. "Drop the main sheet and the jib! Now!"

Duncan and Sasha hurried to obey, struggling with the halyard and the luffing sails, and the vessel slowed, but not enough. It still bounced across the water like a child's skipping stone, slicing through the summits of the breakers and slapping down hard on the other side. Rocks whipped past them so close Sasha could have reached out and touched them. Sai steered too hard to avoid a cluster on the portside, only to scrape the starboard on a nasty stone tooth they came upon too quickly for him to avoid. The railing shattered as they hit it, and a few boards on the deck buckled and split.

"Bare poles!" Sai shouted. "We're almost clear of it!"

Sasha and Duncan scrambled to the aft mast to release the last of the squares of striped canvas. They flapped loudly, as if in protest. Up ahead, the rock wall Sasha had seen loomed over them, and the gap at its center looked just large enough for the ship to pass through. Sai would have to position them perfectly, though. If he miscalculated by even a few feet, they'd be dashed against the stone.

Sasha clung to the aft mast and waited. He could do nothing else, and he hated having his fate in another's hands. The small boat shot toward the towering barricade of stone like an arrow from a bow, fans of frothy sea spraying up on either side of them. Duncan stood watching the horizon with his chin lifted. Though he tried to tell himself he didn't need reassurance, Sasha reached out and clutched Duncan's hand.

They were coming up too fast; they'd never make it into that narrow passage with the waves tossing them back and forth. Even Sasha knew it, though he knew little of piloting a ship. He resisted the urge to close his eyes and cover his head. He would meet Thalil with his head held high and proud and hope his god would accept him. Sasha had left the Crimson Scythe, but he'd never forsaken Thalil in his heart, and he hoped the Dark and Beautiful One would look inside him and see that. Duncan would, no doubt, receive a hero's welcome from his goddesses. He deserved to reside in some eternal, white citadel if any man ever did. They would spend eternity apart. *No.*

I will find you, Sasha swore to Duncan. *I will sneak into the goddesses' palace undetected, just as Thalil crept into the bedchamber of Fayelle, goddess of purity. I can outwit them. Nothing will keep me from you, not even the divines. Let them try.*

Just as Sasha prepared his body for the pain that would precede death, Sai spun the helm so fast the rungs blurred, spinning the ship completely around, into the wind. It slowed almost instantly and headed stern-first toward the small gap. Sai looked over his shoulder as he continued to steer. The side of the ship scraped against the stone as they entered the passage, but Sai managed to guide them away from the edge. The contact left deep gouges in the hull, but did no real damage. A wave swelled beneath them and carried the vessel clear of the tunnel. Nothing but open sea, much calmer than what lay behind them, stretched as far as Sasha could see. He exhaled and let the tension fall from his muscles.

They'd made it.

Sai finally released the helm he'd been attached to for almost two days and two nights. He leapt up and punched the air. "We did it! We entered the Serpent's Belly and came back out! Sweet Emir, we're the first!" He bounded over to them and kissed each of them on the lips, and even Duncan returned what was much more a victorious than an amorous gesture.

"Not we," Duncan said, still clasping the Emiri's hands. "*You* did this, *Sai-Mir.* You are surely the greatest sailor to have ever seen water." He bent down to kiss Sai hard on the forehead, and Sai shivered as he looked expectantly up at the knight.

"Is there any sort of reward, Tam Duncan?" Even near death with exhaustion, Sai managed quite a tempting smile.

Duncan laughed and released the Emiri. "It may not be what you want right now, my true friend, but if I can ever repay you for this, Sai, then I will. Anything. Well, anything but that. You have only to ask. I swear it before the thirteen sisters and all their children."

"You're missing out, *syrai,*" Sai said.

"Are we *syrai* now?" Sasha asked. "You didn't call us *syrai* before, only Yarrow."

Sai looked at Sasha as if he might be a dullard. "We've sailed together, and uncharted waters, at that. *Of course* we're *syrai*. Now, let's have a hot meal, a healthy share of *muri-ku*, and a long sleep. The waters are calm at last, and we all need rest. We should stay on course without much effort from this point on. The currents here are lazy and the winds are dying down."

They ate and drank, and even though the pile of cushions and blankets Sai dragged from the cabin was so drenched it oozed water when they lay down, all of them slept side by side for many blessed hours.

Chapter Seventeen

DESPITE sleeping on a soggy heap of cloth with both Sasha and Sai sprawled across him, Duncan woke feeling refreshed and hopeful. The goddesses had seen them through an impossible ordeal, and he had faith they'd continue to stand by them. They would need every scrap of assistance they could get.

They assessed the damage and planned how best to make what repairs they could. Sai and Sasha worked to spread the wet goods out on the deck to dry, and after Duncan finished patching a section of splintered rail, he went to help them. The three of them worked together to mend the worst of the tears on the sails. Sai went below deck to check for hull breaches and save what he could of their supplies. Afterward, they had a modest breakfast of fish cooked over the brazier; plenty of them had washed up on the deck as they'd navigated the Serpent's Belly. When they finished, Sai went to the helm and guided them along the nameless coast until he found a shallow bay. It surprised Duncan to see dozens of other vessels hugging the shore, but they were primitive: hollowed out bowls with single masts, square sails, and oars extending from both sides.

Sai spilled wind and slowed far from the shore, dropping anchor well away from the other boats. "I have an ill feeling about this port, and I don't wish to dock here. Take the dinghy. I'll get another rowboat somewhere, but I won't sail into this harbor."

Duncan looked at Sasha and wished he could find some suggestion in his lover's flat, black eyes, but Sasha only observed the simple boats moving up and down the coast. Sai had done enough for them, and Duncan couldn't ask the Emiri to put himself in further danger. "Will you be all right if we take the dinghy to shore? How will you get home, Sai? Despite the repairs we made, your ship is badly damaged."

"She's bruised, but hardly broken," Sai said, caressing the rail of his boat and saying a few soothing words in Emiri. "She won't let me down; she never has. As soon as I catch the current, I'll guide her around Espero and back home to the Twenty-Nine. Never fear, I don't plan to try to sail the Serpent's Belly in reverse. Don't worry about me. I'll be fine on the open sea, and in fact I can't wait for that time alone with my thoughts. Worry about Yarrow. Find him. He needs you now." Sai tilted his head toward the dinghy, indicating the conversation was over.

"Fair seas to you, Sai," Sasha said as he turned the lever to lower the small boat into the gentle water.

"And to you, *syrai*," Sai responded. "Maybe the sea will carry us back to each other one day. One never knows, though."

"One never does," Sasha said with an uncharacteristic whisper of regret in his voice. He continued to prepare the dinghy and load their packs onboard without looking back.

Duncan approached Sai and gave him a hug and a kiss on the cheek in the Emiri way. "I'll never be able to thank you for all you've done for us and for Yarrow, but as I said, if I can ever offer you assistance of any kind, you need only come to Windwake and ask. I'm honored to have called you friend, and I would be honored to have you in my home as a guest."

"And me, Duncan. Now is the time for us to say farewell. May the winds favor you, may you outrun every storm, and may your holds be filled with so much treasure it almost weighs you down, but not quite." Sai kissed Duncan again and then returned to the helm, keeping anything else he felt to himself.

Duncan joined Sasha in the dinghy and rowed toward the shore. Sai wasted no time in departing; his ship was only a speck on the horizon by the time they reached the rickety docks, and Duncan wondered what he'd misliked so fiercely. Emiri didn't spook easily.

Sasha looped a rope over a weathered post and gripped it to hoist himself up, as there were no steps. Duncan followed, resting his hand on the sword hilt at his hip. At first, the port looked like any other along the Kanda River or up the coast of Selindria, with men bustling to unload cargo, repair ships, darn sails, and haggle over the prices of their items. Carts and stands hawked their wares, and Duncan smelled the expansive fish market before he saw it. Still, something about it felt very foreign, and

Duncan was glad of Sasha's shrewd eyes and quick blades at his back as they made their way slowly inland.

"Where will we begin to search for Yarrow?" Duncan asked, standing aside to allow a group of dark-skinned, chattering women carrying baskets on their heads to pass. Though none of them looked particularly wealthy, they all wore clothing dyed with expensive plums, cobalts, and scarlets. "Do you understand their language?"

"Now and then, I almost recognize a word from the secret language of my order," Sasha said softly. He risked his life even speaking of his calling in public. "But the cadence is all wrong, and that language has been dead to all but us for thousands of years. But look there. Perhaps we should speak to those men."

Duncan followed the dark line of Sasha's extended arm to a group of Selindrian sailors stumbling out of a brothel. The scantily clad young women kissed their cheeks and waved at them as they departed. Duncan rolled his eyes. Some things never changed.

As they drew nearer, Duncan saw all of the whores wore their hair shaved, and many of them had decorated their skin with swirling patterns. Unlike the paint Yarrow and Sai wore, the designs appeared to have been carved into their dark skin and left to scar on purpose. Duncan shuddered as he tried to imagine the pain. Their thin, richly dyed attire sparkled with rows of beads as small as grains of sand, extravagant clothing for a princess, let alone a group of street slags. The girls tittered and waved at Duncan and Sasha, but they ignored them.

"Excuse me," Sasha said to the sailors. "Are you good mariners from Selindria, perchance?"

"Dear goddesses," said one of them, a tall, broad man with sun-bleached yellow hair and close-cropped whiskers, the captain if one were to judge by the amount of gold in his ears and on his wrists and fingers. "We thought we were the first and only civilized men to ever set foot in this land. How did you get here, friend?"

"We came onboard an Emiri ship," Sasha said.

The big sailor's eyes grew wide. "They're not still here, are they? The Emiri you traveled with?"

Any other man's eyes might have narrowed, but Sasha displayed no suspicion, and his disarming smile never faltered. "No. Why do you ask?"

"I've sailed with a few of the Sea Folk," the blond sailor said. "They ain't like us, but they ain't so bad. They're not safe here. This is a strange and savage land, friend."

"How so?" Duncan asked.

The sailor took Duncan's elbow and pulled him into an alley between the brothel and the small, sand-colored building beside it. Something resembling a cat, but larger and with a longer snout, speckled body, and a striped tail ending in a black tassel, abandoned the garbage pile it had been raiding at their approach.

The sea captain and two of his men leaned against the brothel wall and crossed their arms. Duncan leaned in close while Sasha stayed near the corridor's entrance, keeping watch.

"My name's Bartoum Astir, captain of the good ship *Shadowbreeze*."

When Duncan raised a brow at the boat's name, Captain Bartoum explained. "Look, friend, we're not pirates. We don't steal cargo from other ships, but we're not above taking jobs others find too risky or… legally questionable. Still, we're honorable men, hardened men of the sea, and what we've seen here is enough to make even our salty hair curl."

"I don't presume to judge you," Duncan said, extending his hand. "Duncan Purefroy of Windwake. This is my associate, Sasha. You would be doing us a great service if you could tell us what dangers we're facing here."

Captain Bartoum Astir swiped his hand down his face from his forehead to the tips of his whiskers and toyed with the ends of his beard as he spoke. "As goddess-fearing Selindrians, you deserve no less. From what I could tell from the, er, the working ladies, none of them are allowed hair. Only their rulers. Saw one of them, I did, riding by in a gold and glass carriage. Hideous, deformed thing, white as a fish's belly with a bald skull pointed like a princess's hat. Couldn't tell from the saggy tits if it was a man or a woman. The body was withered. I'd bet gold it couldn't walk on its own. The whores fell down on their knees and covered their heads when they saw our ship's mage. Some of them cried. We felt it safer to keep our poor young enchantress back onboard the ship."

"And the Emiri?" Sasha asked.

"Goddesses," Bartoum whispered, fondling a pendant of Diarana, patroness of all travelers.

"What is it?" Duncan pressed, grasping the other man's thick bicep.

"To tell you they're kept in the cruelest bondage would be an understatement," he said, and his men grunted in agreement, one of them looking away like he might be sick. "I don't know why the goddesses don't burn this horrible place into oblivion. It would be better than it deserves."

The horror in the burly sailor's voice made Duncan's blood run cold; these didn't look like men who scared easily. "Why in the sisters' names are you here, then?"

"Young lad offered us a payment we couldn't refuse, and he had charts to get us here. They looked like he'd drawn them himself, maybe from memory, but they seemed accurate. Had I known what we'd find, I might have asked for double."

"Triple, I say," one of the other sailors said with a scowl.

The golden warmth of hope banished some of the chill crawling over Duncan's skin. "We are here in search of a friend. Can you describe this young man?"

"Well, he looked Emiri at first," Captain Bartoum Astir said. "But I never seen an Emiri, or anybody else, with snow-white hair like his. He's an unusual lad, kept to himself for the most part and got right nasty if any of us went poking into his affairs. Kept us all awake with his nightmares."

"Yarrow," Sasha said, having silently rejoined them. "Was his name Yarrow?"

"Aye," Bartoum answered. "He paid us well to wait here till the end of the moon and headed north in the direction of the hills. Caused a fair bit of trouble before he went, though."

"Of course he did." Duncan pinched the bridge of his nose. "What happened?"

"We arrived here a little less than a week ago. After we docked, me and my men decided to take a look around, see if we might trade with the locals. Have you seen the cloth the women wear? It would be worth a fortune back home. Your friend stayed with us that first night, but then he went off on his own, looking for goddesses know what. Then, a few days ago, we heard a commotion near the center of town, so we went to have a look. Your lad Yarrow took it upon himself to free a few dozen Emiri slaves from their cages and escape with them by basically massacring anyone who stood in their way. He mowed down the guards and left a good chunk of the city burning. Goddesses, the blood—He made it into the hills with the slaves, but they're after him. We had… we had *no idea* of that boy's power. Look, I respect his intentions, but we're just one crew. We can't go against an entire kingdom of barbarians."

Sasha chuckled. "My friend would disagree, it seems. I'm not at all surprised." He sounded proud as he untied a pouch from his belt and held it out to the captain. Bartoum's eyes went wide as he weighed the gold, bouncing it against his palm. "Will this persuade you to wait for us a little longer?"

"Goddesses, this is a fortune," the blond sailor said. "How in their name did you come to carry around so much coin and hand it off like a bag of pebbles?"

Sasha looked up at Bartoum through his lashes as he leaned casually against the wall. "I earned it by doing to other men what I'll do to you if you take my gold and strand us here. There will be nowhere in this world you can hide from me and my *brothers*."

"Blessed mother," Bartoum said, sweat beading across his forehead. "If the sisters see fit to get me out of this voyage alive, so help me, I'm sticking to hauling firewood up and down the river for the rest of my days. I can give you two more weeks on top of what your friend already paid for. If that isn't good enough, take your gold back right now. May the goddesses forgive me for having dealings with the Cast-Down. A righteous man would refuse you."

"That will satisfy me," Sasha said, "and if you keep your word, you'll have nothing to fear from me or my brethren. You have my thanks, but we should go in search of our companion."

"I think that's a good idea, friend," Bartoum agreed. "Keep your heads down."

"You didn't have to threaten the poor man," Duncan said as he and Sasha made their way through the crowded streets. The people they passed, down to the youngest children, wore brightly colored wraps on their shaved heads, but other than that, they seemed happy enough conducting the business of daily life: hanging laundry, tending small gardens, baking in rounded outdoor ovens, and trading goods with vendors.

"We just met him," Sasha argued dispassionately. "I needed some guarantee he wouldn't take my money and be gone with the next tide."

"He seemed a trustworthy enough fellow."

Sasha blew air through his nose. "You trust everyone."

"Until they give me a reason not to," Duncan admitted.

"And I mistrust everyone until they prove themselves worthy of my confidence. For that reason, I'm still alive."

"Oh, and just how many men have achieved that high honor?" Duncan taunted mildly.

"Two."

"Oh." He couldn't help smiling as they walked side by side. Sasha's trust *was* an honor; Duncan wondered if Sasha had even been capable of trusting another person during his time with the assassins of the Crimson Scythe.

"We should stock up on supplies," Sasha suggested, artfully steering their conversation back toward practical considerations. "Food and water. We don't know how long we'll be in the mountains or what we'll find there. Hopefully we won't encounter the guards searching for Yarrow, but, well, we should be ready for anything."

"I suppose that makes sense," Duncan agreed, looking around. Farther into the village, pale golden octagonal stones paved the roads. They followed one of the lanes, and it opened to the strange city's version of an open market or town square. Around a dozen colorful pavilions stood at the outside of the open area, and merchants sat on rugs beneath them. Duncan followed his nose to a canopy where long strips of dried meat hung from wooden poles. It reminded him of the jerky made back home, and he knew it would last on the road.

Duncan pointed to a strip of meat almost as long as he was tall, and the stall vendor, a young man, set his reed fan aside and rose to assist his customer. Like the other residents of the strange port, the young merchant had a clean-shaven head, and deeply carved geometric patterns decorated his sun-browned skin. He wore a bright yellow pair of loose trousers with what looked like layers of skirts over top. Some sort of shimmering black powder lined his eyes, and red paint—clearly not permanent like an Emiri's—accentuated his cheekbones and the deliberate scars on his head. Smiling, the shopkeeper said something Duncan couldn't begin to understand.

Returning the young man's smile, Duncan took a few copper coins from the pouch on his belt. He pointed to them and then back to the meat.

The young man picked up one of the coins and scowled at it. He said a sharp word and pushed it back into Duncan's palm. Clearly he would not accept Selindrian currency.

Sasha stepped in front of Duncan and touched the merchant's shoulder flirtatiously. The brief caress captured the young man's attention, and Duncan blew air out his nose. He supposed if Sasha's approach procured them some food, he would tolerate it.

Sasha took some items—a pendant of Diarana, some Emiri beads carved from shells, a few gold rings and some other baubles—from a small purse and offered them to the shopkeeper on his outstretched palm. The merchant canted his head and moved them around on Sasha's hand with his finger. Finally he accepted the one he wanted—a braided bracelet of gold and silver wire—and held it up with his brows raised. Sasha pointed to the ring and then to the dried meat, and the two of them seemed to strike a bargain. The vendor laid the meat on low table, shook a variety of powders onto it as seasoning, and then wrapped it tightly around a wooden stick, almost like a lady might wrap her embroidery thread. Duncan found it a clever method of storage. Then the stall vendor put the compact package in a coarse tan sack and handed it to Sasha, who stored it in his pack.

They went to a few other tents and, with a great deal of patience, managed to barter for sheets of flat bread—some plain and some filled with what looked like fruit, nuts, and ground meat—fresh water, and dried fruits and beans. The tents grew sparser and farther apart as they made their way toward the outskirts of the village. After a few hours, they left the market and took a bend toward the hazy hills in the distance.

What they saw when they turned the corner wiped the smile off Duncan's face like he'd been punched in the gut. Five Emiri, heads shorn and stripped to their tatty undergarments, hung from their wrists from the supports of a wooden platform. A chubby man in dark trousers whipped each of them in turn. Their chins hung against their chests, and blood streamed down their backs. Some of them barely reacted when the cruel lash tore into their flesh. Dozens of others waited in cages so small they could scarcely crouch, their eyes dead and devoid of hope as they clutched the wooden bars or cowered in the corners. Worst of all, a young Emiri man lay on a slab while his tormentor drove nails into his heels with a hammer.

On the battlefield, Duncan had heard the screams of hundreds of dying men. He'd heard them crying out to their mothers as they tried to keep their insides from spilling out, but he'd never heard anything like the screams of the Emiri on that table. The anguish in those cries cut to his core, to his most primal self, the one that protected innocents from harm and stood against injustice, the part of him that was knight in the purest sense. If this wasn't injustice, Duncan had never witnessed it, and goddesses stand behind him, he would not, could not let it continue. He drew his sword, felt the warm steel against his palm like an old friend's embrace, and strode toward the horrible spectacle.

Sasha caught his elbow, but Duncan didn't stop. He dragged Sasha behind him toward the platform that stank of blood, death, and feces. Despite Sasha trying to hold him back, he'd put an end to this atrocity, free these people from their unimaginable suffering.

Sasha planted his feet in the dirt and spun Duncan to face him. When Duncan tried to pull away, Sasha smacked him in the face with the back of his hand. "I know it's horrible, Duncan. But we can't win this battle. We're two men against an entire empire. Those dozens of guards will kill us, and nothing will change. We either die here for nothing, or we get to Yarrow. I… I will fight beside you if you decide this cause is worthier of our attention, but that will leave Yarrow on his own."

"Goddesses," Duncan panted, barely keeping the contents of his stomach where they belonged. "I have never even imagined anything so deplorable. Everything I am tells me to stop it."

"It is one or the other," Sasha said. "For what it's worth, if we see Yarrow safe, I'll slit these bastards' throats while they sleep if Thalil grants me the opportunity. For now, we must either see to our friend or forsake him."

Duncan screwed his eyes shut, turned away, and tried to block out the sobbing and screams. He couldn't bear to see the light of the sun touching a world like this, a world the goddesses shouldn't allow to exist, so he kept his eyes closed and let Sasha guide him away from everything he felt it was his duty to rectify. He didn't dare open them until the sounds of anguish faded and vanished.

"It isn't right to leave them suffering," Duncan said through clenched teeth.

"I know, my friend, but one battle at a time," Sasha replied, his black eyes unguarded and baring his distress to Duncan.

Duncan bit his lip against the bile stinging his throat and trudged behind Sasha, past the boundaries of the small village. He thanked the goddesses for the rocky plain and the windswept grass around him, absent of the sounds of misery and pleading. Still, he couldn't banish the images of helpless people being victimized, people who needed the help he, as a knight, could and should provide.

"It doesn't sit well with me, leaving them," he told Sasha as they made their way across what looked like an endless expanse of sand and sun-bleached prairie.

"I know. You're too honorable of a man for your own good sometimes. Wanting to right every wrong. I… I yearn to be more like you," Sasha said.

"You do?"

Sasha looked down at his black boots as they carved furrows through the sand. "Who else can serve as an example? My order valued only success. If I have abandoned them and their values, I need to model my life after something. I could do worse than you."

"Sasha… goddesses. I don't know if I deserve to stand as an example to anyone."

"You do, my friend, and I think you know it. I have never known a man so concerned with the welfare of others, even above his own needs. I admit, it is hard for me to understand, but I'm trying. You've at least made me hesitate at times and wonder what's right, and not just what's most effective. That's a step, is it not?"

"I had no idea," Duncan admitted, stunned by his assassin's admission.

"Yes, well, don't expect too much. We should focus on finding Yarrow."

"Agreed."

Together, they traversed the flat, monotone grassland as it sloped slowly into rocky foothills, and then they picked their way over the gravelly trails leading into the mountains. The landscape changed very little as the sun descended lazily to the west, washing the cliffs and gullies in soft lilac. Before long, they had nothing but the soft glow of the foreign stars to light their way.

To the east, dozens of lanterns flickered across the grasslands. Duncan guessed from their formations that they belonged to trained men:

guards or soldiers. When they reached a rocky outcrop with a good view of the plains, Duncan stopped to watch them for a few moments.

"Guards," Sasha said, affirming Duncan's assumption.

"Do you think they're looking for Yarrow?"

"Probably," Sasha said, "though they're going in the wrong direction. Still, we should try to avoid their attention. We can't speak their language, so we'll be unable to answer their questions. We have no idea what kind of men inhabit this land. They may be the kind who kill strangers on sight."

Shivering, Duncan nodded. "In that case, we should move on, and quickly." He pointed to a gently sloping path. The rocks on either side of it would shield them from view for a time, especially if they avoided lamps or campfires. For the next few hours, they walked in silence. Duncan listened carefully for the smallest sound, and his gaze flicked often in the direction of the flatlands. Sasha, too, picked his way silently over the loose gravel, turning his head in the direction of every noise. Desiring distance between themselves and the men seeking their friend, they didn't stop walking until many hours later.

Sasha, several dozen feet ahead of Duncan, crouched and scooped something into his hand. Duncan, though exhausted, jogged up the trail to see what his friend had found and saw a crude campfire, long since burned to cinders, a few feet from the path.

"Lilies," Sasha said, sniffing the ashes. "Yarrow has been here, camped here."

Duncan nodded, recalling the floral-scented blue flames his mage often conjured. He knelt down next to Sasha and lifted a handful of the debris to his nose. The faint, floral scent summoned so many memories all at once, memories of the many nights he'd spent with Sasha and Yarrow on the road, that Duncan closed his eyes against the onslaught. The images continued to assail him, though: just silly things, like Yarrow looking over his shoulder and smiling as he walked along a trail, or dipping hard bread in his broth before nibbling the crust, but every one of them felt like an arrow piercing Duncan's chest. He clutched the remains of Yarrow's fire to his heart for a second before letting them sift through his fingers as he fought to compose himself. "Why isn't Yarrow trying to cover his trail?"

Sasha looked up from the cold campfire and whatever thoughts it had conjured for him, the silver slivers of the moon reflecting from the corners of his eyes. "Simple. He's not afraid. He welcomes a challenge from those who pursue him. Would you expect less?"

"No," Duncan said, shaking his head. "Let's keep going, catch up to him if we can. I'd rather reach him before they do."

"You don't want to camp tonight?" Sasha asked.

Duncan shook his head again. "I wouldn't say this to anyone but you, and I'll probably make a fool of myself, but I… I long to see Yarrow again. Fiercely."

Sasha simply nodded and smoothed an errant strand of hair out of Duncan's eyes. He cupped Duncan's cheek and searched his face for several moments, as if he wanted to speak, but then he turned and continued to traverse the increasingly steep and rocky ground. Around sunrise, each of them took a turn sleeping while the other kept watch. Duncan rested first, then he held Sasha against his chest while his assassin slept deeply, something Sasha rarely allowed himself. Normally Sasha woke at even the tiniest sound, and it pleased Duncan that Sasha placed enough faith in him to protect him while he was vulnerable. Duncan stroked down his lithe arm and rubbed his face against Sasha's silky hair, just enjoying his warm presence as morning brightened into day. When he woke, Duncan took water, a few of the flat, round sheets of bread, and strips of dried meat from his pack, and they ate a somber breakfast before continuing into the hills.

The morning light allowed Sasha to track Yarrow by observing bent grasses or disturbed gravel. Duncan enjoyed hunting and had learned to pursue his quarry, but Sasha's skill in this, like in so many other things, was almost uncanny.

"We're getting very close," the assassin said, plucking a white hair from a thistle-like plant and holding it out to Duncan. "We should catch up to him within a couple of hours."

"What are we waiting for, then?"

To Duncan's surprise, Sasha pressed a palm to his chest and stopped him. He looked as though he'd just eaten something putrid and was struggling not to expel it from his stomach. Duncan pinched Sasha's chin and made him meet his eyes. "What is it, love?"

"I feel a strange dread," Sasha said softly. "It's unfamiliar to me, a chill spreading out from my belly and chest. Thalil, what if he doesn't want us anymore?"

"At least we'll know," Duncan said, though it seemed a poor attempt at comfort.

Sasha shook his head and turned away from Duncan, looking out across the cracked plateau on their right. "This is what my masters always warned me against. Allowing something to become meaningful to you grants others power, because by the Cast-Down it hurts when it's taken away. Even imagining it makes me feel like I've suffered a fatal wound. I don't know how to deal with these things. I never learned."

Curling his fingers around Sasha's shoulder to alleviate some of the tension in his tight muscles, Duncan leaned close and spoke quietly near Sasha's ear. "No one ever learns how to deal with such things. Would you have done otherwise, my love? If you had known last year that you might feel this pain, would it have stopped you from loving us?"

"I don't—No, Duncan, it would not. I would do nothing differently."

Duncan brushed Sasha's hair aside to kiss him on the temple. They continued on hand in hand, and after a few hours, a slight figure appeared in the distance, standing on the crest of a hill and leaning on a weathered branch. Yarrow was even thinner and browner than Duncan remembered, wearing a blue tunic so tattered and worn it looked almost translucent, threadbare trousers, and leather boots caked with dirt. His white hair hung to his chest in gnarled ropes, and he carried a single pack slung over his shoulder.

"Yarroway!" Sasha called.

The mage flinched and looked over his shoulder like he wanted to run. Blue sparkles sprung alight around him. Duncan reached out as if to take hold of him, though several dozen feet still separated them. It was closer than the three of them had been in a year, and Duncan had no intention of letting the chance slip away.

"Yarrow, stop!" Duncan yelled. "At least speak with us."

Yarrow didn't approach them, but he didn't retreat. Duncan looked at Sasha, and they walked slowly toward their friend, as if moving too quickly might send him fleeing like a scared rabbit.

Chapter Eighteen

IS THIS some cruel trick? Even for you, this is excessively nasty, creature.

The creature didn't respond, and Yarrow took a halting step toward Duncan and Sasha, still unsure if they were real. They were even more beautiful than in his nighttime fantasies. Sasha's ebony hair, shining in the sun, fell around his sculpted, golden face. He stood with his elegant fingers spread and held inches from the daggers at his hips. His svelte body formed a delicate, dark curve in his order leathers. Next to him, Duncan chewed his lower lip like a nervous boy, looking fragile and vulnerable despite his stature and broad, muscular shoulders. His gray-green eyes showed Yarrow all the confusion and guarded joy he felt.

None of them spoke. Slowly, Duncan dropped his packs of supplies, raised a trembling hand, and closed his fingers around one of Yarrow's tangled clumps of hair. The knight let out a sigh, as if profoundly relieved to find Yarrow solid. He blinked, and a few tears spilled down his cheeks and into his whiskers as he touched Yarrow's cheek with his finger and the center of Yarrow's mouth with his thumb. Yarrow shuddered despite the intense heat. He'd missed that gentle touch more than he'd ever realized. Gingerly, he lifted his hand and draped it over Duncan's, every bit as relieved as the knight to feel bone, sinew, and warm skin beneath his palm.

Duncan ran his hand down Yarrow's neck and grasped both of Yarrow's biceps, holding Yarrow at arm's length, looking him up and down before finally folding Yarrow in his arms and then crushing Yarrow against his chest. He dropped his forehead to Yarrow's shoulder and choked back a sob. "Goddesses, Yarrow, you… you're very thin."

Both of them laughed, easing the tension between them enough for Yarrow to hug Duncan back. He sniffled as he breathed in the scents of his hair, skin, and the few bits of battered plate he wore.

When Duncan released him, Yarrow took a step to the side, facing Sasha. The two of them regarded each other as if awaiting a duel. Yarrow remembered the icy mask looking back at him only too well. Yarrow had no idea what to say; he'd hurt Sasha. Sasha had relinquished every essence of his identity to remain beside Yarrow and Duncan, and Yarrow had walked away from him. Looking at him now, Yarrow wasn't sure it was a wound that could ever be patched. But then Sasha reached for him and pulled Yarrow against his chest. Their lips met, opened, and interlocked, teeth scraping together. Sasha tasted just as Yarrow remembered: warm and enticing with a hint of exotic spice.

Yarrow and Sasha each reached out one of their arms, and Duncan took his place beside them and wound them both in his thick, strong limbs. For a long time, they just clung to each other like the world fell away around them. For all Yarrow cared, it could have.

Oh, isn't this nice, beloved? Just like old times.

The creature's voice snapped Yarrow out of the warm haze he'd let engulf him, and he broke away from the men he loved and took a few steps back. As soon as he severed contact, he wanted nothing in the world but to be in their arms again, protected and cherished. But as long as he remained a danger to them, he could not.

"Sasha, Duncan," he said, "how are you even here? How did you find the way to this unknown place?"

"Sai is a good friend to you," Duncan said. "He sought us out after you sent him away. He didn't wish for you to face peril alone. He brought us here on his ship."

"You cannot stay," Yarrow said, struggling to sound commanding. He had to make them understand, even if it meant cutting them afresh.

"I will go where I like," Sasha said in a soft hiss. "Even you cannot stop me, Yarrow. I shouldn't have let you go the first time, and I will not do so again."

Yarrow appealed to Duncan. "You swore to me!"

"I did," Duncan admitted, rubbing the crease between his brows with his finger. "I have never broken an oath in my life. But I will break this one. Whatever you're planning to face, you won't face it alone. Not while I live. If I have to be a liar and an oath breaker, then I will."

Watching them, their jaws set in grim determination, their feet planted wide, and their arms crossed over their chests, Yarrow knew they would not be swayed. He would have an easier time melting all the icecaps of the Lapir Mountains than changing their minds, so he said, "I don't want to be the cause of you breaking an oath, Duncan. I release you from it. Goddesses. Do you have any idea the danger you're putting yourselves in?"

"No," Sasha said. "Tell us what we'll face."

"How can I when I don't know myself?" Yarrow snapped, raising his voice more than he intended. He couldn't deny the hope he felt at having these capable men who loved him by his side again, but their stubbornness and refusal to put their well-being above his own irritated the mage.

"Peace." Duncan moved his hand down Yarrow's arm, wiping away Yarrow's anger. The knight looked at Yarrow, then Sasha. "Whatever we must face, we'll face it standing together, as we should."

"How much did Sai tell you of my plans?" Yarrow asked.

"Enough," Duncan said. "He admitted to understanding little of our history and less of your magic, but he knew you'd be facing danger in a strange and uncharted land. He knew how desperate you were to get rid of the thing you host."

"Then you know I may never find Fane, may never be able to reach him, and that he may not be able to help me if I do," Yarrow said. They needed to understand. "If he cannot help me, I can't stay with you. I won't put your lives at risk."

"We can discuss that when and if it becomes necessary," Sasha said.

Will watching them die finally convince you to abandon this fool's errand, beloved?

I will not let them die. I will raze this world and everything in it, myself included, to nothing before I let that happen.

Ha-ha! Now that is something I would like to see! Perhaps it's time for this world to be scrapped and started anew, with us as its ruler.

You will never see that come to pass. I'll be rid of you one way or another.

We'll see, won't we, little Yarrow?

"Yarrow? Are you listening?"

"Yes, I'm sorry. I'm no longer accustomed to speaking with others. What did you ask?"

"I asked if you have an idea where we need to go," Sasha repeated.

Yarrow closed his eyes. If he concentrated, he felt a small pull at his spine just behind his hips, the draw of old, old magic. He couldn't know if it was Fane he felt, but he sensed the source in the direction Hale had pointed out on his chart. "I think we have to continue northwest, into the mountains."

Duncan raised his hand to shield his face from the sun as he gazed at the distant peaks. "Goddesses," he said in a soft voice, "are we truly on the other side of the Lapir Mountains? We're looking at them from the other side? I know Sai said we'd sailed past them, but…. No one in generations has stood where we're standing now. It seems so unbelievable."

"No one from Selindria or Gaeltheon," Sasha corrected. "I've always understood there's no known pass through the Lapir Mountains."

"Yes, that's true." Yarrow answered. "Do you remember when I told you I'd tried to make it over them? When I was exiled, I traveled all the way to the eastern border of Gaeltheon, which is marked by the Lapir Mountains. I couldn't cross and would have died if not for…. Well, you know the rest. The range is vast, though, and if I understood Hale's charts, I shouldn't have to travel so far into them that it becomes dangerous. The highest and most treacherous of the peaks are probably hundreds of miles to the west, and beyond them is Gaeltheon. Hale indicated the site of Fane's fall is not that far into the mountains, though. I think if we walk northwest, we may find it before we have to worry about venturing into the most rugged parts. At least I hope so."

Sasha nodded once and headed off in that direction, picking a path over the increasingly large rocks. The terrain grew jagged as they ascended into the foothills, and now and then they passed rivulets of red-hot molten stone. In the distance, it erupted from the peaks and shot into the sky. Yarrow pulled his much-patched, heavy black cloak from his pack and secured it around his shoulders. The pools and spurts of lava seemed even more bizarre and unnatural when they reached the part of the hills covered in snow. A few feet off to their left, a tiny geyser sputtered and bubbled from the earth, the boiling, liquid rock converting the snow instantly to steam.

"How is it that no one has found Fane's resting place in all these years?" Duncan asked.

"No one knew to look," Yarrow answered, having thought about it a lot himself. "After he fell, the people of the world had to concentrate on survival. From what I understand, they had to relearn the simplest concepts, right down to using tools and constructing shelters for themselves. By the time society advanced enough to concern itself with history, Fane had already passed into the murky realm of legend."

"It's amazing that we might actually be able to see the very spot where the thirteen goddesses defeated Fane," Duncan said, his voice soft with reverence. "We might stand where the holy sisters themselves stood."

Not going to tell him the truth about his darling goddesses, beloved?

Not right now. Why should I? It will only upset him. He finds comfort in believing his goddesses are looking after him.

As I have said before, he's a sentimental fool.

Enough.

"Am I wrong to suspect the goddesses don't want this place found?" Sasha asked. "That it will be guarded in some way?"

"I'm sure you're right," Yarrow said, looking over at Sasha, who'd also donned a heavy cloak. The increasing chill had nipped his high-boned cheeks red, and snowflakes sparkled on his thick, black eyelashes. Yarrow could hardly accept that they were together again. It had been so easy. He couldn't help expecting to wake up from some ensorcelled dream. Only the numbness of his toes and the tingling of his fingers convinced him he inhabited the corporeal plane.

"So we'll have fighting to do," Duncan said, a fur-lined wrap over his armor and his breath coming in long, white plumes. Yarrow wanted to curl against the warmth of his body and take shelter in his gentle arms.

"There's no way to know," he answered. "Not even Hale could say. We should be ready for anything. I hate this. You two, in danger on my behalf—"

"This argument has already been finished," Duncan said, his hand a comforting weight on Yarrow's shoulder.

"We should devote our energy to any threats we might face," Sasha said in agreement.

Fine, dry snow swirled and eddied around them as they continued their trek across the foothills, ascending slowly toward the majestic range in the distance. They walked most of each day and into the night, only stopping for a few hours rest and a modest meal from their supplies long after sunset every night. The air grew thinner and colder with each passing day. Sometimes Yarrow thought he saw a snow wraith materializing at the periphery of his vision, and he kept a fire spell ready. The presence inside him taunted him with every step he took.

Are you enjoying being back in the mountains, beloved? Do you remember the first time you attempted something this foolish? You would have died if you hadn't found me. Do you remember how the cold made your skin crack, bleed, and turn black? Will you like watching that happen to your little friends? Will you like watching them starve out here?

Shut up. You don't know what you're talking about. If Hale's maps are still accurate after all this time, we shouldn't have to go very high into the mountains. It will be nowhere near as cold or desolate as when we first met. I won't be in danger like I was back then. I am much stronger than I was. You won't dissuade me. We're getting close now. I can feel it, and I'm sure you can too. You're afraid.

Hardly. This could work well for me. You know I won't let you die, beloved. I'll just wait until you're too weak to resist me, take control of the flesh, kill your lovers, and roast their meat to sustain us. I wonder how they'll taste. Tough, I imagine, but I'll savor it nonetheless.

Yarrow shivered, fear infecting him. He'd nearly died in a place like this. Sheer will had kept him on his feet long enough to find the creature's prison. The craggy peaks capped in ice surrounding him on all sides looked too familiar. He started to feel trapped, helpless....

No! I am a great mage and I will not be intimidated by ice! These are merely the foothills! I'll let neither you nor my own memory frighten me. I'm stronger now....

Repeat it again, beloved. Maybe you can make yourself believe it.

They reached an impasse moments later. Hundreds of feet of stone surrounded them on every side, and the only way through was a steep, downward slope covered in a roiling river of molten rock. Far below, it flowed into a small opening Yarrow knew he had to enter.

"What now?" Sasha asked, warming his hands over the fiery flow. Stubble covered his chin and dark circles lined his eyes. They'd been walking for days.

"We have no choice but to backtrack and find another way around," Duncan said in a rough, exhausted voice.

"No," Yarrow said. "We have to go this way, get down there." He pushed the cloak he'd let close over his chest behind his shoulders and out of his way. The cold bit his bare arms as soon as he exposed them. Stretching his fingers toward the liquid stone, he began to syphon the heat and energy out of it just like he did when he extinguished fires. A thin sheath of gray stone formed atop the flow, but the hot fluid beneath it soon cracked it, and it sank down into the glowing, red liquid and quickly melted again. Yarrow redoubled his efforts, but he'd never experienced anything quite as hot as this. Fire was weak in comparison. After trying a few more minutes, he knew he wouldn't be able to simply snuff out heat that poured from the heart of the world. He'd always been better with ice than fire.

Ice. Though Yarrow knew he'd never be able to produce enough cold to solidify the flow, crippling cold surrounded him. He just had to focus it. Taking a deep breath, he drew the frigid air to him before directing it at the molten rock. A squall of wind and ice crystals shot from his palms with such force he slid several feet back through the snow. He braced his heel against a frosty stone, bent his knees, and kept at it. At first his fingers felt frozen, then on fire, and finally blessedly numb. The chill spread up his arms, and they began to tremble until he didn't think he could keep them outstretched. He gritted his teeth and refused to succumb to the fatigue.

Finally Yarrow released the magic and dropped to his knees. What had been the red-hot river was now a smooth sheet of black rock, bubbles and whorls frozen in place for eternity. Sasha crouched beside it and ran his fingers over the glassy surface, where snow had already started to accumulate. "It's rather beautiful," he said, looking at Yarrow with wide eyes.

When Yarrow tried to stand and stumbled, Duncan sat down beside him and pulled Yarrow into his lap. He gathered Yarrow into his arms like a child and pressed the side of Yarrow's face to his chest. He closed his cloak around both of them, and Yarrow was comfortable even against his knight's plate armor. Duncan rubbed Yarrow's chilled, bluish fingers between his big hands and blew his warm breath on them until sensation began to return to Yarrow's skin. "Rest, Yarrow. Just for a moment. You're shaking all over, and the stone isn't going anywhere."

Yarrow looked up at Duncan's kind, handsome face, snowflakes skittering across his tanned skin. "We've only been together a few days, and you're already telling me what to do."

"Someone has to," Duncan said, pulling Yarrow in closer. "Goddesses, it feels good to hold you like this again." He kissed Yarrow's forehead, and a shiver that had nothing to do with the cold moved down Yarrow's spine.

"We shouldn't linger," Sasha said with a fondness in his tone Yarrow had only ever heard a handful of times before. "We should wait to rest until we get to shelter." He reached down, clasped Yarrow's hand, and helped him to his feet.

Together, they walked to the edge of the incline and looked down. "Nothing for it," Duncan said with a wide grin. He tucked his cloak around him, sat, laid his sword across his lap, and slid on his backside down the track Yarrow had created. His delighted chuckles echoed across the bleak landscape until he rolled into a snow bank with a grunt just before reaching the cavern's entrance.

Yarrow and Sasha looked at each other, smiled, shrugged, and followed their knight to the bottom of the slope.

SASHA found it eerie to stand sweating in a cavern beneath dozens of feet of ice. His mage's cantrip had solidified the molten rock only as far as the entrance. Inside the huge cave, lava flowed and bubbled freely, giving the strange rock formations a red cast that reminded him of the scarlet light in his order's safe houses. Odd shadows slithered across the floor and slid up and down the walls.

As soon as his eyes adjusted to the light, Sasha began checking the grotto for any sort of trap the goddesses, or more likely, their followers, had left behind. He had seen pressure plates that dropped heavy stone or fired poisoned arrows functioning after hundreds of years, but no matter how carefully he checked, he found no evidence of them here. He also found no evidence of any animals, but then beasts would have had no way to reach the cave's mouth before Yarrow froze the molten river flowing into it. The cavern offered plenty of hiding places behind spindly columns of rock and alcoves dripping water had carved in the stone. Though he knew they were probably the first men to set foot here in thousands of years, Sasha dutifully checked each one.

"I need to sit down for a few moments," Yarrow said, dropping his pack near the cavern wall a few dozen feet from the fiery flow. "I mustn't let myself become too tired."

"We should all take the time to rest," Duncan suggested. "We're as safe here for the moment as we're likely to be for quite some time, and we don't know when another chance will arise." With that, he began working on the leather buckles that held his pauldrons and breastplate in place. The metal clanged as he dropped it to the ground, and then he stretched out in his tunic, trousers, chainmail cuirass, and greaves. Sasha hadn't realized how exhausted Duncan was until the knight stopped pretending.

Yarrow collapsed beside Duncan and edged slowly closer to him, testing how far he'd be welcome, until Duncan finally laughed warmly and said, "What in the goddesses' names are you doing, lad? Come here."

Yarrow smiled as genuine of a smile as Sasha had ever seen on his face as he nestled against Duncan's broad chest and draped his arm over Duncan's belly. His features held none of his typical arrogance, mockery, or scorn as he let the tension drain out of them. The sun had painted him almost as dark as an Emiri, as dark as Sasha himself, but he noted it had engraved none of the lines around Yarrow's eyes and mouth that it usually left on others.

Compelled by something he neither recognized nor fully understood, Sasha reached down and cupped Yarrow's face in his hand. Yarrow looked up at him and smiled sleepily before reaching across and squeezing Sasha's other hand, while burrowing his face into Sasha's palm.

Duncan rested his hand on the small of Sasha's back and murmured, "Come here, my love. You must refresh yourself."

Though Sasha cuddled against Duncan's opposite side and let Duncan drape his arm over his shoulder like a blanket, sleep and rest were far from Sasha's mind. Looking across Duncan's chest at Yarrow, he couldn't resist running his fingertip along Yarrow's white eyelashes. He was so beautiful, so surreal. In response, Yarrow smiled and let out a long, low groan just as Sasha remembered. He hadn't even needed to touch the mage's flesh to coax a pleased reaction from him. Thalil, he loved that about Yarrow.

As Sasha moved his fingers across Yarrow's smooth face and into the tangles of his hair, he tilted his head back against Duncan and regarded Duncan's elegant, powerful neck. An old scar, barely visible and only about two inches long, marred the side of his neck at the base. Sasha knew it well—the result of a glancing blow from a dagger while rescuing an eyrle's son from his bandit kidnappers. By now, Sasha knew every scar and mark on Duncan's body and the story that went with each, but he never grew tired of feeling the satiny, raised flesh beneath his fingers. Duncan rewarded his light caress with a rumble coming from deep in his chest. He looked down at Sasha for a moment before bending to meet his lips.

They bumped their tongues together, letting them press and slide against each other in a familiar, playful duel. Sasha trailed his fingers along Yarrow's bare arm until he reached Yarrow's hand and lifted it to his mouth. He parted from Duncan, dragged his lower lip up Yarrow's thumb, and closed his mouth around the end, tracing tight little circles over the pad with the tip of his tongue. It tasted of the ice the mage had recently conjured. Following Sasha's example, Duncan drew Yarrow's finger into his mouth. The sucking sounds he made sent Sasha's blood to the root of his body so fast shooting stars erupted behind his eyes as if the heavens collapsed around them.

"Oh, goddesses," Yarrow whispered, voice broken, almost crying. "I was so afraid you wouldn't want me like this anymore." He wrapped his leg around Duncan's lap and thrust against Duncan's thigh.

Sasha withdrew his lips from Yarrow's thumb with a pop and caught his chin, making the mage meet his gaze. "We never asked you to go, never wanted you to go. We—*I* never stopped wanting you. Not even for a moment."

"I never wanted you to face all of this alone," Duncan said. "We would have stood at your side through anything. We always will. Yarrow, for you we would walk into the heart of the Shades' Abode."

Though he knew this conversation, and probably many others, would be necessary, Sasha didn't want to have it at the moment. He could express his love for these men best without words. "We're here now. All of us. It has been much too long since I felt both of your bodies moving against me, tasted both your lips. I can't wait any longer." He wriggled his fingers into Yarrow's hair and pulled Yarrow's face to his, jousting with Yarrow's tongue until the mage submitted, as he always did. Sasha kissed him until he couldn't breathe and didn't stop until Duncan tugged at his hair so he could have a turn with Yarrow. Then Duncan kissed Sasha, and Sasha tasted their essences and unique flavors mingled on Duncan's lips. It almost sent Sasha tumbling over the edge. He moved his hand down Yarrow's chest, feeling his pebble-hard nipples through his whisper-thin shirt. Just that tiny graze made the mage tremble and whimper against the side of Duncan's neck.

"How did I live without this?" Yarrow panted.

Sasha wriggled his hand between their bodies and took hold of the big, thick cock curving to Yarrow's belly button, already damp with his first drizzle of seed. "How did I live without that?" He used his other hand to stroke Duncan through his trousers, making the mail tunic he wore jingle rhythmically. "I'm afraid I'm greedy, and I want both of them."

"What do you—" Duncan began, but Sasha rose to his knees and kissed Duncan so hard Duncan's chainmail scraped against the stone behind him. Sasha braced himself against the wall of the cave with one hand and grabbed a handful of Yarrow's shirt with the other, guiding Yarrow off Duncan's lap so they sat side by side.

Sasha moved over and between them, one of his knees between each pair of their legs, his thighs flush with each of their hard cocks. They moved their hands up and down his back, over his ass and across his belly, touching him everywhere, making him flush and tremble in his leather. Returning their affection, Sasha kissed their faces, ran his tongue along their lips and teeth, suckled their necks, and nibbled their ears. He took turns fondling each of their erections through their clothing until he could wait no longer to feel their bare flesh, to taste it.

"Duncan, out of the armor," Sasha said breathlessly.

Duncan faux-scowled even as he grasped the bottom of his long mail tunic. "Assassin—"

"No," Sasha said firmly. "No arguments. No teasing. Off. Now."

From there, Sasha found it easy to tug their trousers down and work their hard cocks and full sacs out over the waistbands. He sat on his heels so he could stroke them both as he watched them kiss, their cheeks coloring and their skin sparkling with perspiration. Their lips grew full and shiny, and now and then Sasha caught an enticing flash of tongue. Yarrow kneaded Duncan's thigh, and Duncan rolled Yarrow's nipple between his thumb and finger.

"I never stopped loving you," Duncan said against Yarrow's cheek. "There wasn't a single night I didn't see you in my dreams. I… I never gave up hope we'd all be together again one day."

Sasha couldn't pinpoint exactly when Duncan's sentimental love talk had stopped sounding silly and evolved into the sweetest, most tantalizing things he'd ever heard. The way the knight's voice grew rough with arousal made it all the better. Sasha groaned and swiped his tongue from the far corner of Duncan's mouth to the opposite end of Yarrow's. Both of them nibbled at his lips, and he kissed one and then the other. "I love you," he breathed. "Yarrow… Duncan… always. Let me show you."

He sank down on his elbows and grasped their cocks at the bases, inhaling the musk stored in Yarrow's sparse white hair and Duncan's thick brown curls. They angled their bodies to assist him, Yarrow with his hand in Sasha's hair and Duncan with his curled around Sasha's shoulder. Sasha drew his tongue slowly up Duncan's erection, across the slit at the top, across to Yarrow's fat crown, down Yarrow's length, and over their balls until he reached the base of Duncan's cock again. Both of them moaned his name and each other's, encouraging him. Sasha pressed their cocks together in his fist so he could lap at both undersides at once, flicking his tongue against the grooves beneath their crowns.

"Goddesses, Sasha," Yarrow said. "Your lips… your mouth…."

"Your cock feels good against mine, my lovely Yarrow," Duncan said. "It feels good to be together… finally."

"Yes," Yarrow said, drawing out the S into a sigh. "Goddesses, yes."

Sasha opened his mouth wide enough to draw the tips of both their cocks into his mouth at once. He bobbed his head slowly, delighting in the textures of their flesh, the ledges of their defined heads. The precursors of their seed mixed in his mouth, the taste intoxicating. Sasha couldn't keep it up for long, but by the time he withdrew his aching jaw, Duncan and Yarrow's bellies were fluttering, and they were pawing at each other and Sasha, muttering incoherently against each other's lips.

It was too much for Sasha, the lust he felt, the overload of sensation. All the love he had suppressed his entire life seemed to rush back in a single flood. The techniques he'd perfected over the years as just another means of manipulation abandoned him, and he licked and sucked at Duncan and Yarrow's cocks, rubbing his face against them with no rhythm or finesse, just enjoying the feel of them, the taste, everything. Yarrow's nails bit the back of his neck as he lapped and slurped.

"Sasha," Yarrow said. "I'm going to—"

Sasha managed a terse nod, and Yarrow exploded across his lips and chin, whimpering and thrashing beneath him. Sasha continued to lick and stroke him as he trembled with release.

"Duncan." Sasha's breath washed over his knight's damp, glistening flesh, making Duncan shiver. Then he plunged down, taking Duncan all the way into his throat.

"I—Ah! I'll let you tell me what to do… just this… one time, assassin." Duncan's seed shot against the back of Sasha's throat like one of the mountain geysers, hot and forceful. Sasha sucked until his knight went almost soft, and then he sat back to catch his breath.

Still dizzy with arousal, Sasha almost lost his balance when Yarrow grasped the buckles of his armor and pulled him close, saying "I need a taste of those lips. Of Duncan. Of us together." The mage kissed him hard, sucking the flavors from Sasha's tender lips and tongue.

Duncan raked Sasha's hair away to nip his neck. "I want a taste of *you*," he said next to Sasha's ear. Before Sasha could answer, Duncan swept him into his arms and arranged him on his back in front of them. Yarrow picked apart the buckles over his chest while Duncan deftly removed his trousers, accustomed to the complex fastenings and straps by now. Both of them pulled their trousers up so their movements wouldn't be hampered, and then they lavished attention on Sasha's exposed body with their hands and mouths. Yarrow pushed Sasha's snug, hooded tunic to his neck and sucked gently on his nipple while Duncan thumbed Sasha's foreskin back and swiped his tongue across Sasha's slit. It was enough to make Sasha's balls draw up next to his body and his inner muscles clench. Words in the dead language of Thalil fell like errant snowflakes from his lips. His scream echoed through the cavern when Duncan took him all the way into his mouth and sucked hard on his crown.

Yarrow's kisses, warm and passionate but as light and taunting as the first warm breeze after a long winter, moved down Sasha's ribs and across his belly. He opened his mouth near Sasha's cockhead to kiss Duncan, and their tongues twisted together around Sasha's crown. They licked down his length and back up before kissing again. Sasha opened his eyes to watch them, white hair and rich red-brown tangling together, pink lips wet and swollen as they moved over his flesh. His stomach muscles tightened until they hurt, and he lifted his hips off the ground as he came hard, yelling their names until his voice cracked and holding on to the backs of their shirts, never, ever willing to let either of them go again.

After a while, Sasha became lucid enough to replace his clothing, but he couldn't stop grinning. Warmth bloomed in his chest every time he caught a glimpse of Yarrow or Duncan, and he wanted to be near them, touching them, a little bit longer. Duncan balled up Yarrow's cloak for a pillow and sprawled out on his back. Sasha and Yarrow took their places at his side as if they did so every night. Hopefully soon they would. Duncan wrapped his strong, gentle arms around them and held them all close together, and Sasha pulled the knight's cloak over them. His feelings, his love for these men would almost certainly cause him pain one day.

He'd been taught life rarely turned out otherwise, and he knew he was leaving himself completely unguarded.

But moments like this, on the road, their limbs twined together and nothing existing beyond, were worth the pain of dying a hundred times.

Yarrow stirred and left the makeshift bedroll. "If we'll all be asleep, I should at least cast some wards around us. We don't know what could be down here."

The mage circled their rough camp three times before returning to rest his forehead against Sasha's, and both of them fell asleep over Duncan's heart.

Chapter Nineteen

DUNCAN felt more hope and confidence as he followed Yarrow through the dark underground warrens than he had since his mage had left his side. He spared a few moments to think of Windwake and hope all went well with his bairny, but he trusted Tam Allwynn, and he knew he belonged on the road like this, fighting as a soldier instead of pretending to be a pompous aristocrat. Not for the first time, Duncan wondered if the creature Yarrow claimed shared his body truly existed. It mattered little. If this quest achieved nothing but giving Yarrow peace of mind, then Duncan was all for it. He found it hard to believe such a monster, let alone Fane, could have ever walked in the goddesses' light.

Duncan wasn't opposed to an adventure with little real danger, which it seemed this one would be. After walking most of the day, they hadn't encountered so much as a bat in these caves.

Not long after they stopped to share dried meat, hard, flat bread, and water, they discovered a grand room the size of Windust's great hall with a circular pool of bubbling, molten rock at the center. Stalactites decorated the ceiling like banners, and striations of ivory, green, and rust sparkled in the reddish light. Just before they entered, Sasha stretched his arm as a barrier in front of them.

"Something about this feels wrong," the assassin said. "Let me have a look around first."

Heeding Sasha had saved his life in the past, so Duncan nodded his agreement. Sasha drew his dagger with the twisted blade as he crept into the chamber, his boots silent on the uneven ground. In no time, the assassin melted into the shadows and practically disappeared.

"What do you know?" Yarrow said under his breath. "Be quiet, or I'll make you. You think so, beast? Stop your prattling, or I'll show you.

Oh? Of course I do. It's no magic I can't handle. No, I'm not asking. I broke Hale's spells without you, and I can unravel whatever's at work here just the same. Ha! What goddesses?"

Duncan had forgotten how unsettling it was when Yarrow spoke to… to whatever he imagined he spoke to. Before he realized he'd done it, Duncan took a few steps away from the mage and gripped the hilt of his sword. Duncan loved him, but the boy might be mad.

Sasha skirted the perimeter of the chamber, running his hands along the walls and crouching to inspect the floors before returning to proclaim it safe to cross. Duncan couldn't dismiss the cold feeling in his belly as Yarrow sheathed himself in blue light, with tiny, embryonic wings protruding from his back.

Their presence almost seemed to aggravate the fiery pool, and it burbled and spurted more violently the nearer they drew. As they passed alongside, gouts of molten rock shot at them so viciously Yarrow had to guard them with a bubble of arcane energy. All of them backed against the far wall to avoid the smoldering globs.

Safe behind Yarrow's cerulean shield, Duncan watched the fount at the center of the pool shoot a dozen feet into the air. Channels protruded horizontal to the floor, and more molten rock fed into the spring, filling it out until it took almost the shape of an enormous man. A skin of gray rock formed around it as it took a lumbering step from the fiery pond. Its molten core bubbled to the surface through cracks in the sheath, and the liquid stone it trailed scorched the floor.

Sasha darted from behind Yarrow's barrier almost too fast for Duncan to follow. The assassin sprinted toward the massive creature and launched himself at it, landing on its boulder-sized fist. It swung wildly, and Sasha jumped to its shoulder, sinking his dagger into its stony neck to hold on. Twisting his body, Sasha managed to get on top of the thing's head. He raised his serpentine blade and drove it into the creature's blazing eye socket, to no avail. It tossed its shoulders to shake him off, but Sasha wrapped his knees around its neck and hacked at it with his knives. His leather steamed where it touched the monster's skin.

Yarrow dropped his shield, and both he and Duncan ran to aid their companion. Duncan drew his sword while jogging and swung as hard as he could at the thing's legs when he reached it. The force of his blow shattered the rock, and the molten center spewed out as the creature dropped to its knees, blistering Duncan's skin where it splashed against his hand. With a hoarse cry, Duncan jumped and brought his sword down vertically, slicing deep into the abomination's shoulder. The arm it had been using to swat at Sasha hung useless. It took a great effort, but Duncan dislodged his blade and prepared for another swing. Before he could connect, the creature caught Sasha in its functional hand and hurled him across the room. Sasha hit the wall, and he tried to turn and land on his feet, but one of his legs gave out and he crumpled on the ground. Forgetting the creature, Duncan hurried to protect him.

Just before Duncan reached him, Sasha lifted his head and pointed. He yelled something Duncan couldn't hear over the bellow of the creature, a sound like the very ground splitting asunder. It gathered a sphere of molten rock in its hand and hurled it at Yarrow. The mage spread his majestic, azure wings and lifted himself out of its path. The projectile solidified, tearing a deep furrow in the cave floor before slamming against the wall so hard it shook the chamber.

Yarrow, hovering a few feet over the thing's head, hurled glowing blue, comet-like orbs at the howling monstrosity. The attacks bounced off without wounding it, and the mage fluttered a few feet back. All the creature's attention focused on Yarrow now. It swung its gigantic arms at him, but Yarrow managed to flit away, barely avoiding the blows.

Sasha pushed himself to a seated position with a grimace and threw a tiny dart in a single, smooth motion. He managed to strike their adversary in the center of its cracked skin, right in the middle of its throat. Whatever poison Sasha had put on his weapon affected the creature, and its glowing core turned a sickly green and dimmed for a moment. Both Yarrow and Duncan seized the opportunity, the mage firing a bolt of arcane lightning into the monster's fresh wound and Duncan sprinting across the room to strike it while it was weak. Yarrow's bolt had widened the crevice in the thing's neck, and Duncan jumped, thrust the point of his sword inside it, and twisted. Bits of rock showered Duncan as the creature howled. He withdrew his blade and struck again. Another of Sasha's darts whizzed past him and lodged in the creature's eye socket, extinguishing the blaze behind it for a moment. Yarrow, back on the ground, shot an icicle into the flickering hollow, and this time the creature's molten center didn't ignite again, but remained cold and dead.

Holding tight to the hilt of his sword, Duncan sliced down the creature's torso on his way back to the ground. As soon as his feet touched down, he wrenched his sword free and swiped at its knees again, provoking another howl but sending the creature staggering forward. Duncan dove out of the way and skidded across the floor on his chest, his breastplate screeching, to avoid being crushed by the thing's hand as it attempted to catch itself. He rolled to his back and shielded his face with his arm as magma showered from its gaping neck wound.

Yarrow circled around behind the creature and rose into the air. A miniature snowstorm swirled around the mage, making his hair whip around his face and shoulders. Icy blue light poured from the corners of his eyes. Duncan dragged himself farther away, barely able to reconcile the radiant being he regarded with the warm, enthusiastic boy he'd kissed and fondled half a day ago.

Spindly needles of ice shot from Yarrow's fingers. Some of them bounced off its stony skin and melted before they hit the ground, but those that penetrated the cracks doused the inner flames, and the thing grew slower as it lost heat. In desperation, it began to stomp around the chamber, bellowing and flailing its good arm in front of it, preventing any of them from getting close. Sasha still aimed his venomous darts at it, but they wouldn't vanquish it on their own. Every time Duncan came within range of the beast, he had to crouch or roll to avoid its swinging arm and crashing feet.

"Duncan!" Sasha yelled. "Be ready!"

The assassin drew his longest dagger and moved in front of their enemy, though with some difficulty as he dragged his right foot. Sasha shouted to draw the creature's attention, moving slowly toward the wall as it took notice of him. It bent almost completely in half and charged. When the creature reached Sasha, it would crush him between itself and the wall. Sasha stood his ground, stretching one hand out in front of him, the other bent beside his head, his dagger next to his ear. He didn't dive out of the way until the thing came within two feet, and he barely avoided it. Its momentum sent it crashing into the wall, cracking the stone and sending it reeling and stumbling.

Yarrow didn't waste any time in directing a stream of frigid air at the creature's feet, just as he had to solidify the molten stream. In minutes, a casing of ice cemented it to the floor. Though it twisted and hollered, it couldn't free its feet from the floor.

Though his muscles trembled with exhaustion and his bones ached from bouncing across the stone floor, Duncan raised his sword above his head and ran at the thing, swinging at its waist and opening a wide chasm. He struck again, but the creature's molten core already welled up to close the wounds he'd made. A fresh stone skin formed over the gashes. Yarrow, clearly exhausted, fell to the ground in a heap, his blue light sputtering out. Sasha limped forward, knives drawn, but he simply didn't have the power to damage the monster. The ice entrapping it sizzled and dripped, great bursts of steam rising into the air. Duncan knew he didn't have much time. The people he loved were hurt, and he had to protect them.

The creature swung its arm, and Duncan leapt to avoid it. Before it could lift its fist, Duncan climbed atop its hand and ran up its arm to its shoulder. Holding his sword firmly in both hands, he chopped at the creature's neck for all he was worth. His sword opened a deep cut, and the thing's head lolled toward its back as boiling, liquid rock streamed down its chest. The heat singed Duncan's soles through his heavy boots, but he held on as the creature collapsed in on itself as what served as its life's blood poured out. It covered Duncan's blade until the sword glowed white-hot, and the heat traveled up the weapon until it scorched Duncan's palms. He held tight against the agony and raised his blade for another blow, and another.

Three hard swings severed the thing's bulbous head from its body, and it fell to the floor like a boulder and rolled until the cavern wall stopped it. The remainder of the smelted liquid filling and fueling the creature drained out, leaving it an empty cask, solidifying as it slowly cooled. Duncan went limp and toppled off its shoulder, smacking his back on the ground.

For a long time, Duncan just lay there, watching steam and sulfuric fumes rise toward the ceiling of the cavern. His ribs hurt, bruised or worse, and every breath he dragged in was agony, but at least Sasha and Yarrow were safe. He could spare a few minutes to recover. He even let his eyes close.

A light touch on his cheek roused Duncan, and he realized he'd lost consciousness. Yarrow and Sasha sat on either side of him, looking worried. A streak of dried blood stretched from Sasha's left nostril to his chin, and Yarrow's lips lacked any pigment. As soon as he saw them, Duncan forgot about his own injuries and tried to sit up. A sharp pain above his left hip stopped him. When he tried to reach for the ache, he realized he still held his sword.

"Duncan," Yarrow whispered, a warning in his tone.

Duncan looked down at his hands wrapped around the hilt of his sword. Intense heat had warped the blade and rippled the metal. Slowly, Duncan uncurled his fingers from his favorite weapon and felt a pain unlike anything he'd ever experienced. Looking down, he saw chunks of his skin and flesh sticking to the blade as he tried to separate from it. He screamed as he ripped his dominant hand, the one at the top of the hilt, away amidst a spurt of blood. He held his ruined hand up, seeing all the skin burned away, and in some places tendons and even bone showing through. Ready to pass out again, Duncan yanked his other hand away from the sword, leaving much of it behind on the warped bronze and steel. Panic gripped him as he understood this injury might leave him incapable of ever lifting a weapon again. He'd be lucky if he could lift his fork. His hands were completely ruined, and he'd be surprised if he didn't lose them to infection.

"Just…. It will be all right, Duncan," Yarrow said, his voice remarkably steady given the circumstances. "Give me your hands."

It took an effort, but Duncan managed to lay his ruined hands in the mage's lap as a surge of cold shot through him. His teeth knocked together, and he shook. All he wanted was to get into bed with his lovers and sleep for a day and a half. He just couldn't stay awake, didn't want to….

A gentle warmth spread from Duncan's hands and up his arms until it filled his chest, making him feel euphoric and invigorated. Goddesses, he felt ready to take on the world, his muscles full of latent strength and his spirit buoyed. The soft light, blue as a fair, summer sky, filled him until it pushed out all the pain. Duncan still felt sleepy, but in the content way of a man stretching across warm grass after a picnic, with nothing to worry about besides napping the afternoon away. When Duncan looked at his palms, the muscles, veins, and skin had regrown, but without the lines and creases he'd become used to. Even the spattering of brown dots had vanished. His hands were as smooth and seamless as glass.

"I'm better than I was, but I'll never be a healer." Yarrow's eyelids fluttered before he slumped across Duncan's chest. It felt nice, and the temptation to doze was strong.

Sasha's muffled grunt as he shifted his weight tore Duncan out of the magic-induced haze he reveled in. He had no business napping when his partners needed him. He pushed himself up on his restored hands, and Yarrow lay motionless atop him, sliding down Duncan's chest as he rose.

"Sasha, are you hurt?" Duncan asked.

The assassin nodded. "My ankle is badly broken. I set the bone, but without dressing, it won't stay in place. Yarrow is too depleted to heal me. I'm going to slow you down. Perhaps it would be wise—"

"No," Duncan said, interrupting him. "I know what you're going to say, and it is out of the question. We're in this together. No one gets left behind. Goddesses, I could never leave you, love, so don't even suggest it."

"I can hardly walk," Sasha protested.

"Then I'll carry you," Duncan said.

"Stubborn bastard," Sasha said, looking away to try to hide his smile. "We should move on. For all we know, another creature could form from that pool, and I don't think we'd prevail a second time."

"Agreed," Duncan said, looking over his shoulder at the churning tarn. He got to his feet and lifted his mage's light body into his arms. He really needed to encourage Yarrow to eat more; the lad's bones stuck out everywhere and he weighed no more than a temperate breeze. Duncan held him tight as he entered a snug passage off the expansive room. They made slow progress with Duncan burdened by Yarrow's weight and Sasha limping along with the aid of Yarrow's branch.

As soon as Yarrow started to stir, he decried being treated like a helpless child, so Duncan set him down. It was hard to gauge the passage of time in the perpetual darkness lit only by the bubbling, red-hot streams, but Duncan estimated they'd been walking for five or six hours. Sasha, supporting himself on Yarrow's discarded walking stick and dragging his gnarled foot, slowed them down considerably. When he felt safe from any immediate threat, Duncan suggested they sit down for a few moments. They shared water, and Yarrow attempted to heal Sasha's ankle. He managed to alleviate some of Sasha's pain, but admitted he hadn't managed to completely fuse the bone back together. After their brief rest, they continued in the direction Yarrow indicated.

Duncan took the lead as they descended a gradual slope. It grew darker as the molten rivers of stone tapered to rivulets. Soon, he couldn't see Sasha and Yarrow following a few feet behind him. He couldn't hear Yarrow's boots scuffing the ground; of course he didn't hear Sasha's. It was odd, but he swore he couldn't feel their presences as he usually did, though he knew they had to be behind him. Ahead, the tunnel opened not to another chamber bathed in fiery reds and golds, but to a hazy gray room. The ground and walls seemed solid enough, but somehow insubstantial and mutable, like images in a dream. Duncan ran his fingers along the uneven stone as he walked, just to assure himself it actually existed.

In the distance, a dark streak gradually took the form of a small man. They approached each other, and Duncan's heart cramped as he recognized the young man's delicate features, innocent, gray eyes, and feathery, light brown hair. *Goddesses, Aubrey.*

Aubrey wore a simple brown tunic with a plain warm cloak over top. A stack of books held together by a set of leather straps hung from his shoulder, as always. He canted his head at Duncan and said, "Where were you, my friend? Why didn't you come? I tried to fight those men off. I told them I didn't have anything valuable. I kept fighting, trying to defend myself, because I was so sure you'd be coming any moment to save me from them. I was sure, right until they cut my throat. Why didn't you come?"

Tears poured down Duncan's face. He wanted to reach out and touch Aubrey one more time, this young man he'd adored, sworn to protect, and failed, but he didn't dare. He had no right to even pinch the hem of his cloak. "Aubrey, I had too much to drink that night. It's a poor excuse, and I won't insult your memory by trying to apologize for it. I failed you in the most disgusting way, and nothing I say will soften my disgrace. I'm only sorry you suffered for it instead of me. I would have died in your place if I could have."

"I cried out for you," the pretty young man said, resentment starting to taint his gentle voice. "I called your name again and again. I never gave up hope that you'd come. Save me. I had so many plans for my life. I was only just starting out."

The pain in Duncan's chest and belly made his burned hands feel like minor annoyances in comparison. "I know," he managed to choke out.

"You were my first love," Aubrey said.

"You were mine."

"You let me die," Aubrey said. "You were supposed to keep me safe, get me to Espero to study."

"And I failed," Duncan said. "I know that. I failed you with my foolishness. I was a very young man."

"So was I."

"Aubrey, I have carried this pain with me for many years now. I wish I could change what happened somehow."

"I wish I would have had those years, even years full of pain. Duncan, I was sixteen years old. I never had a chance to do anything."

"Tell me what I can do."

"Did you love me?"

Duncan nodded. "So much I thought it would tear me apart sometimes."

Aubrey took Duncan's big hand in both of his small, smooth hands and offered Duncan a smile full of innocent hope. "Stay here with me now. I want to experience all those things I never got to try. Will you stay?"

At first, Duncan couldn't see any reason to refuse. Looking into Aubrey's gray eyes, he wanted nothing else in the world. Something scratched at the back of his mind, but he didn't think it could be more important than this. He knew he was supposed to do something, but to the Shades' Abode with it. He'd abandon it, stay with his first love, and finally be free of the deep, ever-present wound Aubrey's loss had left.

"Duncan, say yes," the mage urged. "Tell me you'll stay. Say it."

"I—" He owed something to another, to others.... He'd sworn protection to others....

"Why won't you say you'll stay? It's the least you can do after leaving me to die all those years ago, stealing everything I may have had or been. What's stopping you?"

As Duncan mulled over Aubrey's words, he realized they belonged not to the mage, but to the part of his mind that sprinkled poison into the old wound from time to time. They were the exact words he said to himself as penance when he was alone.

"How can I stay with you?" he asked. "You're dead and I'm alive. I have tried for years to let you go. I have a duty to others now."

"You're planning to abandon me again?" Aubrey pulled away from Duncan and hugged himself, a nervous mannerism Duncan remembered well.

"No, not again. I know you're not really here. You're the part of me that has never forgiven myself for what I let happen. It's been nearly twenty years, and others need me now. Part of me will always love you,

Aubrey, the way a man can only love his first, but I have to let all of this go. It will always hurt me, but I must stop agonizing over things I cannot change and concentrate on those I can. Sasha and Yarrow are depending on me, and I don't want to let anyone else down."

The young man nodded slowly, kissed Duncan lightly, and whispered, "I forgive you." Then he was gone.

Duncan still didn't see Sasha or Yarrow, but even if he had, he wouldn't have been able to stop himself from falling to his knees, burying his face in his hands, and weeping softly until he purged all the poison he'd been storing in his heart over the decades.

AT FIRST, Yarrow thought Sai had somehow managed to follow them into the cavern. Both annoyed and a little touched Sai wanted to help him, he approached the redheaded Emiri captain, ready to ask for an explanation. When he got close enough to see the face and realize it wasn't Sai, he clapped both hands over his mouth and staggered back from what could only be an apparition.

Ho ho! What an unexpected delight, Yarrow! It's our little friend Rini. I never dreamed I'd have the pleasure of killing him again. You should stay with me this time, beloved. You can't imagine how exquisite it was, being inside him as he started to stiffen and convulse.

"Shut up!" Yarrow pressed his palms over his ears as if he could muffle the hated voice, turned his face toward the high ceiling of the cave, and screamed until it felt like his throat bled. "I'll make you pay for it if it kills me! Damn you! I'll tear you out of me and kill you with my own hands! I will not be as kind as your previous beloved! There will be nothing left when I'm done with you."

"Yarrow, what happened?" Rini's bright orange eyes widened with concern at Yarrow's outburst, not for his own safety, but for Yarrow. It hurt much more than if he'd been angry. "We had such a wonderful day, and we were making love. You started to choke me. At first, I thought it might be fun and I trusted you, but then I couldn't breathe. Everything started to go dark and fuzzy, but by then I couldn't ask you to stop. Am I dead, *syrai*? Did you kill me?"

Yarrow's magic flared with his anger, pouring out of him in sizzling, blue waves until it nearly filled the cavern. *This is* my *power, creature. Take note of it.*

To Rini, he said, "I would never hurt you, *syrai-tama*. I loved you more than my next breath, more than anything. I kept things from you, things I didn't understand myself, but I can tell you this: I will make the one who did this to you pay for it a hundredfold. I will make it pay in lifetimes of agony. I swear it, Rini."

"I don't want your vengeance for me to twist you, Yarrow. I want you sweet and free from worry, as you were when we spent our days on the southern shores, doing nothing but swimming and sleeping in the sun."

"It's too late for that."

"I have an idea," Rini said. "You could stay here with me, and we'll forget all about it. We won't have a care in the world."

Take his offer, beloved. I'll even swear not to touch him. I'll let you have the life you always wanted with him.

Impossible. He's dead. Do you truly think I don't recognize the poisoned runoff of my own mind? Even if I didn't, I would trust nothing you advocate. You think this will distract me from destroying you, but you gambled badly, monster. This makes me want to see an end to you even more. So if you're doing this, you might as well save your effort. I conjure his memory myself often enough. It cannot hurt me, at least not more than I can endure.

I'm not doing it, little flower, but I am enjoying it. If seeing him doesn't pain you, why are your insides twisted and tangled like withered vines? Why are you crying?

"Will you stay, Yarrow?" Rini asked again. "I'd hoped we would spend our lives together."

"I—" Yarrow choked on a sob. Suffering so long, spending so many years mad with the pain and guilt had a strange saving grace. This vision didn't hurt as badly, didn't seem as real and alive as the Rini living in his memories. Somehow, it softened the blow. "You are not my Rini. My Rini is resting at the bottom of the sea. You are a watered-down imitation of what I long for. Whatever you are and wherever you came from, be gone."

Aw, beloved! We could have at least tumbled him before you sent him away.

Be quiet. There's a pattern to this magic, or are you too absorbed in your own savage appetites to see it? This spell is similar to the one Hale cast on me and Sai. Not identical, but similar.

Are you saying the same person conjured this? Hale?

No, don't you understand? The framework is the same, but everything on top, the embellishments, are unique. The same person didn't cast both spells, but they may have had the same teacher.

This Fane of yours is a delusion, beloved. Separating us is a fantasy. Abandon it now, before you lose your latest playmates to it. They've already been injured. What horrors do you suppose they're experiencing even now?

They are stronger than you can imagine, creature.

And are you, little Yarrow? You're full of so much fear, and you don't even understand the source. All you really want is to feel safe, like a whimpering child.

I'm a great mage, and I am not afraid. Enjoy the echoes and shades while you can. I have almost found Fane. Feel it. There's powerful sorcery held in stasis near here. Something ancient.

This magic— It cut its observation short before saying something it didn't want Yarrow to hear.

What?

The presence didn't reply, but Yarrow felt curiosity, outrage, and fear moving through it until it made his skin tingle. It only encouraged him. He knew he was finally close to regaining his being, his freedom, his security and the chance to live his life according to his own terms. Everything had been decided for him since before he'd been forced from his home at fourteen. It ended now. He was tired of being tossed about by the whims of others, and from now on, he'd choose his own path.

SASHA'S senses sharpened as he noticed the dozens of figures materializing from the gloom until he heard their every movement, the shuffle of their feet, the rustle of their clothing, even the swish of their hair as they looked about. He didn't hear breathing, and he drew his daggers, ready to face another inhuman threat. His broken ankle would slow him, so he'd have to observe his enemies' every weakness and exploit them to the fullest.

He looked around, gauging the way the people moved, their postures, how they shifted their weight, anything that might give him an edge. They were closing in, walking slowly, barely lifting their feet as they trudged toward him like sleepwalkers. Squinting, Sasha managed to make out some of their facial features and read their expressions, or lack of expressions. Their jaws hung slack and their glassy, unblinking eyes stared at nothing. Sasha recognized some of them as they got closer: Tam Fennsour, Taran Edercrest, and the former king of Selindria, Agarick.

Sasha raised his chin and looked down his nose at the pitiful shades. "Didn't I kill you already?"

"You killed me in my bed," Agarick groaned. "I lived as a warrior, and I deserved a better death than that."

"So what?" Sasha asked. "Your foolish code of honor is not mine. Thalil respects results."

"We want justice!" said a young woman in a fancy gown, Sasha's first victim. "I did nothing to harm you, and you deceived me cruelly. I was an innocent. We want our souls back from your Cast-Down god! Death finds every mortal, but we deserve rest, at least. We deserve justice!" Several of the others muttered their assent.

"There is no such thing in this life. Be gone and don't trouble me."

"I was twenty-five years old," said a knight with a dagger protruding from his eye. "I tried all my life to be an honorable man. I just wanted to die for something worthwhile."

"I had three children," said a noblewoman with a thin, crimson thread around her throat like a necklace. "You took me from them for no reason and left them alone in the world."

Sasha laughed. "Are you honestly trying to make me feel guilty?"

"Any man with a soul would feel some remorse for what was done to us," another man said. "Killed in our beds, never given a chance to fight back! Many of us were righteous and wanted nothing more than simple lives."

"Monster!" a pale priestess of Laud said, pointing her bony finger at Sasha like a dagger.

"May you rot in the Abode of Shades!"

"The goddesses curse you, foul murderer! Cast-Down!"

Sasha sighed, growing weary of the theatrics. "My only crime was being better, faster, and cleverer than all of you put together. I'm not sorry, and nothing you say will change that. Now, be gone. You're tiresome."

The dozens of figures wavered and dissolved until the cavern contained nothing but Sasha leaning on his crutch and Yarrow and Duncan sitting on the ground, pale and shaken, but otherwise unhurt. Good. If the rest of the attempts to stop them from reaching their goal proved as feeble as this one, they would have little trouble.

Chapter Twenty

AT LAST.

The entire mage island of Espero didn't boast as much enchantment as Yarrow felt coming from the end of the corridor. They'd been walking uphill for the past few hours, and Sasha had finally consented to let Duncan support him around the waist. Exhilarated, Yarrow practically jogged toward the end of the channel and had to stop several times so his partners could catch up.

The presence inside him retreated, almost hiding for the first time Yarrow could remember. It was afraid, and that compelled Yarrow forward.

Green-gold light filled the almost perfectly round chamber at the end of the tunnel. Natural columns at regular intervals, carved into lacey patterns by centuries, eons of dripping water, flanked a room that could compete for grandeur with the most beautiful temple. None of the three men said a word as they entered and looked around in awe.

Finally, Duncan broke the silence. "Perhaps the goddesses did make this place. I've never seen such beauty."

"Step lightly," Sasha said in a thin voice, his pain finally affecting him. "There could be traps or other hostile magics at work here."

"No," Yarrow said in a whisper. "Fane is here. Look."

Between two pillars at the end of the room, a pane of enchantment shimmered. Yarrow hurried to press his palms against the barrier and feel the primeval sorcery singing in his veins, filling his body with light and energy, making his feet hover a few inches above the ground. The spell was as old and beautiful as the grotto itself. Yarrow let his eyes flutter shut as he basked in its warmth, and when he opened them, he saw Fane at last.

The old man sat on a simple throne hewn from the rock, his long, white beard and hair almost covering his elaborate green velvet robes. Rows of jewels covered the cuffs and collar, and rings decorated Fane's every twig-like finger. A crown with thirteen spires, each topped with a faceted jewel the size of Yarrow's palm, sat on his head. The ancient emperor's gray skin sagged like wet paper draped over a skeleton, but his eyes were bright and alert. "Go on, boy. Dispel this barrier and set me free at last. I will repay you handsomely."

The spell's construction wasn't complex; it would be easy to negate, but Yarrow hesitated, remembering everything Hale had taught him. He said nothing as he studied the plain man in his fancy clothes. He had never imagined Fane would be so concerned with draping himself in such ludicrous finery.

What are you waiting for, beloved? Set him loose if you're so sure he can rid you of me. What's wrong? Are you disappointed?

Actually I am. I can't accept Fane is an old fop held captive by a spell a novice could cast in his sleep.

All people will disappoint you if you give them time, Yarrow.

There's something else. "If you are Fane, tell me the name of your most beloved apprentice," Yarrow said.

The old wizard staggered to his feet, holding the arm of his chair for support. "You dare question me? I am Fane!"

Undaunted, Yarrow said, "If that's so, tell me the name. Give me that single word, and I'll set you free."

"Boy, I have been here over ten thousand years. You cannot begin to comprehend what that will do to a man's mind. Besides, I had many under my tutelage at the pinnacle of my empire."

"But one of them was special." Yarrow looked over his shoulder at Sasha and Duncan. No span of time would wipe their names from his mind, he knew. He would remember them even after an eternity. "Your favorite. Tell me."

"I don't owe you a thing, foolish child! I'll not play these games. If you wish anything of me, let me out of this cage!"

"No."

"Yarrow, be careful," Duncan warned.

Yarrow couldn't help giggling as he grinned back at the knight. "We have nothing to fear from this impotent impostor!"

"How dare you?" The old man snarled and beat his fists against his arcane prison.

"Oh, and what will you do?" Yarrow taunted, enjoying himself in spite of everything. "Show me, if you can, or go away and stop wasting my precious time."

With a screech like a dagger on glass, the illusion dissipated, and Yarrow stood facing nothing but a stone wall.

"Well done," Sasha said.

"It wasn't difficult," Yarrow said. "I can't believe the… the people who imprisoned Fane here couldn't do better."

"The goddesses, you mean?" Duncan asked.

"If they did this, their magic is shoddy and predictable."

"Yarroway, you cannot say such things," the knight hissed.

"Not everything is as you have been told, my friend," Yarrow said to Duncan. "Besides, I'll say what I want, and if those thirteen whores find offense in it, let them come stop me!"

"Yarrow! Show some respect for the goddesses," Duncan practically pleaded.

"I don't see them rushing to force me, do you?"

"I also don't see this legendary mage you seek," Sasha noted.

"He is here." Yarrow left the cavern through another natural opening flanked by bubbly, wet columns of stone. Soon Sasha and Duncan followed him along a wide, level path free from debris. It led them deeper and deeper into the mountain. After what felt like hours, Yarrow noticed a tickle of annoyance like a rash against the back of his neck. He looked over his shoulder at Sasha and Duncan as he dug at the itch. They leaned close to each other, whispering. What could they be discussing that couldn't include him?

They don't trust you, the presence goaded Yarrow. *They have seen what you can do, and they're afraid of you.*

I won't believe that.

Then you're a bumbling idiot, beloved.

Another half an hour passed, and Duncan came up beside Yarrow. He rested his hand on Yarrow's shoulder and spoke close to Yarrow's ear. "Do you think we can trust Sasha?"

"Why would you ask such a thing?" Yarrow hissed out between his teeth.

"Consider the facts, my friend. He only ever insinuated himself into our trust to get close to Garith. He wanted to leave me to die back in his order's hideout, and he has lied to me dozens of times since then. What if he's still working for their agenda? It wouldn't be unusual for a member of his cult to spend months, or even years, working to secure our trust before striking. For all we know, one of us could be his true target. We should keep a watchful eye on him."

Yarrow nodded. Some of what Duncan said made sense, but he couldn't fathom Sasha betraying him after everything he'd given up to remain by their sides. But then…. It would not be novel for a Crimson Scythe assassin to set up a false persona, even for an extended period of time… in order to complete a job.

They continued on, none of them talking, until Sasha approached Yarrow and stopped him with a serious expression. "Our knight values his duty over our interests," Sasha whispered. "I don't know if we can depend on him, Yarrow. He might find himself in a more agreeable position if we weren't hampering him and his obligations."

"Sasha, what are you saying?"

"Only that we may not be able to depend upon his sword if we find ourselves in trouble. We should be ready to fight without him. Maybe even against him. He cannot accept the darkness within you and me, Yarrow. He doesn't understand."

Yarrow shook his head as Sasha fell into step behind him. Tension and anxiety had coaxed his friends' words out, he assumed. He wouldn't lend them credence; he'd struggled for over a year to get close to these men again, and he knew they could reach an understanding if they tried.

"Duncan would not be here if he cared more about Windwake than us," Yarrow noted.

"Perhaps," Sasha granted.

As they continued walking through the gloom of the cave, Yarrow ruminated on his companions' words, and the more he thought about them, the more his doubts grew, until he wasn't sure if he could really trust either of the other men. Sasha had deceived them from the beginning. As for Duncan, he made no secret of his disapproval of the mage and assassin. So what motivated him to stay by their sides? Each time he glanced at them, Yarrow felt more and more sure they kept their hands next to their weapons. Alone so far beneath the earth, no one would ever know if anything happened to Yarrow….

"Just what are you doing back there, Sasha?" Duncan asked in a harsh tone. "Why do you insist on walking behind me, and why are you holding your weapons?"

"Why do you keep reaching up to touch the hilt of your sword, Tam Knight?" Sasha shot back.

Duncan turned around to face him, squaring his shoulders and widening his stance. "It's habit, assassin. I would feel more comfortable if you'd walk in front of me."

"What, and expose my back to you?" Sasha's chuckle reminded Yarrow of shattering glass.

"Not every man would stab another in the back!" Duncan's voice rose with his anger and echoed through the chamber. Yarrow might not have spent time with his knight in a great while, but what he remembered most fondly about Duncan was his gentle nature and even temper. It wasn't like him to fly into a rage over nothing. "Some men have honor!"

Sasha sunk lower, bending his knees, and pointed one dagger at Duncan like an accusatory finger. "If I'm tarnishing your shining image, Duncan, you could have simply asked me to leave. I gave you ample opportunity. I will not die in this forsaken place so you can return to kiss your nobles' backsides without me."

What was going on? Sasha was cold and calculating in the most strained situations; it went against his very essence to let his passion overwhelm his reason. Yarrow hurried to step between them. "Just what are you two doing?"

Duncan curled his lip. "You. You tried to kill me once before. You have no respect for the rules of civilized society, so why lure me out here to finish the job? Why not just murder me in front of everyone with your unnatural power?"

"Unnatural?" Yarrow hated that word, and the very energy Duncan mentioned broke from his pores with his affront. "I'm unnatural until you need me to defeat an entire army! You only want to acknowledge me when I'm useful for something."

"I know that feeling well," Sasha said.

"Of course you'd take his side," Duncan growled, pointing at Yarrow with his warped sword.

"I never asked either of you to come here!" Yarrow shouted. He aimed a bolt of blue energy a few feet from Duncan, and it struck the ground amidst a small eruption of rubble. "Just go!"

Beloved, what has come over you?

They have it coming! Duncan is always trying to tell me what to do and coddle me like a helpless child, and Sasha has never shown me any real affection!

Listen to yourself, Yarrow! You're complaining that your knight shows you too much concern and your assassin not enough! I could care less if you want to destroy them, but I won't be blamed for it later. This is coming from you. I'll just sit back and enjoy the show.

"You dare to attack me?" Duncan swung his sword, missing Yarrow's belly by only a few inches. "Again? I'll fight you both at once!"

"Bring it on!" Sasha threw a knife, and it whizzed past Duncan's ear, taking a lock of dark brown hair with it. "Just know I won't hold back this time."

"Neither will I," Duncan answered. "You two have much to answer for! I was a good man, an honorable knight before I felt your influence. I have already let myself fall too far."

"You're blaming me?" Yarrow yelled. "You are no better than my blackguard uncle!" He aimed a splinter of lightning at Duncan's hand, just to shock him into dropping his sword. Duncan swung and hit Yarrow in the cheek with his opposite fist, knocking Yarrow off his feet and onto the ground. His skull smacked the rock, making him bite his tongue and taste blood. It also cleared his head. He understood magic was at work, some subtle, ancient curse as faint as the last, dying note of a song. Yarrow tried to dispel it, to negate and banish it every way he knew how, but Duncan and Sasha still traded blows, their altercation growing more and more violent. Sasha nicked the back of Duncan's hand with his dagger, and Duncan punched him in the stomach and made him double over.

"I never should have trusted either of you!" the knight roared, hitting Sasha again.

"You only ever see what you want to see," Sasha hissed, the tip of his knife scraping along Duncan's breastplate.

"Stop!" Yarrow shouted. He couldn't get rid of the enchantment; that was part of its brilliance. It would only dissipate when, and if, those under its effects denied its power. Yarrow could see gossamer filaments of magic draped like nets over his friends, but he had no way to sever them. Duncan and Sasha had to cast them off on their own. Yarrow got between them again even though Sasha swiped at him with his blades and Duncan tried to shoulder him aside. Yarrow used just enough power to sheath and protect himself, but he didn't retaliate. "Listen to yourselves!"

"He is a liar and a murderer," Duncan said.

"And you're a deluded old man!"

"Stop!" Yarrow said again. "You don't mean any of this, not really, and I need you to see it!"

"Out of my way," Duncan said. "You're as mad as everyone says!"

"Maybe," Yarrow conceded. "But do you really want to be rid of me? Think before you speak, look into the true feelings buried beneath the spell. Would you rather be without me and Sasha?"

"I—"

Yarrow turned to Sasha. "You chose us over your order. Are you truly sorry? Was what you had then better than what you have now?"

"In some ways," Sasha answered, the calm creeping into his tone encouraging Yarrow. "It was simpler. Weakness, all weakness, is born from fear. In the Crimson Scythe, I never knew fear because I had nothing to lose."

"What do you fear losing?" Yarrow prompted.

"One day, you two will no longer tolerate me, and then it will have been for nothing. I fear it will destroy me. I fear the intensity of the emotions I experience in regards to you." He reached up and stroked Yarrow's cheek with the back of his bruised and bloody hand.

The clang of metal echoed as Duncan let his sword fall and pushed past Yarrow to embrace Sasha. "Goddesses. I don't know what came over me. I didn't mean what I said, and I'm not going to send you away. Your feelings don't make you weak, Sasha. Opening yourself to them, risking pain, makes you brave. I want to face this with you. I'm... ashamed of my words."

"It was another spell," Yarrow said. "One I couldn't banish. It affected me as well. I also said things I regret. I'm glad you're both here. I was withering away before, being so alone…."

Duncan and Sasha opened their arms, and Yarrow took his place in the circle. They all joined hands and stood silently for a few minutes before Sasha suggested they move on.

Yarrow followed the pulse of magic he felt flowing like a river behind the stone walls of the cavern, running his hands over the surface, tracing the flow until he found a crack in the wall, barely wide enough to enter on his hands and knees. He hesitated, and Sasha and Duncan stood several feet behind him. "I don't know where this might lead me, and to tell the truth, I'm sick at the thought of entering, so the two of you should wait here."

"You're barking mad," Duncan said. "We didn't come halfway around the world to stand idle while you face danger alone."

"How will Sasha make it with his hurt foot?" Yarrow asked in desperation.

"This is hardly the most difficult thing I've faced," the assassin said. "Go, and we'll follow. I will always have your back, Yarrow."

Yarrow took a deep breath and nodded as he crouched in front of the entrance to the narrow passage. Nothing but thick blackness waited a few feet in. Panic made his limbs feel weak, and dizziness blurred his vision.

Go on, little Yarrow-flower. What's the problem? The last time you crawled through tunnels like this, you were fortunate enough to find me.

Bile stung the back of Yarrow's throat as the creature summoned the memories they shared, memories of Yarrow dragging himself through darkness on his elbows and belly for what felt like forever, unable to turn back, unable to reverse out, not knowing if anything awaited him if he continued. If Yarrow entered this tiny chute, he could die wedged between the rocks, starving slowly. Or his creature would keep him alive, suspended in blackness and unable to move for maybe hundreds of years. He could imagine nothing more horrible.

Goddesses, I can't. I can't go in there. Not again.

Then we should turn back, beloved, and leave these caverns the way we came in.

Are you telling me to give up? Accept I'll never be rid of you? Never able to be secure beside the men I love?

You clearly can't continue.

Foolish creature. Watch me. Yarrow wriggled into the passage though he could barely feel his limbs and he heard nothing but his rapid heartbeat. He ignored the fear and concentrated on pulling himself forward on his hands and knees. Sharp tines of rock waited only inches from his back as he worked his way up the steep slope, an inch at a time. He told himself to move forward and ignore the possibility of becoming trapped. An inch, and another. He moved his elbow in front of him and pulled. Another inch. Another. He focused on those inches he gained and blocked out everything else. If he contemplated his situation, his mind would break and the creature would win.

Yarrow reached out and pulled himself forward another inch. His fingers trembled as they tried to claw into the rock. *Keep going*, he told himself. *Fight through. It cannot last. It will end one way or the other.*

The constricting rock and absolute darkness finally broke, and Yarrow giggle-panted as he pulled himself into a small chamber. Unlike the previous cavern, this one was small, simple, and uneven. Yarrow stood, stretched his cramped limbs, and took a few deep breaths to calm himself. Sasha and Duncan emerged not long after, covered in thin layers of dust but otherwise no worse for the wear. They glanced around the room before moving to lean against the far wall. The tinkle of water led him to a recess in the corner. The liquid flowed down the stone, cutting a narrow path in the slimy green fungus coating the wall before dribbling into a pool edged with translucent, glowing mushrooms. Staring into its depths, Yarrow saw a bright smear twisting comet-like through the oily green. As he followed it with his eyes, he felt it brushing against the edges of his mind, grazing against his consciousness in the darkness as if he stood in the water with it.

Yarrow knelt down and held his hand an inch from the water, feeling the chill wafting off it. He felt its voice in the distance, as if it called to him from far away. He let it resonate within him until he began to understand and prepared to answer. Before he had the chance, the presence within him welled up like a tidal wave, and Yarrow might as well have been trying to hold back the sea with his bare hands. Never before had he felt such passion, anger, love, hatred and betrayal from the creature. It took control almost effortlessly, despite the spells Yarrow had mastered to contain it. The mage barely managed to hold onto a small shred of perception and was reminded why he needed this thing gone for good.

You! The presence roared. The emotion and arcane energy it spilled shook the cavern walls, making debris rain down.

The being in the water seemed amused. *Yes. I knew I would likely see you again one day.*

I'm here to make you pay for what you did to me! Yarrow watched his hand plunge into the water and grab for the shimmering ribbon twisting through it. Rage, thousands of years' worth, reduced the presence to a rabid animal. Yarrow tried to communicate with it, to soothe it somehow before it damaged his body, but it ignored him. Yarrow couldn't figure out what had angered it. If this was Fane, how could his creature recognize the ancient mage-lord? From what Yarrow understood, the creature had been cursed and lost its body long before Fane came to power.

Settle down, old friend, Fane said. *You know full well you cannot hurt me with that boy's little hands when I am in this state. At least you should. You taught me the spell, after all.*

And you used it against me! To think I once called you beloved!

It's funny how things work out, Fane said. *I was betrayed in exactly the same way I betrayed you. Being trapped here all these years has almost made me regret what I did to you. It makes me wonder if there's some sort of cosmic justice after all.* He laughed as if the concept was completely absurd.

Yarrow's presence didn't share Fane's amusement. *Your people were little more than animals wallowing in their own waste and sleeping in caves when I took you in and taught you all my secrets. To think I actually trusted you.*

Do not feel bad about that, old friend. I made the same mistake. After I got rid of you, I spent the next few thousand years making the world into a paradise. Civilization reached heights I had never even dreamed of, and I was Fane, ruler of it all. It was... fun while it lasted. But then my apprentices used the knowledge I'd given them to destroy me, just as I did to you. I don't know how I didn't see it coming.

It's better than you deserve!

Probably, Fane said. *Though I'm not sure it's all said and done just yet.*

It is if I have any say in the matter! I am stronger than you right now, beloved! I at least have access to a body that can cast magic. You have no means of using spells. You're less than nothing, and I won't let my new beloved do anything to change that!

Oh? You express a confidence in your control over that boy you clearly do not feel. Tell me, is he as strong as I was?

Yarrow couldn't wait to hear the creature's response. It took a few moments to consider before replying. *Yes and no. You came to me whole, brave and curious. He came already broken. You desired power for its own sake; he hoards it like stones to build a wall around himself.*

Let me speak to him.

What if I don't want to?

Compelled by the need for answers, Yarrow swam through the thick, warm blackness above him even though it felt like he dragged a boulder in his wake. Finally, gasping mentally, he broke the surface and his consciousness surged into his skull, taking control of his eyes, ears and skin. He stared down into the pool, still unable to believe who he was about to speak with.

Hello, beloved. Yarrow greeted him with the only endearment he could associate with him, the one his creature had always used when thinking about or speaking of his pupil.

Hello, beloved, Fane answered.

Were you really my creature's first student?

I was.

Should I call you Fane?

It's as good a name as any. What's yours?

Yarrow.

Well, Yarrow, I have been waiting for you a very long time.

For me?

For someone, Fane clarified. *My treacherous wives were very clever, though, and they hid me well. Tell me. What brought you here? Was it just dumb luck that led you to me?*

No. Hale told me I might find you here.

Hale. I remember him much better than the others. Is he... is he well?

Not really. He suffers from enormous guilt, Yarrow said, a little perplexed by the way the two of them conversed like old friends while the creature stayed silent. He wondered what Duncan and Sasha thought as they stood watching him. *Hale has been punishing himself for millennia. He lives in self-imposed exile.*

I'm very sorry to hear that. He was one of the very few true friends I had.

He remembers you fondly, if that means anything, Yarrow said.

Nothing means anything to me anymore. I don't even properly exist. Why did Hale send you to me, Yarrow? What do you think I can do for you?

The creature, the one who taught you, bonded with me. I let it do it to save my life, but I cannot control it. I've tried everything. It's used me to hurt and kill those I love most, and I want to be rid of it. Hale couldn't help me. He thought maybe you could. Do you... can you help me? You're my one last hope.

I can help you, Fane said. *But I won't do it for free. I'm sorry, but thousands of years of languishing here have dampened any pretense of morality or honor I might have once imagined I possessed.*

Yarrow could hardly believe he'd heard Fane right. *You... you said yes?*

Yes, for a price.

Do not trust him, beloved Yarrow! the creature said. *Look what this wretch did to me even as he claimed he loved me! He might destroy us both! He cares about nothing but himself.*

I suppose he might, Yarrow conceded. *But if I cannot be rid of you, destruction is my only remaining option. What do you ask of me, Fane?*

"Yarrow, is everything all right?" Duncan laid a hand on Yarrow's shoulder.

Yarrow had almost forgotten the presence of his friends. "It's fine. I must communicate with Fane. Please don't worry. There isn't any danger."

"Is there anything we can do?" Sasha asked.

Yarrow shook his head. "I just need to concentrate. It may take a while." Both of them nodded and found a place to sit down while Yarrow proceeded.

Yarrow returned his attention to the pool. *What can I trade you for your assistance, Fane?*

First, you must tend to the wound you've buried for so long. I can help you, but you must face it so you can begin to heal, or being rid of the creature will do you no good. I see a darkness in you, a great fear and rage, and if you do not purge yourself of it you will be just as dangerous to those around you as the one sharing your body. I can strip away all the gauze and reveal the source of this pain, if you are willing.

I am.

Think twice, Yarrow, the presence said. *This is not something you want to know, to experience again. I have helped keep you safe from it. It will shatter you.*

Sometimes a thing must be scrapped and started anew, Fane said. *The choice is his.*

I will take the chance, Yarrow said. *What more?*

You must take me out of this place, end my imprisonment.

How?

Carry me inside you.

Yarrow shook his head. *I cannot agree to that. I came all this way to free myself of one presence trying to control my mind and body. I will not accept another and find myself in the same trap.*

You misunderstand, Fane said. *I have no desire to look through your eyes or act through your hands. I will not whisper inside your head. There won't be enough left of me to do so even if I wished it. No, this whole aspect of me is twisted and flawed after my time here. I'm mad and delusional, but horribly sane enough to recognize it. All I ask is for you to carry a single spark of my most basic essence until I can come back. You will never even know it is there.*

You plan to come back? Yarrow asked.

I must. I will be needed. I need to show people a world without the need for gods or masters. A world where we can take full credit for our triumphs and accept responsibility for our errors. That is all I ever wanted. Help me, and I will help you. As I said, you will not notice my presence.

I... I will do it. What next?

As soon as I join with you, two things will happen, Fane said. *You will have to face the pain you've hidden from for so long. Some of what you suffered is known to you, but I suspect your mind has shielded you from the worst of it, prevented you from remembering. It will not be easy for you to witness, but you must. Then I'll give you the knowledge you need to deal with your creature. You'll have to make a choice. You can destroy it and lose its knowledge and power forever, or you can bond with it fully. It will never again be able to speak to you or influence your behavior, but it will be a part of you, and certain facets of it will integrate into your personality. You will be a single entity, an amalgam. Consider carefully before you choose, Yarrow. This creature is ancient, and its motivations are anything but human. If you meld with it, you may find yourself profoundly altered in ways I cannot begin to predict. Do you understand?*

Yes.

Are you ready?

Yes. Yes, do it.

Beloved— A fear Yarrow had never imagined his creature capable of expressing tainted its tone as it attempted one last plea.

Do it! Yarrow said quickly, before he lost his nerve and changed his mind.

The radiant streak rose toward the top of the water. It breached the surface and broke apart, spewing prisms around the small cave until only a single point of golden light, smaller than a spark rising from a campfire, remained. It drifted toward Yarrow and sank into his belly below the waistband of his trousers. The mage felt only a subtle heat, as if he'd just enjoyed a bowl of hot stew, and then nothing. The warmth crawled slowly up his spine and into his head, and just when he thought it wouldn't be so bad, Yarrow found himself knocked into a nightmare.

He was twelve and visiting his uncle, King Agarick, at his fortress in the mountains. His mother and brothers had retired to their rooms after a sumptuous dinner. He'd expected this and remembered it only too well. Next, the king would take Yarrow to a guest chamber, give him a few glasses of wine, and tell Yarrow he could give him what he really wanted. Yarrow had taken little pleasure in it, but he'd accepted it and moved past it not long after his exile. The king had taken advantage of Yarrow's curiosity, but he could have hurt Yarrow far worse than he had. Seeing it again wouldn't harm him as Fane predicted. But instead of taking the winding staircase to the guestroom, Yarrow descended the narrow steps to the barracks and found his uncle and a half a dozen of his knights seated around a table. He couldn't remember having ever been in the barracks of Agarick's fortress. At first, he felt grown up, special for being included. He took his place next to the king, and Agarick clasped his hand. Though he wasn't sure how he felt about what happened between him and his uncle, Yarrow didn't pull away. He'd been taught to respect his elders, especially the king.

One of the knights slid a goblet in front of Yarrow, and he drank the honey-sweet liquid it contained. When he finished it, they gave him another, and another. Yarrow grew hot and dizzy, and he swayed in his simple, wooden chair. He struggled not to throw up and show himself for a child who couldn't hold his wine. Before Yarrow knew what was happening, someone lifted him from his seat and laid him across the table. The knights tore his clothes away and held his arms and legs when he tried to struggle. Their rough hands bruised his flesh and then—

He screamed at the pain, but he couldn't get away. This was nothing like what had happened with the king; they *wanted* to hurt him. Yarrow waited for it to end, but it went on and on, and there was nothing he could do. He couldn't escape the men's abuse or the filthy, degrading things they said to him. They told him it was his fault, that he deserved it. They told him he wanted it even though he was crying. They called him unnatural again and again. Yarrow called out for his creature. It would massacre them, reduce them to bloody smears. He cried and cried, but it didn't come.

He stood before Agarick's gates again, still a boy. The king arrived to greet his family and escort them to their rooms. He took Yarrow firmly by the elbow and guided him toward the barracks—

The cycle played out again and again, and Yarrow screamed his throat raw, vaguely aware of his physical body curling in on itself while the knights abused the body in his memories. He remembered what Agarick had done, but he'd never recalled any of the others. How? Had this really happened? It couldn't have. Not to him. No. These awful memories must belong to someone else—

I am here now, and I will never let you be harmed again. The creature stood next to Yarrow, beautiful in its awesome might, wings spread wide and blue light pouring from its eyes. It waved its hand, and the naked king and his knights disintegrated.

Yarrow turned to it and hugged it, though it didn't return the embrace. "Thank you."

My power is yours, beloved. Come, let's leave this awful place. With me by your side, no one will ever treat you that way again.

We can't leave. Fane told me what I have to do. I have to decide now. Yarrow broke away from the creature and stood looking at its majestic form and cold, cruel eyes. In this place, in this form, he could destroy it. If he pierced its chest, it would perish, and every trace of it anchored to Yarrow would dry up and disintegrate. Of course it would probably fight back, but Yarrow felt confident he would prevail. His essence was strong and true, while his creature possessed little more than a memory of itself.

"Do you really want to face the world without my power, beloved Yarrow?" it asked. "How will you stop others from using you without my strength? Let us be one."

Yarrow rubbed his bare arms, wanting to scratch away all the skin Agarick and his knights had sullied, feeling so filthy he couldn't imagine ever being clean again. Could he make his way through the world with nothing but his own magic to rely on? Sasha and Duncan would tell him to dispatch the creature, he had no doubt. They would offer to protect him, but could they? They were only men. On the other hand, they might despise him, turn away from him, if they knew he'd made his murderous creature a permanent part of himself, especially if he didn't have to.

It stroked Yarrow's cheek tenderly. "I can never be restored and neither can you. We can only be whole together, beloved. Accept me. I'll be nothing more than an added layer of mail beneath your armor, or a spare dagger when you find yourself in need of one."

"I will be different," Yarrow argued even as he rested his head against the creature's broad chest. "I won't be me. They might not accept me."

"There is always that possibility." The creature stroked Yarrow's hair, its touch so different from the cruelty of the king and his knights. "You must do what you need to do. To be safe. To keep others from exploiting you. Can you trust those two men to save you?"

"No. I need to be able to do it myself. I need power. I don't want to helpless, not ever again. The weak are prey for the strong. Maybe what Sasha said is true and weakness comes from fear. I'm tired of being afraid, afraid of being alone and afraid of hurting the people I love, but mostly afraid of being unable to protect myself."

"Very wise. Have you decided, then, my beloved?"

"I have." Yarrow kissed the creature softly and kept hold of its hand as he lowered himself to the floor and spread his legs. It settled between his thighs, and their erections slid against each other. It lined its enormous cock up to Yarrow's opening and pushed. Yarrow shrieked as it entered him, pushing past his instinctual resistance. He lifted his legs to his creature's shoulders. He couldn't help but enjoy that big cock cleaving him, delving deep inside him, further than he'd ever experienced. As the being thrust into Yarrow, it started to fade away, and Yarrow realized he was absorbing it. He felt it sinking into every fiber of his being, mixing into him like two vats of dye combining to form a completely new color. Yarrow's body burned as his creature thrust, being reshaped like a lump of hot metal on a smith's anvil. The coupling was a metaphor, just a way for his mind to recognize their union. It was painful and beautiful, and Yarrow felt himself transforming, becoming stronger and wiser as the presence dissipated with every stroke, its energy directed into Yarrow, sinking into his flesh and awareness.

"You… you'll always be with me?" Yarrow groaned.

"Always." Its voice was already a whisper carried away by the wind, an echo soon to fade forever.

By the time Yarrow came, he clasped at empty air, and the voice that had kept him company for the last five years had dissolved completely into his being. He clutched it until there was nothing left to hold on to, and then he let himself topple face-first into blessed oblivion.

Chapter
Twenty-One

DUNCAN had been napping against the cavern wall, his cheek on Sasha's shoulder, where they'd both spent the last half a day waiting for their mage to finish staring into the water, when he woke to Yarrow's screams. Instantly alert, he scrambled to his feet and hurried to stand over Yarrow. The young man curled his legs against his chest and pressed his forehead to his knees as he whimpered and groaned. Duncan touched his shoulder, but Yarrow didn't seem to notice. Duncan knelt down and rolled Yarrow to his back, trying to hold him still as he trembled so hard his limbs flailed. Yarrow's eyes rolled back in his head, and he gurgled and yelled.

"What's going on?" Sasha asked. "What's wrong with him?"

"I don't know." Tendrils of blue light moved beneath Yarrow's skin, shooting down his arms and across his face. It flashed in his eyes, and he cried out and thrashed his head. Spittle flew from his mouth, and his body straightened and went stiff. Duncan wrapped Yarrow's cloak around him and scooped Yarrow into his arms, holding Yarrow tight against his chest. He knew little of magic and could think of nothing else to do to help his friend. After a quarter of an hour, he realized the spell wouldn't simply pass. Yarrow lost consciousness a few times and woke again screaming. Duncan could do nothing but pin his arms to prevent him clawing his skin open.

"I've found another tunnel," Sasha said. "It leads up, and the air flowing from it smells fresh. Maybe it will help if we get him away from this place. There's too much evil magic running through here. Who knows how it could be affecting him."

Since he had no better suggestion, Duncan nodded and stood slowly. Though Yarrow didn't weigh much, days without a proper meal or night of sleep had left Duncan weak. They made slow progress with him carrying Yarrow and Sasha supporting himself on his stick, but eventually they emerged from the cavern. Duncan squeezed his eyes shut against the glare. He hadn't remembered the sunlight on the snow being so painfully bright. Flurries whipped around them as they looked out across a row of jagged peaks. Though the cold nipped at his cheeks and made his battered bones ache, Duncan thanked the goddesses for the purity of the wind after days in the musty cave.

"We should get out of the mountains," Sasha said, pointing to the southeast, where the hills tapered off to rounded mounds far in the distance.

Duncan took a moment to get his bearings. It had been nearly impossible to gauge distance or direction in the twisting caverns. It seemed the passage Sasha had found brought them out closer to the base of the mountains and farther south. The grasslands waited to the east, much closer than they'd been when the three of them had entered Fane's cave, and the snowy peaks seemed distant.

"We should move," Sasha repeated. "We'll need to refresh our supplies before long. Besides, I'm eager to see the last of this place."

"Agreed." They traveled until they lost the light and then camped huddled together beneath a small ledge. Yarrow woke many times throughout the night, thrashing and screaming, battering Duncan and Sasha with his arms and legs until he lost consciousness again. Sasha, clearly worried, forced the mage to drink water and tried to speak with him, but Yarrow didn't respond. Whatever he heard, saw, and experienced wasn't the icy cliffs, and Duncan could only imagine it was awful.

As soon as the sun rose, they finished the last of their food. Yarrow remained in his fugue, and so Duncan had to carry him again. Yarrow felt heavier and heavier with each step Duncan took. Duncan heaved a sigh of relief as the ground evened out. They had made it past the steepest terrain, and the slope of the ground grew gentler, meaning Duncan wouldn't have to pick his way so carefully or struggle not to slip. Yarrow's dead weight threw Duncan's balance off, and he worried constantly about falling and hurting them both. He found a flat stone to sit down upon and rest. Though the way would get easier from here, they still had a long journey across the flatlands back to the city and the ship that would take them home, and it would take twice as long if Duncan had to carry Yarrow the whole way. But he would do it if he had to; somehow he'd manage. Sasha sat on the ground and stretched his hurt leg out in front of him, laying the stick he'd used as a crutch next to his thigh.

"Can you take him for a minute?" Duncan asked. He felt like his arms had been bent in the same position for a week, and he didn't know if he'd ever be able to extend them again. Sasha nodded, and Duncan placed their mage on Sasha's lap so he could stretch and twist his waist. His bones popped loudly, and he groaned.

Sasha smoothed the hair out of Yarrow's face and stroked his cheek. A little crease formed between the assassin's slender black brows. "I wish you would come back to me," he whispered.

"S-Sasha?" Yarrow croaked, his eyes fluttering open. Duncan knelt down beside them and clutched Yarrow's hand. The mage looked around in confusion. Tears spilled down his cheeks, and he swallowed a sob. Sasha drew him closer to his chest and kept petting his face.

"What is it?" Duncan asked.

"It's gone," Yarrow said. "Gone. I ask it a question, and it doesn't answer. I call out to it, and it doesn't come."

"But isn't that what you wanted?" Sasha asked.

The mage nodded, sniffling. "It's been with me for so long. I didn't know I'd feel so alone."

"You're not alone," Duncan said, bending in to kiss Yarrow's forehead. "You're finally free. That horrible thing is gone. Its influence over you is gone. You had the strength to give it up, and I'm proud of you. I'm happy we'll have you all to ourselves at last. We should thank the goddesses."

Yarrow nestled his face against Sasha's chest and cried softly. Duncan wrapped his arms around both of them and pressed his forehead to Sasha's. "Yarrow, do you wish to talk?"

"No. Not yet. I didn't know…. Goddesses, how could they? I should make them pay, show them my strength. Show everyone so they all know not to trifle with me!"

"Who, Yarrow?" Sasha asked.

The mage responded by crying harder, and Duncan and Sasha let him go until he finally went quiet, and then the three of them just held each other as the wind whistled across the flat land. Then, in the distance, Duncan heard something else: the sound of hoofbeats. Sasha snapped his head up and looked toward the south. "We should get out of the open, hide until we know who else is out here. Yarrow, can you walk?"

He nodded. "I think so. Thank you both for looking out for me. I'm ashamed it was necessary. I won't let it happen again."

"Hush," Duncan said, helping Yarrow to stand. "We'll do what we must."

"It's unusual for me," Sasha admitted, pointing to a shallow ravine full of brush. "When I broke my leg, I expected to be left behind, even though I knew Duncan would never abandon me. This concept of looking out for others still sits strange with me, but I'm glad to have someone looking out for me, and for the two of you to look after."

Duncan smiled as they crouched low in the bushes. Soon a patrol approached, preceded by a cloud of dust. On his hands and knees, Duncan crawled a little way up the hill so he could get a glimpse of them, being careful to stay concealed by the vegetation. The eight riders reined in their mounts, creatures similar to the horses back in Selindria, but shorter and stouter, with broad, cloven hooves, stubby tails, and pairs of short horns on their foreheads. The men astride the creatures were clearly guards or soldiers of some kind. They wore matching padded leather trousers and boots with nasty barbs on the heels and toes. Their muscular chests were bare, but they wore crimson scarves wrapped around their heads and faces, with conical metal helmets on top. Each of them had a large crossbow strapped to his back, and many of them held long spears similar to halberds but with serrated edges. Some of the weapons crackled with blue, arcane sparks similar to those Yarrow conjured.

Their leader pointed with his weapon and shouted a few words Duncan didn't understand. Lightning arced from the point of his spear. The men yelled something in response and spread out in pairs. Though Duncan didn't know their language, he'd been a soldier long enough to recognize a commander issuing orders to his men. They were clearly searching for something or someone.

Sasha tapped Duncan's shoulder and canted his head toward the other end of the ravine, away from the armed men. Duncan nodded his understanding, and all of them crawled slowly through the underbrush, dragging themselves on their elbows and bellies. When they reached the pile of large rocks stoppering the gully, Sasha held up his hand to indicate Duncan and Yarrow should wait, and then he abandoned his staff and climbed nimbly over the stones despite his injury. The assassin stayed within the crevices and kept to the shadows cast by the irregular rock formations until he disappeared from Duncan's view. Duncan clutched the hem of Yarrow's tunic and held it tightly in his sweaty fist for probably half an hour until Sasha returned and picked his way back down into the depression. He dragged Duncan and Yarrow farther into the brush.

"There are at least two more patrols of eight men each," he said. "Likely more. Well-armed, and some with magical weapons."

"They're looking for me," Yarrow said. "They keep the Emiri as slaves in this land, and they kill anyone with magical abilities on sight. From what I understand, and it isn't much, only the members of their aristocracy are permitted to use enchantment. I freed a group of captives and killed quite a few of the men guarding them. I killed several more when they pursued us into the foothills. I'm afraid I wasn't subtle."

Duncan rolled his eyes. "You rarely are. So, maybe we should stay hidden here until they move on, and then we can make our way back to the city and our ship."

"I'm not sure that's a wise plan," Sasha said. "From what I observed, they're conducting a very thorough search. I'm surprised they haven't given up by now. It's probably been almost two weeks. If they haven't abandoned their search yet, I doubt they will anytime soon. They'll come through here eventually, and they have us at a severe disadvantage."

"Why don't we just kill them?" Yarrow asked.

Duncan flinched. Their mage had always been quick to defend himself or those he cared about, but he'd never mentioned murder so casually before. While he certainly didn't agree with what he'd seen done to the Emiri, if a foreigner came to Windwake and slaughtered a group of his knights, Duncan would find himself in these men's position. He shook his head. "You're weak, Sasha is hurt, and I'm exhausted. Attacking will only give away our position and likely draw more guards. There could be hundreds of them, for all we know. Thousands. So many not even you can stand against them all."

"I doubt it," Yarrow said much more flippantly than Duncan liked.

"Remember, my friend, you no longer have your creature to rely on, to prevent you from getting hurt or heal you if you do."

The mage snorted and smiled, baring his teeth and licking their edges. "I don't need it. I'll crush these worms under my boot, along with any other fools who think they can stand against me. They cannot harm me. I'll soak the ground with their blood."

"And what about us?" Duncan asked, still stunned at Yarrow's blood thirst. "You may think yourself immortal, but I know I'm not."

"I agree," Sasha said. "Engaging these enemies would be foolish. This isn't a battle we can win. We should try to sneak past them." Without waiting to see if they agreed, Sasha crouched low and crept around a copse of trees.

They spent the rest of the afternoon following their assassin, darting behind boulders, crawling through ravines, and slinking around trees that grew larger and more plentiful as they approached the plain at the base of the hills. They spoke little, though a few times when Duncan looked back at Yarrow, he saw the mage was crying. Could he really be mourning the loss of the monster within him, if it had ever existed? A little heartsick, Duncan realized their journey had done nothing to cure the young man's madness.

By sunset, they'd made their way completely out of the hills. Sasha swore softly as they clustered together in the high grass. The men pursuing them lit lanterns, and those on horseback issued orders to those on the ground. The foot soldiers spread out, driving their spears into clumps of bracken and combing through the dry grass.

"What will we do now?" Duncan asked. "Retreat back into the hills?"

"Bartoum and his crew won't wait forever," Sasha said. "If that ship leaves without us, we'll find ourselves stranded in this savage land. The native ships didn't look seaworthy to me."

"We'll have to fight," Yarrow said, staring into his empty palms. "Fight our way across this field, through the city, and down to the waterfront and the ship."

"Impossible," Duncan said. "There are three of us and at least three dozen men on that sward alone. We can't prevail. I think—"

He cut his statement short as six men converged on them. Duncan, Sasha, and Yarrow crouched lower as the soldiers' lights fell across the grass in wavering, golden stripes. The guards came closer and closer; there was no way they wouldn't discover Duncan and his friends' position. Duncan gripped the hilt of his sword. He wasn't about to let everything end when they'd just found their way back to each other, when Yarrow had just purged himself of at least part of the darkness he carried inside.

Duncan said a silent prayer to Myint to stand with them. All he knew in that moment was that he would rather die than fail in his duty and watch another man he loved ripped away from him.

With a soft swish, Sasha unsheathed his daggers.

When the guards came within a few feet of them, Yarrow stood and stretched out his hand. The world shimmied, and Duncan felt his stomach plummet just as it had when Sai's ship dropped from the peak of a huge wave. He blinked and the effect subsided. The six men stood frozen, some of them with their mouths open in midspeech. Even the flames inside their lanterns stood still, the smoke rising from them unmovable smudges against the deepening cobalt of the sky. Though Duncan had seen Yarrow use this spell once before, it still chilled him to his core to watch the blades of grass sticking up as still as tiny spears stuck in the ground while those ten feet away bent and rattled with the wind.

Sasha grabbed Yarrow's elbow, as the mage simply stared at what he'd done, and all of them ran bent nearly in half for a hillock in the distance. The swish of the grass sounded louder than the tide to Duncan, but thankfully no one pursued them. With the exception of the guards under Yarrow's enchantment, the men seeking them were still half a mile away. It would take them some time to discover what had happened to their companions, and Duncan knew he and his friends needed every second they could get. Sasha winced and swallowed a grunt with every step he took, but he didn't slow down, and soon they reached the top of the knoll and tripped their way down the other side.

Duncan pointed with his sword, and they sprinted around another small hill. "We have to go back into the mountains," he panted. "There's no other choice!"

Shouting in the distance told them the other guards had discovered their immobilized comrades, which meant they now knew where Duncan and his friends had recently been. The three of them kept moving, running south toward a wood at the base of an embankment, but before long the sound of hooves joined the men's voices.

Duncan, Sasha, and Yarrow made it into the trees, but a dozen men with lanterns followed close on their heels. Duncan didn't know whether to keep running or try to hide. He followed Sasha from shadow to shadow as the forest floor grew steeper.

"Wait," Sasha said, his voice as soft as the breeze in the leaves. "I see someone up ahead."

Squinting, Duncan managed to discern a group of four people standing between two large rocks. He drew his sword as he approached them with Sasha and Yarrow close behind. His blade was warped and rippling, but it would have to serve him until he found a blacksmith. As he got closer, he saw that the people awaiting them were small, and that they carried no weapons.

"Emiri," Yarrow said. "I think these are some of the people I helped to free."

The Emiri looked strange to Duncan without the long, lavishly adorned ropes of hair he'd become accustomed to seeing on them. Its absence made their frightened eyes seem even larger. Streaks of dirt covered their tanned skin and the filthy rags they wore, but all of them smiled when they saw Yarrow. A female with scarlet eyes and a scar bisecting the corners of her lips said a few words and motioned with her hand. She wanted them to follow her. Duncan looked over his shoulder at his friends.

"This seems the best option we have at the moment," Sasha said. "They at least know the terrain better than we do, and I doubt they have much love for those soldiers."

"I agree," Yarrow said. "We should go with them."

Duncan nodded to their guide and hoped she'd understand the gesture. She said a few more words before turning and jogging into the trees with the rest of her people. They went only a few hundred yards before two of the Emiri men crouched down and began sifting through the leaf litter on the ground. Not far behind them, the guards called back and forth to each other, twigs snapping loudly beneath their boots.

The Emiri found a rope, pulled it, and opened a hatch. One of them propped it open with a stick, and the woman pointed into the shadowy depths. Duncan waited until Sasha, Yarrow, and their rescuers all made it inside, and then he scrambled down a rickety ladder he doubted would hold his weight, closing the hatch behind him.

When they reached the ground, Yarrow conjured a light that bathed everything in soft sapphire. The Emiri gasped, backed away from the mage, dropped to their knees, covered their heads, and whimpered.

"That's an odd reaction," Duncan noted. "I've never heard of an Emiri mistrustful of magic."

"No," Sasha said. "They usually value anything useful to them."

"Don't be afraid," Yarrow said, patting one of the Emiri men on the shoulder. "Look. It isn't even hot." He ran his fingertips over the blue sphere in demonstration, casting strange, shifting shadows on the dirt walls.

Slowly, the young man got to his feet, reached out, and touched Yarrow's light. He looked at his hand as if surprised to find it unharmed, and then he laughed and said a few words to his companions. All of them gathered around to take turns touching the orb, and soon they made a game of batting it back and forth. Yarrow conjured another for their entertainment, this time in a soft lavender. Then he created a rosy pink one.

The multicolored light showed Duncan not just a room, but a long tunnel reinforced with thick branches. "They must have built this," he said to Sasha. "There must be at least some sort of a resistance here."

"Well, Emiri are hardly natural slaves," Sasha said. "We were fortunate they found us, and that they wanted to repay Yarrow's kindness."

"Doing good things for others brings good things back to you," Duncan said.

Sasha laughed and then looked at Duncan with an arched brow. "Oh, pardon me. I felt certain that was a joke."

"Just when I thought your cold heart had started to melt a bit," Duncan grumbled. Their Emiri guides began walking through the tunnel, and he and Sasha fell into step behind them.

"Well, good is a relative term," Sasha said. "How good do you think the men Yarrow slaughtered through to liberate these people found it? It was good for our side when I stabbed Taran Edercrest in the throat and brought your prince his head, but not so much for him."

"Morbid," Duncan muttered.

"Also true," Sasha shot back.

"It's a matter of perspective," Duncan said.

"I don't see it that way," Sasha said. "Good and evil are irrelevant. There are only the victorious and the dead, and no gray area exists in between. Today, we're victorious. It may not last, so let's enjoy it."

Yarrow came back to walk with them. "You know, I'm going to tell Garith about what's going on in this land. He should send knights here and put a stop to these atrocities."

Duncan kept his tone as gentle as possible. "My friend, your cousin has much more immediate concerns. Besides, he's fighting on his own soil to get rid of the Emiri. What makes you think he'd sacrifice his men to rescue these?"

"Perhaps I'll do it myself," Yarrow said dreamily, his eyes either reflecting the blue light of his sphere or glowing with their own. "If I was to conquer this land, I could claim it for myself. Farther inland, there are wonders you can scarcely imagine. I remember them from the last time I traveled here: palaces hewn from crystal and topped with gold domes. Maybe I'll capture one and give it to Sai!"

"You've never had any interest in ruling," Sasha observed. "Why the sudden change of heart?"

"I'm strong," Yarrow said without boasting. "Stronger than any of these people. Why shouldn't I rule them if I can?"

"You never desired it before," Sasha said.

"Besides," Duncan added, "ruling is not about the strong subjugating the weak. That's tyranny. A ruler should protect his people, always putting their well-being before his own. It's something we're entrusted with, not something we take just because we can."

"I grew up among royalty and nobility," Yarrow said. "It never seemed that way to me."

"To me, either," Sasha said. "But maybe it should be that way."

A haunted look came over Yarrow's face, and he scratched at his forearms until he broke the skin. When Duncan reached for his hand to stop him, the mage flinched and his power flared around him. Duncan and Sasha looked at each other, and Duncan said, "I didn't mean to startle you, my friend."

"I'm not startled," Yarrow snapped. Then he took a breath and rubbed the center of his forehead. "I'm sorry. It's been a very long few days. I'm just tired, and I would like very much for us to lie down together somewhere we can be alone."

"That isn't likely to happen until we make it back home to Windwake," Duncan said. "But when we do, we won't leave my bedchamber for a week."

"Not long enough," Yarrow groaned.

Sasha chuckled. "I have to agree. I say we make it a month."

"We'll make it forever," Duncan said, grinning like a fool in spite of everything they'd been through and might still face. He took Sasha and

Yarrow's hands and swung their arms as they followed the Emiri through the tunnel.

At the end of the corridor, they climbed another flimsy ladder and emerged into the bright, pulpy light of late morning. The sea stretched out in front of them, sparkling like a jeweled necklace spread across the horizon. A spit of sand formed a natural pier, and Duncan walked to the tip of it, shielding his eyes as he looked down the coast. About a mile to the east, the simple boats bobbed near the shore, and the city waited beyond them. Duncan could only assume Emiri refugees came here to board ships and escape.

"This is fantastic," he said. "I'll walk to the city, find Captain Bartoum Astir and his crew, probably at the brothel, and we can pick you up here."

"I think we should stay together," Sasha said. "I don't like the idea of us getting separated in this strange place."

Duncan shook his head. "The soldiers here are only looking for Yarrow, and Yarrow is too distinctive to take into the city. I don't want to leave him here alone, though." He met Sasha's gaze and hoped Sasha understood his meaning. Whatever ordeal Yarrow had suffered back in the caverns had left him agitated and behaving strangely. The last thing Duncan wanted was to have to hunt him down again if he wandered off. Looking at the scabs on the mage's arms, he even worried Yarrow might hurt himself. Luckily, Sasha nodded.

"You can always go back into the tunnel to hide if anyone comes by," Duncan said. "Please don't take any unnecessary risks. I'll be back soon."

He thanked the Emiri, even though they wouldn't understand, and shook each of their hands. He planned to ask Bartoum to take the Emiri with them, but he didn't know if they would want to go. He might never see them again, and he owed them much.

Chapter Twenty-Two

THE air tasted of autumn by the time Duncan, Sasha, and Yarrow docked at Greyrclif. Hearth fires, freshly cut hay, and ripe fruit scented the breeze coming off the southern plains. Captain Bartoum Astir had taken them to the Twenty-Nine, sailing all the way around the southern coast of Espero. The blond sailor had had a good laugh when Duncan had asked him if he planned to brave the Serpent's Belly. While his route took much longer than Sai's, Duncan found it much less harrowing. When they'd reached the archipelago at the mouth of the Kanda River, they'd said their farewells to the four Emiri who came with them. Yarrow assured Duncan they would be fine; their countrymen would take care of them just the way Rini took care of him when he'd needed it. Duncan insisted they take the time to visit Sai, since he felt Sai at least deserved to see all he'd done had paid off and Yarrow was safe.

They found an Emiri ship to ferry them to the island Sai and his family called home. When they arrived, Lala told them the others had set sail a few days ago in search of ships carrying weapons from Gaeltheon to the Selindrian coast. Intercepting the shipments not only protected the Twenty-Nine, but the armaments sold for a high profit in the rougher cities, like Felgard. She'd stayed behind to look after Yei. It surprised Duncan when Yarrow spent most of their visit holding and talking to the boy; he'd never imagined his mage being fond of children, but Yarrow's genuine pride in Yei made Duncan grin. Duncan wished he could have seen Sai and thanked him again for all he'd done, but he contented himself with asking Lala to relay their gratitude and repeated his offer to help them should they ever need anything.

After they'd left the Twenty-Nine, they'd purchased passage aboard a merchant ship and sailed along the Selindrian coast. From Greyrclif, they could reach Windwake overland in three days on horseback or about a week in a carriage. They'd had little privacy aboard the ships, and Duncan longed for some time with his partners.

Yarrow had alternated between being distant, leaning on the rail of the ship for hours alone, and clinging relentlessly to Duncan and Sasha like a boy afraid to let go of his mother's skirts. He wouldn't talk about what had happened in the caverns, but he woke up every night screaming. Some days, he refused to leave his bunk, and he lashed out when Duncan encouraged him to eat. Duncan had thought they'd moved past all that silly posturing, but if anything, Yarrow seemed more disturbed than before. Just like before, Yarrow grew the nastiest when he hurt the worst. Duncan didn't let himself be pushed away, though. No matter how much Yarrow protested, Duncan knew he didn't want to be alone. Hopefully, some time to relax at Windust Castle would help him figure things out.

To expedite their journey, Duncan rented a trio of fast horses, and within two days, he saw the peaks of his fortress in the distance. The arn leaves had started to curl and turn orange at the edges, the filbernut foliage was deep burgundy, and here and there briarwoods and maples added splashes of crimson and gold. A few leaves tumbled across their path as they rode. A light breeze rustled fields of grain almost ready for harvesting, just brisk enough to refresh them as they traveled beneath the strong afternoon sun, which hadn't yet relinquished its summer intensity.

Duncan was pleased to be home in time for the harvest and the festival of Berris, which had always been his favorite. He loved the scent of good, Selindrian trees in autumn. Even though he wouldn't be able to dance with his partners, kiss them beneath the wreaths of wheat and small gourds for fecundity, or hold their hands as he offered wine and honey to the soil, he looked forward to sitting beside them at the best feasts of the year. He looked over at their hair, ebony and white, streaming behind them, and smiled wide. His life finally felt full and right, and it had been a long time coming.

The warmth of hope and homecoming fizzled out and died by evening, when Duncan reached his castle only to find dozens of tents on the plain beneath the craggy hill where it sat. All three men reined their mounts to a halt. Knights and foot soldiers moved between the pavilions, sat around fires, and patrolled the perimeters of the camp. The banners were crimson and plum, and Duncan didn't recognize the livery: two rearing stallions with a stylized flower between their heads.

"Do either of you know this heraldry?" Duncan asked.

"It's of Gaeltheon," Sasha said. "Beyond that, I can't be sure. My work hasn't taken me across the river in a few years. There is one valenny, they call them *vaird* there, famous for raising fine steeds, but I don't know who rules it. I can sneak into the camp and find out, if you two would like to wait here."

"No," Duncan said. "I will not send anyone sneaking onto my own lands like a thief."

"It would be the most effective way to find out who they are and why they're here," Sasha started to say, but Yarrow backing his horse away and lifting a hand spouting blue flame stopped him. Lightning danced between the clouds, and thunder rumbled in the distance, to the west over the sea.

"I'll crush them for you," the mage said in a hungry whisper. "They won't lay a finger on any of us, and no one who hears of their fate will threaten us again. I will make us safe."

Trying to suppress a shiver that had nothing to do with the crisp, mountain air, Duncan said, "Peace, my friend. That won't be necessary. This land is mine to protect, and I'll know who lurks at my threshold and why."

Head lifted proudly and flanked by his friends, the two fiercest and most capable fighters he'd ever known, Duncan guided his horse into the camp at a casual walk. The knights and soldiers they passed leaned in to gossip among themselves, but not a single soldier stood or offered Duncan any gesture of respect. He soon realized, in his battered armor and filthy from the road, he probably wasn't familiar to them as the bairn of Windwake.

Duncan reined his horse near the largest and most elaborate tent and dismounted. To the four men standing guard, he said, "Though I am bairn of this land, I don't recall inviting this army. I will speak with the man commanding it."

One of the knights went into the tent and came out with an older man with silver hair but clearly in peak condition beneath his snug trousers and simple tunic. Something about him looked vaguely familiar. Sasha gasped almost inaudibly, but of course Duncan couldn't ask his observations, though he knew Sasha never reacted out of shock. Everything his assassin did was deliberate.

"I am Duncan Purefroy, bairn of Windwake. I demand to know who you are and what you're doing here."

The other man curled his lip and spoke in an oily, condescending voice. "Then I shall tell you. My name is Mauritius Damasca, *vairden* of Foghollow, and I've come to rectify a grievous insult against my household."

"What insult could require such a vast force, tam?" Duncan waved his arm to indicate the hundreds of men.

"The seizure of my sister Lady Ortean's land and entire fortune! Her exile and disgrace! The murder of her associate on your orders! I am here to demand these wrongs be put right!"

Sasha and Yarrow moved a little closer to Duncan, Yarrow's magic held in check but still tickling the hair on the back on Duncan's neck. Duncan begged the goddesses to grant his mage restraint, and then he took a breath to manage his own anger. "I mean no disrespect to you, tam, but your sister committed treason by making an attempt on my life. Her punishment was justified. Mild, the truth be told. Now, if there's nothing else, I'd like you to leave my bairny, and if you care to visit again, do me the courtesy of sending a messenger first. I'll offer you a proper feast, of course. We don't behave like savages here in Windwake."

"I'm not going anywhere," Vairden Damasca said through gritted teeth, stepping closer to Duncan. Sasha moved to get between them, but Duncan lifted his arm to block his assassin. Damasca's men also closed in, their hands near their swords and axes, and tension grew thick in the ensuing moments of silence.

"Tam, I must demand you take your men and go." Duncan pointed in the direction of the harbor.

"And I demand you turn that man over to our custody to face justice!" Damasca stabbed a finger at Sasha. "He is the vilest of criminals, and I will no longer let him cower in your protection after what he's done. Any pretense of legitimacy you've lent him ends now."

Duncan prepared to talk some sense into the irate man, maybe suggest they take the matter before His Majesty, but he never got the chance. Yarrow pushed past him, drew back, and shoved Damasca so hard the older man stumbled backward several steps. The ring of metal echoed as all the guards around him drew their weapons, but the mage remained unfazed, power crackling around him and his eyes so wide he looked completely mad.

"You dare threaten my friends? You'll pay for it!"

"Yarrow, no!" Duncan reached for Yarrow's arm, but Yarrow yanked free of his grasp. Damasca's men advanced, but Yarrow pushed them back with a swipe of his hand. Many of them tumbled to the ground and tripped over each other, but more soldiers appeared from the nearby tents.

Yarrow snorted at them. "You're all dead. I've decimated armies ten times this size. I'll rip you to shreds. You think you'll insult Duncan? Take Sasha from me?" A large, cerulean claw extended from Yarrow's hand. Damasca's soldiers closed around their lord, but Yarrow brushed them away like cobwebs with his mystic appendage. The smell of burnt minerals was strong, and the grass in a two-foot radius from the mage sizzled and scorched black.

Duncan had to stop this. Yarrow killing a prominent noble of Gaeltheon would lead to tragedies he couldn't even imagine. It could dissolve the alliance between the two kingdoms and end the Blessed Epoch before it truly began. Worse yet, it could lead to a war between two evenly matched nations that could rage for generations. All Duncan had ever wanted was to protect the people of Selindria. Though he knew he took a risk, he seized Yarrow's elbows and pinned them behind his back. Yarrow could have easily thrown him off, attacked him with a gout of magic, and in the past, under the control of his creature, he might have. Now, Yarrow just twisted and squirmed.

"Let go of me, Duncan! These worms have no right to speak to you this way! They're not fit to breathe the same air as you and Sasha!"

Duncan leaned close and whispered near Yarrow's ear. "If you ever cared for me, stand down."

The power pulsing around Yarrow burned to an ember and fizzled out. He hung his head, and all the outraged anxiety melted out of his body. Duncan released him, and Sasha moved to stand at Yarrow's shoulder.

Addressing Vairden Damasca, who looked terrified but tried to hide it beneath a haughty veneer, chin lifted and arms crossed, Duncan said, "Please reconsider, tam. What you're doing here could be considered an act of war against a sovereign bairny of Selindria. You have no authority to demand anything of me. How do you think King Garith will react?

Let's behave like reasonable men and take this issue before the king. Let him decide."

"And I'm to believe if Garith orders you to turn over your assassin, you'll just accept it? Because I will accept nothing less than his execution, in public, in front of all the families he's destroyed."

Yarrow started forward but caught himself after a step. No matter how much he wanted to resolve this matter peacefully, Duncan couldn't bring himself to say he'd relinquish Sasha even at the king's insistence. He couldn't even consider agreeing to stand idle and watch while Sasha suffered, not to save the bairny, the kingdom, or even the Blessed Epoch. His words caught like sharp gravel in his throat, and he couldn't choke out a single one.

Yarrow spoke for him, his calm, determined tone more chilling than his anger. "This kingdom will burn first. This world."

"Who is this lunatic who dares to address me?" Damasca said, worry clear in his tone.

"I am Yarroway L'Estrella. I see by your reaction you've heard my name before. Now leave."

Damasca took a step back and fumbled when he hit the flap of his tent. "I will not be intimidated by you. Everyone knows you are mad and unwelcome in your own country, tam. You're a deviant. Unnatural too, I understand."

With a soft swish, Sasha unsheathed his blade. "I have heard all I'm willing to tolerate. Both of these men are heroes. I won't have them slandered."

"Will you murder me while I sleep?" Damasca taunted.

Sasha shrugged. "I might."

"You dare—"

"Enough!" Duncan shouted. "I'll ask you once more to return to Gaeltheon, and we can meet at Garith's court in a moon's time."

"And if I refuse?"

"Then we have reached an impasse," Duncan said. "Your demands are ludicrous, and I have no intention of entertaining any of them. I will return to my castle. If you plan to lay siege, you'll find us ready."

"And you'll find us very tenacious, tam."

Cold and nauseous but determined not to let it show, Duncan turned his back on the other man, mounted his horse, and rode around the edge of the camp to the single road carved over centuries from the ironstone crag beneath Windust Castle.

Seneschal Allwynn met them in the courtyard between the outer wall and the fortress's inner gate after they'd left their animals with servants. "Bairn Duncan," the stocky knight said, shaking his head and stroking the plaits of his beard. "I don't know whether to thank the goddesses for your return or hit you square in the jaw for leaving. I'm sure you know by now this place has gone straight to the Shades' Abode in your absence. As I predicted."

Duncan couldn't help a bitter chuckle. "You've been waiting months to say those words, I'm sure. Now, we must prepare to defend this castle."

"You can't be serious!" Allwynn growled. "That whoreson plans to attack? It's an act of treason against his king and queen!"

"His reasoning matters little," Sasha noted.

"You're responsible for this, you know," Allwynn said, advancing on Sasha.

Yarrow stepped between them. "I don't know who you are, friend, but you'd do well to watch your tone."

"Would I? And just who are you? Another Emiri slug here to drag the bairn off on another foolish secret errand while the rest of us try to hold off his enemies on our own?"

"Goddesses, Allwynn," Duncan groaned. "This is my friend and King Garith's cousin and close advisor, Yarroway L'Estrella."

"I-I—"Allwynn stammered. "The Hero of the Starlight Bridge? Forgive me, tam. I didn't know. But in my own defense, you look a bit more like a pirate refugee than a kinsman to the royal family."

Yarrow grinned and patted Allwynn's broad shoulder. "It seems you've figured me out already. We should get along fine."

"If that will be all," Duncan said, "we should move on to more practical matters. Tam Allwynn, please send couriers to our nearest allies, the valen of Lockhaven and the eyrle of Greyrclif. Choose these men well. They will have to travel in secret, and they may encounter resistance. Pick fleet and clever scouts."

"Duncan," Sasha said, "I'll offer to take a message to one of these men. I can elude anyone, and if I am discovered, well, I can assure you I won't be detained. Unless you'd like to make use of my talents closer to home. I can... cripple the enemy's leadership."

Though Duncan knew what "talents" Sasha alluded to, he saw Yarrow lower his face to hide his mischievous grin and smiled himself, distracted for a second. "No, I don't wish for you to do either of those things. I have skilled scouts to deliver the missives. As for the other, I beg you not to. I want Windwake to be seen as taking no part in this conflict. We'll defend ourselves, but only so far as we must. I don't want anyone to accuse Windwake of antagonizing Gaeltheon. We're the victims, and Garith will see that. Damasca likely has powerful friends in his home kingdom, and I don't want to give them anything to use against either us or His Majesty. I truly hope the presence of Lockhaven and Greyrclif will make him see sense and retreat."

"Until they arrive, we must hold the enemy off," Allwynn said. "Their numbers are significant."

"For now, post men at the gate and along the road. Station archers along the parapets. I must at least refresh myself and change my clothes," Duncan said. "Have some food, whatever is ready, sent up to my chambers. Give me an hour or so, and then I'll meet you and the other knights in the barracks to plan."

Yarrow surprised Duncan by grabbing his arm and sinking his nails into Duncan's wrist. "I would rather meet somewhere else. Perhaps the dining hall or in your library?"

The look of fear on the young mage's face perplexed Duncan. His first instinct was to embrace Yarrow and tell him he'd keep him safe, but he couldn't comfort his friend while others watched. Instead, he said, "Let's go to my room. Have a meal and discuss everything afterward. We've had a long journey, and we all need something to sustain ourselves."

Yarrow nodded, though he didn't loosen his grip on Duncan's arm. It wasn't late yet, and the torches, lanterns and candles still burned brightly, lighting the way for the many servants who swept out hearths, cleared away dishes, and carried baskets of linens and pitchers of water. Their merry chatter as they worked comforted Duncan. It sounded of life continuing, and it steeled Duncan's resolve to protect his people. More than soldiers called this fortress home. Families and even children lived within these walls. It was his sacred duty to keep them from harm, and he would not fail.

Soon after they'd reached his room, lit a fire, and opened the balcony doors to banish the musty, neglected smell, a maid arrived with a pot of thick, pork potage rich with harvest vegetables, a basket of bread, a crock of butter, a tray of cheese, and a jug of ale. It smelled divine. Duncan couldn't remember the last time he'd enjoyed a proper meal. He leaned over the food and inhaled the fragrant steam wafting off the stew while he offered a silent prayer to Berris and the Mother Goddess.

As hungry as they were, they ate in relative silence and finished quickly. Duncan looked longingly at his comfortable bed after months of sleeping in ships' bunks and rough bedrolls on the ground. "What I wouldn't give to get beneath the blankets and sleep until midday."

"Well, let's attend the meeting with your knights and hopefully conclude it quickly," Sasha said, seducing Duncan with the curl of his lips and the flutter of his eyelashes. He made Duncan's blood flow south without even a touch.

Duncan stood from the table and braced himself for what needed to be said. He looked at the coating of dust on his boots. "I'll be attending the meeting alone. This is Windwake business. It is between me and my knights. They'll see no reason for either of you to be there, and it will damage their respect for me. I should be able to lead these men myself. It's my duty, and only mine, to defend this bairny."

When he forced himself to meet his partners' eyes, Yarrow looked like a scolded child when he jutted out his lower lip and knit his brows with offense, while Sasha had donned his emotionless expression and shut off his feelings to protect himself. Duncan wanted to hold them, soothe them, but he stood firm. His responsibility to protect his thousands of subjects had to come before any of their desires.

"I'm sorry," he said softly, "but it must be this way. I cannot bring—"

"What? An assassin and a crazy, perverse mage before your honorable knights?" Yarrow snapped. "I didn't know you found us so shameful."

"Goddesses, Yarrow! You know I don't. But you grew up among nobility and understand about keeping up appearances, even false ones. Illusion can have a place sometimes. As much as I need you, I can't appear to need you. Or anyone. These men need to see me as a leader! I must step up and *be* that leader."

"But we've always fought together," Yarrow said, anger drowned out by hurt.

"And we always will," Duncan said, looking into the mage's glittering ice-blue eyes. He knew Yarrow felt cast aside, just as he had all his life. Duncan hated it.

"The two of us are worth dozens of your knights on the battlefield," Sasha said, all practicality. "It would be a poor strategy not to utilize our skills."

"Ah, friend. I truly hope there will be no battlefield. I only want to hold the castle until reinforcements arrive. When I meet with my men, I'll only be telling them where to stand guard and which watches to take. If there's any fighting, we'll stand together, as we always have. I want you two kept safe as much, more than, anyone else in this land. I just want to protect everyone. You spoke of fear before. Failing in my duty is my greatest worry. Try to understand."

"At least let me place some wards outside the gates," Yarrow said.

"Tomorrow, when I can go with you and make sure you don't get hurt."

Yarrow blew air out his nose. "Get hurt? Duncan, you were with me at Lockhaven."

"But you're not the same as you were then," Duncan said, loath to mention the creature, aware of Yarrow's mixed feeling in its absence.

"There's still much about me you don't understand," the mage said. "But I am powerful. Those peons cannot harm me. I'm a little insulted you'd suggest it."

"I'm glad to see your time away hasn't tarnished your extraordinary amount of… *self-confidence*," Duncan said.

"I don't like the idea of you going alone," Sasha said, a tiny tremor in his glassy-flat tone. "Not while there could still be traitors among your people. I could stay hidden, watch your back as I've done for a year now."

"And I can place the wards," Yarrow persisted.

"You ask me to put my faith in your abilities," Duncan said. "Put faith in mine. I'm a better man because of you both. You've brought things into my life I'd never dreamed of, but I am an able fighter. Need I remind *you*, Sasha?"

Sasha's eyes went wide with surprise but then narrowed as a smirk stretched his lips. "I think we could both use a reminder of your… skills. Get to your meeting, but keep it brief."

"When will you learn to stop ordering me around, assassin?"

"Probably never," Sasha said, grinning and letting his barriers fall away, letting Duncan see the lust, amusement, and devotion in his eyes. "Live with it, my love."

"Yarrow?" Duncan said, turning to the mage.

"I didn't mean to get cross," Yarrow said.

Duncan kissed him on the forehead. "Old habits, I suppose. But you don't have to keep us at a distance anymore. Everything you felt you had to hide is gone now."

Yarrow pulled away and looked into the fire. Duncan would need years before he figured out Yarrow's eccentricities, or Sasha's, for that matter. It might take years before they all completely trusted each other, but at least they had those years.

A sharp slap on his backside interrupted Duncan's ruminations. "I told you to hurry along and get this over with," Sasha teased.

Duncan gave him a deep kiss, letting his tongue swirl around Sasha's before pulling away. It only made him want to stay, just stay by their sides forever. Tonight, with an enemy literally at his gates, Duncan had to put his duty to his bairny first. At least his partners were beginning to understand.

"ARE you going to keep the hair?" Sasha asked, standing behind Yarrow's chair and toying with his tangled locks.

"I don't know," Yarrow said, warm, full, and drowsy. Feeling safe in spite of the army half a mile away. Sasha's fingers in his tresses felt exquisite, the tiny tugs against his scalp intense explosions of sensation, energy flowing from Sasha to him and back in an intimate exchange he'd never perceived before.

"Your hair was so soft before." Sasha's voice grew low and gravelly as he traced the edge of Yarrow's face.

Yarrow felt Sasha's warmth, heard the faint swish of the pulse at his wrist, and swore he could feel the texture of Sasha's fingertips. He groaned and let the back of his head settle against the chair.

Sasha looked down at him, his lips slightly parted, cheeks dark, lips swollen, and eyelids languid over his magnificent ebony irises. He circled Yarrow's lips with his thumb, and Yarrow almost drowned in the scent of his skin. He wanted to drown in the spicy, musky fragrances mixed with leather and death.

"Thalil," Sasha said, "I've never known anyone who relished my touch like you. You make me feel like a god. All I have to do is graze your face and you're moaning and letting your eyes roll back. It's absolutely alluring, and I have missed it so much. Missed you. Are you already hard, my love? I bet you are."

Sasha ran his hand down Yarrow's neck and chest with maddening slowness, and Yarrow slid lower into the chair and let his legs fall open. His skin tingled where the heat and pressure of Sasha's palm permeated his clothes. When Sasha finally grazed his erection, Yarrow cried out loud, the impression of even that tiny touch so deep it almost hurt. Sasha curled forward and pressed his lips to Yarrow's, the flavor of ale and rich stew still clinging to his mouth. Yarrow let his lips part, gave Sasha free rein to explore his palate, suck on his tongue, and nibble his lips. Sasha liked to take charge, and Yarrow loved to let him. His body felt both liquid and acute as he let Sasha run his hands all over it.

I never felt like this before. I always loved him, even before I could admit it, but it was never so powerful as this…. But you're gone. You can't answer. Goddesses, you're really gone, and I can't undo it.

"Yarrow?" Sasha pulled away. "What's wrong? If you don't want this—"

When he reached up and touched his heated cheek, Yarrow felt moisture. Was he honestly crying for the loss of the being that had taunted, tormented, and threatened him? He was, but could he tell Sasha? Sasha had looked into the darkness Yarrow held before and not cowered away. Sasha had shared his deepest secrets.

Yarrow spun his chair to face Sasha. Standing there with his tight leather armor hugging every angle of his body, he was so much more beautiful than even Yarrow's wildest memories. The weak fire in the hearth washed one side of his face in soft orange, leaving the other half in absolute shadow. Yarrow decided to show Sasha both the light and the dark within himself, the ice and the embers.

"The presence I held was with me for over five years," he said. "It was the only one with me as I grew from a boy to a man. For all the trouble it caused me, it kept me safe. I always had someone to talk to, someone who knew every depraved idea I'd ever entertained. Being without it has left a hole in me I didn't expect."

Sasha crossed his arms, rubbed his shoulders, and nodded. "I understand completely. When I was cast out of the Crimson Scythe, I had no idea who I was. I'm still not sure. The hollow place it has left in me still hasn't been filled. Like you, I feel incomplete. You and Duncan are the entire world to me now, but neither of you will share yourselves with me wholly."

Yarrow stood and clasped Sasha's hands. "I will. I'll tell you anything you want."

"Did you lay with Sai?"

Yarrow laughed and rubbed his face against Sasha's cheek before resting against his shoulder. He let his lips brush and tickle Sasha's neck as he spoke, right next to the deep scar bisecting his throat. "No. Though it wasn't easy to resist him. I thought being with him would upset Duncan more than you, however. I didn't do it so I'd never have to lie to either of you again."

"You hold other secrets, Yarrow. I see them in the flitting of your eyes, the way your fingers curl sometimes, the way you worry your lips. I wish you would trust me with them."

Squeezing Sasha's fingers and closing his eyes, Yarrow said, "The creature that shared my body will never truly be gone. It will always be part of me, though it can no longer assume control of me. I will never be the person I was before I encountered it. The things I feel… the things I desire are altered." He felt a little guilty at everything left unsaid, that he couldn't find the courage to come out and tell Sasha exactly what he'd accepted in Fane's cavern. Yarrow's selfishness, it seemed, had not lessened upon bonding with the creature, and he couldn't bear the thought of Sasha turning away from him in disgust. "I wish I could explain it all to you in a more concrete way, but… I can't. But I can't deceive you, either. I'm not the man I once was, and I'll never be that man again."

"None of us are even the person we were yesterday. Every experience alters our aspirations. Do you wish to tell me anything else?" Sasha asked. "Anything about your past?"

"No. What are you digging for? Just say it."

"Nothing, Yarrow. Just know I will always be here to face any enemy you cannot. I'll kill anyone threatening you or Duncan."

"I know. Goddesses, thank you. You can't know—" Yarrow threw his arms over Sasha's shoulders and caught his lips in a fiery kiss. Their mouths wide, they lapped and slurped at each other until they had to break away to catch their breath.

"I'm a man of action, not words," Sasha said, his speech wetting Yarrow's cheek. "I can express my love for you better without talking."

"Do it," Yarrow sighed.

Sasha grasped Yarrow's waist, spun him around, and backed him into Duncan's large bed. When the backs of Yarrow's knees met the mattress, he sprawled on his back across the brocade coverlet and looked up at his partner. Sasha's black eyes glimmered in the dying firelight, and he darted his tongue out to wet his upper lip.

Yarrow grasped the soft dark hair on either side of Sasha's face and pulled him down. Their chests, bellies, and groins ground into each other as they kissed so hard Yarrow's lips almost split.

Pulling away, Yarrow said, "I'm sorry for all you've lost."

"I'm not sorry." Sasha said. He gave Yarrow a quick peck before sitting up and straddling Yarrow's hips. He grasped the hem of Yarrow's faded old tunic and whisked it over his head, leaving it lying on the pillows. When he bent and ran the tip of his tongue up the center of Yarrow's body, along the gully between his belly and chest muscles, Yarrow trembled so hard he had to grab handfuls of the bedclothes. Sasha flicked his tongue across Yarrow's taut nipple, and Yarrow grabbed Sasha's hips and thrust up against him, ready to spill in his trousers.

Chuckling against Yarrow's skin as he nibbled up his neck, Sasha said, "Don't fall apart before I even get you naked. As much as I love the taste of your skin, I want much more from you tonight."

Drawing in a deep breath to ground himself, Yarrow nodded and just concentrated on the feeling of Sasha's hair slipping through his fingers. Their hearts thumped against each other and their erections pressed together. "Sasha, will you undress for me?"

Sasha kissed Yarrow deeply as he traced the shell of his ear. "Take your clothes off first. I want to be able to see what I do to you." With that, he leapt lightly off the bed and stood waiting in a ring of firelight.

Yarrow hurried to toe off his old boots and kick them to the floor. He pulled his loose trousers down and freed his aching erection from the confines of the cloth, grasping it at the base to alleviate some of the pulsing need.

"Not yet," Sasha said. "I can barely see you. Can you make it brighter in here?"

With a thought, Yarrow increased the flames in the hearth and made all the candles around the chamber spring alight. The fire illuminated Sasha, though deep shadows remained around his eyes and beneath his full lips, giving his face the vague suggestion of a skull. He unfastened the buckle over his throat, exposing his svelte neck. Yarrow let his fingers move up his shaft and pushed his hood back. He dragged his thumb over his slit, smearing the fluids he leaked. In his hypersensitive state, he had to be careful or he'd explode just looking into Sasha's black eyes.

Sasha opened the center of his cuirass and let it hang open. His gaze never left Yarrow's as he knelt and retrieved a small vial of oil from beneath the bed. "I want to watch you make yourself ready for me," he said, tossing Yarrow the little glass bottle. "Look at me, and pretend your fingers are mine. Let me see you want me."

"Sasha, I've been without you for a long time, so don't make me wait too long or I won't be able to last. I don't want to come until you're inside me."

At his words, Sasha groaned and squeezed his hard cock through his leather trousers. He swiped his leather armor from his shoulders and let it fall, and then he tugged his hooded shirt over his head and flung it aside. His clean-shaven, willowy-muscled torso sparkled in the flickering light. He'd always reminded Yarrow of a bronze statue; he was just so perfectly proportioned and shaped. The sight of him distracted Yarrow from his task. He couldn't wait to get his arms and legs around Sasha, get Sasha inside him, so he pulled the cork from the vial and drizzled the spicy oil over his fingers. He bent his knees, spread his legs wide, and leaned back against the headboard as he teased his cleft. Yarrow worked a finger inside himself as Sasha removed one of the belts holding his daggers.

The assassin tried to give Yarrow a tantalizing, seductive show as he peeled his leathers from his body, and Yarrow tried to reciprocate, curving his spine so Sasha had a clear view of him pushing his fingers into himself, squeezing his cockhead or balls now and then with his other hand. Neither of them could draw it out, though, not with the desire between them an almost physical force. Finally, Sasha stepped out of his scant black undergarment and tossed it to Yarrow. Yarrow caught it and rubbed the satin against his cheek as he inhaled Sasha's scent.

"Sasha—" He stopped touching himself and reached out his arms. Sasha filled them, rubbing his silky skin against Yarrow, his lips hot, slick, and swollen over Yarrow's mouth. Yarrow lifted his ankles to Sasha's shoulders, and Sasha pressed him against the headboard, squashing their bodies so tight a hair wouldn't have fit between them.

"Yarrow, can I?"

Yarrow could only grunt his assent as he wiggled beneath his partner, rubbing his erection against Sasha's smooth belly. He tried to relax as Sasha guided his cock to Yarrow's opening, but it had been a long time, and it hurt. Sasha stopped and pushed the gnarled hair off Yarrow's forehead. "Are you all right?"

"Sasha, I love you." Yarrow couldn't think of anything else to say. He circled his hips, thrusting back against Sasha and adjusting himself so Sasha's cock caressed that magical spot inside him. Within a few strokes, their bodies seemed to remember each other, and they moved together as if they'd never been apart.

Yarrow sunk his nails into Sasha's hips as their skin smacked together. They kissed hard and then just moaned and muttered into each other's open mouths as their movements grew quicker and more desperate. The combined sensations of his cock rubbing against Sasha and Sasha stimulating his inner pleasure shot Yarrow toward release faster than he could slow his momentum. He'd no sooner left the ground than he was beyond the sun and stars, whimpering with bliss and shaking hard as he came against Sasha. "Goddesses, I love you."

"I love you, Yarrow. Oh Thalil!" Sasha's wet heat exploded into Yarrow. "I'm never letting you away from me again. I'll keep you beneath me just like this if I have to."

"All right," Yarrow said when Sasha's words finally permeated his lust-addled brain. Both of them giggled as they pecked each other's lips and touched each other's faces, their bodies still joined. Yarrow didn't make a move to change that until his thighs started to cramp.

Sasha rolled off him and they turned to face each other. Sasha's seed leaked out and moistened the back of Yarrow's leg, but he was too tired and absolutely content to care. He just lay basking in the warm, golden glow of being back where he belonged as Sasha pulled the coverings over them and snuggled close.

Soon, Duncan joined them in bed, wrapping his big arms around them both with Yarrow at the center. Yarrow stirred for a moment and turned his head to kiss Duncan before settling back in, happier than he'd been since childhood. He finally had a place he fit in, and this time nothing could force him from it. He felt a twinge at deceiving his partners in regards to his creature, but they were safe from it now, and that was the important thing. Yarrow looked at his hand curved around Duncan's neck and remembered the claw it had been. It had torn through and decimated more people than Yarrow could name, and he remembered each of their faces without regret. It was his now, and it would only ever lift against Sasha and Duncan's enemies. Tomorrow, he'd get to test it. Yarrow let himself fall asleep, untroubled by nightmares for once.

Chapter
Twenty-Three

SURPRISED he'd slept so well with so much weighing on him, Duncan awoke refreshed. Yarrow lay sprawled out with his arms and legs askew across Duncan and Sasha. Sasha lay on his belly with his face buried in his elbow. Seeing them sleeping so peacefully made Duncan feel even more sentimental than usual. He hoped they'd wake up like this every day from now on, be the family all of them needed. Despite his full bladder, Duncan just stayed in bed watching them, listening to the deep, relaxed rhythm of their breathing.

A sharp knock interrupted his reverie. Sasha bolted up, and Yarrow grumbled and rubbed his face. Tam Allwynn, with his usual discretion, spoke through the door. "Duncan, you're needed immediately. Damasca's forces are at the castle gates with siege towers, ballista, and mangonel. They haven't attacked yet, but we need to move."

"Understood," Duncan said, hurrying from beneath the shelter of the covers and scooping his clothes from the floor. The cold hit his bare body like a splash of water. "Have the couriers been dispatched?"

"Only hours after our meeting concluded."

"We'll meet you at the southern tower in a few moments," Duncan said, slipping into his mail tunic. He picked up his breastplate and prepared to put it on, but Sasha, still naked, came up beside him and quickly fastened the leather straps that held the armor in place. When he'd finished, he nodded once and went to retrieve his leather clothing. Yarrow dug around beneath the pillows, found Sasha's underpants, and got up to press them into the assassin's hand. All of them dressed and armed themselves efficiently without saying a word. None was needed. They all knew what to do.

Standing on the pinnacle of the southern tower, the highest point of his fortress, Duncan looked down the steep rocks to the field beyond.

Damasca had amassed a couple thousand men, but the ironstone of Windwake's foundation proved an effective barrier. To reach the castle, Damasca's force would first have to take the narrow road winding up the mountainside. When they did, they'd find themselves within a bottleneck. Even an adolescent novice who'd read a single treatise of warfare would know it would be easy to get flanked in that position.

A light rain began to fall from the mottled silver sky. Duncan turned to his seneschal. "I don't want to be overconfident, but I think this old castle will hold until Lockhaven and Greyrclif arrive. Damasca wouldn't make the mistake of trapping his men on the road."

Allwynn shook his head as he looked down the mountainside. "No, I shouldn't think so. But he must have something in mind to ready so many siege weapons."

"They may be just for show," Sasha said. "To intimidate us and damage our morale."

His assassin had a fair point. "So, this is just a case of two angry dogs raising their hackles and growling until one of them puts his tail between his legs and slinks away?"

"Possibly," Sasha said. "His only goal may be to demonstrate his superiority."

Duncan shook his head, his belly curdling. "He won't succeed. Certainly not on my own territory."

Yarrow stepped to the jagged stone blocks fencing the large tower and canted his head as he watched the light shift on his wet hand. Then he made a sweeping gesture, and one of the enemy ballista lifted into the air and smashed against the ground while men ran and dove out of the way. The mage swooned and staggered back until Duncan caught and supported him. Yarrow's eyes rolled back in his head, and he felt as light as a scrap of cloth hanging from Duncan's arms.

"Sweet sisters!" Allwynn hissed, moving away from Yarrow. "That was almost a mile away! I've never seen such magic."

"Be glad he's on our side," Sasha said.

The older knight just turned his back and grumbled. Duncan helped Yarrow lean against the wall until he regained his strength. "Yarrow, I appreciate your intentions, but I don't want to engage Damasca if we don't have to. Please don't attack him again. Our only goal is to hold this fortress until reinforcements arrive. After that, your cousin will have to decide what should be done about Damasca."

"I just wanted to see if I could do it," Yarrow said with a giggle.

"We'll be judged on our actions here today," Duncan said. "This is no joke. If you want to remain here, it will be under my command the same as everyone else. Otherwise, go back inside. Is that understood?"

"Oh, all right, Duncan," the mage said with an exaggerated frown. "You're no fun."

The hours passed slowly, and the rain increased as morning became afternoon, soaking them all to the bone and leaving them shivering on the top of the tower. Below them, along the walls and parapets, the archers huddled together for warmth though they never lowered their bows. As far as Duncan was concerned, if his men couldn't go inside and dry off by fire, neither would he. He wanted his soldiers to see their leader standing beside them, not hiding in the castle while they took all the risks. Servants brought bread, stew and ale, and still Damasca made no move. A few times the enemy commander tested his siege weapons, but they couldn't make it even half the distance to Windust Castle from where they sat at the base of the hill.

By evening, the rain tapered off but left behind a thick, chill mist that seemed to cling to the old stones of the fortress and changed the torches lit along the walls into fuzzy, orange smudges. No division existed between the fog and the low, gray clouds above them, giving everything the impression of an eerie dream. Duncan just wanted to hear the horns of the Lockhaven or Greyrclif forces approaching so he could put an end to this nonsense and find himself a large meal, mulled wine, and a seat by his fire. He was getting too old for this, and the cold and damp made his bones feel as brittle as icicles.

Though he heard the din of metal clanging below, Duncan couldn't see its source through the mist. Before long, a young knight emerged from the hatch and onto the top of the tower, sweating and out of breath.

"Please report, tam," Duncan said.

The lad bent and held his knees as he spoke. "Damasca's moved his forces, Bairn Duncan. They've fought past our guards and taken the road. They'll soon reach the castle gates, and they brought their ballista and siege towers with them. The men want to know your orders, tam."

"I'll come to the gate and take control of our forces myself," Duncan said. Sasha and Yarrow, who'd been sitting against the wall and pressing close against the frigid night, got quickly to their feet and followed Duncan down the winding stairs and out of the tower. Dozens of knights and foot soldiers met them in the field between the outer wall and the fortress, and all of them looked to Duncan for direction. They would live or die based on what he decided to do, and though he'd spent the previous night mulling the possibilities over, he still wasn't sure of the best course of action, and he'd run out of time to contemplate the possibilities. Already the tops of Damasca's siege towers jutted above the fog.

"My orders are simple," Duncan said, his voice strong and clear. "We must keep the enemy from entering the gates or breaching the walls. Do what you must to those ends. Double the archers on the walls, and tell them to take the shots they can. Bring out our ladders to defend the walls. I want at least two dozen knights at the gate. Ready our mangonel."

The soldiers hurried to obey as the first enemy missiles shot over the outer wall. Men dove out of the way of the large rocks, and Yarrow raised a translucent blue shield that not only caught some of the boulders but launched them back at their attackers. It bought enough time for Duncan's men to haul out a trio of mangonels and load their buckets with large stones of their own. As they pulled the arms back and prepared to fire, Yarrow went to each one and enchanted the rocks so they burned brightly. They soared above the outer wall like comets, sending the enemy scattering. Arrows shot by Duncan's archers on the walls whizzed above his forces on the ground, and the invaders they struck cried out.

Sasha yelled to Duncan above the increasing cacophony of the battle. "This could be a grand attempt at distraction! There are a few other places along the walls men could infiltrate. They may have sent spies ahead of them and discovered these weak spots. Soldiers should be sent to keep watch over them."

Though it would thin their numbers at the gate, Duncan had to agree. He knew only too well that it was much easier to hold a castle than to flush out enemies once they made it inside. Still, he wanted Sasha and Yarrow with him. "Inform Tam Allwynn of the areas that concern you. Tell him how many men you feel should be sent to each."

Sasha nodded and sprinted across the field toward the seneschal as the enemy sent a volley of flaming arrows over the wall. Though Yarrow ran back and forth trying to deflect them, one struck a Windwake knight in the face, and he fell backward screaming. Another man took an arrow to the shoulder, right at the gap in his armor. Smoke and the smell of burning flesh filled the courtyard. Piles of straw and some of the wooden shingles above the lower buildings caught alight, and foot soldiers hurried to douse the flames. Luckily the earlier rain had left everything damp, which kept the fires from spreading.

The first four of Damasca's siege towers appeared above the wall. While the road up the mountainside widened out at the castle gate so horses and carriages could assemble, there wasn't much open space between the cliffs around the southern side. Still, Damasca's men in the towers threw ropes down and started to descend. Duncan's archers stopped most of them, and his knights cut down any who made it into the courtyard. Soon servants were dragging bodies to the far ends of the field and piling them up. With the enemy still firing arrows and launching boulders, some of the men lying in that heap wore Windwake livery, and it made Duncan sick. This was all so unnecessary, but he saw no way to put a stop to it.

Two more towers joined the others, filling every inch of space around the inner gate. Men poured over the wall too fast for Duncan's archers to hinder them much, and his knights ran to meet them on the ground. Swords met, men screamed, and more burning arrows sailed over their heads. The courtyard filled with smoke and clashing bodies. Blood spilled and soaked the muddy soil. Duncan looked around frantically for Sasha and Yarrow. Off to his left, bursts of bluish light reflected off the clouds of smog and vapor, but Duncan couldn't see his mage or his assassin.

Something struck Duncan's shoulder from behind, knocking him almost to his knees. Regaining his balance, he turned just in time to dodge a second blow from the mace of a huge knight with the double-stallion heraldry engraved into his bronze-colored breastplate. A helmet with another rearing horse sculpted on the forehead obscured Duncan's enemy's face. They faced off and circled each other for a few moments before the other warrior raised his spiked mace and charged toward Duncan with a bellow. Widening his stance, Duncan held the warped greatsword he hadn't had the opportunity to repair diagonally across his chest as if to meet the attack. He'd been learning much from his matches with Sasha, especially about feigning and misdirection, and he dodged at the last second.

The other knight's momentum made him topple forward. Duncan spun and kicked, knocking his enemy's legs out from under him and sending the other man to his back with a crash of plate. Duncan turned and gripped the hilt of his blade in both hands to deliver the killing blow, but his enemy rolled away. At the same time, one of Duncan's soldiers crashed against his back, almost knocking them both over. Duncan twisted around and caught the man, who was trying to tear an arrow from his inner elbow. He pushed his soldier toward the safety of the castle, and his enemy took the opportunity to swing his mace hard into Duncan's wrist. In spite of his armor, Duncan felt the slender bones snap, and he cried out. Worse yet, Duncan couldn't lift his heavy sword with one hand.

The knight struck again, hitting Duncan in the ribs. Though it hurt, Duncan didn't think any of them broke. Unable to breathe for a moment, he ran a few steps from his opponent, dragging his blade on the ground, before he turned to face the other soldier, basically defenseless. The other man jogged after him, his mace raised above his head. When he struck, Duncan could do nothing but catch the handle of his enemy's weapon on his forearm to avoid being bashed in the head. He kicked the enemy knight hard in the groin, but because of his armor, it did little to slow him down, though it did push him back. As fast as he could, Duncan delivered an uppercut to the man's chin, beneath his helmet. Blood flew from the knight's mouth, and his ass smacked the ground. Duncan kicked him in the neck, and he sprawled on his back.

Another of Damasca's knights rushed forward to defend his comrade before Duncan could finish him, running with his shield raised to his chest and his sword pointed out. Duncan had no way to deflect the blow since he couldn't lift his greatsword one-handed. He backed away while the knight he'd almost defeated dragged himself backward on his elbows. Just before the other enemy knight reached Duncan, a small dagger cut through the gloom and sank into his forehead. The newcomer looked surprised for a few seconds before falling facedown.

Duncan hurried to intercept his original opponent before the other knight reached a cluster of his countrymen. With a great war cry, he managed to hoist his sword up with just his left hand. He brought it down between the bottom of the other man's helmet and the top of his breastplate, cutting halfway through his neck. Blood fountained out, and the enemy knight went still.

His right hand hanging useless and his fingers numb within his glove, Duncan hurried toward one of the outbuildings where the healer Fulgrig and his apprentices had set up a makeshift hospital. Duncan needed his wrist set and splinted, and he needed a crossbow or a smaller sword, something he could fight with one-handed. Defending the castle required every man who could lift a weapon.

A huge boulder struck the castle wall, tearing away a large section of the southern watchtower and sending blocks tumbling into the courtyard. One of them fell on a group of struggling men, killing two of Duncan's knights along with their three adversaries. Yarrow dashed over with his arms raised and caught the rest of the stones on a glowing blue sheet. His efforts saved dozens of men, though it clearly cost the mage. By the time he managed to lower the blocks safely to the ground, Yarrow stumbled and fell to his knees. One of Damasca's men took notice and pointed. Five knights converged and surrounded Yarrow.

His injury forgotten, Duncan felt a surge of renewed battle lust, and he ran to defend his friend. If he couldn't lift his blade, he'd protect his precious partner with his bare hands. He tried to yell to Yarrow, hoping his mage might at least conjure a shield to protect himself, but Yarrow didn't hear Duncan's warning over the sounds of the battle. He didn't even seem to notice the men only a few feet away from him, their weapons lifted, as he clutched his ribs and heaved in gulps of sooty air.

From out of nowhere, Sasha dropped down in front of Yarrow. With a flick of his wrist, he threw three daggers at once, and each of them found a mark: one in a knight's windpipe, another in an eye, and the third in the soft flesh between one of the attackers' cheek and jaw. The knight tore his skin, exposing the teeth beneath it, when he tried to remove the blade. A sheet of blood flowed down his chest, and he turned white and stumbled away, trying to hold his ragged flesh together.

Duncan drove the hilt of his sword into the diaphragm of one of the knights and then struck the man in the back of the head with his fist when he doubled over, knocking him unconscious. In the meantime, Sasha had drawn a long, thin dagger and slashed across the final knight's face, slicing through his eyelid and across the bridge of his nose. Then the assassin thrust the point of the knife through his enemy's throat, where it disappeared behind his windpipe and poked out the other side. Blood sprayed from both wounds when Sasha retrieved his weapon.

By then, Yarrow had recovered enough to grasp Sasha's arm and haul himself to his feet. A crooked smile twisted his lips, and sapphire light spilled from his eyes, flowing down his neck and shoulders like water until it encased him completely. Duncan backed away a few steps; he'd always thought the azure glow had been some manifestation of the creature Yarrow harbored. But now the monster was supposedly gone, and the expression of hunger and depravity Yarrow wore didn't look like it could possibly belong to the mage.

Lifting his hand and stretching his fingers, Yarrow directed three apple-sized spheres of fire toward the roof of the nearest siege tower. It caught alight instantly, and the men inside retreated, screaming and diving from their ladders. Yarrow turned to the next tower, and soon it too burned like a giant candle, sending black smoke billowing toward the sky, where the first stars and rising moon spilled their weak light through the cloud cover. Arrows from both sides continued to fly over their heads. Sasha aided Duncan's men with his throwing knives and poisoned darts while Yarrow prepared to attack the next tower.

Everything around them shook and rumbled, sending a fresh avalanche of debris from the ruined castle wall. At the gate, Damasca's men guided a battering ram so massive it took ten knights on either side to hold it aloft. The heavy metal gates bent and creaked at the impact. Though they held, dust showered down from the hinges drilled into the stone. As the men retreated to prepare for the next thrust, another round of boulders struck the fortress. One of them bounced off the wall and landed on Duncan's mangonel, smashing it and killing the soldier manning it. A small shard of rock struck Sasha just below the eye, drawing blood but not inflicting a serious injury. Sasha pressed his hand to the wound and swore, more out of surprise than pain.

Yarrow's eyes went wide, and he swiped the falling rock away with a gesture, sending it beyond the castle and over the eastern wall. Rid of what he seemed to consider a minor annoyance, Yarrow balled his fists as he looked from Sasha to Duncan, both of them covered in blood and soot and suffering from superficial wounds. The mage's aura flared with his rage, his wings reaching almost from one end of the courtyard to the other. Duncan squinted and shielded his eyes from the sharp glare. Both the Windwake men and the enemy cried out and retreated from the sight of him.

"I think I've had enough of this." Yarrow's voice seemed to come from the sky, the ground, the walls of the castle, everywhere. The crash of the tide, the thunder, and the howl of the wind echoed his words.

"Yarrow, what are you planning to do?" Duncan shouted even though everything around them had fallen unnaturally quiet—even the distant tide, wind and thunder seemed subdued—as if all of nature waited to respond to the mage.

Without answering, Yarrow turned toward the gate and sent a wide beam of scorching cerulean energy toward the men with the battering ram. It not only disintegrated all the enemies for a hundred yards, but also melted the ancient castle gates to molten, steaming puddles.

"What in the goddesses' name is he doing?" Allwynn shouted, stabbing his shortsword toward the gaping hole in their defenses. "For the love of the sisters, stop him! You men! Start gathering those boulders! We have to plug up this hole or Windust Castle is lost! Lost, after everything we've done! Mother help us, that lad is completely insane."

While the soldiers hurried to obey, Yarrow strode calmly to what had once been the gate, blocking the opening with his wings. Damasca's men dropped their swords and abandoned their siege weapons in their haste to retreat. Yarrow reached out with his arcane hand and knocked them off their feet before crushing them with his blue fist. When they managed to exceed his range, Yarrow shot bursts of his devastating power after them, reducing anything it hit to fine, white ash. His laughter range out over the enemies' screams.

"Yarrow, stand down!" Duncan yelled. "They're running away! Goddesses, what you're doing is murder! I demand you stop!"

When Yarrow ignored him, Duncan turned to Sasha. "He'll undo everything I've worked so hard not to allow tonight. If he doesn't stop, we'll be seen as the guilty party in this, killing men by the dozens while they're trying to retreat!"

"Wait here." Sasha's calm in certain situations still astounded and unnerved Duncan. The assassin sprinted to Yarrow, leaping gracefully over both fallen men and debris.

Duncan couldn't believe it when he saw the first glimmer of dawn to the east, over the water. Even more beautiful were the sounds of horns and the appearance of hundreds of knights on horseback: Lockhaven and Greyrclif. Though he should have been relieved, Duncan shook with anxiety. If Yarrow didn't control himself, he'd annihilate not only their allies but possibly one or both of his brothers.

Sasha reached their mage, grabbed his shoulders, and spun Yarrow to face him. He drew back and slapped Yarrow hard across the face. The bright light surrounding the mage, as well as his wings, disappeared like flames doused with icy water. Yarrow held his cheek with both hands and cried softly. Everyone turned to watch him cowering away from Sasha with his shoulders curled forward.

Down the road, the fresh forces surrounded the remnants of Damasca's men, disarming those few who still held weapons and corralling them back up the hill toward the fortress. "Tam Fulgrig, be ready to see to the injured on both sides. Sasha, for the love of all that's holy, get Yarrow inside. His brothers don't need to see this."

Sasha put his arm around Yarrow's trembling shoulders and guided him into the castle. Duncan's men started to clean up the courtyard. The rising sun revealed just how much blood had been spilled over the course of the previous night. Too many soldiers on both sides hadn't made it through to see the dawn, and for what? Damasca would admit defeat and surrender. Duncan didn't have the space to hold him and all of his men, so they'd likely return to Gaeltheon until Garith summoned them all, just as Duncan had suggested before all of this bloodshed.

What had happened with Yarrow? Duncan hadn't expected to see that darker side of his mage now that he'd supposedly rid himself of the other presence. Obviously it wouldn't be so simple, but Duncan didn't have time to ponder the implications. Yarrow's brothers, Rayne and Rowan, approached what had once been the gates to Windust Castle. Between them, Damasca rode with his hands bound in front of him.

Chapter
Twenty-Four

BY THE time Duncan concluded his meeting with Yarrow's brothers, Rayne and Rowan, the valen of Lockhaven and the eyrle of Greyrclif respectively, it had been hours since the midday meal had been served. In an exhausted daze, Duncan sat on his chair in the hall, barely cognizant of Fulgrig setting the broken bones in his wrist. With his entire body aching, the added pain of the physician's ministrations hardly registered. Duncan simply waited for Fulgrig to finish, and then he stumbled out of the hall and up the staircase toward his chambers.

As Duncan had predicted, they'd decided to send Damasca and his men home to Foghollow in Gaeltheon. The man couldn't abscond without forfeiting his claim to lands his family had held for dozens of generations, and the Windwake dungeons couldn't accommodate all his knights and soldiers. In one month's time, both parties would plead their cases before King Garith at his estate in Meritage. Rayne and Rowan, as well as Damasca's sister, Launa Ortean, would attend the council as witnesses. Duncan couldn't imagine what would transpire at the meeting, and for the time being, he didn't have to. With Damasca gone, Windwake was secure for the moment. Lockhaven and Greyrclif planned to stay as guests, along with their substantial forces, for a week, at least, to make sure no one of questionable loyalty took advantage of Windwake's vulnerability.

By the time he reached his chamber door, Duncan barely had the strength to grasp the brass handle and push it open. He expected to find Sasha and Yarrow slumbering in his bed and fall in next to them, but he found them awake, Sasha sitting at the table and Yarrow on the floor in the corner, hugging his knees to his chest. The events of the battle rushed back into Duncan's mind, washing all his fatigue away like driftwood from the shore. The fine hair on his forearms and the back of his neck stood up, and his muscles tensed in preparation to defend himself. Duncan hated feeling that way in response to Yarrow, but after what he'd seen, he couldn't help it. He'd been a soldier too long to dismiss such a clear threat, and even if his mind couldn't quite acknowledge it, his body primed for battle.

Duncan wanted to understand, but he had no idea where to start, what to ask first. He throttled the temptation to accuse his mage of lying, interrogate him about why what he'd claimed to eradicate remained. At the same time, he wanted to shelter Yarrow in his arms and comfort him, as the young man looked so broken and alone.

As he so often did, Sasha stepped in and spared Duncan making the decision, shielded him from the uncertainty. "Have Damasca and his men left Windwake?"

"They have," Duncan answered, both grateful to and annoyed with Sasha for diverting the conversation away from his worries. So often, Sasha's actions proved a blessing and a curse all at once.

"Do you want me to go after him?" the assassin asked. "Ensure he never makes trouble for you again?"

"Goddesses." Duncan collapsed into the chair opposite Sasha and glared at him. "You're not a dull man. Have you failed to grasp how this works? You're not a nameless assassin any longer. You're known to be mine, which means anything you do will be traced back to me. You can't just go around killing on a whim anymore. If you murder Damasca, it won't be a mysterious crime, but a clear act of aggression by Windwake. You don't stand alone anymore; you have connections now, and you must consider them before you act."

"That's why I asked," Sasha said. "I think Damasca is a threat that should be eliminated. Dead, he won't resurface to trouble you in the future. I only want you, all of us, safe. But if you don't wish it, I'll abide by what you say. Hearing you say I'm yours before you can consider what your words mean makes anything worthwhile."

Sasha's statement made Duncan ashamed of his anger. All Sasha wanted was to protect them, keep their enemies at bay. Despite their vastly diverse moral philosophies, they had that much in common. Their methods differed, but Duncan knew Sasha's offer grew out of love, and he reached across the table to clasp Sasha's hand.

Yarrow watched them from his corner with wide eyes, like a scared animal waiting to be punished. Though Duncan's heart softened toward him, he couldn't banish his suspicion. Waiting would yield nothing, so he just asked what troubled his mind. "Yarrow, am I wrong in thinking the thing inhabiting you took leave after our excursion to that foreign shore?"

"No, and… yes," Yarrow answered, digging his nails into his forearms.

"Explain that to me," Duncan said in a tone cooler than he'd intended. "Tell me the truth. Did we go through all of that for nothing? Be honest."

Yarrow nodded, chewing his lower lip. Finally he spoke. "My creature can no longer take control of me. You're not in any danger. But… it will always be a part of me to a degree. We were together so long. It was with me when I had no one else. When I had no one to keep me from harm, it looked out for me. Its voice may be gone, but I will never be completely free of its influence. Our time together changed me. I can't make myself into the person I was before I left Lockhaven. Too much happened to me to ever go back to being that boy. If you cannot accept that, I understand."

"No," Duncan said, smacking his fist against the tabletop. "You're not getting rid of me that effortlessly a second time. I won't let you take the easy path and just run. Help me to understand why you took such pleasure in slaughtering those men while they were running away. If you cannot blame that monster, then why?"

Yarrow got to his feet and paced, making wide, wild gestures with his arms. "I was trying to win a battle! To drive off an enemy threatening your castle! I didn't want to see you or Sasha hurt any further! What's so hard to understand? I fought. We were all fighting."

"There's more to it, and you know it," Duncan insisted, struggling against the urge to soothe his mage's agitated motions. "You were laughing as you cut them down. It wasn't just defense. You enjoyed it."

"And so what?" Yarrow ceased walking and turned to face Duncan, balling his fists at his hips. "Is it such a sin to be strong? To let others know they can't just have their way with you? To the Shades' Abode with those knights, thinking they can do anything they want to anyone. We showed them, and I'm not sorry! I'm not sorry for the power I have! I earned it. So what if I showed them what I can do?"

"But why do you need to show them?" Duncan asked. "Why do you hold so much anger, Yarrow?"

The mage lowered his face to the floor and sucked in great quaffs of air. When he faced Duncan, his eyes burned with azure fire while his features remained frozen. "I was only twelve years old. They put their hands over my mouth. I couldn't even scream."

"What?" Duncan asked, but Sasha squeezed his hand and shook his head, so Duncan stayed silent and let Yarrow continue.

"It was never just my creature," Yarrow said, addressing the blocks on the floor. "I tried to make myself believe it was, but I never could, not in my heart, where it mattered. Hale knew it, and then Fane showed me. Somehow, I made myself forget what they'd done to me, but Fane made me remember. I don't know how I didn't remember before. He said I had to face it. Why did he do that to me? I don't want to remember. I can't even believe it. It couldn't have been me; they must have done it to someone else. I… I would have been too strong. I wouldn't have let them. I would have stopped them. I never would have just lain on that filthy table! I would have cut them down just like I did Damasca's men. I am a great mage!"

"Who?" Duncan whispered, a cold sweat breaking from his pores.

"Agarick! Agarick and his knights! Taran Edercrest! They… they…." Yarrow buried his face in his hands and sobbed, shaking from his hair to the tips of his boots. Unable to stay on his feet, he slid down the wall and burrowed his head between his knees.

Duncan still didn't understand, but Sasha seemed to. He pulled his hand free of Duncan's grasp and went to a chest where he kept some of his belongings. After rifling through it, he knelt in front of Yarrow, wrenched Yarrow's hand away from his face, uncurled Yarrow's fingers, and placed something in his palm. Yarrow stared down at what Sasha offered, and whispered, "I don't understand."

"I killed them," Sasha said. "You can let it go, my love. I have avenged you."

"You… you did…," Yarrow said, sniffling and looking at the item Sasha had given him. "You did this for me?"

"Yes," Sasha answered. "Only for you. I was not employed to do it. I did it out of love for you and outrage over what you suffered. But it is done, Yarrow. He has paid. Thalil will judge him now. All of them. If any of the others still walk in the light, tell me their names and I will remedy it."

Duncan felt left out, unable to enter the dark place his mage and assassin sometimes occupied together, a place he didn't comprehend and wasn't sure he wanted to. "What are you talking about, Sasha?"

Sasha kissed Yarrow's forehead and stood. He closed Yarrow's fingers around what he'd given him, and Yarrow held it next to his heart. Sasha's glassy black gaze met Duncan's, and he spoke without emotion. "Your former king, Agarick, Taran Edercrest, and several others raped Yarrow when he was only a boy." The assassin's words cut Duncan like a knife, a deliberate blow Sasha intended to hurt. "Taran Edercrest admitted this to me on the night I was sent by your leaders to reap his life. It happened more than once, and then they blamed Yarrow for it, called him perverse, and sent him away. I saw they paid for it, and it was the proudest moment of my life when I drove my dagger into Agarick's heart and watched him seize and spit up blood. I offered him to Thalil without any gold changing hands, and I'm glad. Yarrow, he has paid the ultimate price. I know he hurt you, but you are alive and he is dead. You can still make a mark on this world, and he never will."

Yarrow grasped the wall and hauled himself to his feet, and then he clutched Sasha's hand. He opened his mouth as if to speak, but instead he collapsed against Sasha and cried into Sasha's shoulder. Finally, he managed to choke, "This... this is the greatest thing anyone has ever done for me. Thank you. You... you watched him die?"

Sasha smoothed Yarrow's hair down. "I did. I held my hand over his mouth so he couldn't scream, and then I thrust my blade into him again and again. Believe me, my beloved friend, he knew how it felt to be helpless in his last moments. Yarrow, I looked into his eyes as the light faded away. He'll know nothing but the blackest depths for the rest of eternity. Garith owes me his throne in a way he'll never comprehend, but I did it for you. Keep his signet ring, and remember you triumphed in the end. He's dead and you're alive. Nothing else matters."

Duncan hadn't even realized he'd left his chair. As he stood behind it, squeezing the wooden back so hard it creaked, he felt sure he witnessed some fatigue-induced delusion. It couldn't be possible. No. He couldn't accept that Sasha had crept into Lockhaven Castle and murdered the high king of Selindria in his bed. How could he have returned with Agarick's blood on his hands, the king's ring as a trophy, looked Duncan in the eye, and said nothing? No, Duncan felt sure if Sasha had done something so profound, he would have said something. It would have shone through in some way, and Duncan would have known. No man, not even a brother of the Crimson Scythe, could be that cold, and certainly not the man who now held Yarrow so gently and kissed his flushed brow, the love and devotion plain in his onyx eyes. Sasha knew of Duncan's loyalty to the king. Yet, if what he said was true, hadn't Agarick deserved it?

Torn between his feelings of betrayal at Sasha's grievous omission and his disgust that the good man he'd thought he'd served faithfully for so many years proved anything but, Duncan needed to lash out at something or someone. His entire view of the world teetered on a precipice. Unfortunately, Sasha was there and Agarick wasn't. He closed his fist around Sasha's arm and pulled him away from Yarrow. When the mage looked up at him with tear-streaked cheeks, trembling lips, and wide, frightened eyes, Duncan could see the brutalized child Yarrow had been so clearly he had to turn away. If the former king had been in the room with them at that moment, Duncan would have run him through himself. Even so, he couldn't silence the knight within him, the part of him trained since boyhood to defend the king and destroy his enemies. From the time he'd picked up a sword, he'd been taught that protecting the royal family was the pinnacle of his duty. Agarick and fair Selindria couldn't be separated in his mind, and betraying the king meant failing the country. Now, Duncan stood less than a foot from the assassin who'd murdered his sovereign, a man he loved with a fire that almost consumed him sometimes, and he didn't know how to react. His split and twisted emotions took over, and he spoke with thinking.

"Sasha, I trusted you. Goddesses, I don't even know you! You killed the man I swore to protect with my life, and you never said a word to me. How could you do this? You were never meant to murder the king. Rowan paid you to eliminate a traitor, Taran Edercrest, and nothing more."

Sasha yanked his arm free of Duncan's grip, and his face took on the chill, emotionless patina Duncan despised. "He deserved to die for what he did to one of the men I love. I will never apologize for it, not even to you. Agarick was a monster, and if this duty you adhere to tells you anything else, then it has blinded you. I rarely make this claim, but in the case of your blackguard monarch, I saw justice done. I'm proud of it."

"You could have told me!"

"Why?" Sasha asked. "You never want to hear about my work. You prefer to ignore it, pretend it doesn't exist, so you can go on imagining I am other than I am. Tell me I'm wrong. Tell me you truly accept that I'm an assassin, a murderer, a Cast-Down. Listen to me and try not to misunderstand. I am a killer. I like my work and I'll never stop doing it. Tell me you wouldn't have me otherwise."

"I can't say that," Duncan admitted. "You are so skilled. You could use your talents to fight on the proper side."

"On the side of men who violate a child?" Sasha asked, crossing his arms over his chest and lifting his chin in a gesture so superior Duncan wanted to strike him. "Is that who you fight for?"

"You're twisting my words, assassin! I have always fought for the people of this land, those who can't defend themselves. It can be a thankless job, and not especially profitable, so I doubt you can comprehend it."

"Stop it!" Yarrow said in a fractured voice. "Don't. Blame me if you must hold someone responsible."

Sasha turned to their mage and grasped his shoulders. "No. I won't sink to the level of those who claimed you were responsible for your own misfortune. I have witnessed many disgusting and cowardly acts, but these men stunned even me. Thalil, to accuse a child of seeking his own torment! I would kill that pig a thousand times and in a thousand horrible ways if the Dark and Beautiful One would permit me. My only regret is that he didn't suffer longer."

Duncan ground his teeth in frustration, his blood cold in his veins. "Of course I don't blame you, Yarrow. Sasha, I understand why you did what you did. But you should have told me. How did it not occur to you to tell me? Sometimes I don't think you can even comprehend the concepts of honesty and trust."

Sasha whirled and poked his finger into Duncan's chest, his eyes wide and his nostrils flaring with outrage. "You dare to speak to me of honesty, Tam Knight, bairn of Windwake? Every time you lay with me, you claim to accept me for what I am. You lie to me every day! You've never once reconciled my true nature with what you hope I'll become. Why do you hold to the pretense?"

"Sasha, I love you," Duncan said, reaching for him, his concern for his partners trumping his feelings of betrayal and horror.

Sasha evaded Duncan's hand and shook his head. He sounded resigned and genuinely sad when he spoke. "You love my body, maybe.

The idea of me, but not the reality. You never have, despite the words leaving your mouth. I lied to myself, believing you could ever love me as I am. Maybe it's time for me to open my eyes."

"Sasha, no." Duncan's lungs felt filled with icy water, and he choked on whatever he wanted to say next.

The assassin turned toward the door, but Yarrow clutched his shoulder. "Sasha, *syrai*, please don't leave me."

Sasha turned back and kissed Yarrow softly, resting his hand on Yarrow's cheek. "I won't. I swear it by Thalil. I need to be on my own for a while, though. I must think about what I need and value. Who I truly am. I've avoided it for too long. I'm going to the tavern in the village. I want to be alone."

Yarrow blinked back tears and nodded as Sasha opened the door and melted into the shadows of the hallway. The click of the latch when he closed the door echoed in the silence as Duncan and Yarrow stood looking at each other.

Yarrow's flinch when Duncan reached for him cut like a poisoned blade. "I would never hurt you, Yarrow."

"You hurt Sasha. He did it for me."

"I know. Goddesses damn it all, I know! I'm just tired of him lying to me. You both lie to me, don't you? Do you think I'm such a fool as not to notice?"

"Sometimes the truth is impossible to articulate."

"That's just a convenient excuse, Yarrow. I'm sick to death of excuses and half-truths."

"It isn't an excuse. I learned a great deal while I was away. Everyone's past experience, his expectations, color what he sees as the truth. There is no one truth; it's all based on one's perceptions. Everyone's truth is different: yours, mine, Sasha's. To each of us, it's truth just the same. You'd never believe how much of what you think you know is the foulest deception. Everything we thought we knew of this world is wrong."

"How?" Duncan asked.

Yarrow shook his head. "Another time. Look how my own mind deceived me. All these years, I didn't know why I wanted power so desperately, while that nightmare waited in the recesses of my memory.

Who knows how it poisoned the decisions I made, or what I'd have seen differently if I'd been able to face it. It colored my view of everything before I even remembered it happened. It's no different for any man, I suspect."

"Friend, I appreciate some of what you say. But some things are irrevocably true. The truth is Sasha murdered King Agarick and didn't feel I needed to know. That can't be denied. There's no other interpretation. No lukewarm middle."

"He did what was right according to his beliefs," Yarrow said. "I feel responsible for the trouble between you two. You should not have come after me."

"No, Yarrow. Never. I may not always understand everything you do, but I love you, and I love Sasha." Duncan chuckled. "I never intended for it to happen, but one day I just realized you two are all I really care about. Even my duty as a knight falls far behind."

"Sasha would laugh at you for being so poetic," Yarrow said.

"I wish he were here to mock me. I mishandled things with him. He can be difficult to deal with at times and impossible to understand. Ah, I suppose what's done is done. Agarick has been gone for over a year. It seems Sasha meant what he once told me about the bulk of history being shaped by daggers in the shadows. What now, then?"

"We go after Sasha," Yarrow said. "Make him understand we love him. You do love him?"

"Of course. He was the only thing keeping me standing while you were away. I love you both more than I can express."

"We're flawed," Yarrow said.

"We all are, but we're better when we stand together," Duncan responded. "I'm hardly a perfect man."

"No man is perfect, but you and Sasha…. You're perfect to me. Let's go get him. Bring him home."

"He said he wants to be alone," Duncan said.

Yarrow chuckled as he mopped the drying tears from his face. "He's lying."

"Probably," Duncan agreed. "I suppose I owe him an apology."

"He'll revel in that," Yarrow said.

"I know it."

"Well, what are we waiting for?" Yarrow asked.

"I don't know," Duncan admitted, standing with a handful of his ceremonial cloak balled in his uninjured hand. Something troubled him. It wasn't just the smug grin he knew would curl his assassin's magnificent lips when Duncan admitted his mistake and apologized. He expected that bitter tonic, and he'd swallow it, but something else kept Duncan from joining Yarrow near the door. Perhaps Sasha was right about more than one thing, and Duncan really did fear seeing him and Yarrow as they really were. The other two men would mock him for sentimentality, but Duncan knew they needed to sit down for a long talk. Their relationship was unconventional at best, and Duncan tolerated more from his partners than he'd ever imagined he would, but he needed honesty, needed to be able to trust them. Without that, they'd have nothing.

Duncan took one last look at his bed. "Spending the evening in the tavern was at the very bottom of my list of ways to pass the day," he grumbled. "I suppose we should get this over with. Goddesses willing, our cold-hearted friend will be content with a small measure of my humiliation and agree to come back to the castle. I could sleep for a week, and I want both your naked bodies pressed close to me while I do."

Yarrow's smile after his anguish was like a shaft of light breaking through storm clouds to Duncan, and he returned the expression. "Oh, I'm sure Sasha'll watch you squirm for a bit," the mage said. "He's just like that. A little cruel, sometimes, but a good man deep down."

"I know," Duncan said. "I don't suppose the tavern will walk to us if we keep standing here. Let's stop acting like a couple of weepy maidens and go."

Yarrow released all the tension he'd balled up in a truncated laugh. "Agreed. We'll keep this conversation between the two of us?"

Duncan pinched the bridge of his nose. "Goddesses, yes."

Chapter
Twenty-Five

WHEN they arrived at the small tavern at the base of the hill, it was just before dinner and the little wooden building with the thatched roof was filled to the brim with hungry travelers, merchants, soldiers, and mine workers just finishing their day's labor. Many of the knights and warriors who'd fought the night before celebrated their victory over round after round of ale, filling every inch of space in the little pub. Flushed wenches hurried back and forth with tankards of ale, bowls of stew, and loaves of freshly baked bread. A group of old men played a game on the stone slab in front of the hearth. Yarrow didn't see a free bench or stool, and he didn't see Sasha, who would have been hard to miss in his exotic red armor.

Turning to Duncan, he asked, "Do you think he's already left? Headed back home? Honestly, I can't imagine him sitting here by himself and drowning his sorrows. He's not the type. Maybe he went off in search of someone to kill."

"That isn't amusing," Duncan said even as he offered Yarrow a lopsided grin. "Let's get a drink, ask if anyone's seen him, and then head back to Windust. We'll just have to wait for him to return. Maybe he truly does need some time to himself."

Since there was nowhere to sit down, they wandered over to the bar and leaned against it. Yarrow ordered a chalice of the inn's best wine, which he didn't expect to be very good, and Duncan asked for a mug of ale. When the plump young woman brought their drinks, Yarrow described Sasha to her and asked if she'd seen him.

The robust girl with the straw-colored braids set their drinks down. Yarrow sipped his wine and winced. It tasted like someone had dumped the coals from their campfire into the bottle in an attempt to mask the poor quality of the fruit. He almost spit it out, but he didn't want to be rude when he needed information from the barmaid. He forced first a swallow then a smile.

The maiden blushed when she spoke of Sasha. "Aye, I remember him. Dark and very exotic. A handsome man, your friend. All the lasses noticed when he walked in, even the old spinsters."

Yarrow tamped down the urge to just force her to speak, give him the information he wanted. It would be so easy to wrench it from her simple mind, but that wouldn't make it right. He was not a monster and he wouldn't let himself become one, so he just smiled and asked, "Where did he go when he left here?"

She shrugged. "Hard to say. He ordered a mug of ale but barely drank any of it. Seemed sad."

"You were watching him," Duncan observed.

The poor girl's face turned as red as Yarrow's subpar wine. "Just looking, tam. I couldn't help it. The man seemed to need a friend, but he didn't want to talk. Half of a barmaid's job is talking to the guests when they need it, but he was different."

"Where did he go?" Yarrow repeated, trying to veil his growing frustration.

"Outside, tam," the wench responded. "With some men wearing the same funny leathers. I guess he must have known them."

Yarrow and Duncan looked at each other, exchanging worry and wonder without words, as the girl mopped up some spilled ale with a soiled rag and then placed it on her tray. Duncan handed her a few copper coins—the payment for their drinks along with a generous tip. As she moved on to her next customer, Yarrow and Duncan pushed their way through the throng toward the door.

Outside, the sun sank below the western mountains, leaving a few slate-blue clouds with rosy centers drifting across the periwinkle sky. Long shadows extended from the simple tavern and swallowed Yarrow and Duncan as they stood considering the serving wench's words.

Yarrow said what they were both thinking. "Men dressed like Sasha could only mean Crimson Scythe."

Duncan nodded, his brows furrowed and his forehead wrinkled. "No doubt. We should have expected this."

"Should we have? What do you know, Duncan?"

"They've been here at least once before. Sasha said they would never let him go, and it seems they've been biding their time, waiting for him to be alone. Yarrow, they plan to make him pay for his failure. They'll kill him."

"No!" Yarrow had to find him. He looked around for a sign of where Sasha could have been taken and saw a smear of blood on the corner of the tavern wall, violently red against the muted grays overtaking the rest of the world. Fresh and wet, which meant there might still be hope. He pointed to it, and Duncan followed him without question as he rounded the building, his good hand on the hilt of the plain but functional blade his smith had loaned him while his trusted sword underwent repairs. As they moved around the tavern, droplets of blood formed a trail up the rocky hillside and toward the seaside caverns beneath Windust Castle. Yarrow and Duncan tracked them along the jagged stones and pools of brackish water, until Yarrow raised his hand to halt them.

"This seems a little too obvious," he said to Duncan. "The path is far too regular and clear. It's almost as if they want us to follow it. It isn't like their order. They're masters of avoiding detection."

"A trap," Duncan said in agreement.

Yarrow nodded as he sprinted to the next crimson dribble. The blood smell intoxicated him, made him want to sink his azure claws into twitching flesh, especially the flesh of anyone who dared threaten one of the men he loved, one of the two men in the world who'd ever cared what happened to him. His fingers twitched in the anticipation of tearing them to shreds.

"So what if it is a ruse?" Yarrow huffed, running to the next red splatter. "I won't abandon Sasha!"

"Nor will I," Duncan said, close on Yarrow's heels. "I'm just saying we should be ready for resistance."

"Oh, I'm ready," Yarrow said, tingling as he made his way toward a cleft in the ironstone beneath Duncan's fortress. "Oh yes. Bring it on." He ached to tear through flesh, spill blood, just mow through anyone or anything standing between him and what he valued. He and Duncan turned sideways to enter the narrow passage in the rock, marked by another rusty smudge. Only a few feet in, darkness enveloped them, and Yarrow fought the panic it inspired. He wanted his creature to either reassure or mock him; either would have been a comfort, but he'd made his choice, and he was alone. He had only himself to depend upon. But no, that was wrong. Duncan was with him, standing at his back, ready to fight beside him. That knowledge gave Yarrow courage, and he forced himself to squeeze through the channel. No matter what he had to sacrifice, he swore he wouldn't lose either of these men. No matter what it cost him.

After half a mile or so of stumbling through darkness, with only the slimy, lichen-coated wall to guide them, Yarrow and Duncan emerged into an open chamber. The smells of saline and fungus were heavy in the chill air. Though it was still as bleak as midnight, Yarrow discerned the cavern's size by the echo of their breathing. He reached out with his senses, and when he found no other signs of life, he conjured a blue sphere almost as large as his head and sent it rising toward the ceiling. Its light showed them an enormous space with a slender path edging a kettle probably hundreds of feet deep. A few more steps and they would have both plummeted to the bottom. The seawater spiraled below, swirling up whitecaps, too far away for Yarrow to hear more than an echo of its movement. He pressed his chest against the slick wall of the cave as he tiptoed around the deep crevasse. Duncan made his way carefully behind him. Both of them knew one misstep would send them tumbling to their deaths. At some points, Yarrow barely had enough space to rest the balls of his feet on the ledge. Rocks plunged into the water far below as Yarrow moved cautiously along the narrow ridge. In the worst of cases, he could summon his wings and save himself from falling, but that would mean nothing if he lost Duncan or Sasha.

After what felt like hours, Yarrow and Duncan stepped off the slender strip of stone and into a small room. Yarrow's muscles ached and trembled from the strain. Puddles of seawater pitted the uneven ground, and they picked their way carefully around them, following the small dribbles of blood through another passage and into a crescent-shaped cavern.

Yarrow and Duncan stopped at the cave's entrance. Sasha stood lashed to a jutting rock at the center of the space, strips of leather stretched across his mouth, gagging him. His armor had been stripped off, and he shivered in nothing but his undergarment. He writhed within the bonds holding him to the stone, but even his ankles had been bound, and he could scarcely move at all. His flesh bulged out between the tight ropes every time he shifted.

Detecting movement in the shadows draping the perimeter of the room, Yarrow grabbed Duncan's shirt and pressed him against the wall. He extinguished his orb, and only a few sputtering torches provided smoky illumination. Squinting into the darkness, Yarrow sensed a great many lives. The faint sounds of their heartbeats and the scent of the blood swishing through their veins made him salivate. He couldn't wait to crush their bones to powder in his claws. He turned to Duncan and held up both hands, spreading his fingers wide. Then he showed his companion two more fingers to indicate the number of enemies they'd face. Duncan's eyes went wide, and Yarrow knew he remembered the last time they'd faced the assassins of the Crimson Scythe. They'd barely been outnumbered that time, and still it had been a close thing, with a lot of luck involved. Without Sasha beside them, Yarrow and Duncan had no way to know what kinds of vile traps they could be walking into. Worse yet, Yarrow didn't dare give away their position by speaking to Duncan, which meant they couldn't plan their strategy.

Walking straight into that room would be suicide, Yarrow knew, but he couldn't bear seeing Sasha suffer, his bonds cutting and bruising his skin, the corners of his wonderful lips cracked open, blood dripping from his mouth, and errant cuts bleeding all over his body. He closed his eyes for a second to think, and decided to try a bit of magic he hadn't even realized he knew. His creature must have understood the spell he planned to attempt, and now that they'd joined together, its knowledge also belonged to Yarrow, along with its insatiable appetite for death.

Yarrow turned to Duncan and held up his hand, indicating Duncan should wait. The knight's eyes darted back and forth with anxiety, and sweat sparkled across Duncan's forehead. Yarrow studied him: his posture, the way his feet turned out slightly, the way his whiskers curled over his earlobes, the creases time, sun, and worry had carved around his eyes and the lips Yarrow had once found too sensual and expressive to occupy such a stern face. Since the mage couldn't see himself, he decided to use Duncan's likeness for what he planned. When he felt sure he'd memorized every relevant detail of his lover's appearance, he prepared to do the magic, gathering fragments of light, shadow, and vapor. Luckily, a chill mist rose off the damp floor, giving Yarrow plenty of raw material for the enchantment. He compressed the fog, building it up and shaping it like wet clay until it resembled a man. Then he began carving out the details, adding suggestions of color and texture until he felt the copy would deceive the waiting assassins. He transferred a scrap of his consciousness into it so he could direct it, and the effort left his actual body feeling numb and insubstantial. Inhabiting the copy with even such a small sliver of his mind weakened him. He shivered at the sensation of being made of icy vapor held together by coils of enchantment.

Duncan gasped at the certainly unnerving sight of his exact duplicate staring back at him. Yarrow shook his head and pressed a finger to his lips, but the effort left him dizzy. He grabbed Duncan's elbow to stay on his feet while he swooned and waited for the vertigo to pass. The complex magic had taken more out of him than he'd anticipated. Blasting through and destroying took far less effort than creation.

When he regained enough strength to stand on his own, Yarrow directed the illusion he'd conjured slowly into the cavern. Hopefully, it had enough substance to trigger any traps the assassins had laid. Its boots even clunked on the stone as it approached Sasha. Slowly, the brethren slunk out of the shadows, twelve of them, just as Yarrow had predicted, crouched low with swords, daggers, staves, and light, slender bows in their hands. They inched forward, surrounding the faux Duncan, but when they came within a few feet of the illusion, they stopped and waited. Yarrow let a little more of his essence seep into the copy, so he could look at the assassins through its eyes.

All of them wore snug blood-red armor similar to Sasha's, with hoods shrouding their features and expressions. Many of them also covered the lower halves of their faces with strips of dark cloth. Through the illusion, Yarrow sensed the presence of magic, but it didn't come from any of the lithe men and women fingering blades and knocking arrows into place. To gauge how they'd react, Yarrow's illusion drew its sword. To his surprise, the Crimson Scythe made no move to defend themselves. The faux-Duncan stabbed at the nearest one. The slender man leapt back but didn't move the serpentine dagger he held from its place near his waist.

A rush of magic hit Yarrow like a stone wall, knocking his consciousness out of the copy and propelling it back into his own head, where it slammed against the back of his skull and made him stumble and collide with Duncan's chest. The spell tore apart Yarrow's illusion like a bucket of water thrown against thin paper. A fetid wind followed it, cutting a swathe through the mist. The odor of decay summoned a memory in

Yarrow, and he hurried to erect a sapphire shield around Duncan and himself.

"You'll have to do much better than that, Yarroway L'Estrella." The voice echoed through the chamber and cut through Yarrow like a blade.

Yarrow stretched his arm out when Duncan tried to move in front of him. "Stay behind the barrier. We don't stand a chance against them in a fight. Duncan, I will do what I have to do to see you and Sasha make it out of here. You may not like what you're about to see, and I hope you won't hold it against me."

"Just keep in mind they lured us here. They *want* us here," Duncan said.

"This doesn't make any sense," Yarrow muttered. "What do they want with us? And why have they kept Sasha alive? They pride themselves on being efficient killers and nothing else."

"You might as well show yourself, Yarroway," said the voice Yarrow now recognized as belonging to the mage-assassin who had tried to punish Sasha for leaving the order more than a year ago—the man whose arm Yarrow had taken.

"Stay close," Yarrow whispered to Duncan. "I can keep us safe for quite a while yet."

Duncan nodded, and slowly, shoulder to shoulder, they entered the cave and stepped into the firelight. Yarrow noted the position of the dozen assassins and tried to formulate a way to destroy as many as possible without putting Duncan or Sasha in peril. No matter how he imagined it, he couldn't envision a way of attacking without turning his attention away from his friends, and with Sasha helpless and Duncan unable to lift his sword with his broken wrist—

The mage-assassin materialized from the darkness, and not in the way Sasha described, when the brethren hid in the shadows to frighten their prey. The other magician literally solidified from the blackness behind the rock where Sasha was tied, and Yarrow knew he'd been there all along. How had he missed it? His creature wouldn't have, but Yarrow's humanity seemed to have watered down its keen perceptions. The sorcerer's pale face looked disembodied above his dark leathers and long cloak when he appeared next to Sasha. Yarrow stopped and faced him, much more angry than afraid as the mage-assassin fondled Sasha's cheek and neck.

"What do you want with my friend?" Yarrow asked, trying to mimic the brethren's flat, emotionless way of speaking.

"This traitor?" the magician asked, tapping Sasha's face. "He has been living on borrowed time for a year now. I told you the last time we met that no one leaves Thalil. But more importantly, I hoped to use him to entice you here."

"Why?" Yarrow asked. "Are you hoping I'll slice off your other arm this time? If that's what you want, I'll be happy to fulfill your wish. You know you can't stand against me. Not on your own, and not even with all of these others. There won't be anything left of you when I'm finished."

The other mage swore in the obscure language Sasha sometimes used, his eyes going wide and wild. He reached into his cloak, pulled out a long, barbed dart, and stabbed it into Sasha's neck just below the corner of his jaw. Sasha gagged and sputtered, his entire body going rigid. Both Yarrow and Duncan hurried toward him, but the enemy mage left the dart sticking in Sasha's flesh and raised his hand.

"If you harm me, he dies," the mage said. "I coated this barb with a slow-acting but lethal poison. Your friend's blood will slowly start to dry up and turn to dust, and by this time tomorrow, he will die in unimaginable agony, but by then, he will welcome it. I created this toxin myself, and only I have the antidote."

"Oh, and what's to stop me from just killing you and taking it from your body?" Yarrow asked, shaking with a mix of fear and rage.

"Nothing, except that I don't have it with me. If you kill me, I highly recommend you slit this traitor's throat and save him a day of torture."

"What is it you want from me?" Yarrow asked.

The other mage looked quite deranged as he sneered and bared his teeth. "You killed my companions, humiliated me, and took my arm. I want vengeance, of course. I want to kill your friends and mutilate your body."

"You expect me to agree to that?" Yarrow asked. "Why would I let you harm me when you plan to kill my friends either way?"

"Give me your arm, and I'll give you the antidote," the mage-assassin said. "I will free your companion and give you the chance to fight your way out of here."

"Outnumbered four to one?" Duncan shouted.

The other mage shrugged. "You'll face those same odds if he refuses, and your treacherous friend will die of the poison even if you manage to defeat us. Don't waste any more of my time. I have been waiting for this moment. Choose, Yarroway L'Estrella."

Duncan leaned close to Yarrow's ear. "We're left with no choice but to fight them. Anything else doesn't even deserve consideration."

"No." Yarrow reached up and unclasped his worn, black cloak and let it fall in a heap behind him. Underneath, he still wore the thin, faded tunic he'd had since leaving Espero. He stepped away from Duncan, ignoring the knight's hissed protests, and extended his left arm toward the enemy mage. The other man's nostrils flared and his grin grew wide enough to split his face as one of his fellow assassins handed him a vicious-looking cleaver with a serrated edge. Duncan shouted and Sasha thrashed in his bonds, but Yarrow barely noticed them. His gaze locked onto the other mage's black eyes, and the sound of his pulse echoed inside his head.

Yarrow had sworn to himself he wouldn't lose the only people who'd ever loved him, no matter what it cost. Now that he knew the price, he had to pay it.

"Get ready," the other sorcerer said, wetting his lips with his tongue. "It's going to hurt." He lifted the weapon perpendicular to Yarrow's arm, aiming just below the globe of Yarrow's shoulder.

"Wait," Yarrow said. "Give Sasha the antidote first."

The mage-assassin turned and disappeared into the shadows near the opposite end of the cave. His brethren closed around Yarrow, Duncan, and Sasha, training their weapons on them so they couldn't even attempt to escape. Finally the other magician emerged from the darkness holding a small vial of glowing green liquid. He pulled the leather strips out of Sasha's mouth and grabbed Sasha by the hair.

"Yarrow, don't—" Sasha shouted. The other mage forced the vial into his mouth, and Sasha choked down the elixir. Before he could say another word, the sorcerer replaced his gag. Then he returned to Yarrow, picked up his blade, and lifted it to strike.

Chapter
Twenty-Six

THE mage-assassin swung his weapon. Duncan had never felt so impotent or useless. Time seemed to slow to a crawl as the vicious-looking blade cut through the heavy air. Duncan couldn't bear to watch that smooth, slender, beautiful, perfect body he adored and had longed for hacked apart, and yet he couldn't look away. With all three of them wounded, they stood no chance against a dozen Crimson Scythe assassins. What would stop Yarrow from bleeding to death? None of them would make it out of the dank, freezing cavern, and there was nothing Duncan could do about it.

He must have blinked just as the weapon connected, because for a split second everything went black. When Duncan opened his eyes, he didn't see Yarrow bleeding on the ground as he'd expected. Instead, the four assassins closest to him lay ripped apart, as if by a giant talon. Their blood coated the floor. The enemy sorcerer looked both dumbfounded and enraged. Sasha, no longer bound to the jagged stone, ran bent nearly in half through the gore to retrieve a dagger dropped by one of his former brothers. In a seamless motion, Sasha rose, twirled, and sank the blade into another assassin's throat. Duncan didn't understand what had happened, but he didn't have time to ponder it, and he let his warrior's instinct take control as one of their adversaries aimed a crossbow in his direction. Duncan dropped and rolled out of the arrow's path, driving his fist into the gut of another of the brethren on his way back to his feet.

The man Duncan had knocked down was back on his feet in seconds, a matching set of double-edged daggers in his hands. The two of them faced off as Sasha slashed at a trio of enemies, succeeding in keeping them at a safe distance but doing little harm. The poison had clearly affected Sasha, and he moved much more slowly than usual. Even so, he would have still been a match for most enemies, with the exception of these members of his former order. One of the other assassins swung a crescent-shaped blade on the end of a chain and opened a deep gash across Sasha's thigh. Without thinking, Duncan sprinted to his aid, dismissing the man behind him. It proved a grievous error. The assassin leapt into the air, and Duncan turned just in time to see both daggers heading for his back.

With a flash of blue lightning, the assassin was batted out of the air and across the chamber, where he hit the wall hard. When he fell to the ground, he didn't rise again, and Duncan hurried to get to Sasha, bending to pick up a shortsword as he ran. As soon as he got within range, he plunged the blade into the nearest enemy's back, hitting resistance when his steel met bone. He yanked the light sword free and thrust again, making the assassin seize and drop to his knees. Duncan reached around and cut his throat, then raised his weapon just in time to parry a blow from a blood-spattered woman with a razor-tipped staff. With his superior size and strength, he held her at bay until she kicked out at his ankles and knocked him down. Fighting one-handed proved a huge disadvantage for Duncan. His tailbone smacked the stone and his teeth banged together. With incredible speed, the female assassin drove the sharp tip of her staff toward Duncan's exposed throat. It paused only inches from Duncan's Adam's apple as his enemy's eyes rolled back in her head and her grip on the weapon faltered. She fell to the side and landed hard on her hip and shoulder, a knife protruding from her temple.

Sasha offered his hand, grasped Duncan's wrist, and helped Duncan to his feet. They hurried to stand back to back, both of them covered in blood and gasping for breath. The remaining five assassins closed in on them. Two of them trained their bows on Duncan and Sasha, and at their range they couldn't possibly miss. A bowstring creaked and a pair of black arrows sailed toward Duncan's face. He tried his best to shield himself with his gauntleted forearms. He heard a strained cry, and a sheer wall of blue light materialized before him, deflecting the arrows. The mystic barrier flickered, disappeared, then reappeared before fading altogether. Finally Duncan realized what must have happened. Yarrow had used the spell that, as best as Duncan could understand, froze everything and everyone in time. His mage must have used the few moments to cut Sasha free and kill as many of the assassins as he could. Unfortunately, Duncan had seen the terrible toll using that particular enchantment took on Yarrow. He could scarcely believe Yarrow had managed to remain conscious.

"Enough of this!" The assassin-mage's voice echoed through the cavern, stilling and silencing everyone. A thick stream of light cut through the gloom, the color reminding Duncan of the slime coating the surface of stagnant ponds. Just in time, Yarrow folded an azure wing in front of himself and volleyed the spell back at its caster. The other magician, clearly not as worn as Yarrow, wiped it away with a brush of his hand and closed the space between himself and Yarrow, with slow, sauntering steps.

"You cannot win, Yarroway L'Estrella," he taunted, wiggling fingers pulsing with a jaundiced glow. Duncan and Sasha, along with the remaining brethren of Thalil, waited to see what would transpire. "I'll admit I've never encountered a mage with your power, and that power seems to have grown and transformed since we last met, but even you have your limits. Admit it. Whatever you did to immobilize us cost you dearly, and now you're all used up."

A fetid yellow cloud rose from the sorcerer's palm, and he blew on it to send it in Yarrow's direction. It grew in size until the foul reek of decay filled the cavern, making Duncan's gorge rise. Anywhere the miasma touched the pale moss or small mushrooms growing from the rock, it reduced them to black slime, as if they'd rotted weeks ago.

Yarrow laughed, a cruel and bitter sound. "I have more than enough power to defeat someone like you, with your tired entropy." He spread his luminous wings until they filled the cavern, and when he beat them, the fog dissipated. Duncan tingled with cold fire, and he smelled burning minerals as the sapphire feathers passed over and through him. They left a shimmering coat of frost atop his plate armor, and his breath came out in a thick, white cloud even though he felt the stir of warm, rosy embers in his chest and belly: the flicker of hope.

It was a fleeting sensation. Despite his words and the arrogance of his tone, Yarrow swayed for a moment before dropping to his knees with his head hanging limply, as if too heavy for his neck to hold up. His wings drooped and fell at his sides.

The other mage laughed. He shot out his hand, and shards of rock the length of spears broke free from the cave ceiling and soared toward Yarrow. Yarrow closed his wings around his huddled body and managed to protect himself from most of the projectiles, though a final spike breached his weakened defenses. The point scraped along his exposed back, tearing fabric and flesh alike and drawing a ragged scream from Duncan's mage. Blood fanned out from the wound and splattered the cavern wall.

All thoughts of his own safety abandoned Duncan. Only one motive remained: save Yarrow. He barreled into the assassin in front of him, knocking her to the ground. Another of the Crimson Scythe, his face covered in black gauze and his eyes glittering like winter stars, jumped in front of Duncan and swiped at him with the sharp little blades embedded in the knuckles of his gloves. They raked across Duncan's chin. Blood soaked his whiskers, but he barely registered the pain as he backhanded the smaller man in the side of the head and sent him sprawling. Two of the others grabbed Duncan's elbows, but Sasha's dagger found one and sent him facedown and spitting up blood. When Duncan twisted, he dislodged the other and sent him skidding across the ground. As the assassin slid on his back, he reached into his sleeve, pulled out a hidden blade, and threw it at Duncan. Going against everything he'd ever been forced to believe, Sasha jumped in front of Duncan to protect him.

"No!" Yarrow shrieked, scrambling to his feet and reaching out with his radiant claw. After he caught the knife and crumpled it into a steel ball, he swatted the man who'd thrown it aside like a gnat. "I'm finished with this! With you! All of you! How dare you threaten *me*? My friends?"

The clawlike appendage swung behind Yarrow, giving the impression of a trio of resplendent wings, backlighting the mage and making his shadow stretch out in front of him three or more times his height. Cerulean light poured from the corners of his eyes and left comet-like tails when he turned his head. Duncan could barely resist the urge to sink to the ground and cover his head with his hands. Even Sasha, in a rare admission of his vulnerability, moved close to Duncan's back. Yarrow made another swipe with his talon and toppled two more of the assassins. Either injury or good sense kept them down, and the final members of the brethren backed against the wall. The other mage shot a sphere of wormy energy at Yarrow. Yarrow parried it with the tip of his wing. The entire cavern rumbled when the combined forces of their enchantment struck the stone, and dust and rock rained down.

Larger chunks of the wall dislodged when Yarrow attacked his enemy with veins of lightning.

"Thalil curse these mages," one of the three remaining assassins yelled. "They'll bring the whole mountainside down on our heads!"

"This was a fool's mission from the beginning!" another responded. "Our sorcerer was mad before and worse since he lost his arm. We should get out of here! Live to spill blood for the Dark One another day!"

"I agree," said the final female, holding her ribs as she staggered to her feet. She turned to Sasha. "We will see you again, traitor. No one turns his back on Thalil."

Duncan moved to block their way, but Sasha caught his wrist and shook his head. "Let them go. They've done us a favor by leaving us only one enemy."

"If we don't stop those two, it won't matter," Duncan shouted over the clash of arcane energies and the groan of the ironstone as it buckled beneath the weight of the mountain. One tiny crack in the right place would bury them all beneath hundreds of feet of solid rock—potentially destroying Windust Castle in the process. But Yarrow and the other mage didn't seem to care as they dueled with their magics and hurled insults at one another.

"Yarrow is not quite himself," Sasha warned. "His movements are too quick, sharp, and decisive, and his purpose is much more single-minded than usual. Although, in truth, much about him has seemed altered since we left that cursed cavern in the barbarian lands."

"Goddesses, Sasha. Why tell me this now?" Duncan coughed as more fine dirt and small rocks cascaded over them.

"Because you must remember the Battle of the Starlight Bridge! Whatever overtakes Yarrow, it steals his reason. I don't know if he can tell foe from ally. He may not even recognize us."

"I won't believe that of him," Duncan said. "I don't claim to understand this, but Yarrow told me we weren't in danger. I have to trust him. If we can't trust each other, what in this wicked world can we believe in?"

Sasha couldn't answer and merely shook his head. His lack of resistance made Duncan smile, and Duncan kissed him softly before wading into the colliding streams of white-blue and putrid green light.

Yarrow looked to have the upper hand. His icy-hot magic had gained ground against the other's sickly sweet aura of decay, pushing it farther and farther back. The other mage strained against Yarrow's energy, his arm locked straight in front of him but his feet scraping against the rubble-strewn ground as he skidded backward. The back of his ankle caught on a large shard of stone, and he stumbled, his power waffling. Without hesitation, Yarrow seized the other sorcerer in his ethereal hand and slammed him against the wall. The mage-assassin's feet dangled pitifully dozens of feet above the cavern floor. Yarrow drew back and smacked him against the stone again, making him choke on a scream. A large fissure opened across the ceiling, and stalactites fell and shattered like icicles.

"Yarroway, stop!" When his mage ignored him, Duncan reached through the otherworldly material of his wings to grasp his shoulder. Though his arm felt like it dissolved in energy that was both searing and frozen at once and yet neither, something beyond, he didn't let go. He dug his fingers into the stringy muscle stretched over Yarrow's prominent bone and shook. "Stop, Yarrow. If you can't get control of yourself, Sasha and I are lost. We'll be killed! I know you don't want that."

Gradually, the light streaming from Yarrow's eyes reduced to a trickle until only his bright irises glowed. His massive wings shrunk into his back, and he turned to meet Duncan's gaze. Duncan anticipated his mage's confusion, expected Yarrow to look around as if he'd just woken from a nightmare, and the clarity in Yarrow's expression disturbed him.

"The cavern is collapsing," Duncan timidly explained.

"I'm sorry," Yarrow said. "I never wanted to put you or Sasha in danger, but this needs to end here. I won't put up with the annoyance of these assassins pestering me or attempting to bother Sasha. I'll put a stop to it here and now." He tightened his grip around the other mage, eliciting a strangled cry. "I'll show the world the consequences of trifling with me."

"I understand," Duncan said honestly, without any false attempt to assuage his friend. Yarrow had suffered more than he'd ever imagined, and Duncan could appreciate his need to protect himself, and, by extension, those he loved. But he needed to stop Yarrow to protect himself and Sasha. "None of us want to be buried beneath this mountain, though. Is killing this man worth losing Sasha or me?"

"No, of course not." Yarrow colored and lowered his face with obvious shame. He drew in a sharp breath as if he planned to say more, but then bit his lip and shook his head. "I'm sorry."

"We were all fighting for our lives," Duncan said, rubbing the back of Yarrow's neck. "But we need to get out of here now, before it's too late."

Sasha, wounded, practically nude and trembling, stepped up beside Duncan and said, "Get rid of him, Yarrow, or he'll cause us trouble in the future."

Though he hated to admit it, Duncan agreed.

Yarrow stared up at the other mage as he kept him firmly within his claw. "I have another idea."

"Yarrow—" Sasha warned.

"No. I don't want any more Crimson Scythe assassins coming after us. I won't live my life looking over my shoulder." Yarrow turned to the captive mage. "I hope you realize how high a compliment I'm paying you and your order by acknowledging the threat you pose me."

The order sorcerer gnashed his teeth but nodded.

"Get rid of him, Yarrow." Sasha, for the first time in Duncan's experience, sounded almost frantic.

"I think there may be a better way," Yarrow said, his gaze fixed on the other magician.

"No—" Sasha began.

Yarrow turned and offered him an absolutely sincere smile. His eyes crinkled to crescents as he petted Sasha's bruised and bloody cheek. "Trust me."

In response, Sasha just nodded and draped his hand over Yarrow's knuckles. Duncan had realized trust was a choice, and Sasha seemed to agree. It had to be given before one knew what he would get. If one knew what he'd get, trust wasn't necessary.

Yarrow looked up at his prisoner. "I will trade you your life for your fealty and information about your order. You are one of the few mages in a thousand years to impress me, and we can accomplish much as allies. Will you agree?"

"Just what are you asking?" the other mage sputtered.

"Simple," Yarrow said. "Take me to the leaders of your order. I'll reason with or kill them. That's their choice. I cannot find them without your aid. No one outside the order can, not even Sasha."

"You think I'm a traitor like your friend?" the other mage sputtered.

Yarrow shrugged. "It doesn't matter what I think of your character. I respect your magical talent. I can nurture it, offer you knowledge you've only fantasized about. You're astute enough to know I'm not exaggerating."

"You'd let me study with you, Yarroway L'Estrella?"

"If you make it worth my while," Yarrow said. "Will you lead me to your masters?"

"Yarrow, this is a terrible idea," Sasha protested.

"No," Yarrow said in a soft, dreamy voice. "No, it's the only way. They won't stop coming after us. We should take the fight to them."

Duncan didn't know whose side to take. As much as he wanted the threat of the Crimson Scythe eliminated from their future, as much as he hated that damnable order for more reasons than he could list, he didn't know if leaving this dangerous madman alive was a fair bargain. He certainly didn't want Yarrow associating with the other mage. More importantly: "Yarrow, how can you believe anything he says? These assassins are hardly above lying if it will help them accomplish their goals."

"That's true," Sasha admitted. He took a few steps nearer to the mage-assassin and looked up at him. "Your soul, like mine, belongs to Thalil through an ancient pact. If you betray him, you will suffer for it, in this life or for eternity in the next. Will you swear on Thalil's name to stop hunting us and to lead us to the masters of the order?"

"I—I can't," the mage said, squirming in his glowing blue bonds.

Sasha crossed his arms across his chest. "As I suspected. Yarrow, you know what must be done. Would you prefer if I did it?"

"Wait!" the other mage shouted, his voice rough and hoarse from the battle and the smoke filling the cavern. "I'm not ready to go to Thalil!"

"That's hardly our concern," Sasha said, his tone all icy pragmatism. "I'm not ready either, but I'm even less willing to lose Yarrow or Duncan. I'm afraid it's you or us. You understand."

"If I agree to help you, can you keep me safe?" the order mage asked. "The brethren will hunt me as they hunt you if I betray them. Can you swear to protect me from them?"

"I will swear nothing to you," Sasha said. "This bargain, if you accept it, is between you and Yarrow. I'll take no part. That way, if you threaten or harm him, nothing will stop me from punishing you for it."

"I agree with Sasha," Duncan said. "I'll forge no ties to you."

"What kind of deal is this?" the captive sorcerer asked. "Waiting to be killed by my order, or, should I somehow miraculously keep ahead of them, wondering if I'll fall prey to one of you? Yarroway, can you promise me my life?"

"No," Yarrow said. "I'll teach you spells to defend yourself. I'd actually like to learn some of yours. I cannot offer to follow you around like a guard dog, though. Take your chances with your brethren or die here."

"I should choose to die honorably, loyal to Thalil and the Crimson Scythe, but—"

"You're a coward." Sasha finished the mage's sentence.

"I'm not a coward. I'm not afraid to die, but I don't want to. Not yet. There's still so much to learn, so much power to gather. I haven't even scratched the surface. I want to learn all I can before I go into the arms of the Dark and Beautiful One. This world contains things I'm not ready to relinquish just yet. Can you not understand, brother?"

Sasha blew air out his nose and looked away.

"If you find no relevance in my words, why didn't you complete your mission?" the other assassin continued. "You were highly regarded within the order, but you found something you valued more. Something you loved even above serving Thalil. I have also found something like that: magic. I do not know if there is magic beyond the gates of death, and I don't wish to be parted from the only thing I've ever valued. I see the expression of your face, my brother. I'm as adept as you are at reading it. I can see you know just what I mean."

"Stop nattering on and wasting our time," Sasha snapped. "It isn't my fate that will be decided here today."

"Isn't it, brother? The order will not stop unless you stop them. You know as well as I do they'll succeed eventually. They always do."

"Over my dead body!" Yarrow shouted.

"That would be a shame," the other mage said. "All that knowledge lost."

"Then will you agree?" Yarrow asked again.

"Wait," Duncan said, knowing he stood at the edge of a path he wouldn't be able to abandon once he set his feet upon it. He wished the way ahead wasn't so shrouded, with all the divergent trails their decisions might lead them to tread veiled from view. But he knew one thing with absolute certainty. "I will not harbor you in my household or my bairny. If Yarrow chooses to spare you, you must go far away from here. I don't care where. I don't even want to know. Give him a way to contact you, but do not let me see your face until he does. Am I making myself plain?"

"Oh yes, Tam Knight," the mage said in a condescending tone of feigned respect. "Now, let me down, Yarrow."

"No," Sasha said. "Swear first."

"Very well. I swear."

"The whole thing," Sasha said.

The mage rolled his eyes, but when he spoke, his voice was full of reverence. "I swear by Thalil, He Who Stands Just Out of Sight. I swear on the edge of his dagger, which nothing living can escape. I swear on the mountain of skulls beneath his feet and on the endless river of blood flowing about him. I swear on his sweet lips, which utter the whisper heard at the last. Now, let me down."

Yarrow lowered the other mage to the ground and then let his azure claw dissipate. The strain finally caught up with him, and he crumpled like a set of discarded garments. Duncan hurried to scoop Yarrow up and hold him on his lap. As Yarrow's eyes fluttered shut, the two disgraced assassins stood staring at each other.

The mage looked down at the empty palm of his remaining hand. "I am no longer Crimson Scythe. I never even dared to imagine how it would feel to stand outside the order. I—I am truly no longer a blade of Thalil."

"There comes a point where you must stop letting others define who and what you are," Sasha said, a pale wash of compassion coloring his words.

"Can we really bring down the Crimson Scythe?" the mage asked.

Sasha shrugged. "It will be fun to try, and imagine the glory if we succeed."

The mage grinned, nodded once, and turned to leave the cavern. "I will find a way to reach you when I'm sure I am safe."

"Wait," Yarrow said weakly. "I would know your name."

"I have no permanent name," the mage said. "I'm called whatever my mission dictates. I take on any necessary identity."

Yarrow made an exasperated hiss. "I've heard this all before. And don't tell me you don't remember it, either."

"Very well. I was—I am called Corbin. And now, farewell to you, until we see each other again." Corbin limped away and disappeared into the shadows.

"Goddesses help us, what have we done?" Duncan said as he stroked the side of Yarrow's face.

"Nothing," Yarrow said. "If we choose not to pursue the Crimson Scythe, we have only to tell him to stay away from us. He's bound by his oath not to do us harm."

"The others are not." Sasha had retrieved his leather armor and stood looking down at it, a single crease between his slender black brows. "I'm the cause of this, the reason you're both in danger. Your lives are at risk because you chose to keep me in your presence."

"I would do it again," Duncan hurried to say. "A hundred times. A thousand. I don't just love you when it's easy. I love you just as much when I have to fight for you. Please, come here."

Without bothering to dress, Sasha knelt down in front of Duncan so their knees pressed together. He draped one arm over Duncan's shoulder and curled his other hand around the back of Yarrow's neck. All of them leaned in so their faces touched, Sasha and Duncan leaning their foreheads against each other and their jaws and chins on Yarrow's cheeks. For a long time, they just clung to each other in the blood and rubble.

"I will never abandon you," Duncan said to them both.

"Nor me," Yarrow whispered, his voice hitching with emotion. "Never. No matter what."

"This is my oath," Sasha said. "Nothing in this world or any other will keep me from you. Nothing will stop me from supporting you when I can or fighting for you when I must. I wish I had something to give you to seal my promise."

"I don't need anything beyond your words," Yarrow said. "I know you mean them."

"I have your love," Duncan said. "There's nothing more precious you could give me, either of you. And now I suppose I'll suffer your insults for being a sentimental fool." He braced himself to be taunted.

Yarrow brushed his lips against Duncan's neck. "No. No insults."

Sasha pressed his mouth against Duncan's, pulled away, and said, "No."

Duncan chuckled and realized just how bad he hurt—ribs aching, head throbbing, and gashes open and oozing all over. Sasha's poor mouth was scabbed at the corners from the gag, and one of his eyes was dark and swollen. The ropes had torn his beautiful, deep-gold skin and the cut on his leg still bled. It would become infected without cleaning, and Yarrow looked like he needed a week of sleep. Duncan helped him to stand while Sasha dressed, and together, holding onto one another to stay on their feet, they made their way out of the cavern and toward that month in the bedchamber Duncan had promised them and himself. Goddesses help anyone who dared interrupt it.

Chapter Twenty-Seven

AS GARITH watched the late-day light on Sander's hair, he tried to pretend his feelings for his personal guard were his greatest concern. In truth, he'd spent the past week and a half listening to everything from gentle advice to impassioned tirades from his nobles and advisors. None of it had brought him any closer to resolving the conflict between Duncan Purefroy and Mauritius Damasca, and he knew a great deal hinged on his decision. He replayed those conversations over and over in his mind, but he didn't know what to do.

A soft touch on his shoulder startled Garith out of his ruminations, and he realized just how long he'd been staring at nothing. He rubbed his eyes and stretched his stiff legs out straight beneath the table. Sander moved his hand up to the back of Garith's neck and gave the tense muscles a squeeze. "You look so far away, my king. So tired. Like you're holding the entire world on your back. Please, tell me there's something I can do."

Just the sound of Sander's voice, the genuine concern in his tone, drained much of Garith's anxiety away. He smiled despite all his concerns. Right now, he and Sander were alone in his study, with the warm, early-autumn sun shining in golden shafts through the leaded glass. Sander's cheeks glowed rosy, and his blue-green eyes looked right into Garith's heart, at all the tangled emotions, doubts, and unworthiness. Still, he loved Garith; Garith couldn't mistake what he saw in his friend's face.

"Just sit here with me, Sander. Let me just look at you and forget all of this nonsense for a few blessed moments."

Sander smiled, his sumptuous pink lips stretched smooth. "If merely watching me takes your mind off your troubles, I'm happy to sit with you."

"You know it does," Garith said, aware he was saying too much, uttering words he'd never be able to take back, but unable to stop himself.

He'd held it all in for what felt like so long; now, it poured out like the waters of the spring thaw rushing down the mountainside. "When I look at you, I can't think of anything else. It's like staring at the sun. You fill my entire universe."

"My king—"

Garith shook his head and traced his fingertips down Sander's face. His skin was flushed and smooth, with a line of rough stubble following Sander's jawbone. The texture of his emerging whiskers fascinated Garith. "You're so beautiful. So damned desirable to me."

"Garith, no good can come of this."

"I don't care. I have to say it to you anyway. I need you to know."

Sander nipped at his lower lip, and it almost destroyed Garith to watch Sander's teeth denting his pink, puffy flesh. Sander's serious gaze held Garith transfixed as the royal guard spoke. "You think I don't know? That I don't fight the same unnatural feelings every time I'm in the same room with you?"

Garith leaned across the table. His lips were only a few inches from Sander's now, but it felt like miles he could never cross. He clasped Sander's forearm with his free hand. "It doesn't feel unnatural. It feels right, you… us…."

Sander shook his head. "The goddesses say—"

The door creaked softly as Queen Cothryn entered the cozy little room. Garith and Sander sprang away from each other, turning their heads as to not even make eye contact.

"I would speak with you, Your Majesty," the queen said, resting a delicate, rosy hand on the tabletop.

Sander stood and bowed, quick to clap his hands over his groin. He backed out of the room, leaving Garith feeling awful in ways he couldn't articulate. His wife took the seat Sander had just vacated, arranging her pale golden and ivory skirts carefully as she sat down. Then she reached across the table and stroked Garith's fingers. "You're so troubled, my king."

"Yes." Somehow, it hurt Garith when Sander addressed him by that formal title, but not when he heard it from his queen's lips. She rarely called him by his name even in their most intimate moments. "I have a great deal on my mind, and my decisions could affect two kingdoms and thousands of people."

"But that isn't everything," she observed, focusing her soft brown eyes on her husband. "May I be frank?"

"Always."

"The way you feel about Sander is clear to me, my king."

"You…. What?" Garith cast around desperately for some excuse, some plausible explanation.

Queen Cothryn smiled. "There's no need for denial, Your Majesty. I came to tell you to do what your heart compels you to do. I'm not threatened by what you feel for your guard. The love between us is strong enough to weather a dalliance, is it not?"

"I do love you," Garith said. "I could not wish for a better queen, but anything between Sander and me would be more than a dalliance."

"You love him," she said.

"I have never done anything unnatural or violated the sanctity of our union," he protested.

"There's no need to be defensive, Your Majesty. I have never doubted your honor, but I want you to know that I, as your loyal wife, want only your happiness."

"What are you saying?"

"Garith, don't make me spell this out. Take what I'm offering. I offer it because I truly care about you. Your association with the knight won't prevent us from having a long, happy marriage and many more children. I know you need this, my king, so say nothing further. Anything you do from this point on is with my permission. Now, on to far more important matters. Have you decided how you'll resolve the conflict between Windwake and Foghollow?"

He shook his head and squeezed her hand tighter. Of all his advisors, Queen Cothryn and his mother were the shrewdest and the best able to see a situation from all sides, as well as understand all the possible implications and consequences. Garith was glad for her counsel. "I am open to suggestions. Duncan has been a very loyal vassal to me, and I owe him a great deal, as you know. But I cannot show favoritism, or I'll have all the nobles of Gaeltheon against me. There are already whispered accusations that I treat my countrymen better than yours, though I've endeavored to be equal in all things from the beginning. The men and resources I've committed to securing my cousin's South Coast valenny are a mark against me in many men's books, despite the fact that the reason for the union of our nations was to reclaim that territory. I'm sorry to say my mother's Esperon heritage is held against us at times. I've heard some resent that we gave our daughter an Esperon name."

"These are the arguments of men clutching at straws, my king," Queen Cothryn said. "For them to reach to these lengths means they can find no actual fault with you. And who could? You are a fine man and the best king this land could wish for."

"I don't know if I can prove that, my love."

"Of course you can," Queen Cothryn said. "Here is what you must do. Make a small show of catering to Damasca. It will require at least a mock punishment of the bairn of Windwake. I think your friend Duncan will understand that you must do it."

"I'm not so sure," Garith said. "The one Damasca wants to see punished is the man known as Sasha. What do you know of him?"

The queen met his gaze evenly and without judgment. "Enough. I know he has worked for our household as well as Windwake. I am no mere ornament at this court, my king. I am in a unique position to listen and observe, as important men see no threat in a woman. I am of so little consequence to them that they don't even bother to lower their voices when sharing secrets in my presence. They don't realize it, but they give me a great advantage, and one I can pass along to you. Thus, I know that this Sasha creature could cause us a great deal of damage if he doesn't receive our support. He cannot be backed into a corner and forced to reveal what he's done for us."

"How will I avoid that? How can I defend what he's done without showing him favor over Damasca?"

She chuckled. "Simple, Your Majesty. It would be completely unreasonable for you to make any decision in regards to this man's activities without a proper investigation. A very thorough and lengthy investigation. And if this inquiry were performed by a rather inept knight…. Not that I presume to tell you how to conduct yourself, my king."

"No," Garith hurried to say. "I'm so grateful for your counsel. I need direction, and I don't want to have to puzzle this all out on my own. I thank the goddesses for you, my queen. You're cleverer than I am."

"Certainly not," she said, though she looked quite pleased. "Now, I should see to our daughter, and you should speak with Windwake and his companions. They arrived about an hour ago, and Damasca is still en route. I'll stop by the kitchens and make sure everything is in readiness for tonight's feast, and I will see you at dinner. What does your cousin Yarroway like to eat?"

"Cakes and biscuits," Garith said, finally smiling. "The sweeter, the better. Oh, and enough wine for three men."

"I'll see to it," the queen said, eyes twinkling. "That mage is more valuable to us and our future than you have any idea, and we should keep him happy."

Both of them stood, and they kissed each other's cheeks. Queen Cothryn curtsied before leaving the study, and Garith smoothed his red velvet tunic before seeking his cousin, Windwake, and Sasha. He found them together in the guest chamber assigned to Bairn Duncan. When he entered the room, Duncan crossed his right arm over his chest and bent at the waist, while Yarrow almost bowled Garith over when he ran toward him and dove into an embrace. Garith shook his head at the sight of his cousin. Of course, the permanent Emiri paint still meandered down Yarrow's cheek and neck, and now he seemed to have adopted the pirate peoples' hairstyle as well. White ropes studded with clay beads, bits of colored glass, and seashells hung almost to his waist. At least the mage's attire, a clean black shift and trousers with a long, cobalt tunic over top, made some attempt at civility. In contrast, the assassin, Sasha, barely hid his red leather armor beneath a worn cloak. Sasha acknowledged the king's presence with a miniscule nod. Garith sat down on a wooden bench beside the window. "It's good to see you well, my friends. Welcome to my home."

"That's not what you're here to say," Yarrow observed, perching on the edge of the large bed. "Go on, Garith."

"Goddesses, show some respect to your king," Duncan muttered.

Yarrow laughed. "He knows I love him well. After all, we've known each other since we were still pissing our pants and throwing up our wine. Tell him, Garith. Remember how we used to sneak into the cellars at your father's castle to get drunk and pleasure ourselves?"

Though he flushed, Garith was glad his cousin's crude account had broken through the tension. He had no desire for a formal meeting; he needed to speak frankly with men who trusted and understood him. "I suppose so, Yarrow, though you always held your wine better than me."

"I'll wager I still do," Yarrow said. "As for the other part.... So, I'm told congratulations are in order, cousin. It seems you have graduated from your left hand to far better things. Your wife bore a daughter recently?"

Garith couldn't help smiling at the thought of his beautiful baby girl. "Quite right. Her name is Denna Borea, and she's the most beautiful thing. I can't wait for you to see her."

"A mage?" Yarrow asked.

"It's too early to know for sure, but my mother doesn't think so," Garith said, a little bitterly. He knew how it felt to grow up under the shadow of his mother's disappointment that he showed no arcane ability. He had no intention of letting his daughter feel inferior if she didn't manifest the gift. "So what?"

"I just wondered," Yarrow said, clasping Garith's hand. "Anyway, well done. I bet being a father will suit you well."

"I hope so," Garith responded. "It sometimes feels almost as weighty a responsibility as ruling a kingdom. But I need to speak to all of you of different matters."

"Which are?" Duncan asked, finally rising.

Garith raked his fingers through his hair. "This alliance I find myself ruling over is precarious, at best. Both Selindria and Gaeltheon accuse me of favoritism. Any decision I make between you, Bairn Duncan, and Vairden Damasca will be scrutinized. If I don't do something to reprimand your use of an assassin, I'll be accused of showing you preference, and thus evoking the wrath of my Gaeltheon nobles. This Blessed Epoch, as the historians are prematurely naming it, could be little more than a Blessed Decade, maybe less. Forces on both sides seem determined to destroy it before it can even begin. All we hope to accomplish could come to nothing."

"What are you saying, Your Majesty?" Duncan asked.

"I must formally reprimand you," Garith said. "Nothing else will satisfy Damasca. I just want you to be prepared for it. I owe you a great deal, Duncan, and this is something I would rather not do. But if I don't want this alliance to dissolve, I must."

"I will not see Sasha bear the brunt of this," Duncan announced, inviting no argument.

"This political nonsense means nothing to me," Yarrow agreed. "Sasha does. Choose your course carefully, cousin."

"I have," Garith said. "I owe Sasha much, and I've conceived of a way to spare him. But I must level some penance against Windwake. Duncan, you must marry one of Launa Ortean's daughters."

"Out of the question!" Duncan said.

"No," Garith said. "This is the only way to assuage them. Windwake can hardly afford to pay restitutions, and besides, people are already talking about you remaining a bachelor. This must be done, and the ceremony will be held before you leave Meritage."

"I will renounce my lands and title," Duncan said.

Garith arched a brow. "And leave your people to the mercy of a less virtuous ruler? And leave your assassin without your title to hide behind? Without you, he's worse than a common criminal."

"Do it," Sasha urged. "You owe them nothing more. And I can take care of myself. I'm more than eager to prove it, little prince," he continued, turning to focus his unwavering gaze on Garith. "Don't forget that because of me you still draw breath."

"But I do owe my subjects," Duncan said, collapsing on the bed next to Yarrow. "Those poor people have no one but me to speak on their behalf. No one else will stand up for them."

"Duncan, it's your life!" Yarrow shouted. "I hate this political nonsense, and I won't let you fall prey to it. Renounce it! We'll still have my valenny. We'll go there and live however we wish. I've had it with this! We'll choose our own path, and if my esteemed cousin doesn't like it, I will split with his kingdom and form one of my own, and it will be the greatest nation this world has ever seen. Watch me, Garith!"

"I cannot abandon all those people," Duncan said in a shattered voice, shuddering at Yarrow's newfound imperialist tendencies. "But I would rather pay gold than marry one of those women."

"You don't have the gold to spare," Garith said, hating to break Duncan's rosy illusion with cold truth. "And you must marry eventually. Better sooner than later. I… I understand your reluctance, better than you know, but it is time."

"I have gold," Sasha said. "Plenty. Most of it came from your own treasury."

"And you don't think the appearance of such a sum out of nowhere would be suspicious?" Garith asked.

Sasha shrugged. "What do I care? If someone wants to know where I got it, maybe I'll just tell them."

"You dare to threaten me?" Garith raised his voice and balled his fists.

Sasha gave no outward sign of emotion or distress. "Why not? I owe you nothing."

"Enough of this," Duncan pleaded.

Garith sighed deeply, feeling at least ten years older than he had at this time last year. "Duncan, if you wish to run off and live as an outlaw and a vagrant with my cousin and your assassin, I cannot stop you. But if you want to keep your title, or any title at all in this kingdom, you must do as I ask. I did not come to this decision lightly. How long do you expect to be allowed to rule once people begin outwardly accusing you of unnatural acts? Besides, making you family is the only way I can assure Damasca and his witch of a sister won't act against you. Not even those two would sink so low as to sabotage a kinsman. Windwake, please."

"Yes, Your Majesty."

Poor Duncan sounded like he'd just agreed to his own execution, and Garith felt awful. But he had no choice. "Very well. We shall have a feast tonight. Tomorrow, we'll have a meeting with Damasca followed by a wedding. I—we appreciate your cooperation. This union will further strengthen the ties between Selindria and Gaeltheon." He stood and turned to leave the chamber before any of them could protest further. Why should any of them have to sacrifice less than he did? "I certainly don't expect any harm to come to Windwake's new bride," he added as he left the room. "I will know exactly where to look if it does, and I will not excuse another murder. I expect to see offspring, and plenty of them. A son to inherit the bairny, at the very least."

Men married women and had children. It was the way of the world, and life continued because of it. Garith couldn't change that, and he truly hoped Duncan might find his wife as valuable a partner as he'd found his queen. Maybe Duncan would even find some happiness with her, though Duncan's feelings for Garith's cousin and the assassin Sasha were painfully obvious. Still, he had found a way to balance his longing for Sander and what the world expected of him, and Duncan would just have to do the same. Goddesses willing, everything would work out for the best and Duncan would enjoy being a father as much as he did. Garith consoled himself with that thought as he moved from Duncan's room and into the hallway.

DUNCAN waited for the feast to conclude. It seemed to stretch on for days and days, with the nobles prattling on about nothing, kissing each other's backsides and offering empty compliments to the king. What a load of mule dung. Duncan pushed his uneaten root vegetables through the gravy with his knife, trying to disguise his boredom and disgust. His betrothal to Aurauna of Windwake had been announced before the meal, and it had stolen his appetite. How in the goddesses' names would he trick his body into performing? Duncan's guts twisted into knots every time he looked up and saw the girl watching him.

Across the table from him, Yarrow looked ready to vomit as he ground the point of his knife into the wood of the table, digging out chunks of it, which accumulated next to his untouched food. His eyes flared brightly in the firelit room. Only Sasha seemed unaffected, and that worried Duncan most of all. Sasha roamed his black gaze around the hall, studying every face in turn. Now and then his gaze rested on Duncan, but if he tried to communicate something, Duncan had no idea what it could be. He didn't dare contemplate what his unpredictable friends could be planning.

Finally the king announced he would retire for the evening and left with the queen. Slowly, the rest of the guests began to file out, though Duncan's betrothed lingered, still watching him. Eventually Yarrow stood and faced her. "Is there something me or my companions can do for you, girl?"

The smile dropped from her face as if he'd slapped her, and she gathered up her skirts to hurry from the room, her mother and sisters following close behind, all of them shooting Yarrow glares over their shoulders.

Duncan rubbed his forehead. "That was probably unnecessary."

Yarrow dismissed the idea with a flick of his hand. "I was weary of looking at her stupid mouth hanging open like a cow's."

Duncan squeezed the wiry muscles of Yarrow's arm. If he'd learned one thing about Yarrow, he knew the mage lashed out when he was hurting, just as Sasha retreated inward. He hated that he'd caused the men he loved pain, but he couldn't blame Aurauna. "None of this is the girl's fault, my love. She's actually a rather nice young woman."

"Duncan, you can't go through with this," Yarrow said.

"I can hardly get out of it now," Duncan said. "It's been announced. How could I possibly explain declining?"

"I don't care!" Yarrow practically shouted. "I didn't lay with Sai when he slept naked beside me night after night because I knew you wouldn't want me to, and I don't want you marrying that dull, pudgy wench!"

All Duncan heard of Yarrow's tirade was the part about Sai. "You… you didn't?"

"No," Yarrow said miserably. "I refrained—and it was far from easy—because I thought it would hurt you. This hurts me!" In typical fashion, Yarrow responded to the pain with anger.

"It's hardly the same thing, friend," Sasha said. "This is a political matter, a marriage of convenience. As soon as Duncan produces a son to inherit the bairny, he can get rid of the girl. Oh, don't look at me like that, my knight! I promised not to kill her. I'll simply seduce her and arrange for a witness. Then you can dissolve the marriage."

"You can't," Duncan said, still sometimes stunned by Sasha's lack of concern for his fellow human beings.

"Oh?" the assassin asked. "I assure you I could go to her room this evening and accomplish it."

"That isn't what I mean. I mean to say, you can't just ruin her life for our convenience. She's innocent in this. Will you never understand?"

"I don't think I will," Sasha said. "I suppose one day you'll wake up and decide you can't tolerate me anymore. As much as I dread that moment, I expect it."

"Sasha, no—"

Yarrow swung his arm and a whip of arcane energy knocked the contents of the table to the floor. Crockery shattered, stew splashed, and knives pinged against the stone. A pair of hounds yelped and retreated into a darkened corner. Before he spoke, Yarrow yanked at his gnarled tresses and a primal scream tore out of his throat. "To the Shades' Abode with this backward world! It needs scrapped and started over! Tell me why I shouldn't raze this place to nothing and kill anyone who stands in my way! I have the power to make them all kneel at my feet, and yet I let them push and prod me into what they want. Why?"

Duncan hurried to his feet and grasped Yarrow's shoulders. "Just because you can do something doesn't mean you should. You are not a monster."

"Maybe I am. Maybe I don't want to deny it anymore. Maybe I'm ready to take what I want and destroy those standing in my way. The rest of the world does no different."

"Friends, we should move this conversation somewhere more secluded," Sasha said, jutting his chin toward the cluster of servants huddled in the hall beside the large hearth.

Duncan nodded, and the three of them hurried out of the hall and to the ridiculously sumptuous room Garith had provided him. Once inside, Duncan barred the door so they wouldn't be disturbed.

Yarrow wandered over to the spear-shaped window and looked out over the river at the base of the hill. "Let's just go," he said in a small, brittle voice like the first, thin coating of winter ice sparkling on the still-living leaves.

Duncan touched his shoulder lightly, because he was like that delicate frost, the smallest bit of pressure could shatter his mage. Goddesses, he was so powerful but so fragile. "Where do you want to go, my beautiful boy?"

"Just… away. Away traveling. I don't think I've ever been so happy as I was those nights on the road, shivering between you two. I want it to just be us again. To the Shades' with the rest of the world." Yarrow relaxed back against Duncan, giving Duncan unspoken permission to hold him, and Duncan wrapped his arms around his waist and buried his face in Yarrow's hair.

Sasha stood in front of them and put one of his hands on each of their faces. "I'll go with you. I think that's a marvelous idea. I don't belong in this world. I don't think any of us do."

"I do," Duncan protested feebly, but Sasha shook his head.

"You're too pure for it," he argued. "You keep trying to do some good, but you might as well try leveling a mountain with a kitchen knife. A single, virtuous man cannot negate centuries of corruption."

"So I should just stop trying?" Duncan asked. "Just let it continue as it has been, let people keep getting ground up and spit out by the greedy and unscrupulous? I don't think I can do that."

"To make a difference, you have to beat them at their own game," Sasha continued, wriggling his fingers into Duncan's whiskers. "You can't hope to prevail unless you sink to their level."

"I can't do that either," he said, "and I refuse to believe it's necessary. Goddesses, it's so strange being back at this estate. This is where you left us, Yarrow, and now we've come full circle, but nothing feels complete or concluded. I always imagined that us coming back together would herald in some calm period in our lives, because I felt like it was the most important thing in my life and when I accomplished it, everything would be warm and rosy. I felt like this Blessed Epoch might make things better, but nothing has changed or improved. Now I'm rambling. I suppose all I need to say is I still have a duty, and it isn't simply some excuse I fall back on, but a calling I truly feel. I have to marry that girl, and I have to protect the people of Windwake. Where does this leave us?" He couldn't even breathe as he waited for them to answer.

"If you want to do some good, why don't we return to that savage land and fight to free the Emiri suffering there?" Yarrow asked. "Not a night has passed that I haven't felt we did wrong by abandoning them. If you truly want to improve the world, we can start there. We can fight together and no one will need to know how we spend our evenings."

"I must ensure the safety of my own people first," Duncan said. "But I agree with you. The memories of that awful place plague me too, but to attack it could drag Selindria and Gaeltheon into a war."

"I'll stand with you," Sasha said without any hesitation. "In any way you need. For as long as you'll allow me."

"So will I," Yarrow agreed. "But we need to get a few things sorted out."

"Like what?" Duncan asked, warm relief flowing through his veins, melting the ice and making his limbs feel mobile again.

Yarrow spun in his arms and rested his hands above Duncan's hips. His eyes shone brightly. "I can accept, reluctantly, that in order to harvest a crop you'll need to plow the field. But other than your"—he curled his lips as he said the word—"*wife*, it will just be us, yes? Me, you, and Sasha?"

"Of course," Duncan said, pulling Yarrow against him with his splinted and bandaged arm while he opened the other to embrace Sasha. "I have never wanted more. I solemnly pledge myself to both of you. Laugh if you want, but you are my only loves."

Neither of them laughed.

"Sasha, do you feel the same?" Yarrow asked.

"Unless my work necessitates it, I'm all yours," their assassin answered in his velvet drawl. "Though it's hard to believe I'm promising this to the same man who was so worried about me attaching strings back in the order hideout a year ago."

"The same, and not the same," Yarrow answered.

"I'm happy to swear this to you," Sasha said.

"I also swear," Yarrow told them. "I pledge my body and soul to both of you, if you'll accept me as I am now."

"I will," Sasha said, stretching to kiss Yarrow softly.

"I will," Duncan swore as he leaned in, tasting Sasha on Yarrow's lips and feeling like something profound had just transpired between them, that things would never be as they were before.

"I will," Yarrow said, completing their impromptu ritual.

All three of them pressed their faces close, opening their mouths and letting their tongues meet in a wet, sloppy tangle. As they nibbled and slurped, their hands found their way to each other's shirttails and doublet lacings. Slowly, clothing began to pile on the floor until all of them stood in nothing but trousers, underpants, and boots. Duncan reached out and trailed his fingertips along the blue paint winding down Yarrow's side. Yarrow shuddered and rocked his hips against Duncan, and his reaction made Sasha do the same. In minutes, all of them clung to each other, exchanging messy kisses as they rubbed their erections together.

Duncan pulled away and bent to remove his boots. He felt like he had two left hands as he fumbled to pull them off and strip his trousers away, and the bulky dressings on his broken wrist certainly didn't make things easier. As soon as he managed to undress, his hard cock sprang out and smacked him in the belly. Sasha and Yarrow watched him, their arms around each other and their pelvises circling against each other. Both of their cheeks were dark, and their lips were swollen.

"Goddesses, you are both so damned beautiful," Duncan panted, kneeling down to tug off Sasha's boots and kiss along the top of a smooth, golden foot and over the knob of an anklebone. He unbuckled Sasha's armor and peeled it down to reveal his satiny skin. As soon as he saw it, Duncan pressed his mouth against the V of muscle angling down to Sasha's groin. He ran his tongue up over the ledge of taut flesh, and back down into the hot, sweaty crevice between Sasha's leg and the base of his body. As he did, Sasha pulled at Yarrow's crisp, new trousers and succeeded in working them down to his knees. Duncan did the rest, tugging Yarrow's boots off and dragging his trousers to his ankles, where he stepped out of them.

Naked, they collided against each other, and Duncan barely managed to steer them toward the bed and prevent them collapsing on the floor, not that he would have been opposed to the floor, or anywhere else. The few feet they had to cross felt like miles. Sasha and Yarrow moved their eager mouths along Duncan's neck and chest as they groped fervently at his belly, ass, thighs, and crotch. When they finally reached the large mattress, Duncan fell onto it and Sasha and Yarrow sprawled on top of him. Duncan wrapped his arms around their slender bodies as they all rutted against each other.

Sasha squirmed free of the chaotic knot they'd formed and moved up to align his erection with Duncan's lips. Duncan willingly parted them to suck Sasha's delectable erection into his mouth as he dented the flesh above Sasha's hip with his fingers. He wriggled his tongue inside Sasha's hood and drove it back as Yarrow dragged his lips down Duncan's ribs. Yarrow lapped at the underside of Duncan's swollen crown for a few minutes before he positioned himself between Duncan's legs.

"Oil?" the mage asked in a raspy voice that drove Duncan wild. Sasha got up long enough to rummage through his pack, and then he was back on Duncan's chest, his erection commanding attention as he pressed the small vial into Yarrow's hand.

"Duncan, I love you…. I want to be inside you," Yarrow said as he rubbed the lubricant up the length of his impressive erection, pausing only to nip across Sasha's shoulders and back. "Can I fuck you?"

Duncan spread his legs as wide as he could. "Goddesses, I've missed that big cock of yours, my lovely lad. Give it here."

"You asked for it," Yarrow said, lining himself up with Duncan's opening and pushing inside.

Sasha, who'd been rubbing his dick against Duncan's chin, circled the head against Duncan's lips as Yarrow entered him. Duncan opened his mouth to accept Sasha as he relaxed his muscles to let Yarrow into him. Both of them stretched him to the limits of his endurance, and he loved every second of it. He never wanted it to end. Duncan wrapped his legs around Yarrow's waist while he clutched at Sasha's lower back, urging him forth. He wanted, needed, both of them to let go, to pursue their pleasure in his willing body. Being filled with the bodies of the men he loved was wonderful, and Duncan just wanted them to fulfill themselves. He wanted to be the one making these men happy, tonight and for as long as he could hold onto them. He looked up at Sasha's neck, stretched to reach behind himself and kiss Yarrow. If he'd ever thought Sasha cold, a man who veiled his feelings, he couldn't remember it, watching him now. Duncan pressed into Sasha's skin with his nails and dragged them down his back, over his hips, and across his slender thighs. Words in that archaic language rained from Sasha's lips.

To Duncan's surprise, Sasha pulled out of his mouth and bent down to kiss him before turning around and straddling Duncan's face again. That was more than fine with Duncan; he loved to touch and taste Sasha, to wriggle his tongue into his tight flesh. Before Duncan did, he took a moment to admire the firelight on the lithe muscles of Sasha's back and to relish the sensation of Yarrow moving inside him, hitting just the right place with every stroke. Then Duncan cupped the crescents of Sasha's ass and eased them apart so he could run his tongue along Sasha's cleft and around his wrinkled little opening.

"Oh my sweet god," Sasha moaned as he fell forward and caught himself on his hands. Yarrow bucked inside Duncan as he caught Sasha by the shoulder and kissed him hard. At the same time Duncan plunged the tip of his tongue into Sasha, Sasha broke away from Yarrow and bent down. Sasha's tongue felt so amazing skimming up Duncan's shaft that Duncan almost lost himself. He took a few deep breaths to pull himself back from the edge he teetered on.

As if they sensed his imminent release, both Yarrow and Sasha slowed their movements. Yarrow stroked Duncan's hip while Sasha planted light pecks around the base of his erection and inhaled the scent of Duncan's thick curls. In the meantime, Duncan moved his hands up the taut, tantalizing muscles of Sasha's torso. Feeling them just aroused him more, and he gave in, thrusting up toward Sasha's mouth and encouraging Yarrow.

They all gave in, their love and physical needs compelling them to move against each other faster and more desperately. The obscene sounds Duncan and Sasha made as they sucked and lapped at each other filled the room, and Yarrow's skin slapped against Duncan's as his thrusts grew irregular. He braided his fingers into Duncan's above Sasha's hipbone.

"I love you both so much," Yarrow choked out. "I…. Oh goddesses! I can't believe I'm feeling this. I—" His release stole anything else he'd planned to say, and he pressed his forehead against Sasha's back as he trembled and spilled into Duncan, whimpering and shaking with the enormity of it.

With one final thrust up into Sasha's sweet, swollen, hot mouth, Duncan followed Yarrow over the edge. After a few moments of somersaulting through an oblivion where nothing existed by pure pleasure, Duncan came back to himself enough to reach around Sasha, grasp his erection, and stroke him as he drove his tongue into Sasha's delicious little hole. It gripped his tongue in rhythmic pulses as Sasha's seed erupted into his hand. Residual tremors of bliss moved through Duncan, echoing the waves wracking Sasha and Yarrow's bodies. Finally, they separated and cuddled up to kiss, tasting each other on their lips, and then melted against each other in satisfied contentment. To Duncan, feeling Sasha and Yarrow sated and secure atop him was almost as sweet as the passion they'd shared. As much as he wanted to fulfill their desires, he always wanted them to feel safe and accepted in his arms.

"My two beautiful loves," he murmured, stroking the backs of their heads as they nuzzled against his chest and kissed each other leisurely. "I don't know what I ever did to deserve the goddesses blessing me with you both. This is everything to me."

"Always," Yarrow whispered, his eyes fluttering shut as he went still. Duncan reached down and pulled the blankets over the three of them. Soon, it grew warm enough within the covers to lull Duncan into drowsiness. As dreams eclipsed reality and all its worries, he recalled the nights on the road Yarrow had mentioned, because, for the first time since then, nothing seemed to exist beyond the three of them holding onto each other while the rest of the world burned to ash or froze to brittle splinters. In spite of everything he knew tomorrow would bring, the irrevocable changes it would impose upon his life, Duncan slept more deeply and peacefully than he had since the innocence of his childhood.

In the morning, he'd swear marriage vows to a woman he barely knew, but it didn't matter. It wasn't real, just a political maneuvering he'd been forced into. What he'd said to and shared with Sasha and Yarrow expressed his true feelings, and he fell asleep assured they all knew it.

Chapter Twenty-Eight

YARROW felt cold and hollow the next morning as the servants prepared the Meritage estate for Duncan's wedding. He didn't trust himself to attend the ceremony; he feared his disgust at all of it might overcome him and he'd hurt someone. Damn it all, they deserved to see what he could do when one of the very few things he valued was threatened, but Duncan wouldn't want that, so he decided to stay away. For weeks now, he'd hoped for a message from Corbin, something Duncan wouldn't be able to ignore, but nothing had come. Even now, when time had already run out, he racked his mind for a compelling reason for Duncan to abandon this farce.

Yarrow spent his day in the estate's chilly courtyards, among the falling leaves and withering shrubberies. Dead foliage rattled across his boots as he sat on a stone bench, remembering both beautiful lovemaking and older images of tearing through dozens of people with his bright blue claws. He felt a measure of guilt as he recalled the faces of dying innocents, but mostly it made him feel powerful—a person—a *thing*—not to be trifled with. He liked that feeling of immunity from pain, liked being above the mundane worries of others.

Leaves rustled under Duncan's boots as he cut a path through them. Yarrow clutched his dark cloak closer around him. "Windwake?"

"Yarrow, don't."

"Don't you have a wedding or some other foolishness to attend?"

"I wanted to make sure you were all right," Duncan said, reaching out for Yarrow but then letting his hand fall.

"Do you suppose I'm frail enough to just drop dead from melancholy?" Yarrow snapped, his voice echoing across the empty terrace. Duncan flinched at his outburst, and Yarrow forced out a breath to dispel his anger. It wasn't even anger, not really. Anger was just the only way he knew to express the feelings shredding him up inside. Even so, he couldn't bring himself to apologize to his partner. "Thank you for your concern, but I'll be fine. I-I think I'd like to be alone."

"I'll honor your request, even if I don't believe it for a second. Just promise me you'll go and find Sasha if you need someone. Don't sit out here and suffer by yourself." Duncan smoothed down Yarrow's hair and rested his rough palm on Yarrow's cheek for a few seconds.

Yarrow didn't trust himself to answer, and he just nodded in response. Duncan kissed him on the top of the head before turning to wade through the crisp autumn leaves. As he watched Duncan walk away in his wedding clothes, an embellished emerald doublet, snug, rich brown leggings, and fancy knee-high boots, Yarrow wished he could think of something to say to his dear friend. Since he couldn't find those words, he just slid his dark hood over his head.

The day was gradually growing warmer, and shafts of golden light broke through the sheet of dark, blue-gray clouds that just made the warm fall leaves and flowers look more vibrant against them. No young woman could hope for a more perfect wedding day. Though he knew he was being a petulant child, Yarrow wasn't willing to let her have that. Sensing a storm building just down the river, he closed his eyes and concentrated on dragging the cold and chaos to Meritage. When the first frigid droplets fell, he stood to return to his room, where he remained until well after the ceremony and the feast that followed it.

Rain pattered against the window as Yarrow sat on his narrow bed, nursing his second bottle of wine. In the halls beyond his room, the sounds of celebration continued, and Yarrow resisted the urge to violently spoil their fun. In truth, he wanted to knock the castle down as if it had been built from a child's blocks. He missed his creature and the taunts they would have exchanged at everyone else's expense, the bloody fantasies they'd have shared. But when he felt for it, he found it was still there, still living in every fiber of his being and whispering in his thoughts, along with Yarrow's own now, instead of over top.

Someone knocked on the door, and Yarrow turned toward the interruption. "Go away."

Whoever it was knocked again, and Yarrow remembered sitting in this room more than a year ago, preparing to leave his companions.

Duncan had been the one knocking insistently that night. Here Yarrow was again, and so much had changed yet nothing had. His creature was gone, but rage still seethed out of him, still threatened to ruin everything he'd gained. At that moment, he felt as alone as he ever had, and he had to wonder if he deserved it. He could just imagine the cruel barbs his creature would hurl at him over his self-doubt and what it would certainly call whining. Yarrow laughed. He didn't need the presence to tell him he was being a melodramatic brat; he could mock himself just as cruelly.

The door creaked as it opened, spilling a stream of light into Yarrow's darkened room. A woman lifted her skirts as she crossed the threshold.

"I am in no mood," Yarrow hissed. "Leave me in peace or I won't be responsible for my actions."

"I'm surprised at you, little flower."

"Aunt Den?"

"We all missed you at the festivities," she said as she sat down next to him and took his hand, just the way she always had when he'd been a boy, and it still made him feel like he had at least one ally.

Still, he laughed at himself. "You might have missed me, but I'm sure not everyone did."

"Did you not feel well?" she asked. She had always looked out for Yarrow's welfare, more so than his own mother. She had been his first teacher, the first fellow mage he'd met, and also the first he'd confessed his so-called "unnatural" feelings to. Aunt Den, once queen of Selindria, had always been Yarrow's staunchest supporter.

Yarrow shook his head. "I didn't attend because I didn't want to. I won't make excuses. I won't explain myself to them. But I am glad we have the chance to talk a bit before I leave tomorrow. How have you been since the king—?"

Aunt Den looked into her lap and smiled sadly. "Many, many things shape the course of the world. We barely recognize most of them even as they happen, and we have control of so very few. Very few, but not none. When we find ourselves in one of those rare moments when we can make a mark on the future, we should seize them, don't you think?"

He met her serious, dark gaze with a cold shiver moving down his spine. "I don't know, Aunt Den. The consequences of our actions are seldom what we would have predicted."

"Seldom, but not never, little one."

"What are you asking me? We have always been honest with each other. Growing up, you were the only one I could ever trust to tell me the truth."

"Very well." She took a deep breath that made Yarrow dread her next words. "From the time I began to arrange the union between Selindria and Gaeltheon, one of my main goals has been to put a mage on the throne, to have this unrivaled empire ruled by a king with the gift. The queen and I both believe the world will benefit if we can accomplish this. But we need your help, nephew."

"Mine? What can I do?" Yarrow asked.

"Queen Cothryn is a mage," Aunt Den urged.

"And?"

"And my son Garith isn't. But you are. *You are.*"

"Oh, goddesses. You can't be serious! You would encourage your own son's wife to be unfaithful…. With me? What will the queen make of this?"

"She agrees with me," Aunt Den explained. "As for the rest of it, we just want you to pass your magical ability on to an heir. If there were some other way to do it, we would. Unfortunately, I only know of one method of conceiving children. Cothryn and I have been working for weeks to make sure she's receptive and that she'll produce a son. We just need you now."

Garith had, in a way, taken away the attention of one of the men he loved, and Yarrow couldn't help liking the idea of making his wife an adulteress without his knowledge, making him a cuckold for forcing Duncan to marry. More so, he agreed that a mage should guide the course of the world. After all, look what Fane had accomplished. Could that golden age return, with Yarrow's son standing at the helm? But what else might he pass on? Something of his creature? But most importantly—

"I don't think I can. My body won't cooperate. The queen is a beautiful woman, but… but the thought of it makes me feel ill."

Yarrow's aunt reached into a pouch and gave him a small, glass vial. "I expected as much. Drink this and go to bed. We will take care of the rest, and I doubt you'll even remember it. Yarrow, this is our one chance. This ludicrous restriction against our people, those with the gift ruling, must be lifted, and we need a strong enough heir to prove that to everyone. I believe only you can father that future king. Only you can assure a mage takes the throne. What you choose to do in the next few minutes will affect the future, maybe for the next thousand years. Please, Yarrow. Trust me as you always have. Will you help us?"

"Even if this works…. I swore myself to Duncan and Sasha. I don't want to betray them."

"I wouldn't ask you to do that. I'm not asking you to take pleasure with the queen, and I certainly don't want you to offer her love or devotion. I hate to be blunt, but this is a simple exchange of fluids, much like the bairn of Windwake is sharing with his new bride. This is a difficult world to remain idealistic in."

"Yes."

Yarrow turned the little phial over and over in his hands, watching the milky, pinkish liquid flow from one end to the other. A single moment, a single choice that could determine the fate of the world, this decision also represented another secret he'd have to keep from Sasha and Duncan. He'd never be able to admit this to them. But wouldn't seeing his son on the throne be worth it? Thinking about it only led him around and around in circles. He wished he had his creature to speak with, at least. As soon as he thought of the presence, he knew what it would advise. He wriggled the cork out of the vial and downed the potion. Warmth flowed down his throat and heated his belly, making him almost instantly content and drowsy, as well as hard and erect.

Aunt Den smiled, nodded, stood, and kissed Yarrow on the forehead. As soon as she left and closed the door, he stripped his clothing off and tumbled into bed, where he fell asleep almost instantly.

That night, as he perspired and tossed in his sheets, Yarrow's dreams shifted between memories of bloodshed and erotic flashes of twisting limbs and writhing bodies: Duncan, Sasha, Sai, Rini, Jorian, and countless others he'd merely appreciated from a distance. He awoke feeling more worn out than he had when he'd gone to sleep. All his muscles ached, as if he'd been battling for the past day or so, and his head throbbed, probably as an aftereffect of his aunt's potion. He pulled his trousers on and found the first available servant to demand hot water. After he washed and dressed, he packed his few possessions and went to meet Duncan and Sasha at the stables. This estate held too many conflicting memories for Yarrow, and he couldn't leave it soon enough. He certainly hoped to escape before he had to face his aunt or the queen.

Duncan's new wife waited in a carriage, her hands folded demurely in her lap. She looked quickly away from Yarrow, and Yarrow curled his lip. He hoped the girl knew how lucky she was, that she'd keep to herself and stay out of their way. He felt a little better when Duncan mounted a bay charger instead of joining his bride. At least they'd be able to ride together. The girl's presence meant they wouldn't be sharing a bedroll in a small tent the way Yarrow remembered so fondly. She'd probably insist on staying at inns, and expensive ones.

They rode for most of the morning in relative silence as Yarrow tried not to envision all the sweet, erotic things Duncan did to him and Sasha being done to the woman in the carriage. Duncan was so good with his mouth and tongue just imagining it gave Yarrow half an erection. At the same time, the thought of him sharing his expertise with his new bride made Yarrow want to destroy something. He knew too much of Duncan's sweet and gentle nature to delude himself into thinking Duncan would have made the wedding night unpleasant for the girl.

"Do you think we'll get to spend any time together when we get back to Windwake?" Yarrow asked his companions, shifting uncomfortably in the saddle.

"We might have to be patient, my friend," Sasha said. "Ardor usually burns out after a few months, but until then, the lady might demand her husband's attention."

"I will make time for you," Duncan said. "We'll just have to figure out the new rhythm of our life. We'll settle into it. It might be a pleasant change to have some peace for a short time."

Almost as soon as the words left Duncan's mouth, a slight young man on a skittish gray mare rode up alongside Yarrow and said, "A message for you, tam." He pressed a battered scroll into Yarrow's hand, and Yarrow guided his horse to the edge of the road to examine it.

After he broke the wax seal, he discovered nothing but a blank sheet of parchment. A slight hum moving through it numbed his fingertips. Something about it felt familiar. As Yarrow let the enchantment soak into his hand, Sasha and Duncan rode up to watch over his shoulders. It took little for him to decipher the magic and whisk it away.

"Yarrow, what's going on?" Duncan asked. "Is anything wrong?"

"We'll know soon," Yarrow answered. "I'm sure Corbin must have sent this. The echoes of his magic are familiar to me."

All of them watched as a red crescent slowly appeared at the center of the scroll. Three words were written in crimson ink beneath it:

It's time. Felgard.

Check out this excerpt from

Iron and Ether

Blessed Epoch: Book Three

By August Li

Sasha was born to, and has always defined himself by, the secret assassins' Order of the Crimson Scythe. He chose the love of Yarrow L'Estrella and Duncan Purefroy over his duty to his clan, forfeiting his last mission and allowing Prince Garith to live. Now, the order—previously Sasha's family—has branded him a traitor. He's marked, and that means the brethren of the Crimson Scythe won't stop until Sasha is dead.

Garith's twin kingdoms balance on the brink of war, and all three men have reasons to help the king, whether loyalty, duty, the interests of their own lands, or gold in their pockets. Still, Yarrow and Duncan are willing to abandon their reasons to seek out and destroy the assassins' order to keep Sasha safe. But Sasha isn't sure that's what he wants. Loyalties are strained by both foreign invaders and conspirators in their midst. It's hard to know which side to choose with threats piling up from every direction and war looming, inevitable, on the horizon. Their world teeters on the precipice of change, and Sasha, Duncan, and Yarrow can only hope the links they've forged will hold if Garith's kingdom is torn apart.

Coming Soon to

http://www.dsppublications.com

Chapter One

FIERCE wind assailed the mage as he clung to the ice-encrusted rock. It took all Yarrow's strength to hold on and keep from plummeting several hundred feet to the base of Starmont beneath him. His heavy fur-lined cloak whipped out behind him, and ice crystals stung the small strip of exposed flesh around his eyes. Black wool wraps covered the rest of his head and face, as well as his hands and feet inside his heavy leather boots and gloves. When he'd left Windust Castle two weeks ago, the first frost had yet to paint the windows of the ancient fortress, and it only grew chilly enough for a fire at night. Here, at the northernmost border of Selindria and the edge of Yarrow's familial valenny of Lockhaven, the ice never melted. Yarrow squinted against the bright white light and located a narrow ledge a few dozen feet above him. He summoned azure wings made from pure arcane energy, pushed off with his feet, and propelled himself toward it. He beat down with his wings, but they'd never allowed him to truly fly, or at least he hadn't mastered it yet, and he lost momentum just as he grasped the edge of the ridge.

Yarrow caught his breath and waited for his pulse to slow after the shock of nearly falling. Then he pulled himself up on the ledge. Slowly, mindful of the frost beneath his feet, he stood and pressed his back against the rock behind him. Estrella Lake, covered in cloudy ice, stretched for miles below him, as far as the eye could see. At the western shore, near the castle where he'd been born and grown up, the water would be chill but not yet frozen. As children, Yarrow and his brothers had waited until well past midwinter before venturing out onto the ice. Back then, he'd never thought much about Starmont, Selindria's highest peak, though he could see it in the distance from the balcony of his chambers. He'd heard that the Thirteen Goddesses lived at the mountain's pinnacle, but he'd also heard a great wyrm slept in the depths of Estrella Lake. Neither had seemed particularly significant to him; neither really affected his life, and in truth, he had never cared much for unbelievable stories. From a young age, he'd seen them as a means of inspiring fear and securing control. He'd thought himself above them, too smart to be manipulated.

Then. It seemed like a lifetime ago.

Half a year ago, he'd heard the most unbelievable story of all, and the questions and implications it dragged behind it hadn't left him alone since. Unlike the others, the tale he had heard from Hale, a former apprentice of Fane, now living in self-imposed exile, could break the cycle of doubt and manipulation. Hale had seen what really happened when Fane fell, and his version of events had been very different from those Yarrow had heard in the temples as a child. Yarrow felt like the entire world operated beneath a cloak of deception, an illusion no one could see through. It angered him to feel like he'd been duped. He would not be made a fool. Worst of all, he couldn't share his outrage with his partners, because belief in the protection and love of the Thirteen Goddesses brought so much comfort to Duncan, and Sasha's devotion to Thalil was absolute. Yarrow couldn't shatter their faith until he knew for certain he had it all right to the smallest detail. So he'd come here, to the fabled abode of the goddesses, to find out once and for all. What he'd do when he uncovered the answers to his questions, he still hadn't decided.

If Yarrow could believe everything he'd learned from Hale, and he felt he could, the goddesses who he'd been told created and protected the world had once been mortal women. After learning all they could from Fane, they grew jealous of their people's love for the emperor, turned against him, and destroyed him. Well, most of him. If, as Hale suspected, they prolonged their lives and preserved their power by drawing the magic from the world, tapping into the mystic pulse like leeches and leaving little for others with the gift, then what would Yarrow do? He knew what he wanted to do, and he knew his hunger for destruction came from his love of Fane. More accurately, the creature who had once possessed him had loved Fane, eons before the so-called goddesses had been born. Since bonding with the entity, Yarrow had a hard time sorting its memories and emotions from his own, if they could even be sorted anymore. If they were even still distinct. He would get no answers by standing here wondering, though, so he prepared to continue up the mountainside.

Yarrow found a steep, narrow pass between two vertical cliffs. Though he had to crawl on his hands and knees for several hours, it took him closer to the summit. When the path ended abruptly, Yarrow took a moment to sip wine from his flask and choke down a scrap of hard bread. Then he began searching for another way up, eventually locating a cascade of debris he could scale to reach a small plateau. He climbed until well after dark, rested for a few hours, ate more hardtack and dried fruit, and then resumed his ascent. By first light, though his palms and knees were split and bloody and his feet numb within his boots, he hoisted himself over the final ridge and reached the zenith of Starmont.

The thin air made him gasp for breath, and Yarrow pushed his wraps from his nose and mouth as he stepped onto the peak. The frigid air he inhaled stabbed his lungs like iron spikes. At its apex, Starmont was nearly flat. Jagged boulders dozens of feet high wreathed a snow-strewn clearing large enough for several castles, maybe even a small village. Yarrow thought for a moment how impressive it would be to build himself a fortress here, where he could look down on the whole kingdom, and then he turned to take in the view. His breath caught in his throat, and he wished Duncan and Sasha could be with him to witness the grandeur. To the south, even Estrella Lake looked like a small pond, icy blue and glittering in the morning light: just a puddle. To the north, nothing but glaciers and hard-packed snow reached until they curved out of sight with the culmination of the horizon. Part of Yarrow longed to explore land he knew no man had set foot upon in centuries, if ever. He wondered what, if anything, existed beyond their boundaries. He'd learned from his tutors those wastes hadn't thawed since the beginning of recorded time, but if he'd learned anything, he'd come to understand the world was much larger and stranger than anyone imagined. It held many hidden things if one was bold enough to go looking beyond what was written in the books.

Yarrow could contemplate all of that later, though. He'd come here for a purpose: to demand answers, and he didn't plan to leave until he was satisfied.

"You thirteen who call yourself goddesses!" Yarrow yelled, his clear voice echoing across the frozen wastes. "Show yourselves to me! I am Yarroway L'Estrella, and I demand your presence!"

Only the wind, high-pitched, mournful, and sounding almost sentient, answered his call. The unnaturally strong gale kicked up everything in its path and hurled it at Yarrow. Slush, ice, and small rocks battered him until he had to raise his arm to shield his face. Sheets of blowing snow veiled the world, but Yarrow would not be denied. He had suffered much worse.

"Show yourselves, unless you are cowards!" he cried, unfurling his cerulean wings and letting luminescent horns spring from his forehead, reflecting a form that now comprised half of his being. Magic poured from him like a geyser, spilling down the mountainside and shooting into the brightening sky. He knew the power would act as a beacon; no one who sensed enchantment would be able to ignore it. Likely mages as far away as Espero felt the power he unleashed. Not even Yarrow knew what exposure to so much magic might do to the world—or himself. In that moment, he felt like he could haul a castle from the bones of the mountain, and the ground beneath him rumbled at his fleeting desire. He reined it in, had to control it, especially since accessing his full strength made him crave destruction. If he didn't keep a tight hold on his power, he'd level Starmont. The possibility gave him an idea.

"I demand you appear, or I will raze your scared mound to nothing! I will tear its roots from the world and fling it into the sky! What will your faithful make of that? How dare you! I will not be ignored!"

"How dare *you*, little mage?" The answering voice came from the stone beneath Yarrow's feet, from the sky, from the lake waters, from the light on the snow, everywhere. It came out of the ether beyond the bounds of the physical world. Yarrow felt it reverberate through his bones, his guts, that illusive shadow he thought of as his spirit. He fought not to fall to his knees, cover his head, and whimper. No. Never. He knelt before no one. No one would make him kneel. Certainly not this pretender.

A massive form appeared, not only eclipsing the sun but sucking the light from the world. Yarrow tried to look at it, a vaguely female form that shifted and changed as he watched, transforming from a young maiden to a plump mother, then to a wizened crone and back, while sometimes, somehow, displaying all three forms and many others at once. The vision seared Yarrow's eyes until tears streamed down his cheeks and froze to his face, and he still couldn't focus on it directly. It was like a hole burned in reality, a woman-shaped window into the void of eternity. Power like shifting, prismatic flame shot out from its edges until Yarrow felt sure it extended to the ends of the world. It scorched the very sky, turning the clouds to steam.

Still, the mage held his ground. This creature was not superior to him, and he would not let her intimidate him, even though his every instinct told him to throw himself at her feet. Instead, he pulled his magic around him like a net, his wings still extended but ready to fold around him and shield him. "You who call yourself Mother Goddess, I have questions. I have questions, and I will have answers!"

"Who are you to demand anything of me?" The goddess's voice exploded inside Yarrow's skull even as it bombarded his senses from every direction. "You are refuse, and I am the mother and ruler of this entire world."

"That is a lie!" Yarrow shouted. Images he didn't recognize but that felt integral to his being assailed him. "You bitch. You were just a woman, Fane's wife. You learned your power from him and then you— you killed my beloved! My beloved! Do you dare deny it?"

"I owe you nothing. Insect."

"Bitch! Whore! Charlatan! This world was mine! It will be mine again. I will see its people know the truth, and I will bring you down! You and your treacherous sisters are hoarding the world's magic."

"It is our right. We are the Thirteen Goddesses."

"You are no more divine than I am!" Yarrow yelled.

The goddess laughed, and all of reality trembled. Yarrow fell and landed hard on his hip. "Pitiful creature. You have no idea what you are. You do not even know your own heart or your own mind. You are nothing but a frightened little boy. Fane was not so different. Power is much more than something to cower behind, Yarroway L'Estrella."

"I will show you my power! I have wielded it since long before your ancestors existed, since they cringed in the muck and filth like beasts." Yarrow focused his power and compacted it into an arcane spear, which he hoisted and threw into the heart of the nothingness before him. The blackness absorbed the glowing javelin, and the goddess laughed. Yarrow conjured fire, and shot gout after gout at the being, but his flames fizzled and disappeared within her. He shot bolts of lightning at her, but did no damage.

The Mother Goddess chuckled. "I'm growing bored of this, insignificant little worm." She raised her dark hand and swatted Yarrow, lifting him off his feet and sending him flying into the air and over the rocks fencing the mountain clearing. He tumbled down the mountainside, tucking into a ball as he rolled, bouncing off the rocks. He spread his wings to slow his descent and tried to cushion himself with a shell of magic, but he'd used too much power already. He landed hard on a narrow ledge, the breath knocked from his lungs. Ice and stone rained down on him, penetrating the wings he folded over his body and slicing his flesh even through the heavy garments and leather armor he wore.

The goddess stepped down to his level, even her toe towering above Yarrow. "I will crush you into the dirt, grind your bones to powder, Yarroway L'Estrella."

The being's thumb bore down on him, and Yarrow dug deep into his reserves, letting instinct guide his enchantment. He thought of Sasha, of the way the assassin lured his victims close and let them use their own momentum to drive themselves against the tips of his blades. Just as the goddess was about to smash Yarrow into the ground, he conjured a sharp spike from his back. The creature's finger met it, and the goddess pulled back, but only for a moment. It was enough for Yarrow to regain his footing. As soon as he did, he shot an array of fireballs at the Mother Goddess. As before, the behemoth absorbed the energy he directed at her.

You are a taker, beloved, Yarrow's creature had said, back when they could speak in his mind, before they'd fully melded into a single being. With a shrill, triumphant laugh, Yarrow spread his fingers. He located the many magical currents and their tributaries flowing into the dread goddess, and one by one, he dammed and redirected them, letting the energy flow into himself, taking her source of succor. Power sang and crackled through his veins until he felt like he'd burst. The goddess shrieked as she withered in front of Yarrow, and soon a plain, mousy-haired woman, chubby and unremarkable, stood before him. Yarrow raised his fist and smacked her round face, laughing as her lip split and she fell to her knees.

"I knew it," he hissed as he grabbed her hair and wrenched her head back. "Mother Goddess indeed. You are nothing but a hag hoarding the world's magic. I'll put an end to you right now. For my beloved. For Fane, the man you betrayed. To avenge him."

"You ridiculous, broken creature." Blood and foam spattered Yarrow's chest as she spoke. "You cannot even comprehend your own existence. You, the boy living in that small body, never even met the one you call beloved. Let go of me." Stinging heat radiated from the woman, scorching Yarrow's hand, his cheeks, and his eyes. His skin felt like it was melting. He staggered backward, covering his face.

"Fool," the goddess continued. "Insect. You are unnatural, and I cast you down." She regained some of her former stature, and batted Yarrow again, sending him cartwheeling down the hill. All his concentration focused on buffering his body from hitting the sharp rocks and spears of ice, any one of which could destroy his fragile flesh, if not the essence behind it.

As soon as he landed, Yarrow struck. This thing assuming the mantle of Mother Goddess was still weak. He couldn't wait. Ice, for which he'd always felt an affinity, surrounded him, and he used the element he understood so well, breaking off sharp shards and aiming them at his enemy. Soon, the goddess's blood stained the snow, and she hunched nearly buried beneath scraps of the frozen mountain. Still, she laughed at Yarrow.

"You think you're so clever." With a burst of enchantment, she freed herself and sent Yarrow catapulting again. This time, he came to a stop beyond the foothills, almost at the edge of the lake. "You think you understand this world of mine. Let's see if you expected this. Let's see what you'll do now, fragile little flower. Let's see if you can do anything but die."

"You cannot kill me!" Yarrow yelled.

The frozen surface of the lake shattered, thick chunks of ice flying in every direction. The strength of the eruption forced Yarrow's back against the nearest boulder. Frothy water shot from the fissures as something from deep within the lake began to emerge. A talon, old, yellowed, and easily the size of a battering ram breached the surface. Three more claws soon emerged, scarring the stone as the beast dragged itself from the frigid water.

Yarrow spread his wings and drifted onto a boulder as waves of lake water struck the mountainside and froze almost upon impact, leaving jagged, prismatic walls in its wake. Slowly, the head of an enormous creature emerged from the frozen depths. Each of its opalescent scales was as large as a soldier's shield, and its long, narrow head was three times the mage's height. A white eyelid drew back to reveal a yellow iris the size of a temple window, and icicles the size of buttresses hung from the wyrm's bearded jaw. With its huge claws, it heaved itself onto the shore. Yarrow erected a barrier between himself and the mythical beast as the Mother Goddess's laughter echoed around them. He turned to seek her, but she'd already faded away. The wyrm opened its maw and released a great roar reeking of fishy decay, making Yarrow forget the woman as he turned to face it.

The creature's slender, shimmering body extended for probably a half a mile before disappearing beneath the churning waters of the lake. It raised a claw and swiped. Yarrow dove out of the way just in time, but the wyrm's claws cut deep furrows in the rock and sent it showering down, shards battering and slicing the mage's flesh. Its cry of rage made his stomach and organs feel liquefied, and he fought the irrational fear it inspired in him, fought to keep his stomach and bowels from expelling everything they held. He needed fire, and summoned his waning energy to conjure flame from his fingertips. When he waved his burning hand at the creature, it tucked its huge head back against its shoulder. His incantation didn't prevent it from flailing, though, and one of its ice-encrusted whiskers struck his legs and knocked him off his feet. He landed hard, a cloud of snow billowing around him and his fire choking out. The wyrm lifted itself farther from the water, raining cold droplets down on the mage as it regarded him, mouth open to reveal teeth the length of swords. Its rancid breath enveloped Yarrow in huge clouds of mist.

It bit down, and Yarrow's wings closed over him, saving his body from the teeth but not sparing him the impact. He sank deeper into the hoarfrost, and it folded over him like a shroud. For a moment, snow and earth covered his face and stole his vision. He wiped it away and forced himself up on his elbows, digging his way out frantically. Then he gripped the edges of the shallow little tomb and pulled himself up, staggering back onto his feet and facing the beast. He spread his wings and lifted off the frozen ground. The creature swatted at him, and Yarrow dodged to the side, narrowly avoiding its claws. He transformed his wings from sapphire mystic energy to true orange flame. As he extended them, his clothing smoked and his skin blistered, but the wyrm retreated a few feet into the cold water. Yarrow's eyes watered at the pain and stench of his burning skin, but he felt sure he'd driven the beast off at least long enough for him to escape.

He was wrong. The wyrm's head rose from the whitecaps, mouth wide. Before Yarrow knew what had happened, its jaws closed around him, its ancient teeth holding him immobile. It shook its head, rattling Yarrow's brain within his skull, bashing him against the mountain stone. Acting on instinct, he thrashed in an effort to free his pinned arms as the monster's teeth cut his flesh and his blood spilled from its mouth. But it was no use; his body held nothing near the strength of the creature's jaws. Only his magic would save him, and he had precious little left.

Clinging to consciousness, his mind and body begging to pass out and escape the pain, Yarrow fanned the embers burning deep inside his belly. He gave all his energy to feeding that warmth, coaxing it from coals to flame, until he could release the fire. He let it shoot from every inch of his body and smelled scorched fishy flesh as the wyrm dropped him and retreated. Even as it howled, it swiped at him with its claws, and Yarrow had very little strength left to protect himself. He darted behind a wall of fallen rock and snow, isolated a shard of ice, and sent it with all the force he could muster into the creature's amber eye.

The wyrm bellowed in agony as Yarrow's icicle pierced its orb and sent milky fluid steaming onto the snow. In a strangely human gesture, it pressed its webbed foot to its ruined socket and keened, its voice evoking rare compassion in the mage. Yarrow emerged from behind his shelter with his hands held high and his fingers spread open. His scorched clothing hung in ragged strips from his body, offering no protection from the biting wind. The creature, hurt and enraged, lunged for him, catching Yarrow's shoulder with the edge of a tooth and drawing a fresh font of blood that cascaded down the mage's chest. Gripping the wound, Yarrow skirted the edge of the water with the wyrm in pursuit. As it struck again, he dove behind a barrier of jagged stones. One swipe of the creature's claw reduced them to rubble, sending Yarrow fleeing again, his blood leaving a crimson trail in the snow behind him.

Turning, Yarrow concentrated on stealing the heat from the air around the lake water and directed a frigid blast at the wyrm's tummy. He succeeded in trapping it, stopping it from ascending farther from the lake, but as it thrashed, deep fissures cracked the thick ice he'd conjured. The beast's cries felt like they'd split Yarrow's head in two. He ran, doing his best to leap over errant rocks and stay behind what cover he could find. After battling a goddess, even his considerable energy neared its end. Escape was his only option. Besides, a small, silly, romantic part of him didn't want to destroy the magnificent creature, beautiful in its savage power, much like his entity had been before they'd bonded.

Yarrow sprinted toward a cleft in the rocks and what looked like a narrow path beyond. The trail, safely sheltered on both sides by high cliffs of ironstone, lay maybe a half mile away, and Yarrow pushed his body to move faster even as his lungs and muscles protested. He'd almost made it when a huge claw smashed down in front of him, showering him with rime and blocking his way. Seconds later, the creature's head appeared before Yarrow, its huge nostrils steaming and its intact eye regarding him intently. Within that yellow orb, Yarrow saw fierce intelligence, outrage, pain, fear, and confusion. It didn't know why it had been summoned from its slumber and compelled to attack. If he squinted and really opened his senses, Yarrow could see the delicate net the goddess had thrown over the creature's mind: angry, jagged threads filling it with hatred and rage, making it desire nothing but to tear apart any living thing it saw. Yarrow knew that urge, and so instead of attacking the beast again or even preparing a spell to defend himself, he sent a lavender cloud of soothing energy toward it, trying to negate what the goddess had done. At first, it didn't seem to be working, and the wyrm coated Yarrow with freezing spittle as it roared. Fighting his instinct to eliminate the threat, Yarrow spared just enough magic to defend himself and continued using the rest to dissipate the resplendent animal's artificial rage.

He could barely breathe as it thrashed its head and rent the ice with its claws. Dizziness threatened to send Yarrow to his knees, and he clutched a scrap of rock to remain standing. If this didn't work, he didn't know what he'd do. He didn't think he had enough strength left to conjure a wisp of smoke at this point. The wyrm pointed its snout to the snow clouds above and loosed a high-pitched wail that resonated through Yarrow's bones. Yarrow braced himself for whatever would come next, digging deep into his pools of magic for anything he could use to save himself. Bonded with an immortal being or not, he doubted he'd survive being torn to shreds by those massive teeth and claws. He didn't want to survive as nothing but chunks of meat scattered across the mountains.

Slowly, the creature arched its neck toward Yarrow and rested its chin on the frozen ground at his feet. An almost catlike mewling rose from deep within its chest. Yarrow, confused, kept his defenses ready as best he could and waited. Though he expected the wyrm to attack him at any moment, the creature remained docile and complacent. The lid of its remaining eye drooped over its golden iris, and Yarrow reached out with his senses, trying to understand the sudden shift. Grazing the periphery of the beast's mind, Yarrow perceived pride, a singularity of purpose, and, surprisingly, gratitude. It seemed to understand Yarrow had freed it from the so-called goddess's control. Reluctantly, Yarrow took a few steps toward the wyrm and rested his hand against its snout. Much of him still expected it to try to bite his arm off at the first opportunity, but the creature merely huffed out a defeated breath, surrounding Yarrow in a cloud of dank air. Yarrow couldn't help sensing a sort of tenuous bond had formed between himself and the beast.

"Go back to sleep," he said, sending his intent into the creature's mind, letting it know what he wished without language. "Maybe I'll be back for you one day. We'd make quite an impressive sight, riding into battle together."

The white wyrm lifted its head, arched its neck, and looked down at Yarrow. Yarrow detected a mutual respect form between them, and he raised a hand in farewell as the creature sank slowly beneath the frigid waters of Estrella Lake.

Yarrow stood watching until the surface of the water stilled and began to ice over again. Then he collapsed onto a rock and wiped his palm over his face, his hands still trembling. Since bonding fully with the ancient entity he'd encountered as a boy, Yarrow's body had been different. The wound to his shoulder had already closed though the cut had been deep. Before, the presence had healed Yarrow when it grew bored of experiencing pain, but now that they'd become one, Yarrow's flesh mended itself. It wasn't a physical injury that made Yarrow shake and feel like he'd empty his stomach into the snow.

Everything Hale had told him was true; he'd finally confirmed it after the questions had tormented him for months of sleepless nights. Everything his people believed, the very tenets they'd built their world upon, were lies. Those benevolent goddesses everyone believed created the world and looked after its inhabitants were nothing more than opportunistic women who'd stolen power from Fane and then destroyed him. Worse yet, they maintained their strength by hoarding the world's magic. Because of them, mortal casters grew weak, and fewer mages were born with every generation. For centuries, scholars had theorized on the gradual reduction in the world's enchantment. Yarrow now knew the answer those sages sought, but he'd be publicly tortured and executed for even suggesting it.

As if they could execute me.

A few deep breaths of the pure, cold air restored Yarrow's strength, and outrage followed not far behind. He didn't like being duped, and he resented power he could use being stolen. Yes, he knew the truth now, but what would he do with it? He'd be vilified if he spoke it aloud. People liked believing the goddesses watched over them, liked believing the goddesses knew best, so they didn't have to decide their own ideas of right and wrong. Though young, Yarrow had already learned most people would rather be told what to do than have the burden of choosing. They preferred following to forging their own trails.

Yarrow didn't. At that moment, he decided he'd expose the lie if it destroyed him, which it probably would. No altruism or sense of justice led him to his conclusion; he simply didn't like to see the unworthy ordering others around. He never had. After taking a few sips of the wine he'd brought from Windwake, grateful to find his skin canteen had survived the battle, Yarrow lifted his weary body from its perch. He headed in the direction of the small camp he'd made on the western edge of the lake to retrieve the supplies he'd stored there. He'd have to try to repair his shredded clothing. The walk back to Windust Castle would be long and grueling. It would probably take weeks, and Yarrow felt a sudden and severe longing for his lovers. He wanted to lie warm and safe between them for days. Could he reveal to Sasha and Duncan what he'd learned? Would they believe him? Yarrow knew they loved him and that they'd likely give their lives for him, but he also knew they thought him at least half-mad. He wondered what to tell them and just how to phrase it. He supposed he had at least two weeks on the road to sort it out, and he began walking southwest, along the edge of the lake.

After a few minutes, Yarrow stopped and looked back at the apex of Starmont. A watery, lemon yellow sun hovered just a few feet above the mountain's peak, and the world had grown so quiet it almost hurt his ears. He would build a fortress there. Let the so-called goddesses try to stop him. Let anyone. His icy castle would tower above the kingdom of Selindria and the frozen wastes to the north—a wonder worthy of the lost world of antiquity—and he would sit astride the lake wyrm. First, though, he had more mundane matters to attend to. The time had come to return to Windwake and to Duncan and Sasha. They had much to address.

"Watch for me," Yarrow said, squinting into the bright light reflecting off the icy summit. "Your time is short, you bitch. I am Yarroway

L'Estrella. Remember my name and fear me. I will show you no mercy. Expect me soon."

No answer came, and Yarrow wrapped his tattered cloak around himself against the biting wind as he began his long trek home to his lovers and a completely different set of difficulties.

AUGUST (GUS) LI is a creator of fantasy worlds. When not writing, he enjoys drawing, illustration, costuming, and cosplay, and making things in general. He lives near Philadelphia with two cats and too many ball-jointed dolls. He loves to travel and is trying to see as much of the world as possible. Other hobbies include reading (of course), tattoos, and playing video games.

For more info, visit Books by Eon and Gus:
http://www.booksbyeonandgus.com

DSP PUBLICATIONS

visit us online.
WWW.DSPPUBLICATIONS.COM